Praise for *Native Air*

Grand Prize Winner of the 2022 Banff Mountain ...mpetition
Finalist for the 2022 California Book Award for First Fiction

"You know there are people whose obsession is big-wall climbing. You may have seen the documentaries, read the articles, perhaps even read a memoir. But you've never read anything that takes you so deep inside the anchoritic psyche of helpless, abject cliff worship. The narrator is ambivalent, and supremely observant, his partner the absolutist. See Ishmael and Ahab, Sal Paradiso and Dean Moriarty. This is literary fiction of a high order, with a physical immediacy and specificity that never let up, and then a riveting next-generation denouement. The final top-out will destroy you. Climb on."

—**William Finnegan,** *The New Yorker,* author of *Barbarian Days*

"As a lifelong climber, climbing writer and student of mountaineering literature, I want the world to know: Jonathan Howland's *Native Air* is the novel that we American climbers have been waiting for. This book is the first true literary deep dive into the austere beauty, deep friendships and high emotional cost of the lives we've all led in America's great empty spaces, tilting at mysterious windmills, chasing truths and dreams we can never quite name. Howland is the real deal—as a climber, a writer, and a deep thinker about the human condition. *Native Air* belongs on the bookshelf of every climber everywhere."

—**Daniel Duane,** author of *El Capitan,*
Lighting Out, and *A Mouth Like Yours*

"I've read this novel, a story about two best friends who are also climbing partners, twice so far. The first time I became lost in the complexity of the relationships, the heartbreak, the full love, and the bid for repair. The second time I read it for the technical precision, the tension of incomplete ambitions, and the unbearably elegant structure. This novel is a classic. It will be read and loved again and again."

—**Claire Cameron,** author of *The Last Neanderthal* and
The Bear; 2022 Banff Mountain Book Competition Jury

NATIVE AIR

NATIVE AIR

a novel

JONATHAN HOWLAND

GREEN WRITERS PRESS | *Brattleboro, Vermont*

Printed in the United States.

10 9 8 7 6 5 4 3 2 1

Green Writers Press is a Vermont-based publisher whose mission is to spread a message of hope and renewal through the words and images we publish. Throughout we will adhere to our commitment to preserving and protecting the natural resources of the earth. To that end, a percentage of our proceeds will be donated to environmental and social-activist groups. Green Writers Press gratefully acknowledges support from individual donors, friends, and readers to help support the environment and our publishing initiative.

GReen
wrIters
press

Giving Voice to Writers & Artists Who Will Make the World a Better Place
Green Writers Press | Brattleboro, Vermont
www.greenwriterspress.com

ISBN: 979-8-9891784-3-8

Song lyrics on pages 336, 344, and 350 from "Fake Plastic Trees" by Radiohead, and released on their second album, *The Bends.* (1995).

Cover art/design Hughen/Starkweather.
Glossary drawings by Jennifer Starkweather.

Author's website: www.jonathanhowland.org.

for
Mary Howland
and
Courtney Rein

Nothing ever happens once and is finished.

—William Faulkner, *Absalom, Absalom!*

There's Grief of Want—and grief of Cold—

A sort they call "Despair" –

There's Banishment from native Eyes –

In sight of Native Air –

—Emily Dickinson, "I measure every Grief I meet"

But we little know until tried how much of the uncontrollable there is in us, urging across glaciers and torrents, and up dangerous heights, let the judgment forbid as it may.

—John Muir, "The Ascent of Mount Ritter"

Arête—a steep or vertical edge on a cliff or mountain.

Buttress—a square-edged aspect of a cliff that stands out from the rest.

Cam—ingenious device invented in the late 1970's for protecting cracks; brand names include Friends, Aliens, and Camalots.

Chalk bag—chalk is used to keep hands dry; the chalk bag hangs from a climber's waist.

Carabiner—oval ring, made of aluminum alloy, with a gate on one side through which a rope or sling or other piece of climbing hardware can be readily attached or detached.

EB's—a popular and widely available technical climbing shoe, 1970s.

Nut/Stopper—aluminum alloy or brass wedge placed in a crack for protection; a nut is the original type of passive or "clean" protection (1970s), designated such because, unlike a piton or bolt, a nut or stopper does not disfigure or scar the rock and can be readily removed by the second climber who "cleans" the route of the gear.

Piton, pin—an iron blade hammered into a crack or fissure; old-style protection.

SEE PAGE 361 FOR A COMPLETE GLOSSARY.

PART ONE

～

Mount Moriah, Northeast Face Direct—5.11+? (unfinished)

"No," I said, stuffing the letter back into the envelope. This felt a little dramatic, but then I realized I hadn't heard my voice, hadn't spoken to anyone, in several days. I put the letter at the back of the stack of Christmas mail, most of it from former parishioners whose lists I had yet to be dropped from and much of it forwarded from a parsonage I hadn't lived in for several years. Will's note was correctly addressed, and it didn't sit quietly in my stack. My father died around Thanksgiving, and I had just returned from boxing up his things and clearing out the house I'd grown up in.

> *Dec. 26, 2013*
> *Dear Joe,*
> *Or is it Reverend? Rev. Holland? Rev. Joe? Whatever suits you. Dear any and all of you.*
>
> *I don't remember you. Just know you were dad's partner and friend, at least through the '80s. I've seen the old AAJs and Mountain Mags in the library here, the ones where dad and you got ink. So I know about you from those, and a little more*

from Mom. Haven't met you except for the one time. Which I barely remember, and not you.

The climbing pics always seem to be of dad. I guess you hauled the camera.

Anyway, that's then.

To now:

I've got a project in mind. Want to see if you'd be interested in finishing the NE Direct, your and dad's route on Moriah. No one's done it, far as I can tell. Not free anyway. What do you think about it going free?

I scoped it last summer but haven't laid a finger on the face. Most of what I'm going on is from a topo in dad's binder. Which isn't much. Thinking you know more than what's sketched out there.

I can round up another partner if you're not into it. Just thinking yours are first rights of refusal. Don't know if you're climbing. If not, probably too wild a pony.

Thinking late July or August. The wall's good and dry by then, and there's a spring not far from the base that still flows in late summer. Guessing you know that. The aspect, it's true north more than NE—where'd you guys come up with that? Anyway, there's almost no sun, even in June. So mid or late summer prob. best: long days, better temps.

Let me know. Long winter there, I hear.

Will Leap Hunter

In my time with the church I had employed too many mountaineering references from the pulpit by way of analogy to some dimension of the faithful life, but I'd climbed just twice in twenty-four years. I had said more than a few times "the path of discipleship is a path of surrender—that to be faithful is to be open to inspiration, and to change." But these aren't my instincts, or habits.

A massive winter storm, the biggest in years, blanketed the Upper Valley under three feet of snow, and for several days I got to work by skiing alongside freshly plowed roads. In my off hours I checked on elderly neighbors, helped with wood and chores. A couple of times I skied along the quiet river at twilight.

In the deep of the night a slab of new snow slid off the roof and landed with an all-of-a-piece thud like a body fallen from the sky. I knew right away what had made the sound, but the queasy feeling in my abdomen was akin to what I'd grown used to with Pete, that admixture of excitement and wonder and fear—at once quickening and sickening. I didn't need to say yes to Will. Evidently already had. I would go to California in the summer—would begin my preparations the very next morning. However he meant it, whatever he wanted or expected, I saw Will's note for what it was, less an invitation than a summons.

⌒

Our own preparations, Pete's and mine, had been drawn out even longer. By the fall of '88 we were in a tattered stretch of our many years side by side, fully mired amid unspoken strains, halting negotiations, and private plots, mostly mine. We had spent most of the decade together and much of it living out of the trunks of beater cars on climbing junkets from British Columbia to Arizona, Kentucky to Oregon. Months at a time in Colorado and Utah. More than two full seasons in Yosemite. There were weeks-long trips to the French Alps and the Dolomites, an autumn in Peru, and, of course, the requisite weather-plagued pilgrimage to Patagonia. Pete's father had died during our second year of college, and however "dirtbag" our mode—climber parlance for the type of low-budget grunge we embraced—the farther-flung adventures and more than a few capital expenses (gear, cars) were largely underwritten by Pete's tapping his "small but sturdy" inheritance. I don't know how small, but plenty sturdy for our purposes. His father had owned and run several furniture manufacturers around the Great Lakes, a sprawling business of making people comfortable that gave Pete license to practice his own brand. "This bivouac," he once called from a wet and near-freezing hammock about ten inches above my face—we were ensconced in cloud on a variation of Whillans-Cochrane in Argentina—"brought to you by Buffalo Sofabed and La-Z-Boy."

But however generous our roaming, home was the narrow slice of the Eastern Sierra between Bridgeport and Lone Pine, a 150-mile corridor of Route 395 adjacent to dozens of unheralded and even undocumented crags and faces (any one of which would be a destination cliff in Chamonix, Pete liked to say), an easy drive from Yosemite Valley, and only a day or two scramble from the High Sierra peaks on whose obscure steeper faces we climbed dozens of known routes and, in time, established thirteen of our own. In '84, not three months out of college, we put up the first line on the prominent but scary-looking red flank of Peak 11,471 east of Taboose Pass, aand that same fall Light As on Feather Peak—900 feet of clean cracks and polished knobs so obvious and appealing it nearly made it into a *Sierra Classics* guidebook of the fifty best technical routes in the alpine Sierra. In '85 we established the meandering mess of All Premise, No Proof on Mount Williamson, whose mile-wide north face hadn't seen a new route in over forty years, and then another, much better line nearby, Pas de Deux. The working name for the latter was Hunter-Holland in the vaunted tradition of climbing legends like Steck-Salathe, Kor-Ingalls, and Chouinard-Herbert, but after nearly a month of route-finding and cleaning and linking delicate moves on friable rock, Pete insisted we withhold the name for a still worthier route—a decision that became a sort of albatross as each subsequent first ascent ratcheted up the standard for whatever white whale would deserve the eponymous stamp.

By '88 I had lost momentum. It wasn't the scraping by or the itinerant life. We had more or less settled in the Owens Valley during the previous three years, and we each managed a steady if modest income when we weren't climbing. I just didn't know where any of this was headed. Life with Pete, it was like the climbing—balancing amid an improbable arrangement of delicate pressures. Frightening, invigorating, stacked with summits and satisfactions, yes, but even more with pointless exertions and unnerving uncertainties. We met when we were eighteen. I grew up with him. And after a while I began to wonder if I was growing up at all. In July I did some further damage to a chronic shoulder on the punishing off-widths and endless chimneys on Mount Morrison. I couldn't lift my arm above my head without wincing, and couldn't wince without adding a layer to the seethe I felt about Pete's ever-expanding chart of enthusiasms.

In between guiding stints Pete left on days-long forays "into the obscurities" of the escarpment east of the crest. He'd take just binoculars, some food but no stove or cooking gear—Muir-style, he called it—and climbing shoes. He'd leave the dirt bike at a roadhead and hike up into any of the dozen canyons that plunge from the top of the crest to the Owens Valley ten thousand feet below. These drainages are colossal and remote, bordered by jagged peaks too inaccessible and usually too dangerously broken up to have garnered attention from anyone but peak-baggers whose principal aim is to tag the summit by the easiest route. Pete had been tending the lore of Sierra mountaineers for years, and he studied topographical maps obsessively. He had gotten quite good at anticipating hidden and largely unexplored walls and rock faces of worthy scale and character—those that lacked punctuating proximity to a famous summit or the comforts of a nearby roadhead and modest approach. He kept meticulous notes in a leather-bound notebook, including drawings of promising lines, but he never took pictures, and he never talked about his findings with the other climbers in our circle.

Fall had ordinarily been our most productive season, but with my attention divided and my shoulder throbbing, we climbed barely a dozen pitches together, these on the familiar Cardinal Pinnacle just up the valley. When Pete was guiding or away on one of his recons, I was happy to have the time to myself. My tent was just fifty yards from the trailer Pete found abandoned in the pinyons near the rim of the Owens Gorge. We'd built a patio on the Sierra side and lined it with a mortarless rock wall of the sort you see around alpine bivouacs. We made repairs to lawn chairs gathered from dumpsters and Pete installed an outdoor fireplace and grill by getting an auto mechanic in town to cut an old barrel in half with a blowtorch. The patio floor was firm and red and nearly flat. I swept it often and made a low table out of a triangular piece of flagstone into which I etched a chessboard. I frequented this porch, and was often there when the grind of Pete's motorcycle joined and then drowned out the breeze in the pinyons. I'd feel relieved he was okay, but then had to feign interest in his doings and findings. I looked over maps, asked a few questions, but mostly felt glad he hadn't discovered anything to stoke his fire to high heat.

The guiding season ended around Halloween, so Pete had a couple of weeks in early November before he'd start up again with the first snowfall at Mammoth. For a few days he hung around installing a woodstove and chimney in the trailer and adding insulation, and in a furious forty-eight-hour spurt he gathered the wood he thought we'd need for winter—wandering among the pinyons, harvesting only from downed trees and just a few pieces from any one area so as to minimize impact. Then he cut it by hand, ferrying it back to camp in the "Bearpaw Buick," the trunk full and wide open, the back and passenger seats lined with bundled logs and kindling. We stacked the wood under a small lean-to of found plywood, and with another week to kill before he was due in Mammoth, Pete went into the backcountry for a last reconnaissance. This had been his MO for several years: to get something on deck to carry him through the winter—some magnificent project around which the next climbing season would hinge.

At Mammoth, he'd worked his way through the lift-monkey ranks and now got to spend four months skiing around for on-call repairs and adjustments to the lift towers. He said he was a "pig on salary," though he never made more than twelve dollars an hour in what he called the "leisure industry" ("because only an *industry* could in a single generation transform a mountain sacred to Paiutes for thousands of years into an ATM for investors and a sleigh run for South Coasters who consider fifty bucks a bargain for the five runs they take before they get a little winded and head for the jacuzzi—fifty-five with hot chocolate").

And winter nights are long. Without an inspiring climbing objective in mind—one worthy of dreaming about, even training for—I think Pete worried he'd fall in with the burger flippers, ski patrollers, and lift operators who hit the bars at dusk and talk about how much better the snow is in Jackson and how much cheaper it is to live in Driggs or even Park City. Pete liked his beer, too, and with an agenda climb on the horizon he had a bulwark against full membership in the class of softies he privately disdained for four months of the year in order to climb for the other eight.

7

On Pete's third night out I was wishing I'd asked him where he was going. The temperature had dropped, and there was noise in town about a first winter storm churning down from Alaska, due to arrive in two or three days. Bishop is a sleepy town on either side of a corridor of motels and gas stations and amenities that are too many for this stretch of highway but during two stretches of the year, one between Memorial Day and Labor Day when there's a stream of fishermen and hikers with their trailers and trucks, motorcycle bi-way riders, Reno-bound gamblers, and motor coaches with Euros and Japanese on the third leg of their National Park shuffle: Grand Canyon to Death Valley to Yosemite. These stop for gas and a sandwich. The more adventurous might wander into Miguel's or step two blocks off Main Street to browse the gift shops and second-hand stores. Some spend the night. The Vons has longer lines and you don't go anywhere near Schat's Bakery after 9:00 A.M. But this level of activity is more or less pleasant—the buzz of out-there coming in-here to drop some dollars, take in a vista, mail a postcard, and head on.

Winter is the other busy time, and differently flavored: snow-report obsessed, weekend-strapped, weather-maligned. Autumn dusts the crest in a gently transforming visual spectacle until news of a first sizable storm sends a jolt through the valley. The snow itself triggers the roar of Mammoth Mountain and June Lake and Tahoe-bound skiers from Southern California, barreling up and down 395 in a season-long stampede. Bishop hunkers down, feeds and fuels and lodges. The sheriff and Highway Patrol stuff their coffers with traffic fines. Tow trucks and chain monkeys race between mishaps from Ridgecrest to the state line. The noise and nuisance is great for business, predictable as sunrise, and dull. It's tolerable and tolerated because as sure as it kicks into gear, it melts off—and April is peaceful as October, the long high-desert valley fallen off the map, the locals lifting their eyes again to meet one another in grateful restoration.

I was in the town library for much of Pete's fourth day out, working through a small stack of the stuff I figured I'd have to like if I got into a seminary—Buber, Bonhoeffer, Kierkegaard and Kant—but my eyes kept wandering from the page to a strip of pine trees registering the cold wind outside. I decided I'd go looking early the next day if he didn't return that night. If Pete were hurt and needed a rescue, I could at least save the Forest Service a day of aimless wandering by driving up the dirt roads of the likely entries and finding the motorcycle. That night I sorted through his materials in the trailer to see if I could narrow my own itinerary by identifying the maps that were missing—though whether he was using one of these or had merely stuffed them into his saddlebag, I couldn't know. The wind whipped up the valley all night, and when the gusts abated I found myself listening closely for some indication of a motorbike's whine.

At dawn I drove up the Rawson Creek drainage, which became impassable for the Buick after just a few miles. I left the car and ran up the valley's gentle shoulder to the trailhead. Nothing there. This happened twice more, approach roads too rocky for the big car, so by midafternoon I managed just five of the eight canyons I'd hoped to scout. But the exertion of so much running was a helpful check to mounting worry.

Last was the creek that tumbles into the valley north of Mount Williamson. We'd put up routes here several years before, and amid the day's driving and running I had conceived a likely scenario and grew certain I'd find the bike at the Shepherd Creek trailhead. Williamson was Pete's favorite mountain. Our routes there had gotten quite a lot of attention in climbing circles, but we'd never returned for second ascents. We'd not yet savored these as straightforward, un-dirtied lines, the sort that climbers enjoy after multiple ascents clean a route of loose flakes, flora, and dangerous debris. First ascents are long, grungy affairs— spicy for all the uncertainty, but tedious, too. Even a good line involves a ton of work, at least some danger, and, if technically challenging, several attempts in order to link individual sections. Climbing with "beta," Pete said, even if only another climber's hand-drawn topo map, "It's like driving the interstate: efficient, predictable, amenity-laden. 'Curve coming. Wide shoulder. Rest here.' We all do it, but it's not the real deal."

So having failed to identify a project for the next season, Pete must have gone up to Williamson to solo one of our first great routes. Why not? He'd been talking about it for years. It was a form of concession too: indulging nostalgia for what we'd done rather than setting the stage for what might lie ahead. The Shepherd Creek road was washed out, too, though here I had to run only the last two miles to the end, and as I jogged along I felt a surge of joy—both for what I'd figured out and for what Pete's choice indicated: he was making peace with my imminent exodus.

The approach to Williamson includes none of the slot-canyon shenanigans and fifth-class scrambling that many cliffs require just to get in the vicinity, but the routes themselves are sheer and challenging—one a long and sustained linkup of 5.10 cracks, the other a discontinuous and exposed line through the shattered diorite on the right side of the face whose crux goes at 5.11. Pete would rope-solo on this face—if he fell he'd have some margin of protection—but he would also run out the easier pitches to avoid spending a night on the wall, and if he got hurt he'd have nowhere near enough gear for a self-rescue. By now he could have been dangling for two, even three days, just inching himself down the cliff if descending at all.

The end of the road broadens into a gravel turnaround and small parking area. Nothing. But this made sense. The approach trail continues as a gentle swoop up the valley shoulder, a sandy path through sage: Pete would ride the motorcycle up as far as he could and ditch it to the side. So I kept running, taking note of what I could tell Search and Rescue about where they needed to go. The shadows across the valley disappeared as the light grew low. I was in shorts and shoes, no shirt, and for the first time all day the air felt chilly. I had been walking through a steep, rocky section for half an hour when I realized I had long since passed where Pete could have ridden. Did I miss the bike in the twilight? Had he left it behind a bush or boulder, or even before the end of the road—someplace I'd loped past two hours before? I had assumed he was out looking for something to entice me to stick around, but now I wondered if he'd given up on me—climbing alone, not bothering to report to base. I was groping, I knew. Trying to rationalize my way to some kind of peace of mind. Trying, even, to be glad. Pete was no longer depending on me, so I was free.

I called the Forest Service from a pay phone in Independence. I had become certain Pete was on Mount Williamson, but as the dispatch officer talked me through her template of missing-person questions—Which trailhead was the permit issued for? Where was your friend planning to camp? Fishing or mostly just hiking?—I realized I had nothing helpful to say, just that he'd been out for several days, he was alone, and I had many hunches but no evidence as to where they might even begin a search.

The dispatcher wandered from her script. "Sounds like a tough one. Maybe more of a Sheriff's Department matter."

"Huh?"

"More like a missing person than a lost hiker."

"He's not lost," I said, too emphatically. "He's in the wilderness. Probably climbing. Very possibly injured."

"But we have no idea where he got started, or what he was climbing. Correct?"

"Some idea. No, many ideas. Just nothing certain."

"Lotta mountain from 'Whitney to Conness.' Isn't that what you said—'between Mount Whitney and Mount Conness?'"

I said I'd be outside the Inyo district office when it opened in the morning.

Which is where I went next—to fill our water jugs from the spigot outside. Lugging them in pairs, just twenty paces to the car, I felt the full brunt of my fatigue. I'd been out for sixteen hours. I'd run more than twenty miles and hiked another five. I'd built this certain narrative as to Pete's whereabouts but found nothing to verify it. My arms seemed to stretch under the weight of the jugs, and with the last of them in hand I tripped on the hose and dropped it. The plastic ruptured on my foot, the water soaking my shoe. I waited a minute for the rest to gurgle out.

I'd known Pete through dozens of close calls and too many epics and accidents—cold nights on exposed cliffs, mad dashes from (and to) summits in lightning storms, bloodied fingers and hands, plenty of falling rock. I watched him zipper his gear off an aid pitch on the headwall of El Cap, hurtling sixty feet past popping pins and copperheads before my belay caught him, and then whipping in a wild pendulum across the face at just the level of our stance so that when he flew by me, inches away, I could see the fright in his eyes, though when he swung back, several seconds later, he was cackling and howling, thrilled to be alive.

In Zion in '85 I had been out on a lead far too long and finally attempting the baffling moves around a short roof when I dislodged a piece of the corner. Pete leaned to avoid the cantaloupe-sized rock, which flew safely to his side, but he took one of the smaller pieces above his ear. I was sixty feet above, still stretched out on insecure holds, and now less frightened for what I saw below—Pete slumped to the side, the blood trickling steadily over his neck and back and finally into space in a thin line that broke into droplets, as plume from a waterfall—than for my own tenuous position: his hands had relaxed and fallen away from the rope. He was knocked out. I was no longer on belay. With him unconscious, the six feet between my shoes and my last gear may as well have been the full sixty, and I was still several moves below a stance from which I might make another good placement. My left foot had been scissoring on small edges for the last little while, but instantly I was steady, frozen with fright. I slotted a brass nut into the shallow flare below my right finger jam, clipped this to the rope, and with breathless, out-of-body alacrity levered past and above this nut to the bigger holds above. The brass stopper popped out and sailed down the rope as I moved beyond it, but the crack shortly opened to a generous size, and in two minutes I'd built an anchor suitable for a hanging bivouac. From there I lowered to Pete.

I've thought about those few minutes many times in the years since: had I fallen while making the next three or four moves after he was hit, would the rope have cinched or tangled through Pete's belay device and somehow arrested my flight? Would my last piece have held, placed as it was in this famously friable sandstone—and the piece below that, and then the other, and, if not, Pete's belay anchor? In the best but least-plausible scenario, I'd have plummeted forty feet and the sudden jerk and whipping of the rope would have jarred Pete awake and he'd have had the wits to grab the rope from a lower loop so as not to be burned by the furiously unfurling belay line. More likely, I'm injured, or worse, we're both hurtling down the seven-hundred-foot mahogany face, tethered to one another by the umbilical coil of our rope and trailing the clanging detritus of our shattered belay.

Descending toward Pete I could see the full mat of his blood-ied head and the dark back of his soaked shirt. I slipped down to his side and took off my shirt to compress the wound. My climbing shoes slipped on the bloodied rock at the side of the hanging belay. With my fussing around him and the ringing of gear, Pete came to, and inside of two minutes he was not just fully alert, but smiling. He helped me with the cleaning and a quick inspection—a gash, right in the hard part of the skull above the ear.

"Back in the saddle, man," he said. "Getting late."

I must have looked horrified.

"I'll take my leads as they come," he assured me.

I fell three times trying to repeat the moves by the roof, top-rope or no—which Pete followed smoothly, his head wrapped in a shirt. He led two of the next four pitches, we topped out in the blazing desert sunset, and later saw a brilliant moonrise from the trail back to the car.

I tried, there outside the Bishop ranger station, to construct a picture of Pete now. Any number of abject positions came to mind—broken-limbed on a narrow ledge, hunkered down for the night in a boulder field to conserve heat, even inching along on his belly Joe Simpson–style. But I couldn't get him dead, not because it was unthinkable but because I felt sure I'd know it or feel it—some deeper vacancy that would overwhelm the anx-ious-making, trivializing worries that had me scurrying about.

A guy we used to climb with had a girlfriend who fashioned herself a type of mystic. She renamed herself Ciara, pronouncing it "Sierra." She was spry and kind of nosey. She'd stare at you with her dark blue eyes and then not say anything. One evening, after a week of camping nearby, she summed us up. "You two are yin and yang—heat," she said, nodding at Pete, "and cold. Light and dark. Out, in. No wonder you're so joined at the hip."

Pete dismissed her as a quack, but I felt she was onto something. Most everybody else assumed us twins, almost identical in height, hair color, foot size, though Pete was the more agile and expressive. So when I began to pull away from Pete I felt there was some risk to the both of us, a mutual loss of complementarity, and no part of me could compass the prospect that he would engineer it, even by means of calamity.

A short while later I was in the canned-beans aisle of Vons when I ran into Melissa, a climber who waitresses at Miguel's. She said Pete had eaten there two hours earlier. "Dirty, happy. Looks like he's been out a while. He didn't say much. Just gobbled, ordered another plate of enchiladas he said were for you, and left."

"Really?" I said.

"Salsa verde, right? I think you're covered."

"Thanks. I'm hungry."

"You look it."

I nodded, turning back to the cans I'd been studying, their labels now blurry for the water in my eyes.

Nor had said this of him when we were in college—that no one could infuriate her like Pete, even if she'd rather be infuriated by Pete than befriended by most anyone else. She was trying to let me down softly, as though ours were a kind of common alliance vis-à-vis Pete. No matter. I wasn't Nor, and I wasn't going to drive back to camp and be infuriated. He was okay. I had gotten some air and exercise—more than I wanted, but air and exercise nonetheless. I just needed to heat the beans—Pete would have eaten the enchiladas long before I returned—and get to my tent.

The patio fire was ablaze, the tape deck balanced on the trailer steps, but either shut off or dead of battery. Pete wore an unzipped parka and stood up from where he had been hunkered over several layers of topo maps, their corners pinned with empty beer bottles. The parka slipped from his naked shoulder, his wild hair falling away from his face. He switched off his headlamp as I got out of the car. It was nearly still—no engine, the buzz in my head of the past several days entirely evacuated. I didn't feel much. Wasn't angry. The wind puffed lightly through the pinyons, sending sparks sideways out of the fireplace.

"You're back," he said.

"I am."

"You okay?"

"Fine. You?"

"Yeah, good. Beat." I couldn't see his lively green eyes, but felt he was keeping something from me. He nodded toward the fireplace and a foil wrapped platter nearby. "Miguel's there for you."

"Thanks."

He flipped his headlamp back on, first at my face, blinding me, and then up and down my torso.

"Shorts?"

"I was running."

The light rested on my feet.

"Why the wet shoe?"

"Got dark," I said. "Stepped in a stream."

"Well, glad you're okay."

He didn't tell me where he had been or what he found. The storm rolled through the next night, as forecast, and Pete decamped to Mammoth in one of the small windows between waves of snow. He rumbled out of camp on his motorcycle wearing a backpack full of clothes and gear, eyes protected by ski goggles, and we didn't see one another until December. But in those last hours between his returning and leaving again I could see he'd found a project—the light in his eyes, the exaggerated version of his ordinary unflappability in conversation. He was solicitous of me—helped stack the wood, asked about my shoulder—and he said nothing about climbing until just before he set off, hand on the throttle: "Give the cams a lube so they don't gum up over winter, will ya?"

After Thanksgiving I ran into Glen, who works ski patrol, at a gas station in town. He reported Pete was training, and like never before—running the dirt roads east of the highway after work with a headlamp and doing a bouldering circuit at Clark Canyon when the weather allowed. He'd installed gym equipment and fingerboards under the eaves of the dorm where the Mammoth crew lived, and at a party of resort employees he was coy as usual about his climbing plans—but Glen wasn't buying it. He looked straight at me: "What are you guys up to?"

I shrugged. I made like I knew but wouldn't say.

Pete and I hadn't lived together for an entire winter but one, the first after college, but we had always been yoked to plans for spring and summer so as soon as work and weather allowed, generally around the March equinox, we stacked trips to Joshua Tree and Red Rock and Indian Creek in succession.

May was for Yosemite, the Valley of our time locked in its post–Golden Age funk with the legends lurking about and lording over it still but from a distance, as in shared houses in El Portal and retro-fitted vans in the further recesses of Valley parking lots. This was not like ten and twenty years before, with Bachar and Kauk, John Long and Lynn Hill and Yabo, and before them Bird and his tribe of wild ones, and still before them the Greats, Robbins and Frost and Chouinard (each now running clothing empires from industrial strips in Modesto and Ventura)—three successive generations of the boldest and best, plotting and projecting and holding forth around the same dusty and soot-caked Camp 4 fire-rings now tended by streams of anonymous climbers from all corners of the world, some staying the season, but most dipping their toes in for a week or even just a weekend. Gunkies from the East and the North Carolinians from Looking Glass and Linville and Georgians from Stone Mountain, who'd come with all the gear and gusto requisite for a wall but typically balked at the sheer scale if not the proverbial "grease" of glaciated granite that ratchets down most everyone's advertised ability two notches in the first two hours. And the Japanese, Germans, Brits, and Australians on adventures of a lifetime, those who stayed a month or more and generally outclimbed the rest of us and were therefore (and not always wrongly) charged with dubious ethics.

Pete and I kept to ourselves. We camped neither in the climbers' ghetto of Camp 4 or in the parking lots like the elders who were in with the rangers but in the boulders by the chapel or right up under El Cap because in either place the Park Service assumed we'd left our car to do an overnight route on Sentinel or The Captain. Our Valley agenda included nothing fresh or bold. We were out of our league among those pushing grades and putting up new routes, but we had an appetite, even a gift, for volume, climbing more than most anyone and in any case racking up the pitches requisite to what we felt was our true business, which was more or less the course Yvon Chouinard had charted when, in the early '70s, he indicated the future wasn't here in warm, familiar Yosemite but in transporting Valley skills to the cliffs and peaks of higher, more remote realms.

Chouinard was wrong. The "what's next?" for Valley climbers was indeed right in the Valley—not just the still-steeper cracks and seams at still-harder grades in still-further alcoves of the less-developed cliffs, but free-climbing the famous aid routes on El Cap and Leaning Tower and Half Dome, and even bouldering—linking impossibly gymnastic moves around the flanks of house-sized boulders along the valley floor. The first sets of Ray Jardine's ingenious cam devices cut the staying power requisite to protect a Yosemite crack of any size or grade to a fraction of what it had been, opening up miles of once formidable territory to enterprising free climbers.

But the game-changer was Bachar's un-roped ascent of New Dimensions in '76, and then, a few seasons later, his staged solo of the Nabisco Wall on the Cookie. Yosemite climbers had been arranged around a poker table for two generations, watching one another's moves, learning the habits and practicing the requirements of maintaining stature. The risks were ample, but they were contained by a tacit agreement: to see and only lightly raise one another's wagers, if raise them at all, in respectful, cautious, even polite increments. In less than an hour on New Dimensions Bachar had pushed all of his chips into the center. The news rippled through the Valley and would have been received like a rumor of war, but almost no one believed it. At first. And then some did, and in time most everyone did if only so they could claim, by association, a smidge of the glory.

So on Nabisco Bachar told Mark Chapman to lower fifty feet off the left side of the Cookie with a camera and to wait for him. It's not the most famous of the photos Chapman took that afternoon, but it's my favorite: Bachar is sitting, facing outward, on the ledge above Bev's Tower. He's 150 feet off the deck, but the pitch he soloed to get there is far more secure than Butterballs, the one above him, and he can still easily downclimb. He's dressed for the photo shoot: shirtless, just running shorts, climbing shoes, chalk bag, and "drug hat"—a bandana knotted pirate-style around his scalp. Sitting on the ledge, he appears to be wondering whether he wants to go through with this—not whether he can climb the familiar .11c finger crack on a dead vertical wall with no margin for error, but whether he wants to own it, and to forever cast a shadow on all climbing endeavors that don't court a corresponding degree of commitment and danger. Most who see this picture think he's psyching up, or waiting for the temperature to drop. The cynics say he was waiting for the light to get better for the famous photos. I like to think at some point he decided the moment had already passed, on New Dimensions, and this particular affair wasn't any big statement so much as another of the many mile markers he'd pass on the way to a free solo of Astroman.

It was hard for any of us to think our climbing competent with Bachar and Croft and Hersey—the trinity of great soloists—in the picture. To push yourself to the very edge and succeed on something only to have one of them come up behind you unroped—this forced a collective recalibration, their brand of talent and conviction so humbling to so many it colored the course for everyone. If you couldn't get what you needed on your own terms, it was time to get out.

So, yeah: we knew Bachar. Once when he was blowing his sax in El Cap meadow, Pete took his mandolin out there and they played duets until after dark, Bachar leaning back on his horn and Pete swaying side to side on his toes. Another time he was soloing up and down the second pitch of Beggar's Buttress when Pete and I came up from below and he stepped to the side on small but secure holds and watched me grunt through it, a rare 5.11 tick for me. I worked hard under Bachar's gaze, and felt proud not to fall, and didn't need Pete to note what had been on my mind too: given the position of the left-leaning lieback, had I fallen above Bachar I might very well have knocked him off the cliff, and then we'd really have a story.

We knew Yaniro too, and Piana and Skinner, and when Bridwell came through we didn't just nod in appreciation but made a point of shaking his hand. Allen Steck and Steve Roper gave a talk at the Visitor Center, and though we got good seats for the slides, we slipped out as soon as the tourists started with their questions—"How's the first guy get up?" and "What do you do about going to the bathroom up there?" Of the legends, Ron Kauk alone was friendly, recognized us from season to season, lent us some small cams in the Meadows once and talked beta many times. He was the lone bear—impossible to find if you were looking for him but appearing frequently and from who knows where when you weren't. Kauk didn't barricade himself behind reflexive irony and dark humor like the others—an affect climbers adopt less to ward one another off than to add a layer of calluses over their fears. He said the soloing business was foolish, the bolt wars pointless, and the rangers were just doing their job. Pete thought Kauk a bit sad. He called him a preacher without a congregation. In my eyes this only elevated him. Kauk held his own and on his own terms. He established Magic Line next to Vernal Falls, all on gear, then Peace in the Meadows, the latter comprised of tip-sized feldspar knobs up an impossibly steep black streak on Mariolumne Dome. Sure, aspiring hardmen—say what you like about my style. But first climb my routes.

Only once did we stay in the Valley into June, and that time because a stuck rope had cost us two days on the Salathe with no way off but up. Our habit was to vacate before the Memorial Day crush to get back in position on the Eastside and rest up for a week or two. In a normal snow year, the alpine ribs and faces and buttresses at twelve and fourteen thousand feet were just shedding their last hard layers of snow and ice to expose the bare bones of our summertime objectives. Pete studied familiar couloirs on the crest through binoculars, and when the snowfield right of the Third Pillar of Dana had receded into the shadows, we were generally good to go.

This was my favorite time, this interlude between nearly three months of the body-ripping business of so many pitches on so many long and generally familiar cliffs in three or four different states—between this and what Pete called "the best of all breathing," the High Sierra routes on the new season's agenda that often required two days of backpacking just to get to the base and then weeks of work in route-finding and clearing choss and finally linking up the pitches in hopes of having something deserving the attention of other aspiring alpinists if not worthy of Hunter-Holland—and battered hands and chapped faces, clouds of mosquitoes in camp, a broken stove or a stomach bug, always one or another of the aggravating circumstances that keep these high-country routes from becoming popular even if they weren't already too technically challenging for the regular mountaineers and too much work for ordinary rock climbers. The in-between time, that ten- or twenty-day respite in the Owens Valley—this was spring: more or less indolent, full of promise, nearly peaceful. The sage full and green, bright paintbrush and prickly poppy blooming on the side of road. Bathing naked in hot springs at dusk and no Jeep full of skiers pulling up to make a party, as in winter. No work but to sort gear, mix gorp, pack food. Bishop was sleepy again, smaller and toylike compared to when we'd left at the end of ski season, as though our own hands and shoulders, hardened and darkened from the previous weeks in the deserts and the Valley, had recast us into proportions no longer suited for flat streets between trailer parks and motels and auto body shops.

Pete did yoga in the park and took naps. He was unrecognizably lazy, steeling himself for battles to come. I read in the air-conditioned library, wrote letters to my folks in Pennsylvania and grandparents in Ohio, and pulled day-old bread out of the dumpster behind Schat's shortly after the bakery closed.

But by '88 I had resolved to put the next season out of mind. It wasn't just that my shoulder seemed good for nothing more than surgery—the aching woke me at night, and once when I brought an armload of wood into the trailer I wrenched it simply for catching a piece of kindling on the doorframe. Nor was it nerves, though I felt seared from the battering we had taken in August on Mount Morrison, whose upper half involved eight hundred feet of wide cracks and vertical chimneys on decomposing diorite, a vertical bowling alley with infrequent and sketchy protection. The near constant rockfall was murderous beneath Pete but still more frightening on lead, with holds rattling and peeling under your fingers and head-sized stones set to dislodge under the lightest touch, ricocheting into the chamber of the chimney and onto the belay. In six years with Pete I'd worried many times about being seriously injured, but for the first couple of days on Morrison I just wanted an excuse to bail. After cleaning and climbing the first half of the route, we came down to spend a night and a day at the base and to fight about whether to continue. Then we went back to work, and for two days I entered a world I'd known only the edges of in the past: I was entirely numb to the physical pain, and yet felt as though I might at any moment burst into tears.

One guidebook compares Morrison's north face to the Eiger, so loose, dark, and cold Pete suggested we call our route The Pucker Sanction. Until those last few hundred feet, when he was scared, too, he had been thinking our line would be called Shafted because on my leads Pete rigged a belay just outside of the chimney both to avoid the falling rock and to admire the much cleaner crack and corner system he wished we had elected just two hundred feet to our right. During our battle at the base he even suggested we get on this other route instead, but the idea of starting anything ever again was beyond me. We'd invested months on this route—the thinking about it, the preparing for it, and now several days working on (or rather inside) it. The only way we could agree to get out of there was to complete it. I knew I wasn't coming back to Morrison, and Pete even believed me. These were our Gory Days, and the name stuck. And here, almost four months later, I wondered if the pain in my shoulder wasn't some kind of containment of the dread I felt there, which only hastened my steps toward an exit.

༄

An only child, I was too frequently reminded, several times by a Sunday school teacher, that others of my mother's pregnancies had failed (both before I got here and after). Life in our circle was fragile and deeply contingent—the grace of God underlay everything. When I discovered climbing, in college, I found the exposure and mortal perils thrilling, but also profligate and unforgivable. Early on I'd make bargains. Just this, then no more. To domesticate the dangers I began to think of climbing as a kind of meditation, or even prayer, but I never got far from wondering whether I'd fallen under some perversion of faith, some dark and disfiguring spirit whose most avid embodiment was, of course, Pete. In the past year I'd sent postcards to several seminaries and divinity schools and made more than a little noise about making a move.

I negotiated all of this out of a post office box in Bishop— reintroducing myself via mail to the former professors I would need for references, drafting essays for applications in the town library, and exaggerating the time all this took to hold Pete at bay for a while. He chafed and brooded. He traded climbing gear to get me some physical therapy, but I went just once—too painful. Pete got time on rock as a guide, and when he wasn't working or fixing up the trailer he roamed around the Eastside on his dirt bike to identify the various projects that would secure his appetite well into and beyond the foreseeable future and, he hoped, invigorate mine. Only an hour's hike above the paved road south of Tom's Place he discovered an alpine bowl framed by a dead-vertical, entirely undeveloped five-hundred-foot cliff composed of hard orange polish "of the kind you get on the Gold Wall left of El Cap." He talked about it not like we had to go there tomorrow or even before winter but like some private fantasyland we could share in our old age. "I soloed the obvious line. It's clean, hard, and steep on either side. There's five pages of somebody's guidebook to be written there."

Just twenty miles north of Bishop he explored a gorge of steep volcanic tuff on either side of the dry Owens River he thought had potential to become a four-season playground, the sort of place climbers would go to stay primed for their more committing and weather-contingent Yosemite and High Sierra objectives. And along the rim of this gorge, tucked in pinyon pines at the end of one of the dirt roads left by tungsten miners in the '30s, Pete found the small trailer we winched onto a foundation of stacked flagstones we rolled and crow-barred from an acre of high desert. Once he left for the Mammoth ski season, I moved in here.

The storm ran down the spine of the Sierra from the north, and in hours the ski traffic was hammering up 395 as though everyone had been lined up on the other side of Bishop waiting for a starter's gun. I returned to the job I'd had for three seasons at the Sportsman's Lodge. The easier, better money was on the mountain or in the bars, but I couldn't hold my own there—either on skis or in the chatty business of making drinks for strangers. I did a stint as a grunt for a contractor some years back, but when I had a bad year the following climbing season I decided I'd lost my edge on account of being at the end of someone's leash all winter. At the Lodge I just made beds and cleaned rooms—flat rate, cash. Most of the maids in Bishop were from El Salvador and Honduras. In my first season their boyfriends and husbands marked me in town, but Rosa, head of housekeeping at the Lodge, vouched for me when any of them wondered whether I had designs on anything more than honest work and a flexible schedule. Three years in they just thought me odd. I could put in a few hours after the midmorning checkout and still have both ends of the day to myself to read and train and hike. But this winter, lacking the focus and drive of past years, I spent November shuffling between the Lodge, the library, and Pete's trailer.

Around Thanksgiving I got a slip at the post office about three boxes of Texas grapefruits, which I carted back to camp and stacked inside the trailer lest they get frostbitten. A few days later, a note from Pete—pecked out with a manual typewriter on yellowing paper.

Solstice VII—our camp. On Christmas. STOP. Sunset—or an hour after the lifts close. STOP. (I got 12/26 off!) A dozen from the mountain, plus some from over there. STOP. Nor coming too. STOP! Assemble supplies. Will get a keg from Billy's—and

some meat. Get fire and grill going, and the other stuff for the
punch. Grapefruits en route. Make beans. XO. PH.

It's funny. Pete and I shared everything for ten years—not just
our climbing ambitions and the complicated logistics of executing them, but money and gear, food and clothes. We pooled our
cash before counting out the bills for the Buick, and in the years
before we narrowed our activities to the Eastside and I was hundreds short of whatever we needed for a flight to the Dolomites
or Patagonia, he covered me. At least a couple of times each
season we'd curl into one another on a tight bivouac ledge, sharing a sleeping bag to ward off the cold. On other climbs we
dispensed with the second bag altogether just to save weight.
More than one Josh or Valley or Moab climber, running into one
of us without the other, said, "Where's your husband?" Though
if he really wanted to get under our skin, he would instead ask,
"What's next for Hunter-Holland?"—not out of curiosity but
to remind us that for all our first ascents and projects, we still
lacked a route worthy of the proverbial signature.

It was Pete's lead, the sharing. It had never been so seamless for
me. I didn't keep a running tally, but there was still a scorekeeper
in me, registering not just my accumulated debt but how little
I put out. Pete wanted more, gave more, worked harder, spent
more. I acquiesced and quietly resented. He roped me in with
enthusiasm and commitment and mindless generosity. I aided
and abetted, but also contained him. And limited him. Pete was
better. He was stronger, fitter, faster. Bolder and hungrier. Where
I was circumspect and deliberate, he was imaginative and alive,
quickened all the more for the trials and uncertainties he zeal-
ously contrived. He asked very little of me, really—except that I
help him remain so. And then even this started to feel like too
much.

He'd have shared Nor too, except that wouldn't work for Nor. Or for me. They'd been a couple for two years during college and more than one after, and during any number of their turbulent stretches Nor turned to me as a sort of nearest of kin. I met her in a philosophy class sophomore year and was enamored of her long before she knew my name. We went on a couple of walks together on the nearby trails and once ventured as far as some mountains to the east, but however eager I was for things to heat up, the fuel we had for one another was damp as the woods we tramped through on the edges of campus. Plenty for me—but it never yielded more than a semi-soft kiss. I decided Nor was too preoccupied to be available, at least for now. She was an athlete, a serious Nordic skier. She did books, ideas, and friendships. Then she met Pete, and it was wildfire season. Later, I wondered how I'd kept her from him those many months—but that was the year Pete's father had become ill, and Pete took a leave from school. He had been at home during the weeks I'd been trying to get close to Nor, returning late in winter for the spring semester.

That should have been the start to a lonely season, but Pete was no less bent on getting out than he'd been in the fall. We ticked most of the greatest hits in the Adirondacks, and in several weekend trips to the Gunks climbed three dozen routes. Nor came along a few times; that's when I got into the habit of pitching my tent a ways off from Pete's. She wasn't eager about climbing. She knew nothing about method and had no interest in gear—but she was better than almost anyone else we knew, including all of the women we'd seen at the crags. Pete said it wasn't because she was a fierce athlete, even if she was. It's that she didn't care or think about it. "It's the thrashing that causes drowning," he said. "Nor's the opposite. So she floats." In the car and on the trail, Pete and I plotted and made plans, and on the day after sophomore year exams we set out for our first season of all-in climbing—with a standing invitation to Nor but no expectation we'd see her until fall because she was doing two pre-med courses in the summer session. When she showed up at the Boulder bus station in August, I'd never seen Pete happier.

Three years later she drove out of the very Colorado camp we shared that summer. It was a hot morning, still five weeks before Nor was to start med school in New Hampshire. Pete had gotten up before dawn and run up the canyon to scout an approach. I could tell it wasn't going well, but didn't know just how bad. I was making coffee when I noticed Nor stuffing her sleeping bag and arranging her things. When I watched her drive off I didn't doubt I'd see her again, but I figured it would be on the other side of further ranges and adventures, possibly even years hence. Pete was kind of quiet for a few days and, if anything, even more motivated. We were at Eldo, and he started hurling himself at The Naked Edge—a route he might top out on, but not safely, and certainly not without many and precarious falls on a rusty piton someone had placed under the crux in Layton Kor's time. He and Nor had spent too much of the previous year worrying over how they could be together if she were in medical school and he an itinerant climbing bum, and by midsummer they couldn't even agree on whether to heat both sides of a tortilla before filling it with beans.

A couple of mornings later, Pete said, "I'm the only dirtbag who ever dumped a doctor."

"Doctor-to-be."

"Dirtbag-to-be, too. We haven't been at this long enough. We're not certified."

"Maybe dump-to-be, too?" I suggested.

"You know Nor. She means things."

We were standing beside a firepit filled with the ash and foil and burnt cans of previous campers. It had started to rain.

"I think she's gone," he said.

I didn't know all he knew, but this seemed right.

So the news item folded amid the other party injunctions—"Nor coming too"—made for a restless couple of weeks. She had been there for Solstice I, the anti-holiday conceit Pete had cooked up in college to mark the end of exams and the start of winter vacation. The college versions started with some kind of chili cook-off, and once the quorum of climbers was *in situ* there would be interior "buildering"—linking moves around doorjambs and moldings, various features declared off-limits as the night wore on. At some point everyone moved outside, usually to a sledding hill above the cemetery. In two of the first three parties we saw dawn.

Out West the solstice was for a while smaller and more measured—just a midwinter climbers' gathering around a campfire, though once we settled on the Eastside the parties filled out with an expanding circle of friends from up and down the Valley, and lately Pete would rope in assorted refugees, most too busy working the resorts to get home for the holiday. As in college, these became long and involved, blowout affairs whose participants had just one thing in common: they all knew Pete. I was just the climbing partner—standing around a fire with strangers, tending the barbecue, and consolidating empties to a single pile Pete would reconfigure into a sculpture a day or two later and then photograph, commemorating the event in an arrangement of its detritus. Cold wind. Winter stars. At some point the tape deck giving way to guitars and banjos and Pete's mandolin, musicians' hands sprouting out of fingerless gloves. Later I would retreat to the tent I had earlier in the day moved still farther from Pete's, and in the morning I wandered the perimeter of camp to collect the thrown bottles of the truly drunk.

I started pulling together the supplies as instructed. It felt good to have something other than my own upkeep to look after. I wondered about Nor, when she'd arrive, and where Pete would have her go if he was busy on the mountain. I knew they'd been corresponding, but he didn't report much. This was year four of medical school—she was due for another move shortly, and I wondered if she might be headed this way to explore her options.

On the solstice a blast of cold and snow closed the northern passes on 395 and for a few hours even shut down the freeway north of LA. Our camp took a foot or more, a scalloped wall stacking up against the back side of the trailer and the porch filled to the rim like an abandoned kiddie pool. I got to town by snowshoeing through the pinyons to 395 and hitchhiking south. There I got a message the night clerk at the Lodge had scribbled out: *"Hectic here. Equipment probs. Pls. pick up Nor—LA bus to Bishop on 12/21 or 22(?). Sorry. More when I have it."*

It wasn't the first time I'd moved a rollaway into the house-keeping closet on the second floor. I wouldn't be able to get the car out of camp until the sun shone brightly for a day or two—they don't plow anywhere near there—so I shuffled around Bishop between the Lodge, the library, and the bus station, where the Greyhound continued to arrive even with the route to Reno closed off. I cleared a shelf in the closet and started to assemble the party supplies. I got the beans going in the kitchen at the Lodge, and when Rosa advised me to get a particular brand of ancho pepper at Vons I killed another hour walking to the north end of town in blowing snow. Later, not confident in what she saw in my preparation, Rosa took over entirely.

Every few hours I walked the length of town to the one-room bus station on the south side. One time the room was crowded with the newly arrived, most cradling long canvas ski bags and waiting for the Mammoth shuttle. Usually the station was empty but for a vagrant taking shelter from the wind. One bus clipped some road debris outside Olancha, and those onboard were loaded onto the next northbound bus, already crammed with holiday travelers. Cranky passengers poured out at dusk, hauling their things through town along both sides of the main drag in hopes of beating one another to a motel with a vacancy. I got the story as I walked toward the station, checking faces for Nor. I went once more that first night, not long after dawn the next day, and again several times on the twenty-second. By afternoon the weather had kicked off to the east, and shortly the shadow of the Sierra crest fell over town, the setting sun slathering the last of the storm clouds in layers of orange and red and yellow. People stood outside the stores and clustered in parking lots to see it. Then night again, and still no Nor. I figured she and Pete had gotten their signals crossed, or maybe she'd decided to stay to the south—though on account of the weather or something she and Pete were negotiating, I didn't have a clue.

Still, I went back. In the morning there were half a dozen people there, including two I recognized from the nearby Paiute tribe, so I figured they were waiting for an outbound bus. There was an older man with a bolo tie, a young mother and her toddler daughter who climbed around their stack of luggage, and in the far corner the same drunk I had seen when it was snowing. In the other corner, facing him, a woman sat alone, but she was middle-aged.

I turned to walk out.

"Joe."

The woman, standing now—obviously Nor when she removed her hood and turned my way, and yet if I hadn't been looking for her I'm not sure I'd have known. She seemed shorter and leaner than before, and at least so far less quick to smile. Her hair, once silky and long, was shoulder length and tinged with gray, her face pale, even drawn, and her brown, piercing eyes—"Wingate Sandstone," Pete said of them—rimmed by shadows.

"Nor."

She stepped closer. She had a small bag of the sort you use to carry a swimsuit and towel to the pool.

"Hi," she said, throwing an arm open.

I leaned forward, protecting my shoulder.

We walked north along Main Street. Christmas lights in store windows. A wreathed arch over the highway near the center of town. She told me of her tour: Denver, Albuquerque, San Antonio, and just recently LA, each a prospective residency. She had emergency medicine in mind as a "quality of life" option but really hoped to do OB-GYN, and only this week she'd learned that if she were willing to split her time between UCLA and the county hospital in Ridgecrest she could do both.

"I could be up here in two hours," she said.

"For what?"

She looked at me like maybe I knew, and as her brow and eyes grew animated, I instantly recognized her.

We walked past the gift shop—same figurines as last time she was here. A jukebox poured out of the corner saloon where the regulars were having to compete for stools with the stranded.

"At least it's not all cute," Nor said. "Bishop, I mean."

"Wait'll you see camp. Talk about not-cute."

I showed Nor to my rollaway in the closet and packed my sleeping bag, a pad, and two extra blankets from a shelf in the back. There was a storage unit at the rear of the parking lot where I'd slept once before, though not in winter. Nor pleaded—said she could curl up in the corner of the closet, or one of us could take the floor of the laundry room down the hall, but I was wary of pushing things any further at the Lodge.

"Hungry?" I asked.

"Not really, but I'll go with you. Miguel's still?"

"Yeah," I said. "But I'm good."

My head knocked against the naked bulb over the cot. The light flickered, and when I reached up to steady it the bulb popped and hissed in the dark.

"Just a sec," I said. "Extras back here." I felt my way along the shelves—soap, vacuum cleaner bags, boxes of Kleenex. I stepped over bottles of soda water and juice for Pete's citrus concoction, and just as I found the bulbs Nor opened the door and a fluorescent glow poured in. I stood on the cot, but found I could use my bad arm neither to change the bulb nor to steady myself, an embarrassing demonstration of how ill-equipped I'd become for Pete's and my maneuvers.

I tossed my bag and blankets into the hallway. It was early still, and we'd spent barely an hour together, and though in years past I'd spent days scrunched up against Nor on hanging belays or camped in tight quarters, even this proximity seemed too much.

"Anything more?" I asked.

"No. Thanks for waiting around, Joe." She moved to the center of the hall as if we'd be here a while. "And for the closet."

"I'm done here midday tomorrow. Then we'll head out." We'd have to hitchhike, I explained, then walk across the high desert from the highway. If the Buick worked and the road was clear, we'd return to town to pick up the beans and supplies. If not I'd have to get to Tom's Place to leave a message for Pete so he could have someone swing through Bishop before the party.

"Shoestring as ever," Nor said.

"You've no idea. Or some idea. Anyway, right. Same as always."

I was eager to move along if hardly anxious to set up a bivouac in the shed at 8:00 P. M. on one of the three longest nights of the year. My things under my arms, I said goodnight and started down the hall.

"Joe," she called. She was standing in a dim stretch of the hall. "You okay?"

Someone came out of a room behind her.

"I mean, you're thin. And you protect that shoulder like you're carrying a baby."

"It's bugging me."

"Have you had it checked out?"

"Time. Time is all."

"And you seem tired."

I looked at my feet. "You know how it goes. Life with Pete."

She smiled. I could see her teeth in the dark.

I took my things downstairs to the kitchen, stirred the beans and sat on a low stool near the floor with a book. Through the opening I could hear Lodge guests coming and going, some stopping to ask the clerk a question or get a key. Once when I stood I saw Nor sitting in the foyer watching the television, but when I looked again twenty minutes later she was gone. When Barry came around back to fill out his timecard, he asked if I'd seen the lonesome beauty in the lounge.

"Somebody's girlfriend or wife," I suggested.

I gathered Nor was back here because she was again the one. I wondered if, in becoming the other, she might relieve me of my post.

At around ten I took my things out back, pushed aside some of the pool furniture, and set up camp inside the shed. I wore two knit hats and all my layers but my jacket, which I stuffed under the door, but frosty air still blew in around the edges.

～

The improved weather prompted a bigger exodus than expected, so I didn't finish my beds until midafternoon. I

worked steadily but as in a trance. The night had been like one
before an agenda climb—mind crowded with logistics, heart
aflutter. It wasn't the cold or the party. It was having Nor here,
and feeling something again, maybe just proximate tenderness.
She had said of me what I thought of her—she seemed kind
of ragged and wrung out. But she didn't say I was more beautiful than ever.

Midmorning I found the housekeeping closet tidied up, the
rollaway folded in its corner and clear of her things. I was slower
than usual, using my knee and even my foot in making beds
to avoid strain to my shoulder. Windexing bathroom mirrors, I
paused. What was it Nor was seeing?

When I finally finished she was in one of two chairs in the
lobby and Barry was back at the front desk. I filled out my tally,
left a note for Rosa about the beans and other stuff I'd pick up
later, and headed out of the Lodge the front way. I turned to see
the look on Barry's face when Nor rose to walk out with me, but
he didn't believe I was doing anything more than holding the
door for her.

We walked through town to where the highway jogs west
and set our things down to hitchhike and were shortly in the
warm cab of a rancher's truck. It was driven by a small man
from Mexico from whom Nor, her Spanish confident, got some
details about the herd he tended near Bridgeport and even a
couple of laughs. Ten miles north of Bishop I gestured to where
we wanted to be dropped off. He looked to Nor. "*Está bien,*" she
said, and he left us on the shoulder of 395 halfway up Sherwin
Summit.

"You're kidding," she said.

We set off. The snow was ankle deep for the first half mile but
thinned as we angled up through sagebrush and pinyon, and on
the exposed ridge there were just a few inches. Nor had her little
gym bag and a climber's rucksack with the heavy stuff—tortillas,

jars of salsa, some beer. I carried a regular backpack with as much as I could fit. After half an hour we crossed the narrow strand of pavement that is the gorge road.

"Not far," I said.

"How in the world do you know where you are?"

"It's our driveway. Even if it's eight miles long."

We walked up the road a quarter mile, then down a dirt spur that led to our camp. The snow up here had blown around and even melted some, so we were post-holing to four inches, crunching along toward oblivion. Finally the rounded edges of Pete's trailer glowed in the moonlight.

"Holy God," Nor said. "Some little edge of the universe."

In twenty minutes we had the woodstove blazing, kerosene lamps lit, and a pot of canned soup balanced on the tiny back-packing stove we used inside. I shoveled half the patio and then went to work on the car, brushing off snow and chipping at the hard crust of ice underneath. No worry about scratching or even denting it, though I was careful around the rear, where a bear had left long parallel scoriations one summer. The Buick roared to life with the first turn of the key.

"Systems working," I reported.

We sat on two small folding chairs at the kitchen end of the trailer. Between us and the bedside the fire popped and hissed in the woodstove. I turned a milk crate upside down for a table and opened two of the beers she had carried. Nor poured soup into plastic bowls she recognized from years before. She produced a loaf of sheepherder's bread from town and I found a hunk of cheese in one of the military-style ammo carriers we used to secure food from mice and squirrels.

"Party time," I said. "We have orders."

I explained what we had to do the next morning and what I knew about who was coming, and I could see Nor making mental checklists, occasionally interrupting about a detail. "Is there water?" "What's the toilet situation?" She seemed eager to help if bemused we were up to the same business as years ago, something so antic and involved. We opened more beer. Her med-school social life, she said, was "desiccated." When she did anything with anyone that didn't involve memorizing something or preparing for an exam, it was almost always one-on-one, over coffee, and she would often find herself playing cheerleader. A magnet for doubters and sad sacks. Two of the three people she liked most dropped out in the first two years. This being Hanover, she sometimes showed up for things organized by the under-graduates, outdoor stuff, and even went on a couple of climbing trips to Cathedral and Cannon in the Whites. That she'd done time in the Valley gave her station with the youngsters. That she seemed not to care about it, all the more.

I lurched outside to pee. The sky was ablaze, a skunk stripe of the Milky Way across the top. I wondered how my tent had weathered the big snow and headed off to look, but didn't get twenty paces before fearing I'd collapse from fatigue. Even if the tent was fine and my gear dry, the prospect of getting warm in the cold was too painful with the trailer's yellow windows and windless interior behind me. So I turned back, and with Nor standing at the sink cleaning up I fell fully clothed onto the far side of the double bed at the darker end of the trailer.

The next day and night flashed by with fetching and assem-bling and heating up food and stoking fires, and then a string of flickering reunions: "Don't I know you from?" and "Where'd you end up?" and someone else's snow report and "I thought you could do that free with a little variation on the fourth or fifth pitch" and "Want some more? Here, just take it." A few climbers from down at the Pit arrived midafternoon, and a vanload of lift monkeys from Mammoth soon after. Six-packs, guitars, extra clothing. One guy was showing off a pistol, and after he and some others had drained beers they went off a ways to shoot at their cans. The barbecue glowed under a rack of the *carnitas* and *carne asada* Rosa had prepped for me at the Lodge, but the wind was such that everyone stood inside or in the lee of the trailer. I heard Nor explaining who she was to one of the Bishop guys who guides for the same outfit as Pete. She told him finishing med school wasn't finishing anything, really—just a lead-up to several more years of training. The guy looked at his feet, then headed outside for another beer.

Another group from Mammoth roared up in a Ford Falcon outfitted with snow tires, then a little while later two guys I recognized along with a tiny companion, unfamiliar to me, who crawled out of the back seat only after they had unloaded the two duffels stuffed beside her. They had driven from Red Rock, near Vegas, in a single push, and they hadn't been out of their little sedan for an hour before making it known that their small friend had only days before become the third woman to free Levitation 29—"leading every pitch" tacked to the report as it was quietly passed around the camp. It was dark now but not late. I was tending the fire, the Red Rock threesome standing in a tight, mostly mute circle nearby. Then the whine of Pete's dirt bike, not from the south like everyone else but from the matrix of sandy roads we used as a northerly shortcut, and a few minutes later the flash of his headlight through the pin-yons. Nor heard it, too. I saw her through the window at the end of the trailer, dropping whatever she had been assembling at the counter to take off her wool hat and comb her hair with her fingers. She put the hat back on and glanced at herself in the window. The buzz of the bike grew louder, and when Pete pulled up Nor and I were both at the trailer door, his headlight blinding us. He revved the engine a couple of times before cutting it.

"Joseph!" he shouted. "Eleanor!" Pete's signature was his tenor voice, which tonight seemed even to warm the frigid air.

It took him a moment to remove his goggles and helmet. Nor didn't rush past me to greet him, but then I noticed she was in socks.

Pete dropped his pack to the ground. It looked to weigh a hundred pounds. He balanced his helmet and jacket on the bike and tromped over to the trailer with the exaggerated high steps I'd seen him use in attaining a summit after a long slog. His hair was long, his face wind-burned.

He folded Nor into a hug.

When he looked at me, he pointed to his shoulder.

"Been worse," I said.

Pete stepped into the trailer to greet some of the others and strip himself of additional layers. I hadn't seen him in seven weeks. The little blond crow's-feet radiating out from the edges of his eyes punctuated his already lively gestures, and he seemed thinner, not unhealthy, but as reported—like he'd been training. He went right to work on the punch, mixing everything in a five-gallon paint bucket we ordinarily used upside down for a stool. Soon the counters were littered with grapefruit peels and half-empty bottles and the trailer smelled like a citrus orchard but for the stain of liquor. Then Pete lugged the sloshing bucket outside, and the party kicked into higher gear.

I joined the throng, much as I ever do—had a couple of beers and even what Pete would call a thimbleful of his Solstice Citrus Conglomerate. I moved in from the perimeter from time to time to add wood to the blazing fire on the porch or to gather empties for our pile or to check in with one of the half dozen people I knew. There must have been forty in all. Many had brought stools and folding chairs and blankets, and not long after the first round of tacos had been passed around there were three guitars and a flute, bongos, and Pete on the mandolin. Nor had been running the kitchen, but now she came out too and, seeing her, Pete pulled a stool from behind him and patted it with his hand. She wrapped herself in another jacket, took a seat, and sang harmony. After another couple of songs, Pete whistled something to one of the two Kevins, who disappeared in the dark and emerged with a fiddle, and now the band was complete.

The big voices took over for a while, and some even danced, though whether from joy or merely to stay warm I couldn't tell. If anyone laid down a guitar someone else picked it up, keeping things alive whenever anyone went for a refill of what they called "the grog." At some point I wandered off with my headlamp to track the pistol guys' path through the snow and gather the shredded remains of their target practice. I had a peek at my tent, too—bowed but unbroken, looking like it had been pitched there for years. I brushed off the windward side and tightened the guylines. Everything inside was dry and intact.

I circled around the backside of the trailer, found more empties, and came upon the guide from Bishop who had been talking to Nor earlier and another guy I didn't recognize. They were taking a pee and having a chat on this darker side of camp. That's when I heard it first—Maria or Mara, a name I didn't recognize and wouldn't have registered at all but inside of two hours I heard it several more times and always in just that sort of hushed, private exchange between two or three and always between men and usually just the climbers. It was less a flash than a ripple—the first two or three times like overhearing someone's horoscope and feeling curious but uninvested, just more of the regular blabber among climbers who were always spraying about what they had done or projecting about what they were planning to do or referencing someone they knew who did something or was planning to do something, but deeper into the night and long before I slipped off to my tent I realized this wasn't idle or ancillary, this chatter, and the unrecognizable name hadn't been pulled out of a magazine or a guidebook. It was something Pete said to someone who had got him to answer "What's next?"

Later, about midnight, I was studying the stars with binoculars when it came together, all at once like a sobering clang: I hadn't found Pete's bike in October because I hadn't gone up the right canyon. The name wasn't Maria or Mara but Moriah, Mount Moriah. I had seen it on a topo map: just north and east of Dragon Peak, a nondescript, stand-alone mountain east of the crest. Dragon was familiar. We used its southern saddle as the preferred approach to Clarence King and the Kings-Kern Divide and a couple of times summited just for the view. I'd seen Moriah's gentler, scree-laden southwestern flanks several times, and like Pete I'd noticed the tight band of topo lines on the north side, telltales of a promising domain, but there was nothing in the guidebooks to indicate activity over there and neither of us had ever had a visual of the steep side until Pete disappeared for that last stretch of autumn before the snow.

The wind died, the music kicked up again, and I fell into one of the comfortable chairs near the fire. But the name in the air seemed etched across my forehead now, and long before the party wound down I was in my tent alone.

The night before the party, sometime after I'd fallen into Pete's bed, Nor settled in beside me and the bend of the mattress pulled me out of a deep sleep. For half an hour I lay there thinking I should decamp for my tent but hoping Nor would sink into sleep and then I might again, too. Something about her breathing indicated wakefulness.

"Nor?"

"Hi."

The firelight glowed on the ceiling of the trailer.

"Why are you here?" I said.

She sighed.

"To see Pete. And you. I don't know."

Then she said, "I liked it here when we were here. I liked it until I didn't. Until I had to do something else, besides, you know, roam around."

"And scavenge."

"No, I liked that."

"It got worse."

She chuckled. She had rummaged through dumpsters with us in Boulder and hovered in the Yosemite Lodge cafeteria to intercept scraps of sausage and uneaten pancakes from trays left by tourists.

"So what do you think now?"

"School hasn't exactly been a joyride."

"But you're glad you did it."

"Yeah. And now I've got to make another landing."

"Near Pete."

"Well, that's why I'm here. But letters and phone calls, you know, they don't give you much to go on. Even if he does go on and on." They hadn't seen one another in eighteen months, not since Pete flew to Buffalo for ten days in the heart of the '87 climbing season to move his mother out of their family home. Nor had driven over from New Hampshire, though in Pete's version she'd come all that way less to see him than to help his mother.

We were quiet. The fire settled.

"Okay if I sleep in here?" I asked. I was under a down bag we'd patched after a marmot tore a hole in the bottom. Nor lay under a stack of the old-style cotton sleeping bags that smell damp even in the desert.

"Stay, Joe."

In the open space between us her hand was searching, and then her fingers folded into mine.

⌒

If it felt strange to have Nor back, it was also a relief. Hers was a familiar if more tightly bound brand of the anxiety and fear I'd spent years negotiating alone, even though most of the time there wasn't a whole lot on me—except to be scared for Pete at the belay, and to hang on for dear life if he pitched off.

The hanging on was *de rigeur*. The pitching-off—that happened too. We had been in Colorado for a couple of months, fall of '84. On our way west we stopped over at Indian Creek and camped next to a Lester and Bill from England. They were headed the other direction and all high about a canyon on the south side of Red Rock, in Nevada, they'd just come from, one we'd heard of but never with all this gilding. It's hardly unusual to meet up with climbers in one place who are all on fire about someplace else. Every set of crags calls on a particular set of skills. Lacking these, one tends to nostalgia for the last place you had them. But Pete took stock in Brits' enthusiasms as a matter of course. They were unfailingly understated, their talents honed on unfeatured and dangerous gritstone. American crags—big, dry, protectable, even pretty—were gravy to them. (French climbers were the opposite—perfectly unreliable for all their hyperbole, the *très très* steep and *très magnifique*. Germans were sandbaggers, the Japanese bold and productive but self-effacing. Australians, we felt, gave the fairest report.)

Lester and Bill had planned to visit Red Rock for just three days but stayed almost two weeks and discovered their Black Velvet Canyon only near the end. They thought this slice of Red Rock had it all, and when Bill said, "There's so much more to put up," Pete grew more interested. We spent most of this little stint at the Creek together, showed them some four-star out-of-the-way cracks, with Pete pumping them for Black Velvet dope in between our bouts with sandstone splitters. As their hands grew bloodied, they got reinspired, so instead of continuing east per their plans, they agreed to meet us on the west side of Vegas in a week.

An unlikely pair, these two—Lester was taking a hiatus from his physics studies at Cambridge, and Bill came from three generations of ship's mechanics in Portsmouth. Bill had dropped out of a trade school so he wouldn't become chained to work; in between climbing ventures he made money repairing engines on pleasure boats not far from where his father made only a little more money on big ships. They met as eighteen-year-olds on a crag in the Peak District. Each was outpacing his own partner, if not with talent then for sheer appetite, and by '83 they were in their fifth year together.

"My steady," Lester told us by the campfire.

He was the more affable, his eyes darting, his features taut and sharp like his skin had been stretched over his bones. Bill was quiet and feral, though after a beer or two he warmed. Bill was a rhinoceros to Lester's gazelle, his face square and his shoulders packed with muscle and his hands so meaty we later named a painfully wide Sierra crack Bill's Bannister in homage to how readily he could hand-jam the sort of thing we bloodied knees and elbows to ascend. They'd been living out of a tiny yellow Toyota for four months, from Squamish to Yosemite, Joshua Tree, and Red Rock, and when we intercepted them they were headed to Colorado, Kentucky, and finally the Gunks. The car was stuffed with camping and climbing gear. It sat heavily on the tires and seemed even to list, recoil, and recover with each bend in the road—due in some measure to the beer in the back, part of the spoils of Lester's winnings during their Red Rock stay. They'd gone into Vegas for provisions and distraction and it didn't take long for Bill to suggest that Lester, being a numbers guy, might do better than hold his own among the retirees playing blackjack at mom-and-pop casinos on the sadder, west side of town. At one point that first night they were $250 in the black and still managed to get out with much of it, and if two other trips to town were less successful than the first, they were nonetheless "plenty positive for pint provisions," Bill said. When we met their car was freighted with two cases of Boddingtons and one of Murphy's Stout. The Boddingtons they drank warm from tall yellow cans you had to open by punching triangular holes in the top. The Murphys were in aluminum, with modern pull-tabs, but these, they said, were in reserve for the major victories: "Good style on anything hard, English football developments, the queen's birthday—that sort of thing."

We found them outside the supermarket on West Charleston, and I felt glad to see them again. Mixing it up with other climbers is one of the few wild cards in the climbing life that pays benefits—getting thrown in with strangers, sometimes in tight situations that can last for hours or days so that you get to know what they smell like when they're scared. And when it's all done, you march back to your cars together, rinse your face in a stream or from a campground faucet, and maybe share a beer or some coffee and stale nuts someone found between the seats. Then you say so long as you might to a hitchhiker.

In Vegas we resupplied with oatmeal and pasta and powdered lemonade, filled our water jugs from a gas station spigot, and at sunset followed the slow boat of Lester and Bill's little box of a car toward the magnificent, multicolored cliffs and canyons twenty miles west of town. In the morning Pete and I did their last favorite route, the glorious Epinephrine, while they went off to repeat another they liked a couple hundred yards to the left. Epi is no technical feat, but it's almost two thousand feet long and calls for a considerable palette of techniques. That they'd climbed it with only six cams on their rack and in no more time than it took us established their bona fides all the more. In the evening Lester and I made a firepit next to the cars in a dirt lot just outside the mouth of the canyon, and at dusk we saw Bill hiking back up the hill toward us, entirely hidden but for his knees and feet by the tangled nest of sticks and branches he'd managed to gather.

The blaze we tended that night seemed in retrospect to have set in motion much of what followed—not just our hanging around so late into the night as to burn through all the fuel Bill had gathered, nor our cutting into the second case of Boddingtons, but the exchanges and disquisitions and bombast, most of it Pete's. Climbers around a campfire can be a wary, conversationally challenged lot. They take stabs at politics or philosophy or personal history, but these threads fizzle out with a summary remark or dismissive gesture. Only when the elephant is fully invited to the side of the fire do things warm up: your climbing résumé, your climbing ambitions, what you heard somebody else say about something on either list—this is all there is. And corollary domains: style, ethics, history, and weather.

Sometime after dark, Lester brought up the "bolt wars," reporting bits of what they'd heard bandied about at Joshua Tree, including talk of a phenomenon some were calling "sport climbing." Bill and I ventured tentative opinions, each of us mindful that twelve or fourteen hours later this would no longer be a hypothetical matter. Then Pete launched through a brief orientation to Death-Fall Prevention, or "DFP," he called it, and a more elaborate defense of the practice, Lester listening earnestly and Bill poking at the fire with a long stick of manzanita. During the ensuing exchange about how much safety should be a consideration in first ascents, and whether, when, and how much to bolt generally, I noticed the Brits eying one another. The game-altering prospect of someone coming along to retro-bolt the harrowing established lines on their gritstone at home was dizzying—nearly as enticing as it was repulsive.

Then more Pete, now with a sermon I'd heard him deliver versions of several times before and often as not to foreigners and usually by a fire and always with beer: "Because after He made the light, He needed something more, something complementary but also opposite. So He made the rock. Then the glaciers to wax, buff, and polish, and the heat to melt the ice and grow the corn to feed the pigs so Josiah and Clarence and Joseph and the others would have enough dried and salted pork to trade to the Paiutes and Mono Indians who showed them the way up the canyon into the high country where the light He made was like no other on this rocky earth. And in the next generation, John (like a second-gen John of yore: shaggy, wild-eyed, a vagabond—Joe can tell you more about the first later), this John with a Scottish accent and poetic disposition, calling it the Range of Light and wandering for weeks at a time with no more than biscuit and tea and just enough pemmican to stave off starvation, and summiting all the peaks Clarence and William Brewer and the others did but also these others—Ritter and Cathedral and Russell and not just what would become Clyde Minaret fifty years later but each individual nameless spine of the Minarets. And a writer too, this John, so the word got out, and in time it wasn't to explore and map or extol but its own thing, the climbing, and then this, our century: Francis Farquhar and Underhill and theirs, and finally the greatest of all, Norman Clyde, and his.

"And then, after the dormant years, made so by a collapse of the banks and the mobilization that put the Fascists back in their hole for a while anyway, back at Ground Zero: the Cathedral, Jerusalem. Another John, this one Swiss. A blacksmith. Taciturn, gentle, plaid-clad and wool-knickered. Sunburnt, visionary, fearless. Higher Cathedral Spire, Lost Arrow, Steck-Salathe.

All with handmade pitons and hemp ropes. The first gearhead. Doesn't bother forging his own big pitons, just saws them from the legs of iron woodstoves from Bay Area backyards. Thank you Standard Oil for making the woodstove disposable. From what Steck and Roper and others of John's ropemates report, all much younger, mind you, probably the first great 5.10 climber. And his routes had just two flavors: tedious, and terrifying."

Lester looked on with a cool, possibly skeptical smirk. They knew the history, and they understood Pete's was just a version, and one that encompassed almost nothing of what the Swiss Germans and Italians and their own Brits had done to get us to this point. Bill didn't seem even to be listening. He tossed two of the bigger sticks onto the fire.

Pete continued: "And then the Modernists and their so-called Golden Age: Robbins and Frost, and Harding plus anyone-who-would-go-along-with-Warren, and theirs—Camp 4 itself now subdivided into four: orthodox, conservative, reformed, and the bandits, the boundaries entirely permeable, of course, and memberships determined less by what you did in the day than where you happened to wake up the morning after.

"And finally, our people, our forefathers, the free-climbers: Bridwell, Long, and Little Lynnie. Kauk and Bachar. Wild Yabo and ecstatic Tobin Sorenson, R.I.P. Tobin. And the outsiders: Layton Kor and Henry Barber and every worthy itinerant making the requisite pilgrimage to Mecca, and—what, three years ago?—your very own Ron Fawcett."

"Forgot Joe Brown," Bill interrupted, popping another can of Boddingtons.

"And John Gill," Lester said. "Talk about a pioneer."

"Steve Longenecker," I added.

"Who?" Lester said.

"North Carolina. You never heard of him."

"And Ray," Pete said. "Closing the loop: Salathe to Chouinard to Jardine. Where would we be without Ray Jardine?"

"Right where we are," Bill said, a nod to their having just six cams between them.

"I don't mean us," Pete said. "I mean 'they,' the Crofts and Kauks and your Fawcett, the ones at the edge."

We were quiet again for a while. The Brits had gotten more than they asked for and knew better than to throw any more fuel Pete's way, much less say anything they'd be reminded of or have to prove in the morning.

Then Lester, if only out of an instinct for politeness: "But is it good? Did he ever get beyond the 'Let there be light,' and rock, and Friends and say 'it is good' like he did last time?"

"Ask Joe." Pete said. "He handles the commentary. I just do the verse."

We watched the sparks flutter off this latest piece of fresh fuel and crackle in the night.

I was quiet.

"Joe's thinking about seminary," Pete said, drawing out the *s* like it was social work or nursing school I was making noise about.

I said, "Joe's thinking about whether it's good is all Joe's thinking about."

"Good or no," Pete said, "it's better than it was. The pendulum swings about, but imagine it got stuck when Harding was having his way. You'd have thirty-five bolt ladders on El Cap put up by thirty-five different winos. You'd have a *via ferrata* for tourists instead of a handful of Valley hotshots wondering whether one, Harding's very own Dawn Wall, might one day go free."

╰┅╮

The next morning the four of us set off toward the vague if animating idea we'd hatched about a patch of cliff Lester had pointed to the day before—well to the right of the established routes on the Black Velvet Wall. After an hour's hike we dropped our packs by the side of the creek and studied the dark vertical wall that forms the south side of the canyon. From the streambed the line seemed blank above the first obvious corner, but the mahogany varnish on this type of sandstone often looks unbroken and polished from below. *In situ*, plates and fissures appear, and because the smooth outer layer is harder than the grainier interior, these edges, though small, are often positive, sometimes sufficiently deep to take gear and in any case famously accommodating in the way they receive crimped fingers. At Red Rock, climbers pull not just down but ever-so-slightly out, dramatically enhancing their power so that even some easy trade routes here are dead vertical, these composed of larger and more dramatically weathered sections of the patina-plated sandstone.

But Black Velvet Canyon is more weather-protected than, say, Ginger Buttress or the Aeolian Wall, the rock less patterned and in-cut. A few of the newer routes, including Prince of Darkness, were among those raising hackles in climbing circles for being entirely bolt-protected even if everyone agreed the natural protection was wanting or worse. We brought a dozen bolts and a hammer with us, figuring we'd need at least four and probably twice that many for the belay stances between what looked to be about four pitches. In any case, the regular priority, to follow a natural line of the easiest climbing, would be a secondary consideration to finding fissures and seams for nuts or small cams or some kind of protection. As friendly as the Red Rock sandstone is to the fingers and toes, it can be outrageously disdainful of gear.

Pete held out four twigs, making a little ceremony of determining who got which pitch. We stood in a circle, each picking from his outstretched hand.

"Long wins," he said.

"Wins what?" Bill asked.

"Chooses the pitch."

Lester's was longer than mine or Bill's, but the remaining twig was the longest, though Pete disposed of it so quickly no one could be sure he hadn't cheated.

"Number three for me," he said. Lester chose the fourth pitch, which was the only one about which we could tell nothing except that it was unlikely we'd get there today. Bill took the first, and I got number two.

Bill was compact and efficient, more wrestler than climber in build, but, as Pete noted, any Brit on a road trip is nearly always better than any American at home. He topped out on his pitch before I had finished changing into my climbing shoes. He placed just five or six pieces of gear in 160 feet, stopping on a sloping triangular ledge where he built an anchor he said would hold a truck and called down for additional stoppers for the next pitch. Lester cleaned, and I went third in order to get a jump on pitch two while Lester brought Pete up to the first stance.

Bill's corner was harder than it appeared, and the next pitch took me a while, no single move memorable or even sketchy but the protection scant and nearly all of the holds disconcertingly dusted with sand. First-ascent jitters abounding—taking nothing for granted, testing everything, memorizing sequences in case I needed to reverse the moves. I carried the hammer and half the bolts on the back of my harness but finagled adequate gear, including slings on several of the more distinctly eroded plates. About two-thirds of the way through I grew confident and started glancing ahead to the next section, Pete's pitch. It looked still more daunting than it had from the creek bed—several degrees steeper than mine and more polished than anything in these first three hundred feet, and with no clear end point. It took me a while to find my own finish, a couple of casts, some downclimbing and traversing, but eventually I alighted upon the decent stance I sought—a sloping edge that was just two or three feet wide and would be uncomfortable at best for three of us. I drilled the first two bolts on the route, these for anchors.

The sun had dipped behind the ridge by the time Pete started up my pitch, and as he climbed toward the belay I could see him sizing up the stance, looking for any natural gear placements I may have missed or neglected. It was typical Pete: climbing my pitch without so much as pausing, relaxed, alert, assessing the next section. But he didn't say anything at the belay. He just went to work sorting gear and reracking for his lead. I brought up Lester, who stopped twice to take photos of the great wall. Bill had climbed second, and when he was leaning off to the side, watching Lester, Pete silently motioned that he wanted me to handle the belay on this next pitch—a first indication he thought it might be serious.

The next was his fiddling with a nut at the bottom of a seam about fifteen feet off the ledge. He had had to make two committing moves through a bulge to get there, a sequence he pondered for several minutes before smoothly dashing through it. Bill watched this with his teeth clenched and leaning off to the right, as if to move out of the fall line, while Lester studied Pete coolly. Now Pete's left foot was pasted onto a decent but slanted half-inch edge, and with his right he pawed anxiously at the patina to maintain his balance while trying to place a nut. It was a brass nut he finally settled on, among the smaller and weaker of the lot but more deeply secured than a larger stopper would be. The next ten feet of climbing went more easily, Pete following the left lip on the edge of this fissure, but above this lone, obvious gash the wall looked plain steep and blank from our vantage. Lester kept his camera at the ready, and Bill looked rapt, maybe even jealous. A set of circumstances like these, and the kind of focus Pete had to summon— about as real as it gets.

Near the top of the seam he got a small stopper on a long sling, and then it was a matter of plying through *terra incognita*. He was merely forty feet out from the belay now, and as much as we longed for a report as to what he saw or how he felt, no one dared holler up to him.

And then, stuck. He was facing left at a good stance, craning his neck to study the wall but unable or unwilling to abandon this position for what seemed half an hour. We couldn't tell if he was climbing-stuck or gear-stuck—route-finding and courage-summoning, or simply danger-assessing. I wanted to urge him to place a bolt, and a couple of times when he turned to look down I thought, *That's it—he'll reach for the hammer now.* Then, and wordlessly, he started downclimbing, easily reversing the moves to the last stopper, then working his way back over the bulge with some coaching from below to help him identify the little chips for feet. Finally he was back at the belay, and still no communication about what he had seen or worried over. He just said, "It's getting late. And I need a hook."

We rapped to the ground, hiked out of the canyon in mute single file, and got back to camp right at dusk. Pete had hardly put his pack down before he started organizing gear for the next day. I got the stove fired up and heated beans and canned tomatoes and tortillas. At some point I saw Bill hand Pete a Boddingtons, as if in sympathy. Pete sipped it while he racked and drank just this one. He was in his sleeping bag not long after we ate.

It was a warm night, with a blaze of stars overhead and a fuzzy white dome to the east—the lights of Las Vegas spraying out into the desert. On the other, dark side of our camp, the black mountains cut a jagged profile. I don't know how the Brits slept, but I did fine. Pete's saying those four words—"I need a hook"—put my mind to rest. He would climb to near his high point, hook a flake, and stand in slings while he drilled a bolt. The climbing would be what it would be, but at least he'd have something conforming to his DFP standard.

In the morning Pete was no less brooding than he'd been the evening before—restless, ready to go half an hour before anyone else, with dark rings around his eyes as if he'd spent half the night staring at those next twenty feet of steep red polish. Before leaving camp we went through the usual checklist—ropes, gear, shoes, harness.

"Hook?" I said.

Pete pulled it from his pocket. He led the way back up the canyon, Bill keeping a step behind him, then me and Lester. From time to time I heard Bill offering encouraging remarks: "Odd it is here, how you can't see the features till you're right on top of them," and, as we neared the cliff, "You got it today, Pete." Pete's keeping so quiet was the third indication.

By midmorning he was setting off again from the top of the second stance. Lester brought a nylon belay seat this time and leaned out on an extension from the anchor beneath and to the side of us. He also brought a long lens. Once Pete clipped the two stoppers he'd placed in the seam above the belay, Lester watched almost entirely through the telephoto lens with which he took the dozen pictures that would memorialize the route in climbing annals and haunt Pete for years. In a fraction of yesterday's time, Pete was right back where he'd stalled, but this time he hiked through the move as if he'd been rehearsing it for weeks. He reached up and right for a dusty crimp, levered to a high step with his left foot, and then extended his left hand fully with a slapping gesture that appeared at once desperate and confident. Somehow he kept his balance, and shortly his right foot was securely placed on the crimp he'd used for his hand. What next? There was no way he could hold this position handlessly to drill a bolt, and there appeared to be no other features in which to place protection. He made incremental adjustments to his position, shifting a bit to the worse, left foot. Then, reaching blindly for the hook at the front of his gear sling, he removed it, placing the tiny curled edge of the beak on a flake above and to the left.

"Solid," Lester whispered. "He's got it."

A long sling on the hook was next, and we held our breath to see whether the flake would hold him.

But rather than weighting the sling and using it like an etrier, Pete just clipped it to the rope like an ordinary piece of protection.

"Crikey," Lester said.

"Got to be something he sees," Bill said. "Something close."

The hook was mental security at best. In a fall it would be jarred from its tenuous position, and even if it weren't the blunt force would surely fracture a sandstone flake.

I could see Pete gathering himself. I wanted to holler up some encouragement or warning or both, but I said nothing. I looked down to be sure I had adequate slack for him in the belay. My hands were glistening.

Pete made two moves, and with the hook now at his right thigh I thought I saw a little tremor in his legs. I was hoping he'd reach down for the hook and place it higher, on something better and out of our view. Then maybe he'd resign himself to prudence. But he kept on, and without evidence of strain achieved a slightly higher stance so that his right foot stood on the same flake as the hook. Now, unless there was a massive adjacent hold out of our view, there was no way he could retrieve and re-place the hook.

"What you got there?" Bill asked Lester, who had the telephoto pasted to his face.

"Bulgy," he said. Lester had shifted his position, his legs forming the base of a tripod so he stood directly out from the cliff. "Maybe no worse above. But maybe no better."

"Serious bloke, your guy," Bill said to me. "Bring 'im our way someday, for the gritstone. Be right at home."

Then the shaking, at first nearly indiscernible, like wind rippling his pants. I couldn't tell whether Bill or Lester noticed, but I'd watched Pete climb so much and in so many contexts I could see he was doing all he could just to stay calm. The brass nut and stopper were forty feet below and to his right, and the sling on the hook dangled from the rope half a body length below him. He held his position for several minutes, occasionally leaning inches to the side to study the next section, and in time he seemed to steady himself. He knew better than we did a fall would be a test of fate, the hook unlikely to hold him and the nut so far below he'd suffer eighty or ninety feet of air before finding out whether it was secure.

"He's got a plan," Lester said.

"Feckin' hope so," Bill said.

The rope in my hands was moist.

And then Pete stepped out and up with the left foot and reached for something we couldn't see. We held our breath in hopes it was deep and secure, the miracle hold of an in-cut flake or horn. As Pete committed to this left foot and removed his right from the crimp the hook stuck for a half a second to the smooth underside of his shoe, then fluttered down the rope, pinging off the rock harmlessly like the bell a kindergarten teacher uses to call children in from recess. Pete made his next move just as the sling hung up on his last piece of protection, and in several decisive gestures he seemed to be confirming what Bill had said about Red Rock on the hike in—the features appear only when you're on top of them.

"Looking good," Lester said.

"Gear?" I said. "Anything coming up?"

"Maybe it's easy," Bill said.

"Is there gear?" I repeated.

"Oh, wait," Lester said.

Bill and I both looked at Lester. Then we looked up.

Pete was shaking again, and now not subtly. He had turned to face left, the outside of his right foot on a hold that appeared decent and his left pawing at something slightly higher. But the right foot was scissoring.

"Better be a jug," Bill said. "Blimey Jesus."

"Seems not," Lester said, peering through the camera.

Pete turned slightly and looked down. I wondered if he was thinking of trying to reverse the moves to where the hook had been—the last place he'd seemed semi-secure—but this was just a wide-eyed, final assessment he was making, and with that he removed the shaky leg from its better hold and set off on the blank sea of red rock stretching out of our view. A couple of moves later he was making progress, inching through this dark patina. Then he started to shake again, not just his toes now but fingertips too, or at least this is what Lester reported later. It appeared there were holds, if only tiny breaks between the plates, but if Pete could have held them at all he surely couldn't for long with all the clamoring of limbs.

And then he came off.

At first he seemed suspended in air, his slack rope like the tether of a floating astronaut, and fully relaxed, clutching for neither the spare stone he just shook himself off nor the knot at his waist, just waiting calmly for what must come next.

I still hear the audible start I gave—that of a passenger in a car about to bowl over a pedestrian. I gripped the rope on either side of my belay device and cinched it tightly down as Pete flew past us, his hair blown straight up and the gear sling trailing him overhead. If the upper of the two stoppers held, he'd have thirty feet less to fall. But if it didn't, there was a ledge he may or may not clear as well as an awful lot riding on that first brass nut fifteen feet above our belay. If this popped, all four of us were beholden to the two bolts I'd drilled yesterday for anchors.

The entire arcing fall is a silent movie in my memory: Pete's expressionless calm, Bill's refusal to avert his gaze, Lester aiming with his camera. I saw the blurry photographs later, three of them, but never heard the shutter or the snap of rewind. The silence shattered with the small explosion of that stopper popping out of the rock and the sudden crunch of the rope slamming down on the carabiner attached to the brass nut, Pete now swinging left to right eighty feet beneath us on a rope so suddenly taut it might have cut us in half except that he was headed into the left-facing corner that nearly killed him, Pete now passing out of view and then the awful sound, like someone driving a motorcycle into a brick wall, or, Bill said, a cow giving birth.

With the second rope Lester rappelled down to Pete. He had regained consciousness by the time Lester got to him. Lester secured Pete to this other rope and descended to the first stance. Then Bill went down to Pete and hollered up directions, and with two ropes we managed to lower Pete to Lester from my stance. By the time I rappelled off, they had Pete lying on the ground, Bill kneeling beside him with a water bottle, a jacket under his head as a pillow. Lester had run out for help. Later Bill told me Pete said nothing in that first hour except, "It was right there, not five feet away."

"What?" Bill asked.

"Hand crack. Deep as a well."

Then he seemed to sleep, and Bill stayed close, marking his breathing. There had been blood in his mouth and right ear, a stain of it on the rock beside him, but by the time I got there he didn't seem to be bleeding anymore.

The rest was pretty efficient: the Search and Rescue guys with their wire litter, the paramedics and their ambulance parked right at our campsite. Pete was calm through all the transitions, more drowsy than pained. I handled the paperwork while the other paramedic checked out Pete and got the IV going, and just before they pulled out I asked what they thought.

"His vitals are awful."

Bill and Lester had cleaned up most of the camp, and when I was through packing we agreed to meet at the hospital. They set off, and in a few minutes I did, too. A half mile down the red dirt road I glanced down and noticed I was in my climbing harness, the metal belay device with which I'd held Pete still dangling at my waist.

About the next several days all I recall was so much green: the pale green of the hospital walls, green glow of fluorescent light, the green beans in the cafeteria in a stainless steel warmer, these out at every meal and never diminished. And Pete's face. They tested him for everything and found very little, but the medical assessment—considerable and widespread internal hemorrhaging—continued to worry, so they held him for nearly a week, and not just for those days in the hospital but for several weeks after his skin was one or another shade of green. He had a concussion, too, the consequence of his slamming into the corner. I kept pretty close for a couple of days, calling his mom every few hours, watching the numbers on digital displays at his bedside and trying to extract the latest test results from nurses who eyed me suspiciously, as if to say this is what happens when you put your friend up to something ridiculous. During the several-day stretch of outright convalescence that followed, I hung around less vigilantly. Mostly he needed just to sleep. He appeared smaller in the hospital bed, drawn into himself, often tucking a hand under his chin as if his neck were too sore or weak to hold his head even while lying down. Looking at him there I couldn't help but wonder—that straw and that pitch might just as easily have been mine, and I worried I wouldn't have stopped to drill a bolt either, and not for any reason other than some tacit pressure to be bold and strong where I had no business being at all.

Bill and Lester stayed in a Vegas motel for the first two nights, but on the third they went back up to the campsite at the mouth of the canyon, ostensibly to save money, and a couple of days later they checked in once more to say goodbye. I was in the room when they arrived.

"How's the fighter?" Bill said.

His hands were lined with chalk from their day's endeavors. I don't know what I expected them to do with all this down time, but the thought of climbing was sickening.

"Fit as 'ell," Pete said, slurping through a straw from a large plastic cup. He spoke like someone who'd had a stroke.

"Oh good. We worried you got spatchcocked there."

Pete didn't even try to smile.

"Come with us tomorrow?" Bill said.

"If you're playing cards, maybe."

"That's tonight," Lester said. "Last round."

Pete turned on his side and closed his eyes as though they were there to read him a bedtime story. "What's next?" he asked.

"Colorado. Just a fortnight. Then east. Got a mate from home at the Gunks mid-month."

They said their goodbyes no more or less awkwardly than climbers do by the side of a road or in a parking lot, and then we stepped out into the hall so I could report the latest of what I'd gotten about Pete. Lester asked the sort of questions of someone who'd been around med students. Bill paced in place like he'd seen more than he wanted or needed to know, then ducked back into the room. A few minutes later he came back out into the hall, we said so long, and they walked out of the hospital together.

Pete never told me about that last little conference with Bill, and I hadn't thought anything of it until the new Red Rock book came out two years later and the route Pete had careened off was right there, all written up:

Mood Management—5.10d R, 5 pitches. Pete Hunter, Joe Holland, Lester Jameson, and Bill Sewall. F.A. Sept. '84.

We were in Wilson's, in Bishop, leafing through the sticky, freshly inked pages. The Black Velvet Canyon chapter's frontispiece was a full color photo of Pete just minutes before he flew off the cliff. In small letters at the bottom of the adjacent page: "Pete Hunter, about to take medicine on Pitch 3 of Mood Management. L. Jameson photo." We'd seen this and others of Lester's photos before—he sent them from England—but until that afternoon in Wilson's we didn't know they had completed the route, nor when. Nor that they had placed three bolts to protect the section where Pete fell.

Pete studied the page. "10d," he said, shaking his head. "I'm such a puss." He closed the book and placed it back among the other copies.

We never returned to Red Rock.

⌐

On the morning after the party the wind on my tent flap woke me before sunrise. I didn't want to bother them in the trailer, much less survey the damage from the night before. I lay in my bag thinking about a move south. Someplace warm and dry and quiet. Maybe I'd drive Nor back to LA, then head east into the low desert.

When I heard the trailer door I dressed and went in to make coffee. Nor already had. My mug had a dishtowel over the top to keep it warm. She and Pete sat up on the bed with theirs. The fire had been recently stoked but it was still quite cold inside.

"How bad's it out there?" Pete said.

"It's not the Alabama Hills," I said, referencing the post-apocalypse we'd faced three years before. I took a stool by the fire.

"Getting civilized," he said.

"Got a PO box too. At this rate you'll have a credit card inside of ten years."

"Hey," Pete said, raising his mug. "Us three again."

He appeared on the edge of ecstasy. Nor and I were more guarded.

"Let's do something," he said.

"A picture!" Nor said.

He had something more involved in mind, like a drive up to Hot Creek, or a hike.

Nor rolled onto her feet. She put her jacket and shoes on. "Give me a minute."

Pete and I sat near the woodstove, nursing our mugs as on a wilderness bivouac.

"Moriah?" I said.

He'd wrapped his head in Nor's scarf like a Bedouin. He didn't lift his eyes.

"The north side?" I asked.

"Northeast, north." He blew on his coffee. "It's a friggin' uncut diamond. Unbelievable."

"Uncut. And fully in the marketplace now."

"I know. What's wrong with me?" he said. "Was I drunk?"

"Blabber, blather. No one cares."

"Still," he said. "Why talk? Why tell?"

"I don't know. You do it all the time. Everyone does."

He seemed genuinely puzzled.

"It's fuel," I said. "Or at least lube. A way you have of setting up the doing."

The door popped open. "Stand here, you two." Nor's plume of breath disappeared at the threshold.

"The approach?" I said.

"One drainage north of Dragon. Like another century. Bighorn sheep, springs. No hunters' trails. No mining riffraff."

I could tell he was taking my measure. Sure, I was intrigued—though maybe less by the prospect of ticking a worthy route than by making this the last one.

"Come on," Nor said. "Stand over here."

With a blanket she had made a little platform for her Nikon on the gas tank of the motorcycle, and when Pete and I were at the trailer door she looked once more through the camera, then ran over to us. We lifted our mugs toward Mount Tom as if to toast any number of the things hanging in the air. In the seconds before the snap of the shutter, Pete kept rhythm with the barely audible ticking: "Blabber, blather. Blabber, blather. And happy New Year."

⌒

It was a big year for snow and so lockdown cold in the valley that after a while people didn't even talk about the weather anymore but just blew into their hands and got on with their business. Things were slow in town, the combination of constant cold and frequent storms putting a damper on the SoCal traffic. Access to our camp was sketchy too—the Gorge road blown over with snow that iced up when the sun came out—so with the Lodge rarely more than half full I took a room there for much of January. I cleaned rooms in the morning and worked on applications in the afternoon. I got the last of these in the mail on the last day of the month, the very deadline.

In February I drove to the desert, first to the southern edge of Joshua Tree where the camping was free and the temps warm. I hiked in Anza-Borrego during the start of the wildflower season, then drove to Twentynine Palms to see a guy who did body work on Josh climbers. I had to get my shoulder fixed or tell Pete to line up someone else for the coming season. This guy dressed in baggy cotton and beads and talked constantly while he worked on you, but several climbers had told me he was for real, and after two weeks of doing his exercises I could raise my arm over my head with little pain and in a month I was pulling on easy routes at Josh. I sent Pete a card suggesting he find me in Hidden Valley when he was through on the mountain. "*P.S.,*" I added. "*Pick up the mail en route.*" I figured he'd be delivering my fate. Then I started training hard—running up Mount Ryan, doing reps with the gym equipment at the climbers' camp, and taking care not to load my shoulder on anything terribly hard. I met a tireless Brit named Charlie and in two weeks we ticked more than seventy-five pitches on a greatest-hits-of-Josh tour, and by the end of March I had moved from resigned to something like hopeful for one more season before I headed off to school and then, who knows what. For the first time in many years the climbing felt, well, meaningful, if only as a means of extracting myself.

The irony wasn't lost on me: back in my body, long days in the desert, training in the sun, I was the paragon of the itinerant climbing bum. Limber, light, happier than I'd been in a year. I had thought I would continue my winter's reading and make other gestures befitting an about-to-be seminarian, but even after hours on the rock all I wanted to do was look through guidebooks or talk to other climbers about what and when or lay out gear for the next day's doings. Even Moriah slipped along the horizon of my imagination. The sober subjects I'd tackled in the Bishop Library—they never came out of their box in the trunk. When I look back from this vantage, it's this interregnum I find arresting. My liberties were measureless—hundreds of miles from Pete, weeks and weeks without contact. And yet I was holding modest court in a comfortable Hidden Valley campsite, dispensing advice to assorted hangers-on, bouldering in the golden light of sunset. In Pete's absence, I became him.

Then the whir of the bike. I was barefoot and shirtless at the picnic table, making coffee on a hot morning. Pete had driven through the night, again freighted with a large backpack of the sort porters carry in big mountains. In a few minutes a dozen other climbers assembled to say hi, but after dropping his load and stripping, Pete fell into my tent.

"Joe," he called, an hour later. I moved closer by. I could hear him rearranging the bedding. "It's all thin, Joe," he said. "The mail. In the top of the pack."

I found a bundle wrapped in rubber bands. I weighed each of the envelopes before opening any of them. Skunked. Zero for five, with one wait-list, at Union Seminary in New York. The Princeton letter spelled out what seemed intimated in the others, even the one from Union: my undergraduate record was more than adequate, but "what you have done since is not in accord with our committee's sense of what one called to the church does with a five-year sabbatical." Another, Louisville Presbyterian, suggested I consider an internship relevant to service before pursuing the ministry.

"Ouch," I said. As I set the mail down I felt I might fall on top of it.

"Sorry Joe," Pete muttered from inside the tent. He didn't wake up again until dark.

So we went to work—first to Red Rock for a week and then to Utah, where we had an unfinished project on a desert tower near St. George. Pete handled me gently. There was an off-width section in the middle of the tower he suggested I jumar around, but going right-side-in I found I could do it with no more than the usual strain, and we both found the route less daunting than we had on our first attempt two years earlier. Something was working for me. I was at ease on the cliffs again, supple and strong. Some combination of the long hiatus, the concentrated preparation, and the blunt disappointment. I was surprised and relieved, but this translated less to enthusiasm than to a nagging sense of betrayal, my body having the last word: maybe we're in this for good. Pete picked up on this, complimenting the form I'd assumed from weeks in the desert sun. "Man, you're ripped," he said, "for someone so crushed." Later that day, I caught sight of myself in a restroom mirror at the Chevron station—hair awry, beard sun-bleached, and eyes bloodshot from the day's exertions. I looked as suited for the ministry as a baboon.

We opted next for Indian Creek instead of heading back west to the Valley. Pete liked the heat, and I liked the way the heat vacated the campgrounds and cliffs of climbers. We went at it every day, repeating favorites and often taking laps on hard pitches. To mix things up we'd do a multi-pitch on a tower—Jah Man on Sister Superior, Kor-Ingalls on Castleton, the brilliant Fine Jade. On one of these, North Six Shooter, I was inching through the fifth and last pitch, a squeeze chimney, when Pete hollered up from the belay eighty feet below a question that would echo in my mind for the next twenty years and always in his voice: "Why minister?"

"What?" I tried to say, but winded, and hemmed in the chimney, my voice died.

Then Pete again: "Why help anybody?" he shouted. "Or anybody else, I mean."

I had been sweating and grunting, my gear clanging about, but now I burrowed in and relaxed fully into the dark recess. My breathing returned to normal, and through the shadows I could see Pete below, his face sunlit and his hair blowing in the warm wind. He played with the slings on the anchor, adjusting his position restlessly. He looked around the desert over his shoulder. A few minutes later he called up, "That's right, Joe. Just hang tight there till you figure it out."

I rested my face on the cool sandstone, my heartbeat slowing, my position secure as a chockstone, though twenty feet below the chimney opened upon several hundred feet of air. I'd been thinking of little else for months, not with any great consternation but constantly, and I thought I knew the answer. In climbing I had a bridge between proximates and ultimates. The knife-edged ridge and the sky. The hollow, expanding flake to which you commit your weight and the big vacancies at your back. The glimpse of tremendousness you get from a sequence that works only on account of some miraculous braid of strength, technique, and commitment. The exposure we climbed into was palpable and solvable. The other, the cosmic kind, was teasing, opaque, and for distractible young men of my type, avoidable. I wasn't pursuing the ministry to help someone else. It was to help myself—or maybe to be helped by others who could get to those edges without ropes and equipment.

Then I noticed Pete coiling the slack end of the rope. He removed his shirt, rolled the rope into two neat halves, and placed it over his back like a knapsack, the shirt underneath for padding. He was detaching himself from the anchors, preparing to simul-climb—a flat-dangerous technique wherein a fall by either climber is arrested, *if* arrested, by whatever gear lay between the two. We did this often to move with dispatch on easy terrain, but never on anything so technical and exposed as this. The first move off the belay is delicate. He smeared to the left side of the stance with care, marking his toes, then extended through two tricky solution pockets to reach past the first hard move and gain the bottom of the forty-foot finger crack that led to the maw of the chimney in which I was lodged. The first part of the crack was thin-hands and more or less secure, and with his end of the rope running through his belay device, Pete could get good feet to retie his knot every ten feet or so for an additional measure of safety. But then the crack narrowed. Several years before, on our first attempt here, we had both been spit out of this section and more than once. The size—larger than fingers and smaller than hands—requires tricky and painful arrangements of thumbs and forefingers, precise placement of toes, and more than a little staying power. When you come off you don't fall so much as spring out from the cliff. By the time we got into the chimney we were spent, scared, and bleeding, and if the chimney was more secure, it still felt frighteningly slippery.

But now Pete climbed deliberately and with seeming ease, long extensions between finger-locks, attentive in his eyes but without strain. He hiked one foot nearly to his waist, levered off a jam to establish the next, then paused to make small, unhurried adjustments before weighting the new hold. He stopped at each of the several cams I'd placed, first eyeing the gear, then removing it without fidget or fret but rather like a mechanic disassembling some intricate part of an engine. In just a few minutes there were only two pieces between us, and no features near or above me in which to place more. If he climbed into the chimney, we'd be roped together, but entirely unprotected.

"Figure it out?" Pete said.

He fiddled with the second-to-last piece, his face now in the shadows. The cam had walked further into the crack, and with half the rope on his back and the rest hanging on a long coil from a strand between his legs, he had to scrunch up to establish both of his feet, kicking aside the taut strand and leaving the lower coil to sway in the sun below. With a deep fist-jam, he freed up the other hand entirely and then, with a sigh, pulled the cam free and clipped it to his harness. Only one more piece of hardware lay between us, a no. 4 on a long sling in an adjacent, arcing crack near the base of the chimney.

"It's okay," Pete said. "I can help." He reached down as if to retie the knot under his belay device but instead untied the half hitch there, pulled up the dangling coil, and strung it with a sling alongside the two loops from his shoulders so the entire rope could hang beneath him as he entered the chimney. The next move, from the top of the wide crack to bottom of the chimney, was the crux of the upper third of the pitch, an awkward and wild transition. Pete left the last cam in as long as possible, but he'd have to clean it before he was fully established in the chimney. Now he breathed audibly again, raising himself on the last of the good foot-jams and building a ladder of arm-bars to raise his back and butt into the opening. Finally he brought his outer, right knee up, but he could get it only so high. His foot dangled in the air. He paused. He seemed scared, and I wasn't anywhere near secure enough to hold us both if he slipped out. I figured he was about to ask whether I could make any placements from my position or even a little higher, but then he reached back and beneath him with his right hand, blindly found the sling and removed the no. 4. This he let fly, the cam swinging down to the top of the coil in the sun. Now with his right knee quite a lot higher than his waist, his thigh alone was doing the work of maintaining this position. Then his butt slipped a little.

"Pete!" I called, my voice cracking.

"What?" he practically whispered. He placed both palms against the wall in front of him, raised his leg into the chimney, and with a single smooth gesture stood firmly inside, just a body length below me. After catching his breath he made a few worming, undulating moves until he was directly beside me. I had hunkered into a deeper recess, cams and a set of nuts dangling from my now pointless harness. Pete sat in the wider, outer section, laden with the rest of our gear and dragging ten pounds of rope, glistening with sweat and yet entirely relaxed.

"It's okay. I can help you," he said, perfectly calm, like we were fixing a tire.

"What do you mean?"

"I mean, let's do this together."

"Do what?"

He looked down. He seemed to be enjoying this vantage of the formerly treacherous section he'd essentially soloed and the several hundred feet of crimson sandstone to the desert floor below. "This," he said. "Come here."

"Come there?"

"Yes, right here." He moved a few inches farther out, vacating the wider and more comfortable position for me.

"What do you have in mind?" I said.

"Slide in here." He indicated with his head. "Chest to chest."

I did as directed, moving my gear to the side and climbing over his knees one by one. In a moment we were so firmly locked in place that if one of us took a full breath the other couldn't breathe at all.

"Easy," Pete said. "Take turns."

He led with a deep exhale, his mouth beside my ear. "Now you."

He smelled like the desert.

I breathed in, and then we reversed, tentatively at first, but after a few halting tries we relaxed, grew synchronous, and carried on like this as if in guided meditation. Pete rested his chin on my shoulder. I let my arms fall to my side. The muscles at my shoulders tingled and twitched—I hadn't been aware I was using them all this time. We became easy, maintaining even pressure at the breast and falling into a rhythm. One animal, two sets of lungs.

"But they'll never find us here," I said.

"Sure they will. In time. Our bleached remains. Our interlocking rib cages. A ladder of bones for subsequent parties."

My legs were above Pete's, the bottoms of my thighs resting on top of his. "Too much?" I said.

"It's lovely."

He pulled the dangling rope and dropped it over my lap. "Oh God," he said. "So good."

"I'll bet."

"Now, let's scoot."

"Scoot?"

"Mosey, then."

I raised myself a fraction of an inch. "You good?"

"No, I mean together."

Chest to chest we were stuck, if stable, but with incremental adjustments we found we could rise through the chimney more or less as we might alone but for our entangled limbs. Occasionally one or the other of us had to move a palm, knee, or elbow to give the other a better purchase. The rope lay heavily across my lap. I marveled Pete had climbed the finger crack with the additional load.

Some ten feet beneath the flat summit I paused. The comfortable size I'd grown used to pinched down for the final section to either a flaring squeeze with a fist-sized crack in the back or a round-edged, still-larger chimney closer to the face of the cliff. The inner path was more secure but far harder, the outer fairly easy but terribly exposed. With your last gear forty feet below you, it's quite spicy. With no gear it's the sort of thing you bring to mind later only to clean your bowels.

"How about the exit?" I said.

He looked up. "Side by side."

"Fuck you."

"One in, one out. Which do you want?" He had taken the top strand from the coil at my waist, tied a figure eight, and clipped it to the belay loop on my harness to put a couple of body lengths of rope between us. "Inside guy is the anchor."

I felt a splash of sweat on my palms and face.

"Give me the no. 4," I said.

"For what? To fix?"

He was right. Even when finishing this pitch in regular style it's god-awful trying to clean a cam from the back of the flare.

"I'll push it along," I said. "If I can't, I'll rap off to get it. I'm not doing this part naked."

"Jesus, Joe. After all this?" He sighed and started up, the no. 4 dangling from the other side of his harness and well out of my reach.

I wedged in further to get a fist in the grainy, rarely visited back of the crack. I locked a knee bar beneath me and was fidgeting to gain a still firmer stance when I heard Pete directly above me. He was on top.

"Let me pull up some rope, Joe."

I felt a flash of gratitude, but my burrowing had left me gripped and entangled, my head pinched on either side by the narrow slot. I couldn't look down without leaning out, and leaning out I felt I might catapult out from the chimney. Pete tugged lightly on the rope until at last it unburied the knot at my waist—"You're on belay, Joe"—and then I rose, too, easily and without thought, fist-jam, chicken-wing, knee-bar, and mantel, shortly sitting on the smooth summit with one leg dangling in the hole from which we'd just emerged. A blood-red sun bathed the western horizon.

I removed my gear and untied.

"It's all right," Pete said. "Even Siamese twins have to emerge one at a time." He stood against the sun, still shirtless, reracking and taking in the desert vista. He had removed his shoes.

"So what's your point?" I said. "They don't need me?"

"Who?"

"I don't know. The assembled. The seekers and sojourners."

"You mean the sinners?"

"Sure, them too."

He was untangling the rope into two clean loops around his shoulders. We'd have to find the anchors on the far edge and make several rappels down the smooth west face.

"Sin," I said. "What is that, bad style?"

"And litter, and taking too long. Taking more than you need. But these are the easy kind. Sins of a lesser sort. You professionals have to tend to the real kind."

"Like . . . ?"

"Like bailing." Pete lay down on his back, his head resting on the coiled rope. "You wouldn't be able to help anybody with that simply by doing some reading and getting a little certificate."

"You'd have to know it firsthand."

"What's his name, the doubter?"

"Thomas."

"Yeah, that guy. Thomas. And those folks in AA. What do you call 'em? 'Sponsors.' They're credible because they've been there."

"They've touched the wounds."

"Yes."

"And me, because I'm leaving."

Pete sat up, as if to say something. Then he gathered the two loops at his feet and walked to the far side of the summit to find the anchors for the rappel.

"Or was trying to leave," I said, but he couldn't hear me now.

I don't know if he cared one way or another about my lack of options. I had already betrayed him by trying to have some.

In a week we were back in Bishop, in two rested and re-organized, and in three mostly finished with a new route on an unnamed arête east of Junction Peak—a feature I had pointed out several years earlier during one of many back-and-forths across the crest to resupply a project near Clarence King. We had been resting near the pass, Pete cutting salami, and I recall exactly what he said when I directed his attention to the striking line—a steep, arching ridge that bends around a golden amphitheater to gain the three-headed summit: "Sure. Jot that down for later. For when we're old and arthritic." I was angry in the moment but had long ago forgotten about the route. When Pete suggested we start the Sierra season there, I was about as uninterested as he had been. I was feeling good, eager to push it, and this was less technical than old-school adventure mountaineering—the sort of thing I ordinarily like. But at least once upon a time it had been my idea.

So we set aside a week and change to do it, and Late Wisdom (Little Gear) went so smooth and fast we were back in the pinyons in mid-June, racing up to Pine Creek in the mornings just to stay sharp. I ran for an hour around sunset, sometimes ending up in town where Pete would meet me for Miguel's or errands. During the middle of the day we lay around camp, seeking shade and avoiding each other. The mountains loomed, framed by towering thunderheads in the afternoon, but the pinyons were bathed in sunshine, a hot wind blowing from the south. Pete was strangely un-antsy. He'd hold a headstand for fifteen minutes in the shade of the trailer. He looked over the maps and guidebooks and the sketches he had made in October, these in a notebook that had its own place on a shelf in the trailer like a family Bible. Having long since charted and memorized everything there was to glean about Moriah, it wasn't information he was assembling. It was obsession, and psych.

One evening he sat outside on a milk crate, naked but for shorts, filing fingertips and the edges of his toes with an emery board. "Tell me, Joe," he said, looking off where the bright light of the falling sun bounced off the peaks. "What is it that's there, you know, on the other side? Is it redemption? Diffusion? Comfort? That all it is, comfort?"

I too was mostly naked, sitting at the chess table nearby, studying my next move. We had left a game with only a handful of pieces on the board and a perfectly uncertain outcome.

"Whatever it is," he said, "it's not this, right? Isn't that the whole point, it's not this?"

"No," I said. "This is paradise," trying to head him off.

"No, for real. It's not what we have here. Alive, aliveness. Whatever you want to call it. Nothing to squander. Nothing to protect. Just the work and pleasure of keeping the coals burning." He was sawing at his calluses again.

"Moving a knight here," I said, smiling at his relentlessness. I'd begun to accept the prospect seminary would not happen, and for the first time in a long while I felt a stirring. It was good, and maybe good enough. All of it. I was loved. I was in a beautiful place, a kind of home, and my feelings for Pete weren't crowded with the usual complications. Eyes locked on the board, I felt misty and grateful. I could feel him studying me. Later we completed the game by headlamp, and even as he came in for the kill I was happy as I've ever been.

⌒

Sometime around the solstice Pete suggested we forego our plan to explore a line on the Incredible Hulk and instead do a couple of big days in the Meadows and then head down to The Needles. He said this was a better setup—another indication he was all-in for Moriah, though it left me wondering what Moriah could possibly look like if climbing as dissimilar as Tuolumne domes and Needles cracks comprised apt preparation.

"The Hulk's not going anywhere," he said. I couldn't tell if this was accusatory.

Before leaving the Eastside we stopped in town for supplies, and when Pete checked in at the guides' office I walked down the street to get the mail. Two pieces. One was from Union saying the wait-list was now "active." I could continue to stay on it by checking a box on a postcard, which I did. The other was a letter from Nor for Pete. He slipped it unopened into his notebook, pulled it out a couple of times as I drove north, and finally read it when we turned onto 120 at Lee Vining. He looked it over twice more as we rumbled up the Tioga road behind a line of RVs, studying the note as if for something he might have missed. At the park boundary, he said, "She's moving to California in July. Wants some time in the mountains. She says she'll haul gear for us if we wait until the middle of the month."

The sunny domes of Tuolumne were crowded with European alpinists and the usual assortment of chastened Valley refugees, so after just two days we were driving south on 99 through the blazing Central Valley. Pete made calls from a pay phone in

Fresno and once again from the log-cabin country store that is the last point of contact before the long, narrow dirt road into Sequoia. I don't know what they were negotiating, he and Nor, but he grew quiet. On and off the rock he seemed to be pacing himself, containing his expansive appetite as I'd seen him do only a couple of times before and always in advance of something he expected to be possibly too hard. I, on the other hand, couldn't get enough—not because I was feeling born again from what I'd been in recent seasons but also because only the climbing relieved me of the fret, confusion, and disappointment I felt about my skunked exit plan. I fired Don Juan with surprising ease, and afterward suggested we look at the back side of Witch Needle. But Pete kept us focused—one route a day for four in a row. The Needles are a cluster of steep, lichen-splashed granite towers too remote for the uninspired and too technically hard for the uninitiated—the most sparsely frequented high-quality area we discovered in our years together. We were alone but for a fire-spotter in a cabin on one of the spires, and if in the past I'd found these cliffs haunted and intimidating, the wind constant, the rock sharp, the shadows long and spooky, this time I felt comfortable and emboldened. I wondered how long we could stay without resupplying.

And then, early on the fifth day, Pete said, "Let's go back."

"To Tuolumne?"

"Home."

"Why?"

"I don't know. I just feel like it."

"Go ahead? Without Nor, get on Moriah?"

"No. I just want to get ready from over there."

Pete hiked alone the six miles to the crags to retrieve our stashed gear and then drove most of the way home. Twelve hours later we were back in the pinyons—a quiet, starlit night.

I could hear him arranging things in the brightly lit trailer. The following day he went to town and returned with a small chest of wooden drawers and a rig for an outdoor shower. He had picked up another letter from Nor, and with firm dates in mind he said he was going to take a couple of guiding jobs until she got here.

Drop things to guide—in the heart of the season?

"You okay?" I said.

"Come along if you like. Give you some belays. No charge."

Of Pete's maneuvers, this was the most puzzling to me. He'd been locked in for years, systematically organizing the winter to serve his summer climbing agenda. Not so long before he had railed against the "prostitution" of mountain guiding and was long-winded in giving an earful to acquaintances whose own aspirations and projects were always delayed or abandoned in favor of repeated ascents of Whitney's East Face or Cathedral's Southeast Buttress with a covey of "clients" in tow. They got certified by an international outfit, placed ads in the climbing journals, and together supported a little Bishop storefront that took 15 percent for booking the arrangements.

I could forgive Pete's becoming one of them. Ordinary fees were outrageous, and he could charge half again more on account of his reputation—what with his picture in the magazines and our names in the guidebooks. He'd decided the business wasn't unlike resort skiing: at least it consolidated the traffic to a handful of well-grooved runs, and on the rare occasion someone lined Pete up for something out of bounds—a hard or adventurous route—he could double his charge.

So there I was at the end of June, alone in our blazing camp in the heart of the Owens Valley. I thought about making the foray up to Moriah by myself just to get bearings and see what was coming. I thought about working. I spent a couple of days shuffling around town, reading, mulling over a move. And then one morning I decided to just walk out of camp, to gain the high country on the flanks of Mount Humphreys and find Pete and Nor two weeks later at the base of Moriah.

I put a note right beside the one he'd left in the trailer for Nor. His: "*Welcome. If you're reading this, I'm out. Guiding. Lots of work 'round here these days. May not get back until 7/15 but will then. The empty drawers in the blue dresser are for you. P.*"

And mine: "*P & N—Look for me near or under Moriah. Walking. Got ~half the gear—all that's missing here. Expect to arrive 7/17. Joe*"

I was happy to have a project of my own—a John Muir–like trek from desert to alpine summits—and resolved to walk the ninety miles off-road and off-trail. I packed a climber's guide so I could stay sharp on a few routes along the crest, brought too little food and only a couple of other books, but with the climbing gear my pack weighed upward of seventy pounds. I took as much as I could. I figured Pete was in some kind of complicated negotiation with Nor, or with himself about Nor—all this tidying up, getting quiet, taking jobs. But a day or two later, still heading west through the sage and sand, I wondered if it was me he was locking out—in just the way I had him. Here we were, poised for something good, maybe something great—maybe Hunter-Holland—and he'd decided to go into it with an even ante.

Even early on Pete poked at my tendency to position climbing as something philosophical, less a physical endeavor than a form of moral striving. In college I would attend a late Sunday evening compline service on the rare weekend we weren't climbing and I'd hustle there if we got back from a trip in time. More than a few times I drove a little fast and denied his "What's the hurry?" request to stop at a diner. During one May's pre-exam reading period we went to the Maine coast to have at a crag we'd heard about, but the area was a bust—the routes mossy, one-move wonders and the black flies murderous. On Sunday morning, I suggested we bail on the day's agenda and get a head start on the nine-hour slog back to school.

"So you can get to church?" Pete said.

"So we can get out of here." I started pulling up tent stakes. "I could stand to study some, too."

Pete sat on the picnic table while I continued to disassemble the tent. Climbing or not, we had to break camp.

"Can't be salvation you're after," he said softly, as if talking to himself. "You're not enough of a sinner."

I removed the poles from their sleeves and the tent collapsed into itself like a parachute falling to earth.

"Worthiness? Is that what's bugging you? Something you have that needs fixing, like if you can get to the top and see the other side you'll get some giant, godly affirmation?"

I was on my knees, rolling our shelter into a tidy package. I was surprised at how close he was to something I only vaguely understood.

"I want nothing," he said.

I must have looked doubtful.

"Yeah, I want to do more, and get better. But in the bigger scheme, nothing. Because this is it, Joe. All there is. And it's temporary. Just us, just now. And we might as well enjoy it while the window's open, 'cause it's all changing, what with the whole goddamn atmosphere about to shift into overdrive."

I didn't know what he was talking about—something he'd read about in an earth science class. He held the stuff sack for me to slide the tent inside, and together we folded the ground cloth.

"So how 'bout we just match ourselves to now, and you let whatever else is rankling you resolve itself later on? Could be hormones, you know. Give it some time and, *poof*, it's over."

On that weekend we compromised, with neither of us happy. Of the climbing Pete said, "It's what my grandmother says about

Howard Johnson's. Terrible food, and the portions are too small."
We got back to campus too late for church, and the next morning I flubbed an exam, though less for our late return than for ditching two Kierkegaard lectures before spring break to get an early start at the Gunks.

When I got over being afraid of Pete, or of whatever he'd set us up to do, I was impressed, even a little jealous, that he could commit himself to something so hard and demanding and expect so little in return—not even just no glory, but no significance. That climbing could be enough, and no more or less than what it is: improbable, exacting, at once death-defying and life-affirming and more-or-less anonymous, with only you and maybe your partner to validate, judge, and enjoy your work. His was a brand of self-sufficiency I admired and was terrified of. To me it seemed, ultimately, lonely.

In the ensuing years I moved further in his direction than he did in mine, but I never believed this could go on forever, nor ever wanted it to. Even during stretches of relative reciprocity I felt his version of nothing demanded an awful lot of me. I maintained a by-now grossly malnourished idea of myself as someone who could be of service, and not solely to Pete but to a range of people who themselves sought more in life by way of purpose and meaning if not profundity. And yes, I trusted there was something I sought and even got out of climbing that could be rendered accessible in more domesticated forms. What I hadn't realized was how fully trusting and dependent Pete had become—such that my even wanting something else seemed to throw him off his ordinary trajectory. And now with Nor moving here, who knows what he was carting to Moriah. These matters kept me company as I hiked up the Horton Creek drainage and neared the crest, eager to turn southward across alpine fellfields and several lateral divides toward our peak.

No part of a climb is more predictably flavored than the approach, be it half an hour through the underbrush, a two-day slog over mountain passes, or even the sort of far-flung venture that involves days of planes and trains just to get near the trailhead. Straightforward or involved, efficient, onerous, beautiful, or tangled, each gesture, each bend in the road, placement of foot, exhale of breath, swipe of sweat, is shadowed by the knitted-brow imaginings of what the sheer feature will look like and whether your first few moves off the ground will be freighted with consternation or lightened by confidence. The Yosemite formula that 80 percent of climbers who start up a big wall fail neglects a still more daunting fact: half again as many are thwarted by that first view of El Cap from the east end of the tunnel—their portaledges never unfurled, their haul bags never so much as dragged from the back of the car. To climb well and freely is to lock in to the placement of your fingers and toes, your frame of reference limited to the two or three moves above you and that other small distraction—your fall line, your requisite gear, and the constant calculation and recalculation of the risk and consequence of slipping off. A twenty-foot boulder just paces from your campsite or a three-thousand-foot cliff in Greenland—no matter. You climb inside this bubble of intention—ten feet ahead and roughly twice that below—until the terrain eases or the flat summit lies beneath your foot soles. So even the trivial and ordinary maneuvers you make to get to the start of a climb—packing Ziploc bags with nuts, shifting the car into drive, hiking alongside a lively stream—these are stitched with worry, each gesture a kind of practice for the sharp focus you'll assume to get to the top.

At dawn on the third day I reached the crest on an icy, pitted snowfield, a mile north and a couple thousand feet above Paiute Pass where for thousands of summers Indians from the east crossed over to meet up with tribes from the San Joaquin. Natives from our side carried deerskin pouches of the obsidian the others would fashion into weapons for killing the deer and bear whose skins they would later trade for more of the glassy black rock. Pete and I had poked around these meadows for shards and fragments of some young hunter's bored flint-knapping. Once in a while we'd find a nearly complete arrowhead, probably discarded on account of a cleave or flaw we couldn't detect. Pete kept a dish of these in the trailer. From my snowfield perch I watched a string of backpackers approaching the pass from the gentler western side, a dozen ants lumbering along in single file under the shadow of the crest. A group of Boy Scouts on the last morning of a weeklong trip. Probably talking about what they'd eat in Bishop and how good a shower would feel and whether the Dodgers were still in first place. This many days in, their blisters were healed, their mosquito bites rubbed raw. They rose through the last gentle turns in the trail and then walked into the sun. At the pass they paused in a clump beside the battered wooden sign, the tall one standing apart to snap their picture.

Pete was somewhere up here, too, packing and racking for a day on Darwin's east face or Humphreys' north rib or Charlotte Dome, a client or two squatting nearby blowing steam off their coffee. It was a cold morning, but in a few hours he'd be biding his time in the sun while the client worked through an airy section eighty feet below. He would set a series of directionals and use an inverted ATC on the belay so he could lean out or even lower off to snap pictures framed to make things appear steep and severe and heroic. He didn't take ten pictures in ten years of climbing with me, but one of his signatures as a guide were these magazine-cover-worthy shots of clients with hundreds of feet of air beneath them and miles of alpine wilderness in the background, the client outfitted in the latest and lightest technical wear even as Pete climbed in approach shoes and jeans and carried only the handful of nuts and few cams he could place by memory and almost without pause. The payer locked in concentration, breath halting, fingers raw and bleeding. The payee bored in the moment, grateful for the passage of time, musing about Moriah and Nor and all that lay on the nearing horizon.

And Nor, too—in Ohio or Illinois or Wyoming now, punching along Interstate 80 in a tightly packed Subaru, losing track of the miles and hours but not the states she was whizzing through two or three a day. Nor knew about as much of Moriah as I did—starting with the ripple and rumor that circulated around camp in December. She was approaching not with end-of-an-era trepidations like mine but with a roll-of-the-dice sense of mystery, her heartbeat a little quicker for whatever it was she was seeking and wanting here with Pete. She'd drive all day and into the evening and pull over well after dark to lay a pad and sleeping bag out right beside the car. Bread and cheese and soup heated on a backpacking stove on the ground, then stars until she found sleep. From Utah, she'd dive south on Route 6 and make the long, winding traverse through half a dozen nameless Nevada ranges, spend her last night under the new moon, and then chase dawn to the edge of California where a gap in the White Mountains would give her the best and most memorable view of the entire passage: the astonishing escarpment, the splash of glacier under the Palisades, the two teats of Williamson's summit—the long and unmistakable profile of so many Sierra peaks, including at least two dozen she'd ascended, their summits kissed by the rising sun.

Three of us—converging toward the same small corner of a damp meadow bisected by gurgling snowmelt and overrun with mosquitos where we'd make a home under the long shadows of Mount Moriah.

I arrived first. Thunderstorms had been organizing in the past week, growing lower and longer and louder on successive days in a pattern that usually ends in two or three days of steady clouds and rain until the system wrings itself dry and throws open a window for the clear skies and dry air everyone associates with Sierra climbing. I scrambled over the pass in advance of the afternoon's lightning but well after the cloud ceiling had dropped below the crest, navigating not by peaks and skyline features per normal but merely by the shape of the watershed and best guesses. The clouds obscured not just the summits and their shoulders of connecting ridges but even the eskers and boulder fields, and if it hadn't been that my topo map showed this dogleg-shaped lake bound by an amphitheater east of the crest, I wouldn't have had much confidence I was in the vicinity.

But there it was. I dropped my pack and walked to a cliff band right above the bend in the middle. On a clear day I'd be looking across the lake to admire the upper half of Moriah's sheer northeast face where it soared above the gap in the crest, but today I could see only the dark water a hundred feet below and a swirl of fog and cloud rippling the lake's surface and banking up against the ridgeline.

I hadn't eaten since the day before. I was down to three packets of oatmeal, a handful of raisins, two packages of ramen, and two tea bags. Thunder in the distance set me hustling across boulder fields and alpine meadows, and an hour later I pitched my tent in gusty wind and sideways rain. I spent that first afternoon and the next two days more or less in the shadow of the great feature we intended to climb, and with nothing to do but lie still and read and listen to the rain, I knew the smells and sounds of the place long before I could see where I was. I left the tent only to fill a water bottle from the little stream and to circumnavigate the meadow, my camp lost in the cloud from only two hundred yards away. I built a windbreak of stones for my stove so I could reach it from a cross-legged position inside the tent.

I grew so accustomed to the steady patter that when the rain stopped in the middle of the third night I couldn't sleep. I had moved beyond hunger, but lying down it seemed the inner wall of my abdomen nearly touched my spine, and when I stood up I routinely blacked out for a moment before the blood got balanced.

After a couple hours of quiet I peeked out, hoping to see stars. Nothing. I turned on my headlamp—a blinding wall of fog. The rain held off, and as night wore on I lay still and alert, bringing to mind the magnificent face looming nearby until I'd memorized my imagination of it, tracing shattered buttresses and dark overlaps on a mountain I'd never seen so much as a photograph of. Then the two of us, roping up at the bottom. I would take the first pitch, the only one that bore any resemblance to the domes Pete said were relevant preparation, a long arcing seam through steep slabs, me carrying the entire rack despite there being no chance of placing any big gear, simply because on a first ascent half of the objective of any section is to set the stage for the next. Even from the bottom I could see pitch two was a whole other order of business, and higher still the line seemed a maze of unlikely route-finding through discontinuous features and fragmented face.

When I opened my eyes again, it was long after sunrise. The daylight had conjured a breeze out of the west, concentrating the fog, but also something new, a persistent whoosh and moan from the steep side of the valley. I marked it for a while from the warm cocoon of my sleeping bag. I silenced it with the stove, heating water for a used tea bag and the last bit of oatmeal. But as the morning wore on, it grew constant and unmistakable—an insistent coo and prolonged exhale. Moriah would look different from what I'd mapped in my mind the night before, but the voice of the mountain never changed.

Something was going on with the weather, and for the first time since arriving I was feeling impatient. I wondered if Pete and Nor had had a change of heart, or if something had happened to one of them, or more likely to one of Pete's clients. It wasn't like Pete to arrive second and unthinkable he'd be two or three days late. At midday, still ensconced in fog, I worried I'd gotten it wrong and had spent the last three days some distance, even miles, from where I thought I was. I unfurled the topo maps in the tent, poring over details, playing out several prospective and successive missteps from the northernmost of the Rae Lakes, my last point of certain orientation. Now I saw that the dogleg lake I'd passed was one of several that shape and size. The broad boulder field that made for my gentle crossing of the crest had adjacent counterparts. If I was correctly situated, I could descend east and find the approach Pete had used in October and possibly even run into them. But if I was wrong, I'd be roaming down a steepening, unknown canyon like an orphaned member of William Brewer's first party of surveyors in 1864.

I lay down next to the open map and for several hours, drifting in and out of sleep, wondered if I was thinking straight. I'd heard somewhere the starving body, consuming itself, raids stores of things that have been cleverly isolated, the odd chemical stuff that can swirl the mind in hallucination. I shuddered at the clarity I'd had in imagining our route the night before, and just this morning attending the moan of a mountain I might be nowhere in the vicinity of. I was deluded, probably lost. I'd have to stumble back to the Muir Trail and beg backpackers for food, or follow the watershed to the east in hopes of getting safely to eight thousand feet, where there would be monkey flower and miner's lettuce in the streamside shade of laurels, and then to six thousand, for juniper and huckleberry.

The tent fly was snapping in the wind now, and from inside I could see thinning clouds down the valley, but the pass and the peaks on either side remained lost in fog. I passed the afternoon in dreamy retreat, falling at last into the deep and warming sleep that had evaded me during the night.

⌒

Voices. A low murmur washing around my mind well before I opened my eyes. I thought it was the stream at first, or that I dreamed them. But then closer—pleasant chatter in still air. And then not words but cadences, and finally Pete's voice running up and down the register, his excitement touched off by this proximity to the mountain he had been dreaming of for nine months now. When I blinked again, tears squeezed out onto either side of my face. I lay still a while longer, then crawled to the head of the tent and pulled aside the flap to look down the grassy meadow: there, coming toward me across the green, each framed under a towering backpack. Pete cradled a second, smaller pack across his front as well. The sky was brilliant blue and cloudless, the meadow dry, the sun burning into this immaculate alpine nest I was seeing for the first time—a three-sided bowl at the head of a valley with knife-edge ridges and boulder-strewn couloirs on either side. I crawled out further, my lower half dragging the sleeping bag.

"Ahoy!" Pete shouted.

I waved, then lay my head on the cool ground. The grass was spiny and odorless against my face. Only the day before I had wondered whether I might be able to digest it, as marmots do, and if not, what the attempt might cost me were I to become immobilized with stomachache.

I rolled to the side and stood up as they approached, but, feeling faint, I slowly fell onto my stiff knees. They laughed, thinking I was tangled in my sleeping bag. With my eyes closed, my head turned in the other direction from them, I felt the thud of Pete's front pack, and then the big one. Then I could hear him helping Nor with hers.

"Hey, Joe." His hand was on my shoulder. He rested it there a moment. "Joe, you all right?"

"Better than ever," I said. "Hand me a bit of water when you have a minute. And something to eat."

"Jesus," Pete said to Nor. "His lips are shot."

Then she was beside me peeling a banana. "Hi."

I opened my mouth to take a bite, my face still resting on the grass.

"Water, Pete," she said.

I could hear him bounding toward the stream.

"Here," she said. She was breaking little sections of banana and holding them to my mouth. Now I understood what he meant: I couldn't feel my lips for the chap. The first bite of banana had tasted like nothing, just a semi-moist wad I had to gum into paste before swallowing. But each successive chunk was more florid and flavorful, and when Pete held the water bottle to my face I gestured for another banana.

Nor got up to get it, and there, for the first time, the rock face I longed to see and half-hoped never to have to, framed against a clear sky and shockingly close: a Half Dome–sized slice of granite and diorite cut by two gigantic parallel bands like broad blond sashes and iron-stained in the upper reaches, at once strangely familiar and wholly unlike anything I'd ever seen or imagined. I lifted my head to get the level view. It was darker and scarier but also more featured than what I'd conjured the night before, the left side of the face shattered with blemishes and debris-strewn ledges on either side of a long black arch that runs two or three hundred feet across the midsection. Pete's line was well to the right of this and obvious, though nowhere near as clean as I'd expected. It reared right up, beginning with several hundred feet of broken dihedrals and steep corners. The angle looked to back off for a moment in the middle third but then above the second blond band steepened again through a featureless, inscrutable section. There's the business, I thought. Mercifully, three or four hundred feet from the top, a buttress seemed to grow out of the face like a fleshy scar—an emergent, fractured shaft promising a way to the summit if you can only get to its base.

Pete had lit a stove and was heating water for oatmeal. "Got it memorized by now?" he said.

I didn't tell him until later I was only now seeing the mountain for the first time. I alternately stared at the face and watched Pete mix the concoction of oatmeal, peanut butter, and raisins Nor had advised him to make. At first I wasn't even interested, stuffed from two bananas, but after a few bites I was ravenous, and only on Nor's doctorly advice did I wait until late in the evening to have a second helping of the noodles and tofu they cooked for dinner.

Turns out they were only one day late. They had delayed to assemble still more supplies, which they would have to descend to retrieve the following day. It was I who was off. I had arrived early, and by two days. One I quickly figured out: I must have walked out of our camp a day before the date I had written on the note I left for them. In our years of vagabonding this happened from time to time, losing track of the calendar altogether. But the other day was confounding. I could recall and name each place I'd spent a night en route, and yet there was a lost day in there somewhere. Nor said this wasn't uncommon with extreme hunger. "Time isn't hours," she said. "It's meals." This was the following morning, and she was cooking another batch of the gruel she thought I should eat before I went for any of the more conventional things I now craved. "No food, no time. All the more so when you're socked in by the weather you had."

"Like you *say* you had," Pete said, smiling. "We saw a thundershower or two along the crest. Nothing like what you're saying."

Later in the morning I watched them walk out of camp with empty packs. At the far end of the meadow Pete took her hand, and then they disappeared into the canyon. The tent where I'd spent three days in the rain and fog was now adjacent to a compound of strewn gear—three bear canisters of food, their tent, three ropes beside a pyramid of tangled climbing hardware, the water jugs we'd carry to the base of the wall, even two camp chairs. They'd moved in, and as confident as I was they'd be back in ten or twelve hours, I was sad as an abandoned child to see them go.

I spent the morning taking short walks from our camp, amazed at how weak I felt. From vantages around the meadow I sat in the grass with Pete's binoculars to study Moriah in the changing light. The face grows on you under closer inspection. It looked less loose than before, and the line Pete had found was all the more striking in direct sun, features casting shadows on one another—and all the more obvious but for the blank band across the middle that must have discouraged anyone else from claiming it. That section seemed comprised of the yellowing, fine-grained granite I associated with uncommonly textured rock, but I couldn't see any ledges or fractures or other telltales of climbable features. There were several black streaks, these perhaps dotted with the small quartz knobs you find on the water streaks of Tuolumne domes. But two or three pitches of this would be treacherous for a first ascent party: each foot or finger-hold prone to snapping off, and Pete refusing to place the bolts required to make it anything like safe.

At the end of July the northeast face is bathed in the gold of early morning light but shadowed and flat and cold for most of the day. A second blast of sunshine, this one from straight above, lasts about two hours in the middle of the afternoon. I made my way out of the meadow—first time in four days—slowly threading a path through the boulder field toward Moriah's base. The three-quarters of a mile may have taken me two hours, my heart racing when I took more than three or four consecutive steps, but it was warm and still and I was eager to see if the cliff backs off a pace from beneath, as all but the most sheer do. From up here I could see the shimmer of the Owens Valley in the distance and in the foreground the edge of the meadow where our camp was strewn with what seemed colorful but contained litter. Then, with just a bit of a breeze, the mountain breathed again, that moan I'd heard when I lay starving in my tent. Elements of the massive face were fluted and hollow, and as much as I grew accustomed to the steady hum it was less than reassuring to wonder which of the peeling features gave rise to it.

I made my way up to the base of the route where the cliff launches out of strewn detritus that once clung to it. The boulders here were patched over with orange and brown lichen and unusually arranged, not stacked on one another but scattered about, several tabletop slabs with tufts of grass between and around them like you see in the older ranges, the Rockies and the Alps. I lay down on one, using a spare jacket for a pillow, and studied the face from directly underneath, alternately with and without the binoculars. The sheer, cold size was daunting, but at least there was some topography here on the right side, a variety of features and plausible if vague connections between the distinct sections. On most routes, you know right where the suffering will start. Here it was clear where we'd go, and certain we'd have problems—but far from obvious just where the trouble would lie and how long it would last. The other, left side of the face is vast and foreboding. The long arch in the upper third looks still thicker from here, a deeply etched eyelid whose mossy, stained corner gives way to a seepage of water that runs hundreds of feet to the base of the wall and likely the source of the spring Pete had reported.

He had been here in October, possibly on this same flat slab. I was cold now, but it would have been much colder then, the entire formation shaded from morning to night, the air brisk with the nip of winter and perhaps even aflutter with random snowflakes. I walked over to the bottom of the route and sank my fingers into the crack that would give us our first eighty feet, eyeing the edges and toe jams where we would gain stances to place gear. Routes that have repeated ascents have a signature appearance, the rock's aspect different from everything to either side, and not just because they are clear of the loose material and tufts of grass and small bushes that make a home even on a vertical wall. Climbers' shoe rubber scrapes and polishes a cliff of the microflora that gives rock its ordinary complexion—an effect Pete called "paving," which he liked to rail about, especially with climbers who confessed to any difficulty finding their way on this or that trade route. I looked still more closely for signs of activity here, running over each section of the first 150 feet with the binoculars. I had a feeling. The finger crack at the bottom was one of three, and while two were lined with grass, the middle one was a clean slot to the third knuckle. It had been gouged out. Above here, where the route kicks left to an amber dihedral, one side of the ledge appeared clearer of the loose rock I could see stacked on the right side, and, sure enough, a small pile of broken stones lay twenty feet to my left, as if tossed from the ledge by a first ascensionist.

I brought the binoculars to my eyes. It's easy to trace where a climber's hands will go, but it's the feet that leave the indications, sometimes with smoky black smudges along the side of a crack, but just as often to one side or the other of the obvious line where they rub the rock smooth and raw. Not much doing here. But in the middle of that gorgeous corner, about fifty feet from the ground, I thought I saw black scuff marks on either side of a foot-sized jam, and then, just a little farther, a splash of red nylon wedged in an incipient seam. Pete was sloppy that way, neglecting to burn and seal the frayed strands on either side of his water knots. The hairs of one of these had gotten tangled in some grit, and Pete, impatient to descend, possibly cold or even in the dark, had left a track. That he had climbed in October didn't surprise me—I just wondered how far he'd gotten. I backed away from the base to get a better vantage, but short of any garish signature—a blond scar from something trundled, or a nested set of slings for a rappel anchor—I wouldn't be able to gauge his high point from this vantage at the bottom.

And then I stopped caring. This would be no more or less a first ascent than any number of the others we had done: Pete identifying the cliff, working himself into a fever on the recon, and over a period of weeks to months pulling me into the fray. Neither would it be the first time he had soloed good measures of a route before I even touched it. With Tower of Glower on Mount Williamson he'd done all but the last three hundred feet before we went together early the following summer to complete it, and to document and publish the details. I used to think it generous he never told anyone ours had been more of a second ascent, and submitted the route description to guidebooks as another of ours: F.A. Hunter and Holland, 1985. But as I made my way back down to our camp, wending through the boulder fields and shivering now under the shadowed face, I got it that this was merely part of his operation, just another way he had of roping me into his enterprise.

One time we were about to work a new route on one of the unnamed spires on the Sawtooth Ridge. It was the end of our second full year on the Eastside, and I was stewing over what I saw of the future: not the variety and spice of climbing but the days and weeks and months of plotting and training and endeavoring that were starting to feel as uniform and inexorable as one of those long, two-lane roads that arc across the Nevada desert. We were packed and about ready to hike into Yosemite when I phoned my parents just to say hello and got it from my father that my mother was going to have surgery the following week. Something they wanted to remove, a woman's matter. He didn't encourage me to fly home, but I did. I exaggerated the seriousness to Pete in order to fend off his disappointment. I suggested he get a proxy for the spire, perhaps Mark, a talented younger charge we cragged with from time to time but never invited for one of our bigger objectives. Two or three weeks later, when I saw Pete's notes, it appeared the climb went smoothly. I wasn't even rankled when I saw he'd scribbled the Hunter and Taylor that would make it into the guidebooks. But then I ran into Mark at the grocery store. "Scary as hell," he said. "Pete, he's like, rabid. Way different than being with the two of you."

I asked Pete about this. He said Mark was taking too long and making dumb route-finding decisions, so finally Pete just took over. "Tangled ropes, sore toes. The usual bullshit," Pete said.

"Like we never have," I said.

"It's different. And you know it."

I didn't counter. He was right. A belayer is one thing, a partner another. It's not just holding a rope. It's encouragement, advice, succor, and witness. And then, the sharing of the route—someone else to appreciate, admire, and document. The contract is umbilical. I won't just climb safely, or reasonably safely, but I'll go fast (or reasonably fast), and I'll do it in good style, and you will help me and hold me accountable. It's a lot, partnership, and lacking the whole package many climbers would just as soon not bother. Hence the legendary soloists, Muir and Norman Clyde in the old days, Bachar and Croft in our time. When I first started thinking about making other plans I didn't much think or care about how Pete would manage without me. When it seemed likely I was leaving, I rationalized—it may take him a while, but he'll find another partner. Possibly a better one. And then when I got the rejection letters in the spring, I was just angry. I couldn't help but read between the lines, which, distilled, seemed to say: You can't be with us, because you've been with him.

I heated up the last of the gruel and watched Moriah turn black in the twilight. I was starting to get some juice back, and yet still felt tapped by the day's little outing. Drowsy with images of the route, of darkness and falling rock, of the mountain's cold expanse and spooky moan, I crawled into my tent to wait for Pete and Nor. I thought of Pete being up there alone in October to clear out the cracks with an old piton and a wire brush, blowing on his hands, having to climb everything at least twice as one does in a rope solo but probably several times to clean it, and maybe even exercising some care to leave little trace. With my eyes closed I could see it all from many angles and vividly. There was fuel in my brain again—enough to worry. At some point I'd be able to translate this to my fingers, and then, in time, and without even asking him, I'd find out just how far he had gotten and why he had to turn back—and then I'd know what it was he needed me for.

Then the rearranging of gear and clinking of carabiners wasn't in my mind but near my head. Pete and Nor were back; he was adding things to the pile in our camp. I heard the snap of a can of beer, and in a little while another. Nor said thanks, but quietly, as if to not wake me up.

"Hi," I said from inside the tent.

"Hey, Joe," Pete said. "Got chocolate. And beer."

"I'm good," I said.

The stove kicked to life, followed by little waves of steamy miso blowing through my tent. Another beer popped open, waking me again, but when I opened my eyes next it was in the deep of the night. I dragged myself out to pee, standing in socks in the cold meadow some twenty paces from our camp. A carpet of stars stretched from one horizon to the other, interrupted only by the circular, looming void of Moriah.

⌐

In the morning Nor studied my face. "You've got color again."

Pete was sitting cross-legged between two piles of gear, adding lube to our cams with an eye dropper—the job I was supposed to have done in winter. "Yeah, black and white don't suit you."

"I feel better. Waddled around some yesterday. Got up to the base."

"And?" Pete asked, his eyes unlifted from the mechanism in his lap.

"And nothing."

He held a cam at eye level for inspection. "Nothing," he said, shaking his head deploringly and dabbing oil onto the tiny springs.

"Looks good," I said. "Clean for a while, and obvious. And then not."

"Yep." He set the cam alongside others leaning against a rock to prevent oil from bleeding onto the cam surfaces. "Feast, then famine."

"Jungle, desert," I said.

"Dinner, no dessert."

Nor was making coffee. "Science, religion," she said.

"Science, religion, and architecture," Pete said. "You take the binoculars? See that crazy buttress up high?

"Sure. The architecture of 'if.'"

"As in 'if' we can get to it?"

"Uh huh."

"Then we'll be the first," he said, snapping the oil off a cam. "First to sink paws in those parallel cracks. First to stem the corners."

"And how 'bout all that desert/no-dessert/religion underneath us?"

He didn't say anything this time. He knew as surely as I that whatever we had to accomplish or endure to get established in that upper feature, *if* we could accomplish and endure it, would be at best merely memorable but far more likely some darker shade of unforgettable.

"Bolt kit?" I asked.

"Yep," he said. "We've got two dozen. May need a pendulum or two. And anchors, if we have to. And DFP, of course."

Pete would drill bolts, but never to render an otherwise unprotectable route safe, the style that was coming into fashion in the '80s. He had one pretext for placing bolts mid-pitch: Death-Fall Prevention. On first ascents, he was more than content with the "R" designation, for "run out," a rating that lightens the traffic and puffs out the chest. He aspired only to avoid the "X" rating indicating a fall will result in severe injury or death. This was no point of contention between us. I was comfortable and even happy on long run-outs, so long as the terrain was manageable. But I had no taste for Pete's derring-do on 5.10 face and such. The main thing, and the point of singular agreement between us, was to climb in good style: with as little thrutching and thrashing as possible, and absolutely no weighting of gear.

A couple of years earlier, in Indian Creek, Pete found a hard-to-get-to crack that ended with twenty feet of brutal fat fingers—on a guidebook-photogenic wall deep in an obscure canyon that glowed in the late afternoon light. Red rock, blue sky, yellow amphitheater. We worked the pitch several times over the course of a week, loving the first 130 feet only to be crushed in the last little bit. We tried various taping strategies both to protect and to fatten our fingers until Pete declared this was bullshit: "If we're going to get this thing, much less claim it, might as well do it right." On our last day there he made it to within two moves of the anchors, alternately stacking fingers to position a toe and then liebacking with his upper hand. Placing gear was unthinkably tenuous, and on his last attempt he ripped out what he'd thought was the most solid placement. But falling wasn't the only danger. I thought he might permanently disfigure himself for trying—tendons, ligaments, bones—and it just didn't seem worth it.

So we left it for next time. We didn't tell anybody about it, but Pete had placed anchors, and people were on the hunt, and in time we heard about a Jamie we'd once met who sent the route, supposedly after only a few tries. But what we also got, this from some climbers at Josh around Thanksgiving, was that he'd taped one of his ring fingers around a metal splint of the type this crack might have you wearing for months in the aftermath. "Not just for protection," the guy reported. "For leverage."

I didn't care what these guys thought. I wanted Pete to know I remembered how hard he'd worked that section, and that I'd tried myself, and that of all the equipment shenanigans, well, this was horseless-carriage nonsense. Anyway, none of this would have mattered except that Pete grew determined to get the first true free ascent, so that winter he went bananas in training, especially on this impossibly steep finger-crack machine he built on the side of the dorm at Mammoth. I visited a few times and could barely get established on the thing, much less make a move. By midwinter Pete was running laps.

Then back to Moab in the early spring for another go, and we hadn't been in The Creek for two hours before intersecting, of course, Jamie and his partner. The parking area by Cat Wall—not three cars in the lot. They were making coffee on a little camp stove beside their truck. Pete and I stood at the back of our car building a rack for a training day—the aim was to get back on the crack-in-question, but not until Pete felt ready. For twenty minutes they were like dogs, Pete and Jamie, sniffing each other from afar, each wary and neither quite sure who would make a move or how. At some point, mug in hand, Jamie called over, "It's a helluva find, that one up Lavender Canyon."

"Yep. We didn't get it. Last time."

"What are you calling it?"

Pete looked at his feet. "Fail," he said. "For now, anyway. That's all anybody's done on it."

They migrated toward the middle of the lot. Jamie's partner and I marked one another wearily. We didn't want any part of trouble.

"I'm just hoping it's in the condition we left it in," Pete went on. "You know, how metal works on sandstone."

"Fuck you, Pete," Jamie said, turning away. Now that it was out, Jamie looked ill.

"We'll see."

"No more damage than skid marks from the cams you ripped out of there."

Pete cocked his head, as if to consider, then tended to the gear at his waist. He knew he had Jamie on the ropes.

"It was a tiny sleeve," Jamie whined, holding up one hand. "On one finger." He appeared to be talking to himself. "Anyway, I hope you Royal Robbins it this time."

"That's the plan," Pete said. "No aid."

It seemed to me Jamie was trying to pull himself away. He'd made a decision months ago he'd had to live with all winter, and now the inquisition, and it was basically over and should have been painless. But sanctimony is hard to stomach in any circum-stances, and from climbers, with all their rules and traditions, it can be unbearable. Jamie scratched at the red earth with his foot. "It was a little fucking splint, Pete. I wasn't going to pull my finger apart on it, so I figured something out." He waited, gauging Pete's reaction, but Pete had turned his attention back to the cams on his gear sling. Then Jamie added, "Just the kind of thing I hope you guys are wearing. You know, with what's going on these days." In the mid-'80s, even adventure outposts like Moab and Bishop had posters about HIV.

So Pete launches at him, the gear flying around their heads. They didn't land blows but just kind of wrestled in the dirt until Jamie's partner and I pulled them apart. We didn't have to work all that hard—even they seemed to realize how stupid this was—and then Pete was sitting off to the side in a pile of cams, his face stained with red clay. "So if I were a fag, what would that be to you?"

"Nothing," Jamie said. "I'm sorry."

"No, seriously. How's that figure?"

"I don't know, man. I don't care."

Pete got up, the gear jangling around him. He seemed relieved, like the formal business was done with. He walked over to Jamie and offered him a hand. "What do you think, Joe, should we tell them? Just come out with it?"

"I'm sorry, Pete," Jamie said, still sitting. "I really don't care."

"Joe? Ready to do this?"

"Let's do it," I said. I didn't know what he was talking about. Pete helped him up. Jamie couldn't even look at him.

"So, how's it start? I take thee, Joe . . ."

"C'mon, man," Jamie said. "I said I'm sorry."

"All right," Pete said. "Besides, the light's not right. We want it, you know, like at sunset. When it's pinker."

They stood near one another and awkwardly for a moment. "Hey," Jamie said. "Tell me how it goes, will you?"

Pete looked puzzled.

"This time," Jamie said, "I hope you crush it."

But that was the last we saw of them, and three days later Pete did only a little better than he had the previous fall. And not for lack of training or technique. It really just came down to finger size. When I got as close as Pete to completing the pitch it was on account of a wad of tape around a bleeding knuckle. Walking back to the car in the twilight, battered and spent, we felt less disdainful of Jamie even if not converted to his particular brand of ingenuity. Pete dropped his things by the car. "He breaks our rules, we break his. Or he thinks we do, anyway. In the end, we do as we do." Pulling away, he added, "My hat's off to anyone who so much as hikes to the bottom of that thing."

Pete sent details to the guidebook author, and only when the new edition came out did I see his choice for a name: Fail Better.

⌒

Was he more cautious in the later years? Did he adjust the protocols for Death-Fall Prevention? I never again saw Pete shake like he had that time with Lester and Bill, and I wonder if his peeling off that route mostly had something to do with the company we were keeping—feeling he had to finish the pitch or turn it over to one of them. When it was just the two of us, the other nearly always took a crack at what one of us was backing off of, though in my case this was a mere formality and gesture of respect. I completed Pete's pitches not five times and usually on account of some hidden hold he hadn't found; he finished mine more than I care to remember.

So on the morning we started up Moriah I wasn't worrying the prospect of spare protection and long falls, or at least no more than usual. I felt lightheaded and weak, and if Nor hadn't been there to help us freight the gear and ropes and water to the base I'd have wanted and maybe even asked for another day to get my system in order. But she was, and we did, and so just two days after they'd found me starving in the meadow I was a hundred feet up the first pitch—admiring between my legs the string of evenly spaced and readily placed cams, and Pete belaying on the slab of white granite at the base, and behind him Nor lying down in a puffy down jacket, and behind her, a thousand feet below us and half a mile away, the swath of green meadow where we made our camp—when I realized how light and easy I felt on the rock, the axiomatic biking or swimming feeling: focused, balanced, relaxed. Yes, this again. And now no doubt Pete had climbed here the previous fall: the center crack delightfully clear of dirt and grass, but dark stains in the interior from the material he had gouged out, and here and there a tuft of loosened green matter with soil still attached. I pocketed the fray of red sling I'd seen the day before, as if conspiring to keep his secret, and if the ledge I'd noted from below was less obviously tidied and rearranged than I'd imagined, there were indications I wasn't the first to set foot here: loose rock on the left side arranged closer to the wall than to the edge, and a shadow stain in the sand where a larger slab had been slid a few inches back from the perch where it had lain for centuries.

So that was one surprise—that after not just days but weeks of little to no climbing, and some trials along the way, this was pleasant and painless. The second was a few minutes after I hollered off belay and completed the next set of routines—backing up the anchor, getting comfortable to bring up Pete, and taking up slack in the rope—it was Nor in climbing shoes and tied to the end of the rope and Pete in the prone position on the slab. I hadn't noticed her pack a harness and shoes—had assumed she was along purely for portage and that once we were on the wall she'd return to camp. Nor hadn't climbed with us in several years, and here she was in her puffy green jacket which, unzipped now, billowed out like a tiny parachute to either side and appeared even to expedite her smooth and steady ascent, that familiar light touch with which she rises, seeming just to stroke the holds Pete or I grasp or jam or lever onto, her fingers and toes alone in a sort of delicate play—a fly or mosquito to our gecko.

In twenty minutes she was beside me, the gear arranged neatly on her harness but for two pieces she had clipped the trail line through for Pete. After securing herself on a comfortable tether, she threw her hood on, zipped up the jacket, and pulled gloves out of the pockets. But Pete wasn't thirty feet off the deck when the sun bolted over the visor at the top of the cliff, and by the time he arrived we were warm and limber and smiling. Pete climbed with a pack full of water, food, and extra gear for the upper pitches; our intention wasn't to get all that high on this first afternoon so much as set up stores for the middle section we expected to demand some time and attention.

Are there ordinary days of your life you can recall like no other—not for where you were or what happened, but for the seamlessness? The first of the many we spent on the northeast face of Mount Moriah, July 21, 1989: several hours and four pitches and six hundred feet of climbing, fully half of it in the warm Sierra sunlight. Clean, sticky granite ribs and cracks and shallow corners offering varied positions and distinctive features. The climbing friendly but, as Pete would say, not too friendly. Pete and I swapping leads without fret or negotiation, and Nor climbing between us to clean each pitch and extol its virtues. And the belays like happy little reunions so that when I was first or last at the stance I was eager as a child to be joined by Nor as she approached from below or to hum along on top-rope to belong again to the two of them above. It was as if each of us had graduated from something he or she had to do alone to get to this day where we could enjoy ourselves and each other without interference for what anyone wanted or remembered or needed—a temporary and unforgettable joy born of braided history and trouble and happy amnesia, and for at least these few hours un-muddied by ordinary worry over what's next and consequent plans and promises. If I had been nothing else these many years, I'd been Pete's, and not just his sidekick and companion but his steady. If those Valley climbers' quips about him being my husband had been far-fetched and playful several years earlier, by now it was a simple fact. Moriah was the last cliff we'd start up together, and with Nor along, too, we'd wandered into a crossroads beyond which we would join ourselves to the rest of our lives. But for one day, anyway, we were in the intersection together, and happy to be there, and blind to whatever lay off in the other directions.

Nor got to the top of pitch three with a sheen of sweat and a happy smile: "Do you guys have fun!" This was the best stretch of the lower third of the cliff, a steepening set of thin parallel cracks that look improbable but for so many sharp edges for the feet you can't see until you're right on top of them. I was perched in a small triangular alcove, the most cramped of the stances. Nor tucked in tightly and leaned on me as she stretched out from time to time to photograph Pete, who hiked the pitch with what seemed (and was) rehearsed celerity. He took the gear from beneath us while still on belay and slotted the pack onto our feet as he climbed through.

An hour later we were together again at our high point for that splendid day—an ample ledge here, perfectly cut and nearly level, two feet wide and more than ten feet long. It had a tidied aspect Pete couldn't have mustered while belaying Nor and me—he'd gotten at least this far the previous fall—and before we left it was stocked with the contents of the pack: four full water bottles, a stash of food encased in a hard plastic box to protect it from rodents and birds, and some extra clothing bundled in waterproof nylon. We left all but the gear we'd need to get back here the next day, and then he and Nor simul-rapped the upper pitch, easing down side by side on single strands, talking and laughing and finally disappearing over a lip. I studied the next day's doings on full display above: a cryptic passage up and left on steep face to the base of this wild columnar feature, and that seeming to end abruptly with the strange and sudden ironing out of features into the broad, blank midriff of stone I'd admired from below.

We got back to camp just as the sun was bending behind the crest—the stove kicked to life, warm clothes assembled, cans of beer pulled from the cold stream, our day's doings too readily ascribed to recent history and happy memory. Years later I learned this bottom section we'd established would constitute its own route: the four pitches to the big ledge sufficiently appealing in their relative ease and remote vantage that climbers would hike all this way to accomplish just a fraction of what Pete and I had in mind. Afterward they would return to this very meadow to admire the cliff in soft twilight and revel in their good fortune. But our evening was already shadowed by our plans and ambitions, the light banter of today's pleasure pock-marked with quips and questions about the morrow, the turn of the sky and the brilliant first stars both decorating the moment and signaling its proximate demise.

We were blowing on warm mugs of miso soup, Nor telling us about a patient she'd tended in a neurology rotation who fell off his bike, hit his head, and lost not just his store of memory but the very capacity to record anything to memory. "Perfectly functional in the moment," she said. "He could feel pain and express discomfort, but he had no fret or distress. He was curious, but not about anything in the past. Or about why he was in the hospital and getting all this attention. As the weeks rolled by he fell into some predictable routines. He tended to eat the same things, watch the same movies, read the same books over and over. But he could be spontaneous. He seemed drawn to complex arrangements of color. He was always going out around twilight, and anytime it rained he'd want to be outside right when it stopped."

"I think I've got that," Pete said, touching his head.

She wouldn't be interrupted. "His family would come around. They were nice to him, but privately they acted like he had died and they were left with just the body. But us, the doctors, we were fascinated. Neuro's full of bad stuff, most of it headed to awful. This guy was a pure mystery. We wondered if he might be more himself in this condition. He took up watercolors, which he'd never done before. He didn't have the anxiety he'd been treated for in the past. He lost weight without trying, his blood pressure falling back into normal range, which was what he was trying to accomplish with the bike in the first place."

"He get better?" Pete asked.

"Probably not. Most don't. I was in OB-GYN next, several floors up. I'd see him out by this little pond in back of the hospital, sometimes with his easel, sometimes just watching the trees and sky, but I never got anything more on him."

I was in my tent with a headlamp and a book when I heard Pete open another can of beer, and then they were talking in voices too low for me to hear, and laughing. I fell asleep. Sometime later I heard Nor. She was just a bit louder than the nearby stream, breathing loudly, then gulping air. A short while later she was giggling, and then Pete's low voice and more laughter. I was awake now but didn't want to turn on my headlamp again. I lay there thinking about the man with the paintbrush and what it was like to be in his head, to have that kind of mind, and whether he was relieved altogether of feeling shy or afraid or alone.

Nor came with us the next day, but you could feel the weather turning, and even with the earlier start and the sun on the rock it was like climbing into a refrigerator—blowing on hands, bundling up at the belays, turning your face away from the lightest of breezes. We got to the big ledge midmorning and I took the next lead into this unexplored section. I aimed for an incipient crack that looked promising, but as I got closer I could see it pinched down to a seam. Only the curious pillar I wanted nothing to do with would facilitate a passage through here, so for some thirty feet I aimed in that direction on crimpy edges and an occasional pocket and placed several crappy small stoppers en route. This is ordinarily the type of climbing I like—feet, trickery—but with the grainy texture and scant protection it was terrifying. I stalled, trying to persuade myself to work out a better sequence, to figure out rests, to remove from my mind the picture of what I must look like to Pete and Nor from below, and how cold they must be. But most of all I was just looking for a confidence-enhancing placement or two. On one of these, a thin stopper, I lowered off.

Nor was blue, folded into herself, her arms and face inside her jacket and her head bowed. Shortly after Pete started up the pitch I could see why. It would be a while yet before the early afternoon blast of sun, and with the fallen temperature and the breeze we were in full alpine mode. This is an awful condition on a belay ledge, but for a climber it can be focusing, your fingers numbed but not yet insensitive, your shoes as sticky as they get. Pete scampered through the part that had stymied me, his toes working the edges with balletic precision. He found holds well to the left I hadn't thought to investigate, and along the way he replaced most of my gear, managing even to deploy a small cam in a hole I had been too frazzled to recognize. Above this, past my high point, he stalled for a while just as some frozen spittle filled the sky. The precipitation relieved us of having to negotiate what to do next; we left a fixed line to his high point and started the long rappel to the ground. Pete and I watched Nor carefully, double-checking her rig for each rappel as well as one another's. Wind and cold can chill you to stupidity.

When I intersected with Nor again at the second stance her teeth were chattering. Pete suggested she lower all the way to the ground, after which he and I would take the time to do the two rappels necessary to get the ropes down, but she refused. "Go first and go fast," she said, and he did. I pulled her close to me on the small ledge. The wind was swirling, and with the updraft the air would clear for a minute, followed by waves of white pellets, something between hail and snow cascading around us and gathering on our shoulders and feet.

"At least the start of that pitch is behind you," she said. Her words sounded hammered off a typewriter.

"Behind Pete," I said. "I couldn't do it on top-rope."

"Disappointed?"

"He's a better climber."

She looked up to see if mine was a shrug, a gripe, or a worry. "And he did it in October," I said.

"Oh?" She appeared to shudder, though whether from what I said or to shake the pellets off her jacket, I couldn't tell. "Alone?"

I didn't answer. Didn't need to. It was like I'd said he had an incurable disease. There was nothing more I could tell her about it or about Pete that would make it anything but what it was: this thing. This defining thing he lives for. This defining thing he will die from.

When Pete phoned me four years later about their wedding, I didn't think about the many months we three had spent together in college and after, nor about our last trip, including that glorious first day in the sunshine on Moriah. He wanted to know if I would officiate. He assumed my divinity school degree conferred that type of license. It didn't—I was still a year from ordination—and so it wasn't much of a negotiation. We hadn't talked in a while. It was late at night, he sounded a little drunk, and I couldn't really tell how onboard Nor was with his thinking about marriage. In the moment I just felt lucky I wouldn't have to stand between them, administer their vows, and remember Nor's eyes when I said, "He did it in October."

I regretted telling her even as the words crossed my lips, and when we got down and walked back to camp and rearranged our things it was all I could do not to crawl into my tent and bundle up alone. Nor was fidgety and wary, transformed from the day before, and Pete was oblivious and businesslike as ever, ascribing the change in her to the stress of so many hours on the cold cliff. Over dinner she told us she'd opt out of the next day—no big surprise. The next section was going to involve a lot of waiting around on still more uncomfortable stances if we could gain them. Pete and I talked weather and what to do if the route was climbable in the morning. Ordinarily we would avoid three days in a row, particularly if the next part looked to be demanding. But a pattern like this usually hung around for a while—cool and clear in the morning, unsettled and thunderstormy in the afternoon—so it seemed best to make progress in the short spurts available to us, at least through the middle section, and then perhaps we could pull off a single base-to-summit push with a predawn start that would launch us through the clouds.

There was no laughter that night. The couple of times I got up the meadow was encased in fog, but when Pete and I met between the tents before dawn a blanket of stars stretched overhead, and we wordlessly packed our things and left camp before I heard or saw Nor. We packed extra layers this time, including thick socks and approach shoes for the belayer. We simul-climbed pitches one and two, conventionally belayed three and four, and clipped the anchors on the big ledge just after the sun hit the wall. The efficient move from here would have been for Pete to hike through to his high point, but when he offered the pitch to me I couldn't say no. Whether it was for watching Pete the day before, or not having Nor in the gallery below, or feeling guilty about tattling on him, I was more bold and fluid this time—even the gear fell into place—and I got to the last placement just as the sun bathed us in a golden morning light. The air turned frosty for half an hour like it does at dawn, but it wasn't the cold that stopped me. These transition moves to the bottom of that steep, scary column were, for me anyway, inscrutable, and I lowered again.

Pete was buoyant, dropping outer layers and feeling hopeful about the opening window around us, blue sky, calm air, climbing with dispatch. But to this point we'd ascended seven hundred feet of Romanesque variety, and the next stretch was a Modernist skyscraper—a patch of glass that stretched two or three hundred feet before breaking up around that emergent buttress on the upper third. In a river this would be the mysteriously calm eddy where rafters gratefully assemble to gather their wits for the next turbulent stretch.

Pete studied the wall from the belay. He knew that once he got above his last gear he'd be groping and improvising, weighing prospects for protection against the requisites of upward prog-ress. He racked more gear than he'd like, even a few larger pieces that seemed pointless given the terrain, and just before leaving he handed everything to me for a moment to strip himself of another layer of clothing. I was relieved to see he had the bolt kit, too, on the back of his harness, and a light hammer.

The very first moves off the ledge involve long reaches between half-inch edges on an upward left traverse. The footholds are spare or worse, some just a coin's width, others mere smears on the vertical wall—but Pete monkeyed through this section again without hesitation, and thirty feet up he reached a still higher left-facing flake whose open side you couldn't see from the belay. He placed two small cams on a long tether, one at either end of the feature in hopes of equalizing the load so the rock wouldn't blow apart. Then he turned his attention straight up. From my vantage this looked horribly unlikely, but as I couldn't see the flake where he'd placed the protection I assumed he was onto something obvious, to him anyway, and promising.

With steady movement he gained another forty feet, his protection neatly spaced. I had no idea whether any of this was good, but the ease with which he placed and clipped it indicated something was working. A dark and wide discoloration in the cliff here narrows into a pillar in what looks from afar like an upside-down funnel. Pete's path intersected with this narrow-ing column, which he liebacked for the most part, sometimes wrapping one heel around it to pull himself in and a few times finding good stances on small quartz bands that wrapped the feature like rings on a dark finger.

Then it ends, suddenly, and with a flat top: the tip of a pole pointing to the broad, blank, white face above.

Pete appeared quite comfortable here. He used an edge at the back for a hand and one of the bands for his feet, leaning out to examine the terrain above. He also looked down, especially to the right. All of this looking about—he was at the end of a cul de sac. Then, with a single dramatic move I managed to capture with the camera, he manteled the pillar to stand atop this tiny diving platform, fifteen feet above his last gear and seven hundred off the deck. With a blank wall above, he had to gingerly pad the face for balance. I wondered if Nor had caught this through the binoculars, though, from a distance, even tentative, intricate gestures can look like a happy scramble.

Then the *tap tap tap* of the hammer. I locked Pete off at the belay and unwrapped a peanut butter sandwich. I wondered why I had told Nor about Pete's soloing the first several hundred feet in the fall. I was pretty sure it wasn't just to explain why he danced through a section that stymied me—I'm not that small. I think it was a warning, to the both of us, about the risk of loving Pete. The sun swung behind the mountain, abandoning us to shade, but the valley was still bright: a broken ridge of iron-stained parapets on the north side, broad swaths of white granite boulders below, and the patch of green where we were camped nestled at the base of these, and the laurel-lined cascades to the east where several alpine streams intersect for a long, loud plunge to the Owens Valley. And in the distance, that valley, where even morning temperatures would be climbing into the nineties, and semi-trucks hauling up 395 from Long Beach to Reno, and SoCal families in their vans and station wagons and campers just two hours now from June Lake and Bodie and Yosemite. Schat's would be a mess at this hour, and the Highway Patrol would be raking in fines north of Bishop where a long stretch of open road beneath the vast Sierra makes even eighty miles an hour feel like a crawl. Twice I caught sight of Nor in the meadow, once shuffling to the stream, sometime later sitting on the center of a large, flat boulder at the far edge, probably with the binoculars. Then Pete shouted "Tension!" and with one hand I released the knot at my belay device and looked up. He hollered a plan: to lower thirty or forty feet and pendulum left. He added there wasn't anything obvious over there but the cliff seemed more featured in that direction. It was a single quarter-inch bolt he was lowering off—standard for the day—but with two free hands he managed to back it up with a sling wedged behind the dark pillar some six or eight feet below, and then he started the route-finding.

Pete was cautious for a while, perhaps mindful of a vulnerability in the bolt he'd drilled, or maybe because he thought the likely line wasn't all that far left of the trajectory we had followed to get to this point. He held the rope with his right hand and tensioned off to the left, reaching with his free hand for edges and scanning for weaknesses and fissures we might be able to link together. A couple of times he slipped or skidded off, catapulting across the face on the forty-foot tether, but then he got his balance again and gingerly pawed his way back into an oblique angle left of the anchor. After a while of finding nothing promising, he had me lower him further, sixty or seventy feet off the bolt, and then he started running back and forth in a proper pendulum.

In Yosemite tourists cluster in the meadow to follow these maneuvers on El Cap, most of which are concentrated on the King Swing of The Nose. But that's a well-defined and predictable affair, normally just a couple of wild dashes across the face and the climber dives into the objective, an ample corner with a hand crack in the back. To do a pendulum in genuine reconnaissance is a whole other matter, groping and grasping for features far too small to see from below and almost always without success. Today Pete managed to unweight the rope only one more time, this on a broken ear of a flake he levered onto by hooking his left heel over the side. Once on top he called for a little slack and made a couple of delicate moves up and right, but with nothing promising for protection, much less a continuous set of linkable holds, I could see this was the sort of gesture you attempt only at the end of a long top-rope, and when he fell this time he left some skin—a cherry-streaked abrasion on his left forearm. I lowered him to the belay.

Pete didn't ask if I wanted to have a try. He drained most of a liter of water and ate some nuts from top of the pack that was clipped to the anchors, and then he reached deep inside and pulled out a pair of etriers and several hooks.

"What's the angle?" I said.

"There's something up right, in that white patch."

"And from there?"

"More. More of the same."

He busied himself rearranging the gear on his rack. "Someday, somehow, someone's going to free this thing. But not me. Not this time, anyway."

Laden with the additional gear, Pete strained even to repeat the first moves off the belay. He went on tension well below the arc of his earlier pendulum and hooked through a section, but the next thirty or forty feet below the dark patch he was aiming for proved blanker than hoped, and flaky, too. He was still well below and left of the single bolt, so when he came off the consequence was a mere jolt and a wild swing to the right, but the higher he got the harder it was to regain his line. After a while he had not just hooked this stretch several times in succession but inadvertently cleared it of several useful if sketchy placements. The prospect of this kind of aiding above the single bolt—well, it's what the best of the bold do on El Cap, but it wasn't our type of thing. And drilling a line of bolts, or even just the handful it would take to make this sort of hooking safe—simply untenable, at least to Pete.

We left the fixed line—we would return for one more try—but even the rappel was gloomy for this reckoning with an unbridgeable impasse in the middle of our route, and when Pete hooked through the same section the following day he was reckless and thrashing and angry.

The wind had kicked up during the night, and we were again semi-hypothermic in the middle of the day. Pete wore a helmet, which at the time I found more frightening than reassuring, though later I saw this for what it was: a gesture of resignation, an indication he would have to live for something else. My images of him that day are pictures of defeat, the ends of his hair blowing up and around the sides of the helmet not just when he fell and swung across the face but even as he lifted a hook toward another micro-edge and blasts of cold wind pummeled us from below. On the approach pitches he'd asked to carry the camera, which he never did. I figured he wanted to use the long lens to scope something in the hard section, but as I was following the third pitch I noticed he was leaning out to take pictures of me. When I got to the ledge he turned his attention to the gear rearrangement and didn't say much. Only when I stopped some fifteen above him to place a first piece did I see his eyes were pink and his cheeks wet with tears.

In camp the evening before the last day there had been a bowl of peanuts and raisins sitting on a bear bin, like an hors d'oeuvre. Nor was shuffling things on and off the stove to warm a three-course meal she had prepared. She had watched enough of the day's activities to know not to ask much about them. Pete and I went down to the end of the meadow where two streams conjoin in a small pool. It wasn't fifty degrees out, but we stripped ourselves of our climbing clothes and stood in the stream and with a plastic bowl poured water over one another's shoulders. Then Pete dunked his head in the clear pool, submerged in water that only hours before had dripped from the snowpack above us.

I wrapped my long-sleeved shirt around my waist like a towel and wore my jacket, too. Pete walked back to camp naked. He came after me and slowly, shaggy hair and hard arms and dark face and neck and hands weirdly disconnected from the tender white of his belly and butt and thighs. He sat on a sleeping pad while Nor picked through his forearm with tweezers for grains of rock lodged amid the greasy red striations. She cleaned it again with water and then a layer of antibiotic cream.

I ducked into my tent to grab clothes, but not until later that evening did I see the stack of mail. Nor had placed it there sometime during the day, but it was nearly dark when I found it, so I got up to rummage through the climbing pack for my headlamp. I could hear them talking in their tent, not words but low voices, hers consoling, his resigned.

There were about a dozen pieces, everything but the single fatter envelope incidental, and I'm fairly sure they wouldn't have brought the rest but for this one. It was an acceptance from Union in New York, postmarked a week before. The envelope had been opened. They'd done me the favor of seeing I wasn't missing any deadlines—I had a few days still to make a deposit and until the end of the month to get situated in Manhattan— and they included the bus and train timetables I'd need to get east. Pete must have persuaded her we should first get an attempt on Moriah, though now I understood his was far from undistracted. Later, when I got the film developed, I discovered he hadn't taken any photographs on our last day. He'd used the camera's long lens just to watch me, just to commit a stretch of this to memory.

I have a picture of Pete from that day on the wall above my desk. It's a bit blurry—I caught him in the middle of a move. He's about thirty feet off the belay on his last attempt on the unfinished pitch, free climbing here but beleaguered too for all the gear he had to carry for the aid section above. I like the photograph because it catches his face in profile in the middle of something he knows can't end well, and yet his eyes are more determined than disappointed or angry or afraid. He's got the helmet on, which he almost never wore, and the hammer at his side, which he almost never carried. It's not a heroic shot—I've dozens of those—but there's something true here in the concentration and contending despite the certain outcome. Only an hour later we were pulling the rope through the bolt off which he'd been penduluming and hooking for two days, and by midafternoon we were at the base of the wall amid several piles of our gear.

Nor had seen us in retreat. She arrived at the base just as we did. She brought two empty packs to help assemble and carry things back. By midafternoon we had gotten all of the gear, climbing and camping, stuffed into or attached to someone's pack, and then we started the long walk down the canyon to the valley. Pete was subdued. He knew I had gotten the news. He didn't say anything about it but once, just before the bend in the canyon would put Moriah out of sight for good. He stopped ahead of me, got me turned around, too, and once more we admired the great face. "We could call it Hunter-Holland (unfinished)," he said, "except that would be a kind of promise. And also kind of lame."

I think he understood even more than I did this was it. I was on a bus to Reno inside of forty-eight hours and from there a train to Denver and New York. We didn't talk for almost a year. It was exhilarating at first—to be in charge, to have pavement and purpose. Later, once they were married, Pete worked harder at keeping up with me, harder than I did to keep up with them, anyway. Will was born in the Mammoth hospital where Nor did emergency medicine. They had a house in town, Pete still guiding in summer and working the ski mountain in winter. He would talk about wanting to find something else, but he liked the flexibility. He was still feeding the climbing bug. One of the old-timers in the area called Pete a "dean of Eastside climbing."

When my mother died in '96, I was undone. It was sudden. A car accident. Middle of the day, her fault. I had spent the previous two years as a campus pastor in Hanover, and when Mom died I was in my first month at my first and only church. Pete reached me down there in Shillington. I'm not sure how he found out, but I was surprised to hear from him—the phone ringing in my parents' kitchen. I had been there with Dad for two days and was in a raw way, finding my own thinking and theology inadequate to this sudden maw and the drumbeat of the Presbyterian funeral service sadly thin. Pete's call was a glass of cold water—the familiar if forgotten reservoir of airy exposure and charged feeling we'd known and shared and feared for so many years. Oh, this again. Danger, injury, uncertainty. The nearness of loss. Loss itself. He reached me just hours after the service, and we didn't talk for ten minutes, but afterwards I went out back in the twilight where the house I grew up in falls away into the hayfield of a nearby farm and I wept into the evening. For a while he called more regularly. Once he reminded me I'd been helpful to him in college, when his father died, even if we barely knew each other then.

But when Nor called, two years later and almost nine to the day we packed up at the base of Moriah, I didn't feel much of anything but kind of cool and numb. Pete was missing. They weren't sure where he'd gone, but he was climbing, and she was worried. Then, two days later, she called again—they'd found his body at the base of Clyde Minaret. I drove to the Burlington airport in the morning and was in Mammoth that night.

The details came later. For the several days I was there it was all friends and relatives and arrangements. Another doctor, someone who worked with Nor, picked me up at the small airport south of town. No one had told me Nor was seven months pregnant. When I got to their place, she was wearing a bright shirt and jeans with an elastic waist—I never saw her in black—and she looked drawn but stoic and focused. Will was four, alternately bounding around the house and yard and burying his face in his mother's lap or sitting close to one of her and Pete's adult friends.

She wanted me to officiate. She didn't think I'd want to but thought it would be important for Pete.

This was Wednesday, and the service was to be Saturday. She didn't know how many people, but the internet was alive now and his death had been flagged on climbing websites—so she had a friend reserve a section of the campground at Lake Mary and we went up there the next afternoon to look it over and to think about what to do. Crystal Crag and the Mammoth Crest were framed by blue water, fitting, but the grander profile of Ritter and Banner and the jagged Minarets were obscured by the ski mountain. Pete had been on the Southeast Face of Clyde, either on or near a long route we'd done together and one he'd soloed in the past. At a picnic table by the lake Nor told me they'd been going through "a hard time," some of which she traced to their expecting a second child. She said she thought Pete felt some pressure—to get on with things, into a steadier way of life—even if this wasn't her agenda.

"The one thing we had was an agreement about soloing," she said. "At least after Will."

Several gulls circled the lake and over the far shore a larger, steadier bird, probably an osprey, studied the dark water.

"I knew he didn't keep to it. Well, obviously. I guess I just didn't want to know. And I wanted him to be careful."

I knew it was ridiculous to think about whether if I were still here Pete would be, too, but that's where the mind goes. I wondered but didn't ask whether Nor's had gone there too.

She hadn't seen Pete's body yet, and wasn't eager to, but the doctor in her believed it was important and she asked me to come along. It was her territory, the hospital. She knew everyone by name, and once the attendant showed us which of the metal encasements was Pete's, he cleared out so we could be alone.

We stood side by side. Nor pulled back the sheet. They hadn't dressed him up or anything, and he looked like himself but for the bandaged back of his head where there was some damage.

"Ah Pete," Nor whispered.

I'd expected he'd be more battered and disfigured, a broken bird. But he was intact, firm of body, tan lines delineated. But for the awful stillness he seemed himself—sharp line of jaw, the wrinkle in his brow he called "my seam," and that jagged scar above his right thumb. This same hand lay outstretched and stiff at his side as if he were still reaching for something, but now with two fingers smashed and unnaturally awry at the middle knuckles and blood-stained.

Nor touched his shoulder, her belly brushing the edge of the gurney. I took her elbow with one hand and placed my other palm on his cold chest.

Pete was cremated that night.

Dozens of friends and acquaintances, mostly climbers, gathered at the lakeside on Saturday with Nor and her parents and her two brothers. Pete's mom and sister, too. I stood beside a picnic table to read the pieces Nor and I had assembled. Others of their friends read other things we'd chosen. We had some silence, and there was a time for people to share memories, but I didn't wander from my script. It all felt un-ballasted to me, and I couldn't or didn't summon a slice of something from our years together. I was among strangers. When the service was over, people stood around chatting, drinking lemonade, and checking in with Nor. I went down to the shoreline with Will to poke sticks in the mud.

Only the next morning, alone again, did I feel the sting. I was waiting outside at the Mammoth airstrip for the plane to Reno, standing on a bolt of hot concrete surrounded by sage and high desert with the grand sweep of the Sierra crest in the distance: at my left the steep north side of Mount Morrison, where we had dodged bowling-ball-sized detritus in the chimneys, and just beyond Mammoth the twin monoliths Ritter and Banner and the signature scrawl of the Minarets—all of it spectacularly featured and safely remote, a landscape of two dimensions, painted, peripheral, removed. I watched my little plane chug by to get set up for landing, and then turned my eyes back to Clyde Minaret, remembering being there with Pete, and, digging deeper, the inclination to be there at all—to haul oneself and one's gear up alongside the noisy cataracts and blue alpine lakes and in the early morning leave a bivouac in a clump of whitebark pine to traverse hard snowfields to the base of the wall—and then, the thing itself: the joining, the rising on sharp edges to inhabit the airy spheres.

For many years I had been telling myself I was grateful not to have the appetite, but here on the edge of departure I felt twice-grieved. Sure, Pete was going through a "hard time" with Nor, and maybe "he died doing what he loved," as any number of the testifiers had said the day before, but these salves were hollow and insufficient. Pete was very much alive, not clutching at scenery but fully inside the many-dimensioned world that becomes available only by that appetite, conjoined to and inextricable from the mountain—until he fell—while I had taken shelter and made a home indoors, devolved to metaphor and memory and postcard renderings of wonder.

The pilot wasn't twenty-five years old. He came jogging toward me, in a clip-on tie and a set of plastic wings. He grabbed my duffle and ushered me inside the four-seater Cessna. With a deafening engine and the pilot locked into his headset, we were mercifully separated. He had to circle twice to gain the altitude we needed to climb out of the valley, so I had two straight shots at the dark Southeast Face of Clyde and the apron of snow where Pete's body lay for three days before they found him, and in the grind of our steady ascent I was crying less for losing Pete than for what I had forgotten about the life he wouldn't or couldn't let go of until he did.

PART TWO

ᔥ

A Fine Line

Faith is a many-legged structure. Doubt is molten. Until it's not.

My own doubt had bled around the edges more or less harmlessly all along but hardened all at once into some dense, cutting crystalline form when Pete died. Maybe in homage to him—a sort of headstone. Or a kind of scar tissue. A knife goes in and comes out, fast and clean. Severs nothing, changes everything.

I hadn't seen Pete but once since he left me at the Bishop bus station in '89—hadn't talked with him in the last several months before he fell—but I was not for a single day unaware of him, and all of the not-seeing and not-talking only served to reinforce an expectation that we'd have another phase, some further twining of our paths in which to rehash and reconstitute and even enjoy the luxury of some forgetting instead of the mere and awful catalog of what I became determined to remember, which, shortly after I returned from his service, I wrote down with feverish persistence until there was no more—just words, nothing living and breathing, only so many episodes and adages of what I could have and hold in a chapbook whose empty pages are many more than the full.

For one: "The rock doesn't care. Been here a long time. It'll see us through and outlast us." He was never outright disdainful of my religious impulses and habits—didn't think me ill-advised to want what I wanted even if he thought I was unlikely to find it. Pete was just twenty years old when he stumbled into some of the earliest published material about what at the time was called the "greenhouse effect." So on the occasions I described or tried to explain my own orientation, he listened with interest, asked questions, didn't argue—though more than once he noted that the mere gesture of driving to church hastens the very end-times more than a few of the believers had assembled to prepare themselves for. In the '80s these exchanges went long into the night, usually around a campfire, often after a day on the crags. In the '90s they were infrequent, clipped, phone-bound, and sober. Pete described the receding glaciers under the Palisades and the odd patterning of some favorite alpine species—the chirping pika and fat marmot at ever higher elevations, and our nemesis, the maniacal Clark's nutcracker, pestering his bivouacs well above eleven thousand feet now. Next to these considerations I had nothing, and if his queries about me grew ever more perfunctory, I held nothing against him. My country church was doomed, and I was living year to year, while he was thinking about protective measures for later generations. And yet our exchanges rarely ended without Pete saying something to puncture the solemn tones. My favorite: "It might be an awesome enough responsibility just to enjoy your life, Joe."

So when in the space of a few seconds on a summer's afternoon he'd gone from bracingly alert and alive to a broken corpse in a snowfield, I got stuck there, too: had he been enjoying *his* life? The marginal distance from him I'd spent nine years achieving and protecting was instantaneously vast and now irrevocable, and for months I lay awake at night amid the memories and conversations, these blending into such noisy, swirling forms I was sometimes afraid to sleep. I learned to relax by not hanging on, not sifting, sorting, and organizing, but by going with him, slipping out of the house long before Will was up, driving through the dark to the trailhead at Agnew Meadows. Hide the truck key under a loaf-sized stone. Walk alongside the frost-kissed cascades of Shadow Creek at first light. The winter had been wet, the snowpack deep, the meadows now lined with the shooting stars and tiger lilies of midsummer and the creek loud and full. Inside of two hours the first lake, its gurgling outlet lined with granite stones. Pause, catch the breath, watch the morning breeze ripple across the surface. Then to Ediza's rock-lined basin, the lodgepoles thinning out and the water an even deeper luminescent blue. The Minarets' serrated signature teases into view, only to disappear again at the upper end of the lake. Then, half an hour more, Cecily's black water, the roundest and most still of the three. Here we made our camp the first time, and though he's been back dozens of times in the fifteen years since, Pete stops right where we slept as a matter of habit. He drinks half a liter of water. From his small pack he takes out climbing shoes, a chalk bag on thin webbing, and a light windbreaker. The headlamp falls out from the top flap of the daypack, and with little consideration he zips it back in. No imaginable play of circumstances warrants carrying the extra stuff—he'll be home before Will wakes from his afternoon nap. He stashes the pack behind a nearby boulder, brings his feet one at a time to a downed log to tighten his shoelaces, then picks up the narrow climbers' trail again. The woods gather in one last dense clump before giving way to a lichen-splashed boulder field that defines the upper reaches of the basin. Pete skips along these, breath full, steps light. The tops of the spires are visible again, ochre and yellow in the light of morning, but the ridge still seems far away and static, more like a photograph on a kitchen calendar than the talismanic, ever-closer objective of the day. In ample sun now, the ridge marks the western skyline from the porch at home. If Nor's outside she can see it—the agreement he's breaking in order to keep another promise: not to back off, not to be entirely domesticated. Not to lose touch with how it feels to be alive.

Then snow. Hard as rock at the edges and just starting to glisten with the slippery sheen of a new day's melt. The grade increases, the suncups grow icy and deeper. He steps along crunchy ridges between these pits, several times sliding into one and always careful to relax the higher leg lest he twist a knee or be thrown into the splits. Halfway across, the inside of each pant leg is wet. But now Clyde Minaret's entire Southeast Face looms, and brilliant in the early light: a dark tower rising out of the snowfield whose sides steadily narrow, cut like a gemstone designed to play in the light and appear twice as high as its already titanic eighteen hundred feet. The full view quickens the heart, and Pete slows his pace in equal measure, reminding himself to savor the closing proximity. This we bring to climbing only in middle age: the pleasure of the wanting. Not training and preparation, not logistics and arranging, but the austere beauty of the hunger itself. He's been here with the wanting so often and in so many places that he's confident of only one thing: nothing compares, and once he starts the climb it is only a matter of time before it is finished, and from the summit and the other side there is no satisfaction like this and memory is the distant and much poorer cousin of an imagination joined to an appetite.

A bergschrund at the top of the snowfield divides ice from rock. In places it is two yards across, and if narrower near the base of the route it's still too wide to leap over safely. Pete kicks steps in snow fifty feet farther to the right, where he can hop across to rock, then traverses back on scree-littered ledges. He can feel the cold at his back and twice turns to admire the deeper, blue ice where the gaps are wide. This is the dangerous part, he knows, not soloing the route but getting to the bottom. He wouldn't die if he fell here and may not even be hurt, but tunneling out from underneath the cavernous bergschrund or being found there before freezing would be a roll of stacked dice. So he's cautious but not slow, and in moments he's on the clean ledge at the bottom of pitch one. He sits to change his shoes, securing his approach shoes to a carabiner on his belt and slipping bare feet into climbing shoes. He laces them more carefully than he would on a roped ascent and twice removes the left to shake out tiny pieces of gravel. He reties them once more, less firmly this time to favor comfort on a route that involves steep edges more than delicate footwork.

Pete stands. He faces the rock and bows his head, reminds himself of the soloist's mantra—three limbs on until he's off the steep. He turns once more to admire the snowfield and the lakes and the enormous volcanic mound of Mammoth Mountain in the distance, on the other side of which Will is by now lying on the floor in his pajamas, watching cartoons, and Nor probably on the phone with a nurse at the hospital or weeding and watering the garden and in any case uncomfortably guarding her distended, pregnant belly.

The first finger-lock is above two pin scars where the earliest parties anchored their belay. With fingers sunk to the second knuckle and his right toe on a sharp flake, Pete steps off the ledge at the base. The Southeast Face Direct takes a water-worn corner that is steep from the start and intimidating to many, but for Pete it's a familiar and comfortable dance he knows by heart even if he does it just two or three times a year, typically with a client, and a little differently every time. Ten and twenty feet up he feels the regular stir in the belly and momentary halting of breath, and with small testing gestures he takes measure of his finger strength and stamina; there is a technical crux at about two hundred feet, and while not necessarily a threshold above which there is no prospect of downclimbing, he knows it would be tricky and dangerous to reverse these moves. His body is warm and the rock cold. Everything sticks, and he rises easily, climbing through the hard section without pause or further consideration. The wind kicks up, cooled by the snowfield at the base, and at three hundred feet the route angles straight left to join the Southeast Regular via an easy ledge traverse. Here the rock changes from a darker brand of the granite common to our beloved Eastern Sierra to the Minarets' distinctive mahogany tuff. This face is more featured, often with plates and thin parallel cracks and square edges that seem cut for climbing, but it's also more friable. Weakening granite tends to flex in a useful if heart-stopping telltale, while metamorphic rock is more intricately and mysteriously attached, sometimes fracturing several feet from where it's weighted and even large sections sloughing off with little or no warning. But the Minarets are oft-climbed, the Southeast Face alone ascended by dozens of parties each season, so the routes are generally washed free of dangerously loose material, and Pete is neither more nor less aware of the danger of a broken hold up here than he is on a fifteen-foot boulder near home.

Above the traverse a short but secure off-width makes for some harder work. Pete pauses to catch his breath—he's above eleven thousand feet now—and to appreciate that he is just where he pictured himself when, earlier in the week, he thought it's a good time for Clyde: alone, unprotected, seven hundred feet off the deck, calm, and just two body lengths below his favorite section, some three hundred feet of face-climbing on dark red panels. In a few minutes he's there, and with no injunction to place gear or to accommodate a partner in tow, he can wander, linking generous holds in fresh patterns and taking note of prospective placements and airy stances for the next time he guides on the route.

Here my hands grow moist, and my perspective shifts: I weigh and balance the tactile play of his climbing, the wind in his hair, the fingers on rock, marking every move not from above or beyond as before but side by side with him. He appears to grow longer now, reaching past an adequate hold for something still more secure and making decisive moves between these so that his feet are often near the same level as his hands. From afar he looks like a frog on a dark pane of vertical window glass, alternately scrunched up and then fully extended, and as he grows more relaxed my own heartbeat deepens, until he enters the final section and we are face to face: I the rock, not indifferent and unfeeling but attentive, benevolent, even loving: "Here, Pete, for your hand, an incut flake. Now up and left, and carefully."

⌒

I was at my desk, as on any Saturday, Pete alone on the Southeast Face. I was writing a sermon. Pete careened from the cliff. I was arranging some words about some words someone arranged two thousand years ago about some words attributed to a man with a message. Something broke, or somehow he slipped—it couldn't have been fatigue. He weighted a hold and in an instant became captive to horrid momentum. I stepped into the kitchen to make tea. My morning had dragged—it was by now early afternoon in Vermont. I had three pages. He had a few seconds, maybe two, maybe ten, depending on how he fell and where he first impacted. I returned to the study with a steaming mug, sat down, reread, crossed out some words. Was he scared? Angry? Sad?

"Everyone falls," Pete said. "Fall. Fall again. Fall better." He thought if you're not falling, you're not at the edge—another point of contention between us. Because I rarely fell, and when I did it wasn't akin to his dramatic spring from a cliff but a dejected relinquishment, a shaking, clutching, sliding off from a stalemate of exhaustion and paralysis and usually with ample forewarning. Walking back to our car after one such episode, he said, "You didn't fall. You f-f-f-f-ell."

"Mine's not a sharp end," I said. "It's the blunt edge."

But Pete remained constant with encouragement, even cheerful: "You got it, Joe," he'd holler, in those desperate seconds before I came off. "Way to work it!"—even when I hadn't.

I've grown accustomed to the prospect that mine is a fall, too, not dramatic and catastrophic like Pete's but in its own way dangerous and in any case life-altering. That hard nugget of doubt— some piece of it lay there. I got home from California, put one foot in front of the other, but something fundamental had been altered. I felt numb and dumb. Unable to write a fresh sermon, I resorted to recycling old ones. Unable to pray, I wrote out and read aloud those I needed for services lest I fumble entirely.

Then Carol. We met eighteen months after Pete died, she at Dartmouth, me at the Thetford church a dozen miles north. For a spring and summer and fall she taught her classes in the morning and worked on her dissertation in the library in the afternoon and went home to her college-owned apartment promptly at 5:00 P.M. and most always wanted me there and usually wanted me naked—and before long not just for pleasure and satisfaction but to conceive. She had an oval face with kind, unembellished eyes like those of the poet she so earnestly admired and feared, and the child and the marriage and my country church would comprise her fortress against the poet's famously passionate loneliness. I found her own brand of passion alluring and her ideas about family at once mysterious and grounding. She grabbed my attention and deployed my energies like no one I'd ever known except for Pete, and I grew drawn to the idea of inhabiting a bookish, New Englandy form of Pete and Nor's compatibility. A wedding, some travel, and complicated career arrangements. Carol had a degree and an academic book with a spicy title—*Sexual Silence and Sexual Noise in Emily Dickinson*—but her job prospects were spare.

The baby wasn't to be. It didn't take, and then, with as much conviction as she'd wanted a child, Carol decided she didn't—wouldn't shoehorn herself into motherhood against whatever it was her body, or being, resisted. My letting go was slower, and tangled up again with Pete, with his losing and being lost to Will and Astrid, who were nine and five in a Christmas card photograph that arrived only days after Carol told me of her decision. I'd imagined in a child some ballast, not just against the church of old people I drew my living from but against the larger prospect of my irrelevance. Carol could be an itinerant professor. She could "deal her pretty words like blades" in Rochester or Reno. I would be the parent—stable, alert, provident. I'd have and hold. I'd catch.

Then, after Christmas 2005, she went to Berkeley for a stint. She'd been more than two years free of the baby we wouldn't have and I was still marking people with small children, watching and wondering. Carol would be there a calendar year, and by the time I joined her for two months in the summer she was busy and happy and more than well established. She taught a seminar on the American Romantics she loved, enjoyed the company of her students and colleagues, and refused no opportunity to do career-making rounds among the university's well-regarded professors. I wandered about, too much time on my hands. This was my first return to California in the seven years since Pete died. I had thought that after two or three weeks in Berkeley I'd drive over to the Eastside, revisit stretches of the old domain and stop in to see Nor and the kids. But I kept putting it off, kept feeling I needed a firmer foothold on the now before an enveloping confrontation with then.

So a fall, mine, that had started with Pete's and was briefly forestalled by Carol maybe ended on the thickly padded floor of the Berkeley climbing gym. I'd read of these gyms in the climbing magazines back East but couldn't fathom the prospect as anything other than an overbuilt playpen for children's birthday parties. The conceit sounded to me like those cycling outfits where thirty people ride exercycles while a "coach" shouts encouragement—a curious if spurious facsimile of the activity they claim to embody. The Berkeley gym was on the corrugated-roof side of town by the bay in a drafty, capacious building that once housed a smelting factory. One side of the interior was like any other deluxe workout facility: two levels of equipment and machines, a smaller section of barbells and free weights for the serious lifters, racks of jump ropes and medicine balls. But on the other side were the "walls," sculpted and painted to look like rock and as much as sixty feet high. The individual routes consisted of patterns of plastic-molded holds, each route delineated from its neighbors by splashy strips of duct tape. And each named, per real cliffs, and marked with a rating using our same Yosemite Decimal System. Bizarre—and yet this "Iron Works" gym had a weirdly familiar flavor, which I initially ascribed to various of the atmospherics: posters of Yosemite and the Tetons, a messy bulletin board of rides offered and climbing partners wanted and gear for sale like a tidier version of the one in Camp 4, and an alcove stocked with new ropes and hardware and guidebooks.

On my first visit I wandered about, perplexed. It was midafternoon on a weekday and the gym nearly empty when I walked in, and in this state it seemed laughably overbuilt. But two hours later there were dozens of people climbing, and in only minutes of watching I recognized the manners and gestures of a familiar tribe—their backs and shoulders muscled disproportionately to their otherwise slight frames, their standing about in simian repose and too-casually playing at Our Serious Business, whether flaking ropes, assembling and locking in belay devices, or spotting one another on the first sketchy moves off the ground.

I had spent most of the intervening time near the entrance with my nose in the rack of guidebooks, all but a couple new since our day and almost all authored by people I'd never heard of. Our books had terse verbal descriptions and poor, hand-drawn topographical renderings of routes. These featured splashy color photographs and precise, digitally rendered maps. I scanned indices for our routes and counted more than a dozen Hunter-Holland attributions. I found no descriptions that didn't square with my memory and only one meaningful rating change (a notch harder than what Pete and I said, a sort of compliment). And then there were these others, thirty or forty, with Hunter but no Holland, most of them just a pitch or two and many a grade and two harder than anything we ever climbed. A few Pete had put up solo, some with a David Goldstein I'd never heard of, and several with as many as three other partners, as when a set of climbers discovers and develops a new area. Two jumped off the page, both from the early '90s: Just This, a long moderate on the south flank of Lone Pine Peak, and Inventing the Difficulties, a hard-to-get-to eight-pitch route high on the Wheeler Crest, both attributed to Hunter-Rhodes. Pete had climbed these with Nor in the years between my departure and Will's arrival. In the forewords and afterwords of each of the Sierra guides, I found acknowledgments addressed to Pete for what he provided by way of "beta"—climber parlance for route information—as well as history, drawings, and even encouragement, and in the back of one of the guides a memorial page with a blurry black and white photograph of Pete in Yosemite. At the top: "Pete Hunter—1962–1998," and under the picture: "Pete in the day." I recognized the scene, and then recalled the photograph: I had been on the other side of our pile of gear, at his left, now cropped out. It was from our second trip in the Valley, just after we returned to camp from several days' climbing and clinging to El Cap. Pete was ecstatic, face darkened from sun and oily hair awry.

Just to see my name in all these books was startling, and when I stood again after two hours and saw the thirty or forty climbers who had come in after work, I felt less anonymous than I had in months, maybe years. I was unknown to any individual but, by virtue of our doings twenty years ago, somehow relevant to the assembled. I also felt like I had missed out on something. I wasn't jealous or resentful Pete had taken up with other partners, but surprised and disappointed to see his production had fallen off, and that so many of the routes were single-pitch, cragging lines, and only a few bore marks of the type of adventure and enterprise we aspired to in ours. Unless I was misreading the annals, or missing something, it seemed he'd been limited by my leaving.

A week later I went back to the gym with Jeremy, a roommate of one of Carol's students. I warned him I'd have to get a belay certification first—that I hadn't so much as seen a gym until a few days ago. "I know your résumé," he said. He described a website I'd never heard of that functions like an online guide and community forum for climbers. "I figured it had to be some other Joe Holland. But you, well, you look like yourself. Maybe a little thinner here." He pointed to his temples.

"And here," I said, pointing to my bicep.

"Must be strange, a climbing gym," he said.

I was about to agree, but he went first: "Not as strange as not climbing, though. Not for me, anyway."

Jeremy was a software engineer by day who lived for his next adventure. In street clothes he was khaki-and-polo nondescript, but pared to T-shirt and shorts he bore the signature taut of the climbing-obsessed. He was kind around the eyes and solicitous of me even if he had a discrete series of routes, part of a work-week training regimen, that he would center our session around.

I hadn't so much as tied into a rope in fifteen years. Still, the business of being oriented and certified to belay was mildly humiliating. I'd been benighted mid-pitch on The Sentinel in frayed slings before you were born, I wanted to say to the teen-ager telling me where the brake hand belongs on the rope. In twenty minutes I had a freshly laminated card hanging from my harness and a small stack of indemnifying forms in their file cabinet, but then we had to take another, special test so we could "lead climb," using our rope to clip the fixed quickdraws on the way up instead of top-roping on the gym's lines.

"You first," Jeremy said.

I started up the requisite .10b test route—a respectably chal-lenging grade in my day—more than a little aware of the audi-ence of Jeremy's gym-mates behind us. Since a fall and catch are mandatory, and most everyone in the gym has endured this rit-ual, all eyes are drawn to the tidy drama of the lead test. Jeremy was earnest and encouraging, and one of the gym managers stood nearby to evaluate me. I could hear Jeremy talking to the manager, "Joe was Pete Hunter's main partner," perhaps think-ing the favor of reputation might trump any concerns about my competence. If the climbing mind is largely neutered on a gym route, with every gesture ordained by a designated color of tape, the body is nonetheless stressed in eerily familiar ways: strain through the abdomen, taut calves, and the inimitable forearm burn. The cerebral and mysterious "how to" is bled out of the enterprise, and yet the spare athletics of linking prescribed holds feels strangely analogous and arresting.

I clipped the fifth bolt, climbed six feet farther, let go, and fell halfway to the floor. We repeated the drill with Jeremy on lead, and then, with a second laminated card at my waist, we were free to wander the facility, dragging our rope around on a small tarp between the elements of Jeremy's routine. Most everyone knew Jeremy, and many introductions were exchanged. A couple of the older climbers recognized my name, and one mentioned Pete as well. "I met him in a gym!" he said. "In Sacramento." Pete had been there to do a slideshow of Sierra technical routes, a wintertime activity he described to me on the phone—proud that the first and last of his slides featured pictures of me. "I watched you lead-test earlier," the guy said. "I thought you looked familiar." Later I ran into the same guy by the drinking fountain. "You know, I think that was the same year Pete died," he said. "When I saw the slideshow."

Jeremy got us moving along from these exchanges—he had a workout to accomplish, climbing two or three routes to every one of mine. But the activity was beside the point. I could think of little else but this tightly knit world we inhabited and the mythic status Pete had achieved in it. I recalled what he'd said to me about artificial climbing walls, because by the mid-'90s there was a little one even in Mammoth: "I'll hang up my shoes before it comes to that." But this gym was vast and well equipped next to whatever Pete had been complaining about, and as the summer wore on and my visits became more regular than I care to admit, I worried over this dichotomy, not for what it suggested about gym climbing but for my life and work back home: these indoor routines we accomplish in veneration of what we can know only out there, on rock, under sky—the synthetic business, even if situated in a cathedral, at best a place to practice and at worst an elaborate tease.

So after three or four invitations I finally said yes to join Jeremy for one of his weekend trips to Yosemite, and one Friday evening in early August we drove into the Valley at midnight and parked next to the El Cap meadow where rangers wouldn't be able to tell Jeremy's car from those belonging to climbers on multiday ascents. We walked into the dark oak forest toward the toe of the great cliff, and in the moonlight I could see outlines of the matchless topography through the trees and smell the familiar pine and cedar and campfire smoke, the aroma of adventure. I slept no better than I did on other nights in the Valley that would end with a predawn hike to the base of one formation or another. When Jeremy and I walked back toward the meadow it was darker still, the moon long since set and only the night still and calm because what I felt in my stomach was the same curl and twist I'd never made peace with in many years with Pete.

Jeremy had proposed an agenda suitable for an "off the couch" climber: on Saturday the East Buttress of Middle Cathedral, and if we were fast, maybe part of Central Pillar of Frenzy, too. Sunday I could belay him on his project, a hard, bolt-protected route near Bridalveil Fall. If I had any steam left, there were easier things nearby.

No matter that I'd climbed the East Buttress many times, I was breathing hard for merely thinking about it. We moved the car a couple miles east and ducked back into the cool woods at first light. Jeremy sensed my nerves and took control: he found the approach, led the way, flaked the rope, racked the gear. He didn't even bother to ask whether I wanted to lead the easy first pitch. Snapping on his helmet, he looked me in the eye and said,

"It's an honor, Joe. To be here with you. Truly." And then he was gone. Did I see him again? Not much: he climbed so fluidly and fast, reracking at the belays and never more than the half dozen pieces he'd placed, and then he was off again. For me, the first two hundred feet were exhilarating—it had been so long—but in an hour I was tired and in two just scared, less by the hundreds of feet of air we had gained above the ground than by my diminished powers even on a moderate and familiar route. Across the valley, El Cap soared dramatically, and the higher we got on the buttress the more unthinkable it was that I'd ever been more or less competent and comfortable in such a vast vertical wilderness. My hands bloody, feet on fire, I huffed and puffed my way up to Jeremy at each belay. He took pictures of me I'd never want to see and said things like "Attaway" and "Still got it, Joe." But I didn't, and I knew it. When we reached the top and traversed east to the gulley rappels, I was more eager than ever to get back to the broad and level valley floor. Hours later, resting on the open back of his small station wagon in bare feet, I lifted a beer to my lips. "Still got nothing."

But the appetite is stupid, and if I was in no condition to climb the next day, or really the rest of the summer, something had been awakened—some long-dormant sap starts running again and you can't look at a bridge or a building, much less a mountain, without assessing prospective lines. Sure, it's a physical call—assuming a musculature adequate to your intentions. But it's also aesthetic—a sequence of holds, discovered, arranged—the architecture of *if.* Most of all, and most troubling to me, were the metaphysical dimensions of what I'd been joined to and inspired by and fled from, a way of being in the world that somehow feels more honest and animating for its proximity to the void. I started dreaming about climbing for the first time in years, and at the gym I became a regular—as much to peruse guidebooks and magazines and listen in on the banter as to use the equipment and climb the walls. A whole-sale reacquaintance. Carol complained she saw more of me in a single day in Vermont than a summer in Berkeley, even if to me the distance was nothing new. I'd grown accustomed to our parallel lives as a sort of protective arrangement, if only because when we were together I felt, often as not, the object of her pity. But in California, where even professors are outdoorsy and athletic, and where the aloof tribe of climbers maintains a further cachet, even Carol's curiosity was aroused. At the beer gardens and potlucks where she intercepted her students she heard more than a little about this climbing business, and for the first time she showed some interest in what was depicted in photographs on the parsonage walls at home. I was growing fitter and stronger in ways she hadn't known me to be, the gym sessions returning a measure of form to my long-unmuscled arms and shoulders and hands. Here in California I was some-thing other than the ineffectual minister and childless father. I was a climber—or at least a former climber. I knew some words she didn't. I had done some things other people were curious about. In corresponding fashion, I was finding her enthusiasms increasingly leaden, the career-focused appointments and uni-versity politics rather pale compared to the poetry-passion she'd been in thrall to when we met. For all of her preoccupation with who's working where and what he or she did to get the job, Carol too, it seemed, had migrated from the real deal into a sort of gymnasium.

Most of all, I grew curious about Pete. What had it been like for him in the years after I left, and what I had missed for leav-ing? So when Jeremy invited me to Tuolumne later in August, I figured I'd go and just keep going—over to the Eastside to look around, and at some point stop in at Mammoth to find Nor and Will and finally meet Astrid. When I told Carol about my plans, she said, "So this is what it's like to be married to a climber."

"It's worse."

"Oh right. They used to call you his husband," she recalled.

Later, when I was packing a rental car with gear, she followed me outside. "Onward into the past?"

I laughed.

"Wow. Must be weird."

Sure, weird. Not just this activity I had once been identified with, but history as well—famous places, long friendships, death. Her *wow* may have been facetious or jealous or some combination—no matter. On the long drive to Yosemite I nursed my own wordless sense of wonder.

Jeremy was meeting a friend, a climber from Colorado who lived out of a van except for winter stints tending bar in Aspen. He and Sam had cooked up a plan to have me join them on the famously scenic Oz on Drug Dome because Sam read that Pete and I had done one of the first ten ascents, in 1985. So this was a "twenty years after" conceit, the sort of thing climbers indulge less to tap the tiresome nostalgia for those who came earlier and the "Golden Age" they were believed to inhabit than to rationalize whatever it is they'd like to do *now*, no matter how familiar and, for them, rudimentary. I noted that when Pete and I first climbed Oz it was already yesterday's news and on no one's list of hardman ticks, but Jeremy didn't care. That we had done the route a long time ago and without small, finger-sized cams gave it a worthy, daunting aspect to him. I didn't complicate the picture by recalling the many fixed pins lining this and so many other Yosemite routes at the time.

I found them beside the large, canvas-covered wooden frame that is the Tuolumne Meadows store, Sam's van one of several among a dozen vehicles in a pop-up climber's camp that materializes in the small lot most mornings during the season. Jeremy was making coffee on a stove by the van and blowing on his hands to ward off the late summer frost, Sam sitting in a folding chair, back to me, shoulder length hair flowing out from under a wool hat. The panoply of domes and grass and forests around the Meadows looked and smelled like a home I once lived in and loved and never expected to leave. I had driven up the day before, several times pulling over to admire one vista or another—roadside cliffs where Pete and I tested gear, creeks where we filled our jugs, cliffs where we learned to handle ourselves on Yosemite rock out of sight of accomplished Valley climbers' eyes. I hiked up the southern slabs of Daff Dome to look across at Fairview. Under brilliant sunshine, four evenly spaced teams on the Direct North Face were another indication of what a popular pastime ours had become. In the early evening I walked the short trail to Drug Dome to get a preview of Oz. The forest floor near the road was moist and mossy, the boulder field en route to the cliff dark and lichen-splashed, just as when Pete and I first traversed this stretch. Drug Dome is one of several great cliffs south of the road, so Pete and I had walked through here probably fifty times in both directions and in various states of excitement and anxiety and joy and relief but always confident we would be back, today's just one more approach or descent in an endless liturgical rite. But here I was alone, thinking I've probably stepped on this very stone before and surely hopped over this stream. I recognized the play of light through the lodgepoles and the corn lilies beside a swale, flowers grown from seeds of those we once trampled. And the smell, too—dry forest and wet meadow and clear air with just a trace of campfire smoke drifting west from the dozens of campsites behind the store. Then the trees fall away and the steep north face of Drug Dome rears into view, the glorious wall, yellow now in the early evening light and free of clinking climbers' gear and splash of their loud clothing, just still and severe, serenely etched and wholly unchanged. I sat by a clump of deer brush and watched the sunlight die on the cliff. I had binoculars in my pack but didn't bother; in twelve hours I'd be back, inching my way onto the feature and in time gaining that intimacy with edge and wrinkle and crack only the climber knows. After sunset I meandered back to my car, and sometime later walked back behind Puppy Dome to sleep near a cave Pete and I frequented to hide from thundershowers and avoid rangers.

Jeremy had left Berkeley late, and Sam was coming from the Eastside, so they too had guerilla-camped off the road at opposite ends of the park and were just getting reacquainted when I pulled up. Jeremy had told me Sam was his favorite and most reliable partner. They'd met several years before in the Meadows, and in recent years spent a good chunk of August together. This was their meet-up for the start of a two-week climbing trip. I parked nearby and rummaged in the back seat for my mug. Jeremy saluted from across the lot, raising his coffee, and when Sam turned toward me something on Jeremy's face mirrored back my own puzzlement and I instantly knew to act unsurprised Sam was a woman. From behind there had been no indication: shoulders sturdy and hair longer than most men's but shorter than many climbers' and unkempt as most. She wore a heavy woolen sweater and the sort of weather-resistant, stretchy pants climbers sport nowadays.

Jeremy reached toward me with the saucepan of coffee. "Cowboy-type. Let it settle."

Sam extended a gloved hand. She had bright cheeks and warm, blue eyes. I couldn't tell if she was twenty-four or forty-four.

"Take my chair," she said. "I'm going to use the loo."

The van's open side doors were hung with black netting and stuffed with clothing. I peeked inside. The interior had been custom outfitted in fragrant wood. She had a large bed and a colorful quilt tucked in at the corners and a tidy array of pillows against the far wall. Gear bins under the bed, two bookshelves, and a recess for cooking equipment beneath the counter. It was like the hold of a wooden sloop, cozy and efficient. On one wall she'd tacked a Sierra Club calendar and on the other a sort of diploma, evidently a gift from climber friends:

SAMANTHA 'SAM' NEUWELD

MASTER OF ARTS IN STEEP ROCK

DOCTOR OF FINGER CRACK

(WUSS OF SLAB)

LONG MAY YOU ROAM

UNIVERSE(ITY) OF THE HIGH DESERT

DECEMBER 2002

The words were composed in calligraphy and the margins filled with colorful, hand-drawn flowers and trees and the outlines of crags. In the bottom right corner a pen-and-ink sketch captured Sam's high rosy cheeks and playful smirk.

"You didn't tell me," I said.

"Why would I?" Jeremy said.

"I don't know. Because there weren't so many back in the day."

"Pete was married, yes?"

"To Nor. Eleanor. I'm going there next, to Mammoth."

"She climb?"

Sam was back, standing near us in a forward bend. Even with palms pressed flat on the ground her elbows were bent.

"Not really," I said. "Brilliant ability. Not much appetite."

"Who?" Sam asked.

"Pete's wife," Jeremy said. "Or widow, I guess it is."

Her face still near her feet, Sam said, "Speaking of the will and the way, I was across from Kauk last night. In that pullout the other side of the pass. Says he remembers you, you and Pete."

"Sure," I said, my skepticism poorly disguised.

"Why not?" Jeremy asked.

"I don't know. Maybe Joe DiMaggio remembered a minor leaguer or two."

Jeremy tossed a bag of gear onto the pavement and started selecting pieces for a rack. He knew exactly which he wanted.

"Nor didn't care about climbing," I said. "Though she was with us on our last route together. Helped portage, did the first pitches."

"What was that?" asked Sam.

"Moriah. Northeast Face."

"Which has a big problem section in the middle?" Jeremy said, more excited than daunted by the prospect.

"I heard the bottom pitches are stellar," Sam said.

"So what is it," Jeremy said, "above there?"

"I got onto the fifth a couple of times. Way beyond me. Beyond Pete too. But he thought it would go. Someday."

"But didn't return?" Jeremy said.

"Was saving it. Used to say it would be there when I got back in the saddle."

"You never made a plan?" Jeremy said.

"No. He mentioned it when I saw him in '95. He came through with his mother, to see the leaves. I saw him twice in a week. Next time was in the morgue."

Sam stood erect now, her eyes locked onto my face.

"Two kids, too," Jeremy said, as if to compound the blunt summary. "Joe's headed over there this week."

Jeremy tended to the gear while Sam remained quiet and still, her face warming in the morning sun. I couldn't tell if she was waiting to hear more about Pete or merely abiding the sudden solemnity cast over our introduction.

"Drug Dome will be a freezer for another two hours," Jeremy said.

"Mind if I walk?" I said. "Meet you there?"

"Go," Jeremy said. "See you at the pullout. Put your pack in the van."

Sam was looking off at the meadows.

⌒

I found them on the sunny side of the sandy lot midmorning, Jeremy on the ground with a book and Sam now in full yoga mode nearby, gliding through her poses with the alacrity of a grasshopper. I had hiked on a trail paralleling the Tioga road, though well enough to the south I might as well have been in wilderness. At stream crossings I marked the play of morning light in the cold water and crystalline patches of frost alongside shaded banks. I was nervous about the climb, if still a bit puzzled as to why I had catapulted out of the morning rendezvous, but then within a mile of Drug Dome I remembered this was how I came the first time. Pete had run down to the Valley to meet family friends from back East in Curry Village. He was gone a couple of days, me alone in a campsite just paces from where I'd found Jeremy and Sam this morning. We had agreed to rest in anticipation of giving Oz a try, a big deal for us at the time, and on the designated morning I walked exactly the path I was taking now. Not long after I arrived, Pete pulled up in the Buick, hopped out, and popped the trunk. "Hungry?" Three open boxes were stuffed with supplies—bags of dried noodles, cans of soup, enormous tubs of peanut butter and jam. A family pack of Hershey bars. A case of beer. His friends had come to Yosemite bearing this pantry, something engineered by his mother. We were set for weeks. We debated driving the groceries up to the campground to store them properly, but itching to climb, we decided against it, and nothing about that first time on Oz was so memorable as the long scoriations left by a bear across the back of the car, parallel stripes that rusted in time but never provided less than a happy marker.

Odd to have a life measured this way—the same jitters along the same path toward the same route on the same cliff. And yet this time I had so little at stake: Jeremy and Sam would handle the real climbing. All I had to do was get through it, and avoid the expectation that it would be painless or easy.

They had decided to wait a while for the air to warm up. On this, their first morning, neither was anxious about the day's activity. Their objectives lay elsewhere—Oz a mere warm-up and acclimation they'd arranged on my account.

Another car pulled in, and without speaking we were underway. The last thing we wanted was to be stuck behind others on a cold cliff. In twenty minutes we were at the base of the feature and warm from hiking, and before I had even stepped into my harness Sam was working her way into the first challenging section. She protected a hard move almost without pause and stepped past it easily, scampered up to the ledge and was off belay before I had even changed shoes. In our day we thought Oz the rare climb that has it all: a tricky section off the deck but then a hundred feet of fun seams and ledges. The second pitch is the supposed hard one, a pair of steep mantels on slippery granite shelves, these moves mercifully bolt-protected. Third is the famously photogenic corner with a narrow crack splitting two hundred feet of blond, lichen-splashed granite so clean and vertical it's as if God had made the dome, cleaved it of its northern half, and cracked it: "Here. Climb this." Above here, a roof arches out over the top of the route and makes for two possibilities: the standard way veers left, delicate steps protected by bolts and fixed pins and final easy moves to the summit, while the Gram Traverse goes right over big air—solid jams in the crease but almost nothing for the feet. Going the harder way, you also have to navigate around several heart-stoppingly loose blocks pinned beneath the roof, any of which, dislodged, might miss you but just as easily cut your rope. In the '80s you couldn't report having climbed Oz without an immediate retort: "Did you do the Gram?"—a ritualized exchange Pete dubbed "The Gram jury."

I went after Sam, and though stalled momentarily at the first crux the pitch was more manageable than I'd feared. It seemed my gym-going was proving useful, and in moments I was sharing the long narrow ledge with her, facing out, legs dangling.

"Familiar?" she said.

We were above the trees, admiring sun-splashed domes and forests north and east of us.

"Except harder," I said, unlacing my shoes.

I massaged my feet and recalled my first time here, twenty years earlier, how fit and purposeful and anxious we were. Pete was in his ethics phase, determined to utilize as few of the fixed pins as possible, and if either of us fell or hung our effort would get a taint, which would require a subsequent, clean ascent. I was just impressed, then and now—by the severity of the steep cliff, by our being one of the first parties to attempt the route, by our being here at all.

After another hour and another pitch, situated on a tight stance directly beneath the great corner, I was worked and bleeding. Here the dark lichen gives way to a pastiche of yellow and red-splashed granite in the upper reaches of the face. In 1985 there were three large pitons in the first fifty feet of the crack, and above these we could see just the heads of several Lost Arrows stacked in the steep, narrow part of the corner. We'd heard about small edges for stemming through the steepest section, and with the line of fixed gear and the rumor of good feet, we were excited for what lay before us. I remember reracking for the pitch and looking up at the corner, less to admire the clean, steep feature than to avoid Pete's eyes, certain he'd try to buy it off me. But he didn't.

Sam set off, Jeremy followed, and when I went on belay I saw him lowering on a strand to the side with the camera. I didn't protest, but with a top-rope only the wholly uninitiated would see these pictures for anything other than what they were: an old poser who happened on climbers patient and generous enough to haul him up the famous Yosemite corner. Still, Jeremy's dangling overhead with the camera both took me out of my own body and endowed me with form, as an audience for an actor, and for the first time in fifteen years I was really climbing: fluid, clever, mostly unafraid, and improbably capable despite steep walls and spare, sharp features. I enjoyed the prospect that I, anyway, might appreciate the visual record of this passage, and a couple of times I paused longer than I otherwise would have, even in the middle of a hard move, in anticipation of Jeremy's snapping shutter. In the steepest section he had left one of Sam's cams for a directional lest I fall and have a hard time gaining the crack again, and as I approached I worried this would flummox me—having to free a hand to remove even one piece of gear. God bless Sam for placing it from a decent stance, with stemming edges on either side of the crack. Done. In a few minutes my bloodied fingers and happy grin were scooching onto the tiny belay ledge.

Sam knew joy. She smiled at me and said nothing.

Jeremy climbed back up to us on his tether, a maneuver that should have given us pause for the shock-load to the anchor that would result should he fall, but there are times in the climber's life when the unthinkable is simply unthinkable, and if Sam was worried she didn't let on, didn't quickly back up the bolted anchor or ask him to pause a moment and allow her to put him on belay.

Shortly he was alongside us. Even before he clipped in, he said, "Want it?" nodding to the fourth pitch.

I thought no, but studied the rock to our left, and with my end of the rope on top and Sam already having me on belay, this made the most sense. Without replying I took the few pieces off the rack I'd need for this short section—a forty-foot traverse past two bolts and some easier climbing to the greenery at the top.

As I started off I glanced down. The two guys we'd seen in the parking area were in full retreat, one already lying on a boulder at the base in bare feet, the other on rappel just beneath the first anchor. I turned back to my little project with a hollow in my throat. The initial moves off the belay seemed coated in a waxy sheen. I leaned awkwardly from a secure stance to clip the first bolt, then spent several minutes trying two variations to traverse past it before committing to a third, obvious option, a set of moves no more difficult than crossing a stream on secure, evenly placed stones, though the rushing waters stir the imagination.

In minutes I was sitting at the edge of the great cliff, secured to a dwarf limber pine. Then Sam, and finally Jeremy. We changed shoes, added a layer, coiled ropes, and reracked gear in the cooling light. Our late start and my slow going through the hard sections had put us on top in the late afternoon. We found the mountaineer's descent trail and got back to the boulder field just in time to see the north side of Drug Dome fully bathed in sunshine, the hard edges and sharp features we'd climbed buffed and softened by the setting sun. At the pullout the two guys who had retreated were sitting on the ground between their car and Sam's van in jackets and bare feet drinking beer.

"No problem," one said to Sam, a nod to her acumen.

Sam smiled. "We had the benefit of a first ascensionist."

"No way," the first guy said, looking at me.

"Hardly," I said.

"Back in the day, anyway," Sam said.

"No benefit, I mean. I aided the mantel."

"What's the deal with that?" the other guy said. "I couldn't get even to Simon's high point."

His partner grunted. "Don't compare us to them."

"Nor 'them' to 'them,'" I said. "I'm not fit to drive the van."

Jeremy spoke like the seasoned veteran. "Everybody's project is someone else's warm-up."

"Right," the first guy said. "I'd like to see the guy who warms up on your project."

We said so long and turned east toward the crest, twilight now and a nearly full moon sitting above Mount Dana. Jeremy ran into the Meadows store for beer and a bundle of firewood, then we followed Sam over the pass. The thought had been to sleep where she'd seen Kauk the night before, but with several vehicles there Sam motioned to us to keep heading down. The moon was well above the horizon and the sky clear, granite basins high above us lit as if by soft electric light. We drove slowly down the east side, Sam in the van, Jeremy in his little station wagon, and me in the rental. A few miles this side of Lee Vining the eastern desert opens into view and finally the great black mirror of Mono Lake, shining in the moonlight. When Sam took a dirt access road descending east into the basin, I hung back a bit to allow the billowing dust behind them to settle but not so much as to get lost. Warm sage filled the car. A series of turns on intersecting roads, and then a singular high-desert oasis—four cottonwoods and a cluster of small aspens.

Beside the van was a small fire circle made of round stones, and near this a couple of flat, leaf-strewn tent sites. Just beyond the grandest of the cottonwoods, the bounding waters of Rush Creek flow through a rock-lined streambed. Before the reservoir was built, ten miles upstream, this unbroken tributary of Mono Lake had for thousands of years been lined with Paiute settlements, the weather gentle and the fish abundant. Sensing the great lake's salty water, trout crowded these lower reaches of the stream, at times swimming so hard in the other direction that Natives could catch them with bare hands. I'd never camped in this very site, but the ecology was identical to any number of Pete's and my Eastside haunts—and as far from New England as I'd been in years.

Sam stayed in the van awhile, candle flickering inside. Jeremy and I set out the stove and other gear, laid out our tarps and sleeping bags, and then I took a beer and walked out onto the sandy plateau on the other side of the road. Along the small ridgeline just east of us I could hear only the soft wind in sagebrush and some gulls down by the lakeshore. The lake's surface rippled and shimmered, and now the Sierra Crest glowed too, proud profile of the Third Pillar of Dana cut by the moonlight. I circled back, intersecting the creek again, then walked along the stream toward the canopy of trees that marked our camp. Several times I dipped my tender fingertips in the cold water. There would be no climbing for me the following day; even to tie my shoes would be painful. I wasn't twenty feet from Sam before I saw her, then fairly paralyzed: she was naked, ankle deep in the stream, pouring water over her hair and back with a small plastic bucket.

I made a move to head back but feared she'd see me and think I was ogling. I crouched for a while, then sat in the sand, turning to face upstream. The water was loud. I couldn't hear Sam and had to look from time to time to tell whether she was still there. Clothed, she had seemed a rugby player, naked, a dancer. Her skin glistened in the dark.

"Hey there," she said. She was wrapped in a towel. "I didn't see you. Hope I didn't invade your little hideout."

"No. Just taking care of my hands."

"Bad?"

"Same old sting."

"Yeah, my deal at the bar is no dishwashing after Presidents' Day. Then I go to work on them. Sandpaper, and this little device I made."

We climbed the bank to camp. Jeremy had a pot of rice on one burner and an iron skillet of vegetables on the other. He was grating fresh ginger over these.

"Almost," he said.

Sam slipped into the van to change.

I went to my car to rummage for a plate, and when I returned Sam had taken over at the stove and Jeremy was down by the stream. As on the cliff, I was an interloper, like one of many strays Pete and I had entertained through the years.

"Take a chair," Sam said, gesturing with a spatula. "In there."

I looked in the van. It smelled of incense. She had a rolled-up blanket on the bed, and a couple of paperbacks there too, including *Amaravati Chants*.

"You're a meditator," I said.

She fluffed the rice. "I'm ambidextrous. Climbing, bartending, Buddhist chants. Many practices, no rules."

"But the one," I said.

She looked puzzled.

"About dishwashing."

She ducked into the van, returning with an eight-inch square of wood with about fifty nails of various diameters hammered into one side, each one trimmed of its head.

"Not as awful as it looks," she said. "Even if any one of them would spear you. Bed-of-nails premise."

"She does fingertip push-ups on that," Jeremy said. He seemed both impressed and disgusted.

He scooped rice with the wooden spoon and plunked vegetables on top. We sat on the ground in portable chairs, and with no headlamps or fire the night sky was ablaze.

My own fingertips burned under the warm plate.

"What's next?" Sam said.

"South. You?"

"Tomorrow a cliff I bet you never heard of. Just under the Tioga road, but way up by the pass. Monday we're walking into the Hulk."

"For?"

"Polish Route first. The big deal is Positive Vibrations. Was that up in your day?"

"Just. One of those everyone talked about and no one climbed."

"Not like we haven't been talking about it for, what, three years?" Jeremy said.

"Well, I can't help you," I said. "Not even with the mythology."

"We're all set," he said. "Only thing to worry about is the climbing."

"We used to say that. It was almost never true."

Jeremy brought the iron pan around and pushed the remaining food onto our plates.

"South where?" Sam said.

"Mammoth."

"Where Nor is," she said.

"And Will. And to meet Astrid. Nor was pregnant when Pete fell."

"That's a lot," Sam said.

We each turned to our plates.

"What about you?" Jeremy said. "You and Carol? No children?"

"Thought about it. Tried. Then changed our mind."

The wind had died, and the night felt still warmer.

"You?" I said.

"Me what?" Jeremy said.

"Kids at some point?"

Sam laughed. They caught one another's eye. I wasn't the first to presume they were a couple.

"Sam first," he said.

"I'd more likely solo The Naked Edge," she said.

"When Collins did, it was for longing," Jeremy said.

"Or maybe grief," Sam said.

Each glanced at me. Of course I remembered: Jim Collins' solo of the iconic line, supposedly driven by heartache.

"We were there in Eldo not long after, Pete and I. It was like someone hung a shroud on that route. To do it regular, like we hoped to, you might as well be nailing into the Sistine Chapel ceiling."

"Glad that's all done with," Sam said. "It's a favorite."

We had coffee together at first light, and they were pulling out before I even started packing. They were eager to climb in the morning's cool sunshine and spend the rest of the day provisioning for their trip to the Hulk. When the sun hit our campsite, the temperature soared, and I headed south.

I was agitated for where I was going, the sort of buzz and churn I used to have driving to one cliff or another. I knew I should go straight into Mammoth, Sunday perhaps a good day to find Nor, but I also knew I wouldn't. I passed the exit, still without a destination in mind. I drove slowly, admiring the age-less landmarks—the dark north side of Mount Morrison, Lake

Crowley's marshy, treeless shores, and the turn in the Sierra Crest by Sherwin Pass where the massive cone of Mount Tom sits off to the right and finally Mount Humphreys' grand profile rears into view. Bishop appeared unchanged as well, but I didn't stop, not for another thirty miles, and then only when the sign for Goodale Creek called out to me. This is one of the wild canyons, and not until I had spent much of the day hiking along the narrow mountaineers' trail beside tumbling waters did I recall it was first of the several drainages I'd explored on those frantic days Pete had gone missing, the time he'd found Moriah. On the day I was last here, Pete may very well have been climbing the lower half of the route—he ecstatically embracing his next project, I anxiously scurrying around the Eastside for evidence of his whereabouts.

So I finished this day exactly as I'd finished the other: drove my little rental straight to Vons in the early evening. Jeremy had lent me a little camp stove. I'd pick up some things and head up by the Gorge and find our camp. In the market I studied faces, recognizing no one in particular and everyone in general: backpackers and climbers gathering noodles and energy bars for their adventure, others from around the valley with their cereal, soda, and frozen pizza. I found the Gorge road where it swings off to the east. The narrow lane had been paved recently, and there was a parking lot and access trail that hadn't been there in our time. Pete got it right about these short, steep cliffs that line the edges of the once dry and dirty gorge: the place had become a climbing mecca thanks to the "sport climbing" style that was emerging about the time I pulled out, and now the Eastside was, like Joshua Tree and Yosemite, another little slice of California teeming with climbers from around the world. In the twilight of a warm summer's evening, I mindlessly navigated the maze of dirt roads that led to our camp, the sage and pinyon-dotted hills above the gorge familiar as the shape of my hands.

The trailer was gone—it had been for years. Pete lived in it for several seasons, and when he moved to Mammoth to be with Nor had it hauled there on a flatbed truck in hopes of making some improvements. It sat on their driveway for two years before Nor finally persuaded him to let it go.

I parked a ways off. I was hot and spent from the two days' outings and eager to find a flat, wind- and sun-protected place to spend the night. But it's rare you get fresh proximity to an old home, so I paused to allow the ritual to unfold. The lay of the land here unmistakable, clumps of pinyons as dwarf and wind-battered as ever, high columns of basalt on the horizon indicating the gorge's farther rim. It's a massive sky from this vantage, fourteen-thousand-foot peaks to the west and the equally high if lumpier White Mountains to the east. Looking south you see the shimmering lights of Bishop clustered at the head of the broad valley.

Still, the missing trailer left a jarring vacancy. I was in a frame whose picture had been removed. I tried to imagine it into place but was lost for details, couldn't recall even the aspect of the side door. A berm of coarse sand had buried the stone wall we built around the porch where we cooked and played chess and hosted parties. I scraped some shallow pockets nearby until my tender fingertips found the hard patina of flagstone. The pre-twilight glow turned everything rosy, and when I stood again it was with awe—what a glorious world we'd inhabited.

Before the sun hit my tent I was driving along a dirt shortcut to 395 and north toward the Mammoth turnoff. In town I found a coffeehouse fashioned out of a shack between two gas stations. I got a sandwich for later and used their phone book to verify Nor's number: "Rhodes, Dr. Eleanor, Will and Astrid Hunter."

I drove up past the ski area, and then down the back side to the wilderness trailhead. I wasn't fit and fast enough to get to the base of Clyde Minaret and back, but I could go a ways. I wanted to trace the steps where Pete had taken his last.

It was seven years, almost to the day, since Pete pulled up in the little sandy lot. Did he park there, in the sun, so by afternoon these pines would shade the truck? Or did he back into this little alcove and point the car out in anticipation of his homeward jaunt?

But walking, I lost him. Meadow, stream, boulder, sky—these, along with my breath and the sweat of steady upward trekking, wresting me back to now. At midday I sat beside the outlet of Iceberg Lake to refill my water bottle. At 2:00 P. M. I stepped onto the snowfield whose upper end is the steep headwall of Clyde, and at three I was right there, where Pete landed. The snowfield had long ago dissolved and recast his imprint, and the rock face looked no more or less sheer and magnificent than the last time I was here—to climb the route with Pete some dozen years before he fell off it. I bowed my head, but the gesture felt formal, empty of loss. I stood there on the snow as I did at weddings and funerals, assuming the contrived solemnity with which I made my living. Then I studied the cliff from directly beneath it. It was unimaginable—that Pete had pitched off this face, and that he wasn't torn to shreds on the way down for all the ledges and buttresses. I wondered if we knew anything about what happened, and why. Then I set my daypack on the snow and took a seat, gazing east toward the San Joaquin headwaters, grand Mammoth Mountain, and the Nevada desert on the horizon.

A short while later, bounding and sliding down the snowfield, I was relieved to have this errand behind me and even felt a touch of the Sierra good tidings John Muir extolled. The snow had softened in the sunshine, the air now thicker and my lungs full again. What remarkable vantage lay around the next bend?

At twilight I intersected three climbers at Shadow Lake and walked behind them and their headlamps for the last three miles back to the car. They had left the trailhead before dawn to scramble up one of the easier Minarets. Fourteen hours in, tired and sunburnt and approaching the end, they were chatty, hungry, high with accomplishment.

I got a site in the municipal campground, near a shopping center, two gas stations, even a McDonald's—rather like a Yosemite campground for the smell of dry pine and the groan and rumble of traffic on the other side of the trees.

Early the next day, in the same coffee shack as before, I was reading on one of their couches when a woman in hospital scrubs came in with her empty thermos. Even from the back I instantly recognized Nor, my breath suddenly shallow as I anticipated her surprise. She wore clogs, her hair as much gray as brown and longer than she wore it in the old days. She said hello to the woman at the register in an efficient exchange, placed some bills on the counter, and waited for her full thermos in what seemed a morning routine. The woman said, "Hope it's lazy over there today." Nor said thanks, then left without looking around to see who else was in the café.

I stood to watch her drive off.

At noon I walked to the hospital. Two ambulances pulled up in the fifteen minutes I was there. Dr. Hunter wouldn't be available anytime soon. Leave a message? I said I'd call her later. I fell asleep for a good long while in my tent. The past several days had been the most active I'd had in years, and when I got to a pay phone it was early evening. Nor sounded exhausted. She seemed surprised to hear from me, not happy like I expected. She had to be at work early the following day. We could meet afterward, at a restaurant between the hospital and home.

We were on the phone just two or three minutes, but I could hear her through the night—clipped, even annoyed. She had to drop the phone once to explain something to Astrid. She didn't apologize for not being readily available. She didn't try to hold me on the phone any longer than necessary.

On a time-killing walk the following afternoon I stopped at the mountain shop in Mammoth, quiet inside but for the young guy beside the register. Climbing hardware dangled from the wall behind the counter, new ropes hung from the ceiling, but most of the interior was taken up with racks of colorful, expensive technical wear now that everyone everywhere dressed like they were en route to alpine adventure. In an alcove at the back I found the books and climbing guides, and there, on the wall over the top shelf, Pete: an enlarged, framed photograph of his face, the same one that ran in the climbing magazines after he died. Beneath the picture someone had tacked a memorial on a piece of cardboard:

PETE HUNTER—1962-'98
TOWNIE, CLIMBER, GUIDE
EASTSIDE OG
GOOD FRIEND
OF MAMMOTH MOUNTAINEERING

"Help you?" the kid called from behind the counter.

"Just poking around."

He reached to a low shelf for the thick *Sierra Mountaineering* guidebook and flipped through some pages at the back.

"That you?" He held the page open to a photograph of me and Pete from 1986. We were standing in a meadow about a half mile from Feather Peak, each of us pointing to a section of the "Northeast Face Direct," the route we had put up the day before.

"It is," I said.

"You here awhile?"

"Couple days."

"Too bad Will's away. He's seen this. I think he said he didn't even know you."

"I live in Vermont."

"Cool kid," he said. He couldn't have been more than twenty himself. "Still climbing?"

"No." I turned to the index of routes in the back for others of Pete's and my routes. "Got dragged up 'Oz' the other day."

"That's pretty good for no. Will's a little spider. Sends hard boulders. Lives at the gym. Pretty rad on a snowboard, too."

"He's eleven?"

"I think so. He's away now. Goes to some camp in the East."

"I'm here to see his mom."

"Tell her hi, from Blake. She calls over here when she's looking for Will."

I reached for the newest Owens Gorge guidebook. "Can't believe how thick this is."

"Marty Lewis, Inc.," he said. "Those guys are animal. Been down there?"

"Twenty years ago. Scary-looking, I thought. And bone dry."

"Want to climb later? Not there. Sport crags up near the lakes, granite. I'm going after work."

"Thanks. My tips need a few days. Or maybe another fifteen years."

On a paved bike path around the perimeter of town I walked the long direction, then took a spur to the lakes. At Lake Mary, where we held the service for Pete, fishermen stood on the muddy shore and a couple families had spread their things on the tables. I sat for a while, listened to the gulls and watched clouds gathering around Crystal Crag. When I asked one of the picnickers about the time, I was surprised to learn it was well after three, but in running shoes I could trot down the bike path.

Still, I was late getting to Mulligan's, and sweaty. The air was crackling with thunder, but it was warm in town except for the periodic pulse of the cold thunderstorm blasting by. Nor's car was one of a few parked out front. I found a restroom in the bar, washed my face, removed my shirt, and patted myself dry with paper towels. The restaurant was empty, but on a porch out back there were several groups of people sitting at round tables under umbrellas. Nor was at one of these, alone, on the far side. Facing the Mammoth Crest, she had half a glass of white wine on the table beside her.

When I put my hand on her back, she appeared to recoil.

"Joe," she said, turning around.

"Hi. Sorry. Running late, literally."

She was wearing jeans and a blue athletic top with "Eastside Tumblers" stitched across the front. I couldn't see her eyes behind the sunglasses.

I faced the mountains as well. "I went up to the lakes."

"How was that?"

"Same. I mean, familiar. Everything is. Tuolumne, Bishop. Your little mountain shop."

"What'd you expect?" she said, lowering her sunglasses and studying my face.

A tall waiter approached, dreadlocks piled under a ratty knit hat. "You okay, Nor?"

"He's a friend," she said.

"How about you, friend?"

I asked for a lemonade.

"It's strange, too," I said. "Seeing it all again. I walked up to Clyde yesterday."

"Jesus."

"Yeah, well, I guess I always had it in mind, once I got here."

Thunder resounded around the peaks, surely frightening for any climbers up there but from town just idle entertainment.

"Maybe why it took me so long."

She lifted her sunglasses to her forehead. There were creases in her face, concentric bands by her mouth and eyes, her skin tighter around her bones than I recalled. Instantly I felt self-conscious, wondering what she saw in me that had evolved or seasoned or died.

"Tumblers?"

"Astrid. She's a gymnast," she said, tugging at the logo on her sweatshirt. "Couple of years ago another of the parents, a climber, saw Will messing around on an apparatus at a meet in Reno. He invited Will to our little climbing gym in town. Will thought that was kind of boring, but when they went to some boulders around Sherwin Summit . . ." She threw her hands. "Hooked."

She looked at me to see how this landed, Will's interest in climbing.

"Now he's at the gym all the time. Mountain shop, too."

"Blake says hi. I had some time today."

She drank some more. "So you saw the little shrine to Pete? A bit much, don't you think?"

"I don't know." To me it had seemed modest, and endearing. "Blake recognized me, from one of the guidebooks."

"Well, so welcome back," she said. "Here among the living. Astrid. Me. You. Will's at camp."

"I heard."

"In Maine, same place I went. He wanted a full month this time, though after he got all into bouldering he didn't want to go at all. But I hear he's made a pal there, a counselor who's taken Will under his wing. Climber, of course." She shook her head.

"But the kids around here, they all do something dangerous. Motorcycles, skateboards. Snowboarding. What was I going to get, a stamp collector?"

She finished her wine.

"It's safer," I said. "These days."

"Yes and no. We get way more broken ankles than backs. So yeah, the sport climbing thing, it's safer than what you guys were up to. But now there's highball bouldering, and kids Will's age aren't exactly good at risk-assessment."

Neither are some thirty-six-year-olds, I thought.

"And of course there's the soloists. John's still at it, Bachar. Lives in town here. Lonnie Kauk's carrying the torch. Will follows him like a rock star."

She looked off at the peaks, now mostly ensconced in dark clouds. "It was always Pete's, this," she said. "I wanted to leave, soon after he died. Maybe should have. But people are here for you. I think I got Will hooked up with the summer camp hoping he'd make best friends and that would be a pretext for a move. He's always been kind of, not lonely, but more of an on-his-own type of kid. No team sports. Not big on the birthday party circuit."

She looked at her watch, sat up straight, and placed her hands on her knees. "I have to get Astrid. She's the one not lacking for pals."

Bright holes were opening in the clouds overhead and a fresh, cooler breeze blew down from the mountains laced with the humidity of rain fallen somewhere else.

Nor stood. "You coming?"

I must have looked like I wasn't sure.

We drove back up toward the lakes and through a housing development that might have been in an LA suburb but for the backdrop—large houses indistinguishable from one another, most of them too close together and all with oversized garages. Nor pulled into one of these. It was a stretch to think of Pete making his home here.

"Give me a sec," Nor said, ducking into the garage.

One side of the driveway was bordered by a deep, green lawn, a set of uneven parallel bars set there. In the garage half-a-dozen bicycles of various sizes and shapes were strewn about, and on a piece of throw carpet a short section from a balance beam, just a foot off the ground. Getting out of the car I realized I was nervous to meet Pete's daughter.

In a few minutes Nor came through the garage followed by someone else's mom and then two girls, Astrid last and shoeless. While I was introduced to Karine and Sophie, Astrid attempted a handstand on the balance beam.

Nor held Astrid's pack. "Shoes?"

"We're not going out to dinner, are we?" Astrid said. When she came into the light I was startled for how much she looked like Nor, bold eyes and tanned face and sun-streaked hair she flipped out of her face with one hand.

"Astrid, this is Joe. We went to college together."

"Hi," Astrid said, looking at her feet.

"Thanks, Karine," Nor said, and, to me, "Astrid lives over here."

Karine called, "Good to meet you, Joe."

Nor snaked backed down a different route through the development, crossed a busier road, and entered another set of homes. Things started looking vaguely familiar.

"Your house," I said. "Wasn't it . . ."

"Not-yellow," Nor said. "Now it's not-green. We did it ourselves, two summers ago. Would have been cheaper to hire the job out, what with all the ice cream and movie bribes."

Astrid disappeared while Nor went to work on dinner. She had most of a cooked chicken in the refrigerator, and while warming this she assembled a salad and opened a bottle of wine. I used the bathroom and looked around the house. After several days without a shower, I felt like a shaggy dog that had sneaked inside. There were no indications of Pete, no photographs of mountains or cliffs or even of just him and Nor and Will. I wondered if Will's only encounter with his father's image was at the mountain shop.

I sat at the counter. Nor asked about me, and I gave her the summary—my floundering church, meeting Carol, the business about children and then not children. At some point she said, "A preacher and a professor. Sounds fun." I thought she either isn't listening or I haven't been telling the truth—I felt I'd been talking about being at loose ends.

"Children," she said. "They do ground you."

"I can see it'd be hard to move."

She drank her wine. "It's them, really. I can travel light. They're the ones with big, full lives. And it is a good place to grow up. Even with DFS."

I cocked my head.

"Dead Father Syndrome," she said, her voice dropping. "You get anything and everything you want. From everybody. Except of course the thing you don't have. And in Astrid's case, don't even miss."

The timer went off. Nor placed the steaming chicken on the counter.

"And there's this mythology-of-Pete around here. Which, the older Will gets, the more interested he is." She stared out the window. "I hoped they'd be into team sports. But even Astrid, it's the routines she likes, the physical stuff. Other girls on the team are more into each other. Hair ribbons, cheers."

"Pete was the gregarious one. Of us two, anyway."

"Yeah, well, Pete's gregarious is anyone else's hermit."

She tossed the salad.

"He wasn't the pied piper for climbing they've made him out to be," she said. "And then, with Will, he couldn't stand the little toddler play groups he had to cart him around to. I was working all the time."

She went over to the hallway. "Dinner!"

Astrid came flying out. "A guess: chicken and salad."

"Set the table, please," Nor said. "Hands washed?"

Astrid spun around, threw her hands under running water, and reached into a cupboard for plates.

"You're there, Joe," Nor said, nodding to the chair opposite hers.

"That's Will's seat," Astrid said, gesturing to the empty place. She had put a plate there as well, but no glass or utensils.

They held each other's hands. Nor reached across for mine and, after an instructive glance from her mother, Astrid took my other hand. Nor bowed her head, and Astrid did too but just for a moment, and then she looked at me. I held her gaze while Nor withdrew for a moment, and Astrid's eyes appeared to soften in the forced quiet. Then, with a squeeze from Nor, we were called back.

"We keep Will's place set," Nor said. "You know, to bring him home."

She refilled her glass.

"Where did Dad sit?"

"Right where you are."

"So I'm in the bad-luck seat?" Astrid cocked her head, looking at her mom like she had her pinned.

"Your dad didn't die of bad luck," Nor said, too firmly. "You ready for this weekend?"

They were headed to a meet in Lancaster, where a Rachel on the team was going to unfurl a new trick everyone else was trying to learn. Astrid gobbled her dinner and in moments fled back to her room.

Behind Will's chair, sliding glass doors opened onto a back patio and yard with a vantage of the Mammoth Crest, more or less the same view as from Mulligan's. The thunderstorms had blown through, the evening sky brilliant blue and shot through with the last of the sunshine, this already dissolving behind the mountain.

Nor rested her face in her hands, elbows on the table. "You know, what I've learned is all anyone remembers about you when you're dead, it's not you." She took a breath and looked at me. "It's someone else. Or something about themselves. They remember someone they want or need to imagine, but it's not Pete."

Nor went to the counter and lifted the bottle of wine. "Want some?" she asked. I declined. She poured herself a splash and put a cork in the top.

"They weren't the best years, the last few." She sat again. "Then I got pregnant with her."

"Our last was rough, too." I instantly realized how lame this was.

"What is it with Pete and endings?" she said.

"His favorite subject, apart from climbing."

"Big-idea banter," she snorted. "At least you had that."

I felt accused.

"Climbing was foremost," I said. "At least for Pete."

"Exactly. The other stuff, friendship, family. Doesn't measure up."

Nor stood, took our plates, and kind of lurched into the kitchen. I felt I should rally to Pete's defense. From the sink she called, "Grab the glasses, will you?"

"Sorry to drag you back," I said.

She handed me a dishtowel. "Doesn't take much."

"You carry on," she said. "You hope the time will just accumulate, the way snow does around here. Something to make a big insulating berm." She handed me a plate. "Then it just avalanches."

Nor smiled, amused by her own embellishment. "I've said many times the only thing worse than being married to Pete is being married to his memory."

I dried each dish as she handed it to me and arranged them on the counter.

"It's not him I blame. He wasn't dishonest about who he was or what mattered. If anyone held back it was me, even when things were pretty good. Even after Will was born. You know, he was way more into Will than he expected. Hovering over him, rushing home after he'd been out. It was a crappy season on the mountain, that first winter. We spent a fair chunk of it on a ratty couch in our basement apartment."

Nor made a second round wiping counters.

"When his mom offered to help us with this, the house, how could we refuse? But the whole deal scared him, I think. Some horizon he didn't recognize, or like. That's when he decided to get out of the resort, make more of a go of it guiding. But that was just a ruse. He was doubling down, on climbing."

The kitchen was hospital clean.

"Can I take you now?"

"I'm fine walking."

"You can stay here. I'll drive you over to get your stuff. You can have Will's room."

"I'm all set up. It's fine."

"I've got to be at the hospital early. When Astrid gets up she calls Karine and gets picked up."

"I saw you, yesterday. Getting coffee, at Stellar Brew."

"Yeah, most mornings."

"Campground's right behind there."

"Come on. Let me take you."

Nor went to Astrid's room, and when she emerged again Astrid was on her heels. "Nice to meet you, Joe," she said, as if reading a cue card.

The night air was clear and warm with traces of sage and pine. The best of all breathing, Pete would say. I wondered about Nor driving, for all the wine she'd had, but she seemed no less steady than earlier. We swung east of town, one side of the road abutting the hospital, the other glowing with creosote and small white boulders in the moonlight. I recalled driving this way with her once before, on the day we saw Pete's body.

"Will I see you again, Joe?"

"I need to head back," I said, though I didn't.

"Well, when you get out here again, stay awhile. Bring Carol. It's a nice place to be, especially in summer."

We waited to cross the four-lane highway. The stoplight took forever.

"You really loved him," she said.

Her eyes grew moist. "I didn't. Or didn't allow myself to, to get all the way there."

I wondered if I was supposed to contest her version of things.

"Burns me now. Not thinking I should have or couldn't. I just wouldn't, and I was never entirely square about it. Now I'm all set up here. Our children. In the town he wanted to live in. All the shell and none of the goo inside." She wiped her nose with her forearm. "It's not that he's dead. You get used to that. It's me. Being so self-protective. If I were just mad at him, I'd be over it."

We made the turn into the campground. Nor leaned forward, peering, and crept along. Small fires glowed to either side, the dark outlines of campers beside them.

"Far end," I said. "By the fence."

"We've got a lot of stuff, Joe."

"The little white rental there. Want tea? I have a stove."

"I've had enough for one night, don't you think? And Astrid's alone. But sometime. Maybe not seven years this time."

"Okay."

She reached across to my forearm.

I covered her hand with mine. "Thanks for the lift, Nor."

⤙

Most climbers proceed by means of the obvious array of hand-holds and footholds, making a ladder of a route—pull here, step there, reach past a crimp to gain that flake. If they're powerful, they can be quite talented. If they're tough, they can climb a variety of features and formations. Others—a small minority, including the best—ascend by matching themselves to an intricate arrangement of available, often inconspicuous elements. Less monkey, more spider. They appear relaxed where others are strained. They sometimes neglect a generous hold in favor of an obscure sequence that proves less taxing.

Finesse, we called this, as distinguished from the mere, sheer conventional power widely assumed prerequisite to success. But it's really a form of savvy, or even sorcery. Climbing IQ. Pete had it. I didn't. Sam had it in spades. However muscled her teenage-boy shoulders, however rough her hands and lumberjack-strong her grip, to watch her climb was to see a dance—undercling, sidepull, smear, and backstep. The splits. Her left fingers caress a sharp feature not twice the thickness of cardboard, and with the outer edge of her right foot she pivots on a crystal no larger than a swollen mosquito bite until the razory angle becomes useful, and Sam rises above a blank section to sink three fingers into a deep pocket. High-step with the right foot to a chip, and she's levered through to a secure stance.

Pete said it was like sight-reading in music: you can practice, and you should, but it's a gift some have and most don't and never will. You can sometimes look the part through intention and imitation, but inevitably your true character will be fully disclosed and most often in desperate, clawing gestures before you either punch through a crux or career off the route with a suppressed, defeated yelp. The savvy climber adjusts the placement of a foot, drops a knee, and improves their position on a tenuous hold near the chest. I grip harder and grunt upward for the flat edge just inches out of reach, a good enough hold in ordinary circumstances but now next to useless for all the juice I've used to this point, and I come off.

Jeremy told me later that summer he'd learned more from watching Sam than he'd gleaned from countless books and videos and all the lore of experts. "She has eyes in her feet," he said, "and this crazy way of staying balanced, like she's surfing a route. All the little gestures. She's Bridwell *and* Baryshnikov." A famous photograph from the '6os came to mind: burly, bearded Chuck Pratt juggling three balls while balancing on the tourist handrail above Glacier Point. And the proverbial slackline rigs in climbers' camps.

For a year or two after our visit to California I thought maybe I'd have a second coming, and this time I'd build a foundation less of the calisthenic routines and hand-strengthening exercises I used to do in the off-season in favor of yoga and a strong core. I'd assume a beginner's mind. I'd learn, as Pete used to advise, to climb like a girl. But I did nothing. I'd been unable to write a fresh sermon since Pete died, and I managed to avoid divulging my paralysis to the vestry only through a delicate combination of recycles and the Internet. In any case, my church was falling apart, and Carol had all but left me. Only once after our summer in Berkeley did I step into a harness and flake a rope—in 2007, when Lester came through.

But I rekindled a vicarious engagement, following the climbing news with greater attention than even when I was a part of it, and between the two monthly magazines I could peruse at the bookstore in Hanover and a few burgeoning climbing sites on the web, I got regular dispatches from California that not infrequently referenced a Will Hunter of Mammoth Lakes. At twelve, thirteen, and fourteen he made lists of top indoor climbers in the West for his age group, the rankings based on competitions in large, state-of-the-art climbing gyms in LA, Boulder, and Seattle. And when he was fourteen, fifteen, and sixteen, there were several little press notices featuring his outdoor accomplishments, mostly bouldering close to home but sport routes, too, and at least one new line, a single pitch crack near June Lake he was credited to have first-ascended with Peter Croft, though it seemed far-fetched to think Will had much to do with the project other than cleaning Croft's gear. And in many of these, "Will Hunter, former national-class gym climber," and in some, "son of '80s/'90s Sierra climber Pete Hunter, deceased." And sometimes a picture too, not of his face, but of his lengthening form mid-move on some improbable granite boulder, and entirely familiar: a sort of shrink-wrapped version of Pete for the wild hair and abandon but shot through too with Nor's birdy litheness. Once I saw an online video of him sending a treacherous twenty-five-foot boulder problem he'd been working on for more than two years, and then a short interview. He was breathless with surprise and delight, his voice rising and falling to either side of the register between childhood and adolescence. It was a rough-cut film and very homemade, wobbly camera and all, and at times I felt I was watching a home movie of Pete—hair, eyes, gestures—except that Pete didn't climb before college and didn't get anywhere near Little Egypt, east of Bishop, until he was twenty. Neither did Pete climb V9. Not ever. Nothing close to that hard.

Then, later that year, an item about a sport route at the Gorge, a crimpy thing said to favor small fingers, and another boulder, this one out near Benson, something obscure and so strangely featured that older, more powerful climbers had shied away from the line on account of holds that were said to flex and fracture. But young (and light) Will was able to piece it together. And then another: a dangerous highball whose location the magazine wouldn't divulge for fear of appearing to promote a route some subsequent climber might die for attempting.

And then nothing—for several months, a year, two years. Just the annual card from Nor, at Christmas, always with a photo of the three of them in an outdoor locale and usually in the snow, but no news or notice anywhere referencing Will and climbing, and I figured maybe he'd quit. Moved on. Got a guitar or a girlfriend. His mother could breathe again. When I saw her in 2005, Will was just happening upon the edges of this, his father's realm, an entire cosmos, and Nor was clearly anxious but also steely and resigned. So maybe he had gotten all he needed, and climbing could be for him a mere childhood obsession like a model railroad or a skateboard rather than the full-blown, ever-abiding, insatiable appetite that owns the fly-fisherman, the golfer, the bridge player, for life. I missed the notices in the magazines, and maybe even more the excitement of looking for them, as when a great and favorite athlete retires and the sports pages are no fewer in number but suddenly wanting. Still, I was relieved for Nor.

Carol left in 2007, in the end for career reasons—a university job in Tallahassee. We didn't end it right away, but when we did it seemed long in the coming and not overly sad except that in my mind it was mixed up with what Pete had gone through with me twenty years earlier, though now I was on the other side: Carol's forays into schools and jobs making for a steady stream of mail and many applications and lots of consideration about logistics and my moving or not moving and our being married but far from one another. And the disappointments, the not even getting an interview, and the pressure I felt to make our life together sufficient. So when she got the job I was glad for both of us. We planned to carry on somehow rather than dissolve via telephone, which, in the end, we did, and when three years later I learned she was wife to a dean and stepparent to two preteen girls and an eight-year-old boy, I was neither hurt nor sad and only a little surprised. No weirder than I had been: the little grumbling noises I made for years about the ministry, and thirty-six months post-Pete I was campus pastor at St. Thomas' in Hanover before being installed at the little Thetford Church I had for almost fourteen years.

At the height of the leaf season in 2009, I got the terse, typed note from the vestry I'd been expecting for some time: I had four weeks remaining in the pulpit and a little longer in the parsonage, if necessary. By the time I finally moved into town, I had become fully trained and employed in elder care—perhaps the one thing I'd had some facility for as a pastor. New Horizons, the assisted living facility in Lebanon, was aptly named, for me anyway: clean hours and an honest exchange of pay-for-services-rendered. No pretense of growing old together, as with Carol. No messy business about meaning and ultimate destinations, as with parishioners. And none of the offices—the periodic funerals and infrequent baptisms, and the steady parade of out-of-towners' weddings because our spare country church was charming and because I was in no position to turn away a little extra income.

And then, late December 2013, back in Vermont again following a third and final trip to Pennsylvania to clear Dad's house of his things and make arrangements for the sale, the Christmas mail, and the letter from Will: *Come to California. Help me finish your and Dad's route.*

A yoga teacher came into New Horizons twice a week to lead an exercise class residents could do in their chairs. The next time I saw her I asked if she could give me private lessons. I went to the co-op and bought running shoes and strap-on gadgets for our snowy, slippery roads. I inquired over at Dartmouth about the use of the gym, including the indoor climbing wall, a *de rigeur* perk at private colleges now, but the monthly fee was too steep. Then I recalled my instinct of several years before: to get supple and lean, and then climb my way into fitness. I knew any pretense of training for Moriah was absurd—that even at my peak I was able to make only a few moves above the fourth pitch, and these only after a full preview. But this felt like as much of a calling as I'd ever gotten. I would support Will. I would see Nor again, and Astrid. In one way I could readily afford it, thanks to a shot of income from the sale of my father's home. In another, I wasn't sure what I was doing or why, though some part of me understood it wasn't only for Will that I agreed to go.

I replied with a postcard: just tell me when to be where, and for how long, and try to give me several weeks' notice.

⌒

Reno in mid-July was enveloped in a dust-storm, with driving winds out of the Nevada desert. The midsize jet I was in aborted an approach before, in the pilot's words, threading the needle between gusts.

Will was at the curb outside baggage claim as promised, leaning against his small black pickup. Seeing me, he waved— trucker's hat over unkempt hair, golden skin and ratty jeans, one foot in a beater sandal and the other in an orthopedic boot. He hobbled over.

"Just these?" he said, hoisting my two duffels. After tossing them into the cargo bed, he turned back to me. "Will," he said, his hand extended. Brown leather, a climber's hand. He held my gaze, as though he were trying to remember me, and I found myself staring at his mouth. He'd said three words, but it was all I needed: Pete's voice, coming out of this scruffy teenager.

"Joe," I said.

"Glad you made it."

I pointed to his foot. "How bad?"

"It's nothing. Sprained. I was worried for a few minutes."

"Recent?"

"Four days ago, in the Happies. Unlucky landing is all."

We drove off, Will's boot covering the clutch. "Crazy-ass weather," he said. "Got stuck a while, north of Mono. Semi blew over. Just lying there on its side."

"By Lundy Canyon," I said.

"Good guess. Right before you start up the pass."

"Saw it happen. Your dad and I did."

He sat a little forward and gripped the wheel at two and ten like he was taking a driving test. "We can supply up here, at the Costco in Gardnerville. Or south, at home. Preference?"

I was staring at him.

"What?" he said.

"Sorry. Just your voice. I haven't heard you talk, except the one time." But it wasn't just his voice. How he sat in the car, knees bouncing. Bend of his neck. The raised veins along the backsides of his hands that would mark him for an older man but that his dad had these, too. Some part of me felt stuffed into my own twenty-year-old self, locked in a passenger seat beside Pete on one of our early sorties in the wild Sierra.

"Things are cheaper here, but it's a scene. Didn't have these mega-stores in your time."

"No."

"Country then, right? Gardnerville, Minden, Carson City. Even Reno's exploded. The Biggest Little City that ain't no more."

We scooted along an access road and shortly joined 395 south, brown clouds of sand and dust blowing left to right. Tumbleweeds were pinned to fences along each side of the highway.

Will went on. "That's how I got out of high school. Did this research thing on all this: geography, demographics, resources. I wasn't going to make it otherwise. Mom persuaded them to have me do a custom program. Good enough to get me a spot up here at U Nevada."

"I thought you were at the JC?"

"Started here, anyway. I'm not like you and my folks. Not from what she says. Three hours in a library isn't work to me. It's torture. My buddy says with a doctor in the family what do I have to worry about. But Ricky's a whole other case. Really on his own."

It was heartening to me Will felt he wasn't.

"No car insurance. Figures he's got nothing to lose. His mom's a cocktail waitress, dad's a seasonal on the mountain."

He looked at me to see how this landed.

"I know," he said. "Mine was too. But it's different if you've got options. And if at least one of them's a realtor or doctor or something. Fair chunk of Mammoth is that way, people just getting by. You don't see it unless you know where to look."

For the past three winters Will had worked as a snowboard instructor, and in spring he did some rigging and repair on the lifts. Sometimes he hung drywall for a contractor in town. He lived in a cabin up from one of the lakes, which in winter he had to ski to, though he was quick to add he could always stay at home with Mom and Astrid in serious weather, and often did.

"No big objective here. Just see where it leads." He drove slowly and always at the right, his little truck chugging along with the RVs and semis while others our size sped past us.

As we ran the canyons south of Bridgeport I told him I'd seen him a handful of times in *Rock and Ice* and on some websites. "Not recently," I added.

"You get to that place. They say it's between indoors and out, but really it's about making headlines and buffing a reputation, or just climbing. I'm lucky. I didn't waste a lot of time at something that didn't mean that much to me. I mean the scene. Competitions, sponsorships. When I bailed I just got so much more into it. A lot of that just being out, looking for things. And stopping trying to impress anyone."

I felt myself cheering for him.

"Better for Mom, too," he said. "She doesn't have to torture herself over what someone shows her on YouTube. I'm not like total vanilla, but there's no one following me around with a camera."

He laid out our plans. A summer thunderstorm cycle was moving in for a few days, so rather than wait out rain near Moriah we'd warm up on some crags near Mammoth and then hike in supplies until the drier stretch materialized.

"You can come to the cabin with me. It's tight, but not like a bivy. Or you can stay at Mom's. They're away. You know about Astrid?"

I didn't.

"She's the one you can find online these days. Running. Mom and her are at some big meet in Pennsylvania now. Looking at colleges after. She's got grades, too."

"Trains at altitude."

"There's a whole scene here. Olympians, even. They put a track in out by Hot Creek couple of years ago. Astrid's down there all the time. Mom said to say hi. They're back next week."

He licked a finger and held it up as if to gauge the wind. "Right about when we're topping out."

At the supermarket in Mammoth Will zipped about efficiently: noodles, dried soup, some kind of miso paste, bricks of pressed, marinated tofu, energy bars, and cheap steaks and fresh corn for tonight. In the checkout line two small boys threw themselves at him, kids he'd babysat when they were toddlers. When I took out my wallet he suggested we settle up later.

I elected to stay with him, so in the early evening we drove through the village, up past the first two of the lakes and then into the woods on an obscure dirt road. Will humped up a section I'd have thought too steep and rock-strewn even for the truck, and there it was: a squat and square cabin with a corrugated metal roof, half of it shiny and the other half covered in moss and bent at the edges as from the weight of so much snow.

"Base camp," Will said, turning off the engine.

He put a small key into a beefy padlock and the thick wooden door swung on creaky hinges. The cabin had been assembled from big logs, so the inside was tight and tidy—smaller than Pete's trailer but reminiscent of it, too. And weird how Will had sawed a bay window into the south side and, like his dad, lined the sill with little potted plants. A small wood stove sat to the right, an old Coleman cookstove on top. Table by the front door, woolen rug on the floor, and a single upholstered chair faded and frayed as if from several years on someone's porch. A loft attached to the back could be raised via a rope running through block and tackle of the sort used to hoist a sail. Will lifted the bed and the cabin was instantly spacious, his clothing and gear arranged in stacked bins underneath.

"Who do you rent from?"

He chuckled. "That's just it. Not just off the grid here. Off the books. Forest Service, the water people in town, no one wants to deal with it. I do some things for them in winter. Clear a path to the instrument cabinet on Lake Mary, sometimes flip a switch or jot down numbers. I got it for finding it and fixing it up, and mostly for keeping a low profile. One guy told me it would take them years of paperwork to do anything about it, even tear it down. I just think it's easier for them to pretend I'm not here."

"Fire's all they care about," he said, crumpling newspaper into the bottom of a rusty charcoal chimney. The barbecue was nestled between stones on the ground. "I'm super-careful. Not like folks down around the lake. The water's a pain, though."

"Climber's lament."

"What'd you do, back in the day, when you guys had that trailer?"

"Filled jugs at Tom's and in Bishop, depending which direction we were coming from. One year there was a leak in the penstock pipe at the rim. Huge waste, but handy."

Will blew on the charcoal and motioned toward the side of the cabin. "Check out the facilities. Crapper's over there." He pointed to a five-gallon paint bucket with two boards nearby for a toilet seat. In a stand of pines he'd assembled a variety of training apparatuses—several hangboards, gymnastic rings, dowels and cantaloupe-sized balls on ropes for pull-ups, and two sets of parallel boards on end—"crack machines"—whose angles he could adjust from vertical to overhanging via a set of pulleys and winches like the one on his bed. A tarp stretched between trees way overhead kept at least some of the rain to the side.

"Shower, too," Will said. It was a wooden pallet on the forest floor beneath a black, water-filled bag dangling from a retired climbing rope. A couple of towels rested on another line between the trees. "Water's warm by now, on a day like today. Not so in the morning." He leaned over, disassembled his plastic boot, and stepped out of his pants. Then he lay his shirt on the plastic boot. His body was sinewy. I turned away, like I was seeing Nor naked for the first time and only now remembered that I ever wanted to.

When he came around front again he was wearing just the towel and carrying the plastic boot. His foot was stained purple and visibly swollen.

"Ouch," I said.

"Looks worse than it feels. There's another shower in there if you want one."

"I'm good."

"Mom says compared to Dad I'm, what is it? 'Fastidious.' I guess you guys were the real dirtbaggy deal."

"We'd rinse off if there was a stream or lake handy. It was a bit more of an effort at the trailer, but we made stops at Hot Creek, Wild Willie's."

Will stood nearby, his sandal in one hand and his clothes in the other. He studied me, as though realizing I had something he didn't ask for and hadn't known he wanted, surprised less by what I said than by his own interest in what I had to tell. Then he ducked inside for clothes.

We ate the steaks and corn outside on camp chairs, Will's slathered in hot sauce he poured from a jar. The last of the charcoal glowed. Lights from cabins along the lakeshore shimmered through the trees.

"Give me some more," he said.

I reached for the grill.

"No," he said. "I mean about you and Dad."

"Okay." I took my steak with my fingers to rip some off.

"Peaks and valleys," he said. "Some best, some worst."

I felt I was the one in the towel now. I was both eager to share and afraid of what I might report, not for what I might reveal about Pete than for how naked it felt to reconnect. And all the stranger to be invited to that time and territory by Will, whose cut of jaw, dart of eye, and tangle of hair were so redolent of his father. Then the meat got stuck in my throat. I stumbled out of my chair toward the trees to dislodge it, but in moments I was gasping—this is serious—and then, with Will's arms wrapped around my midsection, not gasping. Later Will said I just sort of collapsed into him, and as he lay me down on the forest floor the chunk fell harmlessly out of my mouth.

When we sat down again my clothing was damp with sweat and I was suddenly cold. I moved closer to the coals.

"You have to chew it," he said.

He didn't ask more questions and I didn't volunteer anything. It was midnight where I'd come from. I needed to sleep.

⌣

Midmorning we drove to nearby Lake George and walked a mile to the Dike Wall, a short, steep granite cliff where Pete and I had climbed once or twice and one I'd have forgotten about altogether except it was cited in the papers when John Bachar took his fatal fall here in 2009. A tragic loss, to be sure, but also ridiculous—like Al Capone getting arrested for tax evasion. Through the pines we could see people projecting and top-roping, and as we approached someone belaying at the base called out a greeting to Will. The climber lowered just as we reached the crag, and, seeing Will, said, "We're set now." But as she was untying her knot she took notice of Will's plastic boot. "Oh no. You okay?"

"That's what we're here to see," Will said. Though he didn't mean it, it occurred to me this was a contest of two liabilities—his foot, and my climbing.

"Joe," he said. "Natalie and Rafe."

Then Will was on a sport route. He hadn't even asked me to belay, indulging some tacit arrangement with them that after a warm-up he'd put a rope on their project. He had slipped his feet into climbing shoes, not bothering to tie them, though the left couldn't get much more snug on account of the swelling. Even this easy route was more overhung than not, with big gaps between good holds, but Will climbed with his body well away from the cliff, placed his toes purposefully, and made bold, certain gestures as though repeating a series of steps in a habitual dance. In just minutes he was back on the ground, reattaching the boot and getting caught up with his neighbors.

"You, Joe?" he said.

"I don't want to hold things up."

"Take a turn. Then I can set them up," Will said.

I changed my shoes and tied in. With my feet on a cinder-block-sized stance, I leaned into the cliff with my palms flat against the smooth stone. I felt entirely unsuited to the task. Will was belaying, but talking with them, so he didn't immediately see how flummoxed I was.

"Wait, Joe," he said. "It's deceptive, the start. Step way left," he pointed. "The rampy thing. You get a sidepull for the left hand." He had moved closer to indicate the foothold, a half-inch edge so rounded and oblique I'd not registered it. But with more than a little effort I made the moves in just the sequence Will had described, and in moments I had two hands on a generous incut above the cavelike overhang that had thwarted my first attempt. My left foot straddled the small dike below the magical sidepull, and I pawed at the cliff with my right toes for something to lever onto. I wasn't desperate, but I couldn't hang here forever, so I surrendered to a thin edge and pulled upward. The cliff flew by, the rope went taut, and with a single soft bounce I was back at the bottom, nearly knocking Will over as I gained my balance.

"That thing's way hard," Natalie said.

I coughed.

"Black Lassie's easier," Rafe said, referencing a nearby route. "And it's 10d."

"They're right," Will said. "Let me put draws on this other one for these guys, then we move up there."

"Once more," I said, still catching my breath.

This time I got above the first fifteen feet by moving fast, but I wasn't to the third draw before I stalled again and only then appreciated how steep the cliff was. Lowering again, I ended up in the boulders several feet behind Will. Climbing, Pete liked to say, is an endless courtship with your inadequacy. Still, it was disappointing to have my reacquaintance so emphatically affirmed in these first fifteen minutes with Will.

Will glided up the nearby 11c for his friends, pulled the rope from that route, and reclimbed ours, which he cleaned on the way down, all of his movements decisive and relaxed. As we hauled our things up the talus along the base of the cliff, he said, "Remember: it's my backyard. My jungle gym."

What I remember, I thought, is that I never climbed like you. Nor did your father. Pete and I got started on mossy cliffs in upstate New York where you'd be on a route for twenty minutes before you could even see over the trees and most of this time fiddling with stoppers, and if we hadn't had stiff shoes and limited gear we'd have had to ascribe our awkwardness and fright to its true source, not just lack of talent, in my case, but the alien aspect of it all: the wild steep, this linking together precarious positions in a vertical world. Pete and I were children of the Northeast woodlands. Maybe in time we could have become acclimated and more or less native to the long bands of short cliffs in our vicinity. But in the expansive Sierra, no matter how well acquainted with the terrain and certified by accomplishment, we would always be immigrants. Other climbers, especially the younger ones, thought Pete a local—again, "a dean of Eastside climbing"—but neither of us entertained the illusion. If it didn't feel big, strange, and scary, it could become so at any instant, and with that the reminder of our provisional status: you can play here on these grand granite cliffs as long as you like, but you'll never belong.

Will was a child of the West, a climber at home. Young man in his yard. The air wasn't thin and dry, it was just air. The cliff not pumpy and devious, but a "jungle gym." He had by birthright what his dad sought to acquire and I had attempted and fled. I'd been with him for less than twenty-four hours and climbing not for twenty-four minutes and understood only too well how poorly suited I was for what he'd invited me to do.

The three routes at the upper end of the cliff were more manageable, one even fun, and by noon we were back in the truck and headed down the Owens Valley to ferry a first load. Will was buoyant—however dark and swollen his foot, it hadn't been painful or limiting. He had it in mind to drop a cache of supplies a couple miles up the canyon toward Moriah, and then to walk down from our high camp in subsequent days to draw from it as his foot improved and my lungs got accustomed to the thin air. We stopped by Nor's on our way out of town—Will had been using her garage as a staging area for the gear and the food we'd haul in. While he rearranged things in the truck bed, I ducked inside to use the bathroom. The same pine chest as before was arrayed with family pictures, several of Will and Astrid in various stages of childhood, a couple with Nor too, one of her folks, and one of Pete's mom with the kids. Another of Astrid alone, on the track in her Mammoth Huskies singlet. She had a mountain tan like her brother and Nor's lean frame, but it was her eyes I found arresting. Pete's brow, and that signature furrow of concentration, on a teenage girl. She appeared to be protecting a sizable lead.

Only on the way out of the bathroom did I see the other photo beside a hall light switch, which I flipped on: the two of us on either side of a pile of gear, Pete beaming and me looking exhausted if glad to be down and alive after the last and most ambitious of our climbs in Argentina, 1985. We had walked for three days hauling all our gear before getting to an outpost where someone snapped the photo, and most of the time one or the other of us had been sulking: Pete when I sounded anything short of enthused, me when I privately agreed that his argument for resupplying and going back in for another two weeks made sense. The story we told was that the weather had won—it was February already, end of their summer—and inside of twenty-four hours the first of a series of storms washed out the road to this little bodega and stable, and we ended up having to walk two more days in the rain to get to a road north.

"Hungry?" Will said, stomping through the living room. "Check out the fridge. Seeds, berries. It's like two birds live here. If Astrid had been first I'd've starved to death."

"Remind me to tell you the back story of this," I said, gesturing to the photo.

"Tell. I brought eggs. Want some?"

I took the photograph from the wall and sat at the counter while Will cut onions into a saucepan and started cracking eggs.

"Your dad's hand was bandaged." I turned the picture and pointed to where Pete's right hand was hidden behind his back. "He ripped a gash above his thumb on a junk pitch in the Torres del Paine three or four days before. When we got back to camp we decided to walk out, not for the hand but because we were nearly out of food. Then the cut started oozing, though by the time we got here it was crusted over. Ugly, but seemed okay.

We were in a tussle about what to do next." I didn't tell Will everything—not even the tame parts, like how that night after dinner Pete did several reps of pull-ups on the porch rafters of the *posada*. He acted like he was just working out, but he was staking a claim for another route, showing he still had it. "I was fried. Maybe you can see. Scared, too, but mostly just fried." In the picture my eyes are shaded under the brim of my hat, but the dark does little to hide my fret, captive as ever to Pete's bottomless appetite. In memory the trip was a turning point.

"So who won?"

"It started raining the next day."

"But he wanted more."

"Pretty much always."

Tending the eggs, Will smiled a little. "I can get like that. At least compared to much of what goes for climbing around here. Herds with their pads around the boulders. On a big day they'll give a project five tries, the crew with their arms in the air. Then they wander off to smoke a bowl and nurse their sore 'tips. Maybe, if it's not too hot, repeat a couple easy favorites."

I laid the photograph back on the counter.

"Can't believe what you guys got," Will said.

"Hardly a blank slate, not even down there," I said. "Thank God."

"Still. Adventure. Travel. Something fresh!"

"Felt like that. Even if we were far from the first."

He flipped the mash of onion and egg. "Now it's charted. Everything! Not just the route. Tricky placements, hidden holds."

"Approaches, descents," I said.

"Rack specs," he added. "Weather reports. Where the water is. GPS coordinates."

He went out to the truck, returning with a bottle of the hot sauce he'd smothered his steak with the night before.

"I lost my shit last year when a guy I was with in the Sads topped out on a project and immediately whipped out his phone to post it."

"Your dad used to make a stink about summit registers. Refused to sign them. He didn't even like that Indian Creek thing, where they scratch the route name and grade on a slab of sandstone."

"But that's not spray. Or at least not only spray. I think it's kind of cool. Paleolithic, anyway."

He opened the fridge again and I saw what he meant—storage jars of various sizes and none with an ordinary supermarket label.

"But he wasn't around long enough for us to fight about that," Will said. He brought the saucepan to the counter. "Like this? Or with the sauce?"

"Little of each."

"So then you flew home?"

"By the time we got to LAX his hand was big as a thigh. The doctor said he had maybe two or three days before it would have had to come off, though maybe just to get his attention. We spent two weeks on a guy's floor in Santa Monica. Your dad walked to the hospital twice a day for an IV. It was spring in LA. Warm and clean and dry, and all I remember was feeling soaked to the skin, cold and mad. I couldn't shake it."

"Mad at Dad?"

"Yeah. Otherwise I'd just have me to be mad at."

The eggs with sauce burned my lips, and as I moved them to the side Will put his plate next to mine and scooped them over.

"It's like any couple," I said. "Or partnership, or marriage."

He seemed startled by the analogy. Will had pieced together enough of the record of Pete's and my climbing activities to know they stretched over ten years. But names and dates in guidebooks are washed clean of the interstitial business—getting lost, cold nights under stars. The blisters and bad water, shared triumphs, tantrums.

At the sink again, he said, "Well, I'm not asking you to move in. I just need a decent belay."

"Which is how these things typically start."

When he gave me a look, I shook him off: Yes, I'm kidding.

Will cleaned dishes and wiped counters, left a note for his mom and locked the house. Only when we were on the highway did I remember I'd forgotten to return the photograph to the wall.

In the late afternoon we hauled the first of two loads up the canyon I had descended with Pete and Nor twenty-five years before. The roiling stream and gold-striped rock bands were unchanged, of course, and the trail, if anything, even more ramshackle and hard to follow. But Will had the area wired. Two miles up, just above where the canyon walls slide together, he pointed to some flat grass alongside the water and motioned me over to a pair of boulders in the stream giving us access to the other side. There, in a stand of aspens I remembered from years before but had never bothered to approach, sat a small cabin, abandoned and sliding off its timber foundation.

"Miner's cottage," Will said. "Got a tip about it last summer, from a fisherman."

Will had done some repairs, covering the empty window frames with chicken wire and getting the door back up on a hinge. We dropped our packs and arranged the contents on the dirt floor inside, and while Will soaked his ankle in the cold stream I sat nearby.

"That Dike Wall business this morning give you pause?" I said.

"If you can climb the first four pitches from memory, we'll be right where we need to be. I figure it's what comes after that that will give me pause." He seemed neither eager nor scared.

Thunder up the canyon sounded like rockfall.

"And if not?"

"You've jumared miles more than I have."

"And I'm not here on account of pride."

Will pulled his foot out of the water. It was pinker and more swollen than yesterday. "I've got my own little handicap here, too."

"Yours doesn't include a climbing résumé with a quarter century of blank space."

"Blank?"

"A dozen pitches, nearly ten years ago. Saw your mom, finally met Astrid. You weren't around. I think you were in Maine."

"Camp."

"Couple years later a guy your dad and I knew, a Brit, came through. We did a day on Cannon, in New Hampshire."

"Who's that?"

"Lester. Lester Jameson."

"Mood Management," Will said.

"That's the one."

"There's a photo of Dad in the old guide. You started it, but they got the FA?"

"They did."

"And Dad took some horrendous whipper?"

"He did."

Will winced.

"Yeah. Scary. Hauled out in a litter. He spent a week in a Vegas hospital."

Will dunked his foot in the stream again.

"Who came up with Mood Management?"

"They did."

"'Cause Dad didn't keep his cool?"

"Not exactly. Lester told me, this last time, in New Hampshire. Said it was more about what his partner Bill did than what your dad didn't. Part of which was to put several bolts in the section your dad climbed with no pro. Lester said he'd never seen anything like the brass nut that held your dad, which saved us all from who knows what kind of shock load on the anchor. Welded, like someone brazed it there with a torch. God knows why the rock itself didn't blow apart."

"I didn't know he got all messed up."

"In bed for most of a month. Completely out of commission for two. A long, in-season re-hab. So miserable he even managed to recalibrate."

Will lay back, resting his head on his hands. "Not so much he didn't solo Clyde."

"No."

"Jesus. My dad. Guess he was lucky he had you around."

"He was a driver, but not reckless." This was a stretch, but not an outright lie. If Will wanted the story of his father, I felt determined to rinse it of my own fears and fingerprints. "Except maybe for the aversion to bolts."

"Not my program," Will said. "I've heard that about his routes, though seems like he mellowed or got smarter or whatever it takes. After the '80s, I mean. I meet these older guys who say they climbed with Dad. Whenever I ask what they did it's always something in the Gorge, or Pine Creek, or Clark's, back when the sport routes were going up by the armful. Then again, most of the time they weren't even with him. They just saw him crossing a creek or flaking a rope or drinking a beer in a parking area. Anyway, anything interesting, anything multi-pitch, seems it was mostly with a client, and mostly repeats of your routes, and the standards."

"Well, that's how he got into the pickle at Red Rock anyway, the bolt allergy."

"This will *not* be our problem," Will assured me. He reached into the water past his elbows to massage his foot.

"There's a steep, blank section," he said. "What do you got on that? And is there anything fixed, anchor-wise, above the fourth pitch?"

I described what I could recall: gear at the top of the pitch one, and pairs of three-eighths bolts at two of the other three stances, including the big ledge. "On pitch five there's just one bolt. At the top of this crazy columny thing. Quarter-incher, probably. No idea how sturdy. I never got there. And your dad never got above it."

"You bailed mid-pitch?"

"We had 5.12 appetites, or he did. But we weren't 5.12 climbers. Not on a first ascent, anyway. Much less at 12,000 feet."

Will pulled his foot from the water. I lay down on a mat of leaves. The sunlight was slanting through the aspens and would soon fall behind the ridge. I didn't see how we'd have time to make another trip to the truck and get back before dark.

When I awoke it was much cooler, all shadows, and Will was gone. I crossed the stream and started down the trail. He had taken the larger of the packs and closed up the cabin. I grabbed the other pack and hoped he hadn't tried to dash up the canyon to get a look at the cliff, five miles farther and almost three thousand feet higher. The kind of thing Pete would do.

Will was just a year older than his dad had been when we met in college, and if fresh and unknown to me, he was also eerily familiar. He appeared to have Pete's focus, the unabashed, quirky intensity, and yet it seemed there was something softer, too, maybe more restrained. A something I connected to his being native to these parts and these activities. And then of course his mother, who of all of us was the most grounded, graceful, and disciplined.

I was just getting to the mouth of the canyon, where the broad alluvial fan opens up to the valley, and here was Will, under another ungainly load, humping up the sandy trail toward me. He was using ski poles this time to take some of the burden off his foot, and he'd ditched his approach shoes for sandals.

"You looked pretty comfortable there," he said, drawing close. "Figured there was time for another haul." His shirt was unbuttoned and his chest coated with sweat. We were standing in the last of the day's sunlight. "Truck's open. See you in an hour and some."

It was twilight when I heard his footsteps again, and I was in the truck's open bed watching the light die on the White Mountains across the valley. A planet sat low in the southeast, just a pinprick when I first saw it but a beacon by the time Will returned.

He tossed the empty pack into the back. "Miguel's?" he said.

We got inside the cab. I could feel the heat from his skin.

"Or would that bring on some kind of PTSD?"

He eased the truck over the ruts at road's end.

"Been thinking about you guys. Can't believe my dad was so high maintenance! How crazy for you. And now me, hauling you back for more." He smiled. "Listen. Your, what do you guys call it, 'Golden Age'? It's done. This isn't an 'extreme sport' anymore. That would be big air on a snowboard, BASE jumping. Even ATV bullshit. We don't just 'go for it' these days. We don't 'manage our mood.' We just figure shit out, get it right."

He was driving at a walking pace down the pitted road.

I pointed to his foot. "Figure it out?"

"Could have been the curb. Yeah, there's Bachar and Hersey, or there was. And now Honnold. But really, this thing has changed."

Sweat-smelly and tired, and with the steady hum of the engine in the near dark, this felt no different than driving off with Pete amid one of his post-climb disquisitions.

"I know," he said. "Some say this isn't 'the business' we're doing. Whatever. I can't get caught up in it. It's not worth the trouble. And you can't win. When I was younger I did. Once I ended up rolling in the dirt with some douche. Another douche, I should say. Outside the gym."

"About?"

"Well, that *was* legit. A kid from the climbing team, jawing on about soloing. Always found him annoying, so probably it was about that, too. But one day, you know, lying around on the pads complaining about being pumped, he let it drop he heard Dad was a suicide. That he wasn't soloing, but exiting. Said his mom told him. Well, anyway, that was okay, because that was the beginning of the end for me, of the whole indoor scene."

I couldn't be sure, but it felt like he'd just given me an assignment. "Your mom help you out with that?"

"Yeah, but that part's hard for her. She doesn't mind me thinking climbing's dangerous, and that soloing's suicidal. Or something like that. Later that same summer Bachar died up at Dike Wall. You probably heard what they did, a service like Dad's. On the lake. Though Bachar had this crazy hall-of-fame crew showing up from all over. Lynn Hill, Bridwell, Kauk."

"You remember your dad's?"

"Tiny bit. Bunch of people I didn't know and haven't seen since. You too, I guess. I remember for days there were lots of grown-ups around, then all the sudden not. And then Astrid. It was like that: I had a dad. Then a sister."

༄

So that night I started in about Bill, Lester's old climbing partner. Or at least what I got from Lester about Bill. I think

I wanted to tell about Bill not just because he was one of that other breed, the kind to lay it all out, but also to provide a foil to the rumors Will had heard about his father. We were sitting across from one another at a table Pete and I had shared, Will doctoring Miguel's salsa with still more of the hot sauce he'd brought in from the truck.

Lester and I hadn't seen each other in years—Mood Management was 1984, his visit to New Hampshire 2007—and had corresponded infrequently. He was a professor of physics now, wife and two children, comfortable, still climbing but nothing untoward or unsafe. The things he liked were long, established alpine routes in the Alps, but he frequented crags near home on weekends to keep the fire lit. For years after our Red Rock adventure he continued to climb with Bill, though less and less like the old days—just cragging from time to time in the UK and a few longer stints in summer, all long ago.

"I was preparing lectures and changing nappies," Lester said. "Bill, he was committed." Bill had left the seaside years ago to be closer to good rock, cobbled together a living for a while as a welder and mechanic, then got his guiding certificate. "He hated it. All the waitin' 'round for some whinger from London with money, a new harness, and notions about a hobby." Then he lucked into a job with a German climbing gear company. He could work the rainy days and climb the dry. He moved to Nottingham, and he got really good on the gritstone, which is famously hard to protect. And the ethic there doesn't just favor but insists upon natural protection. "They don't chop the bolts and call it square," Lester said. "They chop the head off anyone who places them." Two or three seasons in and Bill is a serious player at this high-stakes table.

Lester told me the bulk of this on Cannon Cliff in New Hampshire. It was two years after my summer in Berkeley and the first time I'd roped up since Oz with Jeremy and Sam. I had asked about Bill the day before when we met in Hanover, but we got onto something else, and I asked again on the drive up and he said yes, he'd tell me about him, but then he changed the subject. Finally, on the approach trail, he started, but at first it was just about where Bill had moved to and how he made a living and what they'd done together in the years after Pete and I were with them in Utah and Nevada when we were all young and free and determined.

It was a cool, cloudless, late September morning. We were climbing the Whitney-Gilman, a long arête that's more or less the Grand Teton of the Northeast: famous cliff, easy route, spectacular position. Weekday, no one around. Lester said, "Bill worked the routes on top-rope. He'd dial in key sequences and practice the placements. He was absolutely not stupid about it. Still, scary as all hell. Makes our Red Rock route seem tame. Honest. Of course, it wasn't me on the sharp end of that pitch Pete flew off of. But even following Bill in the Peak District was . . . well, after a few visits I just quit going. Very severe, all of it. Even the stuff within my limits, just an awful fright." The deciduous trees in the valley had begun to turn amber and orange, and we were in no hurry, so at each belay he'd tell me a bit more, and then one of us would climb off, and when we met again at the next stance he'd pick up from where he'd left off.

"So there was one route Bill was keen about for a long time, more than a year. A ninety-foot arête, a tad over vertical, and just one solid placement in the upper half, at least in the hard part. A micro-cam you have to place blind and on a long sling way out left on the main face while you're stretching off an awkward heel hook. Mind you, this just *maybe* to protect the bloody thing. Then you climb through, and he said you get a glance at your gear but you're nowhere near it now and you've no free hand to make any adjustment, so it's just got to be solid, else above there you've got no chance if you fall. Sixty, eighty feet, right onto the boulders. There's mental pro in the upper third, and finally one more good cam near the top. But by then the hard stuff's under you. No traffic, this route. None. And Bill's got it wired. He can top-rope it blindfolded. But he's never led it, and he's maybe the second or third ever to try. 6b+, 6c. It doesn't matter. It's just one of those things you don't want to get near. I've been there. Not a decent hold you can see from below. And of course you have to hit it just perfect, too—temps, humidity, angle of the light.

"So he gets it. There's a big party at a pub for him. He phones me a day or two later. Doesn't tell me right away. He asks about my kids and what I was up to and all that. But he was dead chuffed. And you know how that goes. What now? A couple weeks later some blokes ask him to do it again, on camera. The film guys, they love gritstone. It's not like a big wall, where they have to work for days just to get in position and then the light's bad or it starts rainin'.

"And this time Bill handles it like before. It's a musical instrument he's been playing forever. But that horizontal placement, it's not quite right, maybe just a bit off to one side or the other. But he figures he doesn't need it. Still, it's in his head. He said he looked at his right toe, getting ready to launch into the sequence that starts with stepping on a polished crystal, but then he returned to the heel hook on the edge to have a second go with that cam."

And then Lester took off. We were on the third pitch, of seven. He was ten feet above me and turning a corner to the other side of the arête, and still talking.

"Stop!" I hollered. "Can't hear you!"

I heard a carabiner clip into something, and then the rope uncurled from the pile at my feet. Lester reappeared on my side of the ridge but now thirty, forty, and soon a hundred feet above me, his climbing no less lithe and efficient than years before. Then the "off belay" in his British accent that always sounded oddly proper to me, like we were on a golf green or tennis court.

When I got to Lester this time I feigned some trouble with my shoe just to get more of the story. The stance was so small I had to lean out on the anchor to unlace and remove it. "Bill," I said.

"Bill what?" he said.

"He didn't like that cam."

"Oh, no. He didn't like it. He told me later it wasn't a regular feeling. Not that dark way we have of sandbagging ourselves. Nor the cameras and all that buggery, either. They had three, one from the top, one at the bottom, and another guy with a long lens from another formation. Each one positioned so the others wouldn't creep into the frame. It was a feckin' Hollywood set." Lester sounded angry—the first indication this doesn't end well.

"The cam?"

"He gets a better look, and it's just off, half slotted in there and the other half at the very edge like a mouse trap. Or a suicide. That's how Bill said it: 'Right at the lip, poised to jump.'"

"And no way to fix it."

"No. But he knows he can do the moves. Still, he's worried, if only a tad. Not the full burn where he's got to move fast or figure out how to downclimb to where he can jump and still have a chance of getting caught and at least not die. He knows he used up some juice when he didn't just climb past the piece but stopped to look, so now it's like a first try on this section, whole new go." Lester looked off at the valley. "Way later he told me he wondered if it wasn't on account of the other blokes. Not posing, or not meaning to, but just enough aware of other eyes to maybe add something extra. He saw it all, you know, the movie."

"Did you?"

"No."

"Why not?" I said.

Lester nodded upward. "It's you now."

I had been slow getting assembled to lead the next pitch, a short connector ramp between the better, steeper sections Lester would take. But even on this easy scramble my palms were sweaty. I'd place my foot on an incut of the sort Pete would call "big enough for a bivy" and grind my shoe onto it before committing because my mind was there with Bill on the pinpoint precision of his holdless arête. Something wasn't right, and now he was above that questionable cam.

At the next stance Lester didn't indulge me. He climbed through without pause, and then, just two pitches from the top, we were where our route steepens and a once-upon-a-time climber has to concentrate. So I finished my pitch and for a few minutes even managed to forget about Bill. But by the time I built an anchor, put a jacket on, and started bringing Lester up, my palms were sweaty again for remembering him on that dicey sequence.

When Lester arrived he was grinning. "That's more like it," he said. "The next one that good?"

"I don't remember. I think so. What happened to Bill?"

"Yes. Bill." He was taking the gear piece by piece from his harness and methodically reracking, occasionally looking up as if to scope his first placement. We were in the shadows, the wind had picked up, and the air was chillier. Lester had his hood on under his helmet. "Bill," he said, then sighed. "Well, he fell. He got through the crux, placed the two brassies, and even got to where that one last good piece should go. But he didn't bother with it. At that point it was a race to the top. If he so much as paused he'd have blown off."

"Goodness."

"Yes," he said. "Goodness." Then he stepped past me, and while he completed the last and best part of the Whitney-Gilman I imagined Bill's fall over and over again and from every angle, and I realized I was shivering, though whether from cold or fright I couldn't tell.

When I got to the top, Lester was nestled in some scrub and anchored to the exposed root of a tiny fir. The Presidentials were glowing in the fading light to the east, and we'd be descending in the dark if we didn't hustle along. We coiled and packed and changed our shoes wordlessly, and only after we were well on the trail and in the lee of the mountain did I ask for more, Lester just paces ahead of me.

"'Goodness,' you said."

"Goodness?" Will said, our plates long cleared and other customers come and gone since we'd sat down and now nothing but a pitcher of melting ice and two empty glasses between us. Will had been transfixed by the story about Bill, and though nowhere near as drawn out as Lester was in the telling, I too had paused several times to pursue tangents but also just to be quiet until he couldn't stand it any longer.

"Yeah, the last thing Lester said at the stance near the top of Whitney-Gilman: 'Goodness,' I reminded him. 'About Bill. You said goodness.'"

"You did," Lester said.

"Fine. Goodness again. What about now?" I demanded. "Is he okay?"

Lester was balanced on a small boulder in a steep section of the descent trail. He turned and seemed to be looking at something in the underbrush. "Bill's dead."

"He died?" My voice cracked, and I felt water rush into my eyes. Will too had a flash in his, and then he closed them and turned to the side like he might be sick.

"But you said he watched the film," I said.

Lester faced me, placid. "He did. The fall was a long time ago." Then he stepped off the boulder and started down the trail again.

Somehow Bill's surviving the fall conferred instant relief, changing everything. I set off after Lester.

Will sat up straight again, revived.

"Tell me the rest," I said, a little too loud. "He cratered, right?"

"Lost the race to the top," Lester said. "Peeled off just a few moves below the lip. And these not even the hard moves, mind you. Nowhere near. He ripped the brassies. Pulled the cam too, though from that height it made no difference. He landed on boulders, way left of his belayer."

"God," I said.

"Edward. The belayer. The plan was to turn and run if Bill peeled. Only way you might pull that much slack in. They'd even practiced. But at that point it wasn't going to help. He froze. Just watched it."

We were walking into the bowl-shaped flank of the valley where the glacier had cut a line so smooth and clean the path down is like a ramped sidewalk connecting the base of the cliff to the dark forest at the valley's bottom. For a while we walked side by side.

"I got word the next day," Lester said. "By the time they got him out of there and to the hospital and in and out of surgery, it was, well, it was the next day."

"How bad?"

"Gruesome."

I didn't press for more. I slipped behind him again, and we walked the rest of the way in silence, arriving at the car shortly after dark.

Halfway back to Hanover Lester said, "Bill talked about you guys, you and Pete. That episode at Red Rock made an impression, but even more the way you two handled those cracks at the Creek."

I wanted nothing to do with inspiring Bill.

"When Bill finished that pitch at Red Rock, Pete's, I think he thought maybe he was okay. Not just another wanker."

"How long was he in the hospital?"

"Weeks, months. Broke his back, down low. Had to use a chair. Still quite the athlete. But, you know, never satisfied. Like before, but now, with no way to get better. Really better. And everybody saying how lucky he was. No helmet, and he didn't get more than a little concussion. If his spine had been crushed a bit higher he'd have been a quad. The docs, his family and friends, all of 'em. 'Wow, so lucky. Could be so much worse. . . .' Bill nodding and saying thank you. For two years he worked like mad to get onto his feet. In the pool, therapists. Trying everything."

I struggled to bring this image of Bill to mind.

"Never walked. Climbed, though. Even soloed. He had these braces that locked his legs stiff, like pegs. He'd wheelchair himself as far as the chair would go, then crutches and his braced legs. Sometimes just dragging himself across heather and stones, two or three hours to do what takes fifteen minutes. Ripped above his hips, like before but times ten, and just withered in the bottom half. He climbed by pulling himself up, and then kicking one of those peg-legs onto a hold if he could. He fell a lot, but it was all on a top-rope." Lester talked softly. He sounded exhausted just for telling it. "I helped him. Miserable business. He'd get bruised, cut up and such."

Will said, "Some friend."

"Lot of mileage, those two. But then Lester quit, at least with Bill. He started making excuses. Kids' soccer games, work. He couldn't stand it. It wasn't the effort it took Bill to assemble the gear and haul himself out of the house. It wasn't the stuff he had to do just to get near the crags and get a rig set up. It was the wanting it still, like before."

Will stood up suddenly, as if he couldn't stand it, either. We walked out of Miguel's and drove the hour back up to his cabin in silence. The night was warm. I worried I'd told Will too much with this thick story about obsession and death. When we got back he arranged the last of our loads under a tarp in the bed of the truck, and just before he climbed into his loft he told me tomorrow would be a rest day. If the forecast held, we'd head up to Moriah the day after.

I dreamed of Pete that night—the two of us young and scared, but not for our lives. Just pride on the line. We were in the desert towers, in Utah, on something I didn't remember or recognize. Pete was encouraging me, my sweaty fingertips tracing a seam too tight for jamming. I was smearing my feet and just trying to scooch along to where the feature opened into a shady maw, and then I slipped. He hollered, "I got you." I woke up, my heart thumping, and then remembered where I was: on the floor of the cabin, listening to Pete's son's steady, restful breathing.

When I awoke again the sun was pouring through the window above my head and there was a note tacked to the inside of the door: *Errands. Back after noon.* I made coffee and walked the half mile down to the lake. Mammoth vacationers were at full throttle, boaters and picnickers and fishermen. In the small parking area two big cars sat idling, waiting for someone to vacate a space in the lot. The air was drier today, and there weren't any thunderheads building. In twenty-four hours we'd be setting up camp in the meadow below Moriah, and in two days fully under the shadow of the cliff, climbing into trouble. It would be several days before I discovered Will's "errands" involved two more hauls on his bad foot up to the miner's cabin with food and gear.

I was napping outside the cabin when I heard the truck. It was getting on toward early evening.

"Hey," Will said, standing beside my sleeping pad. "You feeling it, yesterday?"

"I'm fine."

"I got a couple things to do here, then we can grab something in town. There's a taco place by Snow Creek."

So that's where we were when Will asked about Bill again, at a roadside picnic table near the taqueria, and I told him how Lester and I sat in my car outside the library in Hanover following our Whitney-Gilman day. We had stopped in a mill town for dinner and now it was late.

"You want the rest?" Lester said.

"Yes."

"So after he falls, Bill pretty much quits drinking. He always liked his ale. You know—the cases we carted around the States. He got so disciplined. Course he had to, just to survive. He'd have a pint still, but never two. And when he gets to trying again, arranging things to even dream of climbing, he doesn't drink at all. Has a basement apartment that suits the chair, home gym on the rafters. Gets crazy strong. That's when I started worrying. The fourth anniversary passes okay. We talked that weekend. He sounded kind of mute. Not complaining or anything. Just worn down. That's how I remember it anyway."

Lester sighed, and I grew afraid for what was coming.

Three students clambered down the library steps beside us. They walked loosely, books under their arms and small packs on their backs. One gave another a gentle hip-check as they turned the corner and disappeared in the dark.

"It was a couple weeks later," Lester said. "Shot himself."

"Jesus," Will said.

We sat quiet at the picnic table for a moment.

I didn't tell Will the rest of what Lester had said. No big gesture in advance. No note. Bill had tidied up the apartment. He racked his gear neatly, like it was for sale. Even spread an old tarp on the floor to contain the mess.

I ferried our paper plates to the garbage. When I returned, a young couple was standing beside the table talking to Will. Sunburnt skin, sunglasses at the ready, sandals—a climber couple. I sat on a tree stump closer to the taco shop while they pumped him, Will explaining with his hands something about a route or how to get someplace. The woman ran to their car to get paper, then sat at the table to scribble some of what Will had to say. Then the obligatory "What are you up to?" and Will offering little or nothing.

He appeared locked in thought when I returned.

"They're everywhere," I said.

"Oh, you have no idea."

I did. In our day Pete entertained these queries all the time.

"As it was and ever shall be," I said.

"Yeah, at some point I want to hear about that. The ministering."

Back in the cabin Will lit a candle beside the small stack of maps and topos he'd assembled on the table, and for a while he sat there, unfurling one and then another to select those he wanted to bring with us. I brushed my teeth out among the trees. When I came back inside, he was still studying maps.

"So that's how I know your little friend was wrong," I said.

"My friend?"

"The kid you got in a tangle with."

"Yeah?"

"Your dad, he wasn't done."

"Probably not sober, either."

"No. It wasn't all sunshine and sage. But his soloing wasn't suicide. Not by far."

"You don't know."

He was sitting with his back to me. I placed my hand on his shoulder. Apart from our greeting at the airport, it was the first time I'd touched him.

"He had a lot to live for."

"Ever try that on Mom?"

He blew out the candle, then went outside.

A bit later, climbing into bed, he said, "Why'd Lester tease you along like that? Why didn't he just tell you?"

I was on the floor in my sleeping bag. I started to say it was because Lester was surprised I didn't know, and he wasn't sure how to tell me, so he stalled. But now *I* stalled. I wanted to get this right. I knew the story of the end, the one the kid was reporting about Pete—it's too easy. It's clean. Or at least cleaner. But it's wrong.

"When I first asked, if he'd just said 'Bill's dead,' that would have been the end of it. We'd just have got stuck there, at the end, at the collapse and the grief."

Wind pushed through the pines around Will's cabin.

"So Lester took his time because he wanted to tell me what Bill lived for, which takes a while. But it's the story that makes a heart beat and your hands sweat, and it's the one about Bill."

Will grew quiet. Then he rolled over, and I figured he'd fallen asleep. Sometime later, in a near whisper, he said, "You don't really know, and all your storytelling won't persuade me one way or the other."

We locked the cabin at dawn, stopped for oatmeal at the hippie coffeehouse on the edge of town, and gassed up nearby. As we waited to pull onto the four-lane road, a white van rolled slowly through the intersection. My eyes met the driver's just as the windshield glare dissolved. If it wasn't Sam in the van then of course I would conjure her just hours before attempting to join the climbing ranks once again. Will thought he'd seen the van before. He'd heard of Sam, but didn't know her.

By midmorning we were halfway up the canyon, our shirts streaked with sweat, our awkward loads requiring periodic adjustments as ropes slipped and tethered gear shimmied loose. Will's black plastic boot was strapped to the top of his pack. He used a pair of ski poles for support and seemed to limp or at least favor the bad ankle. Still, I couldn't keep up. I often found him sitting on a rock, not to rest but to be sure I didn't get tricked by an animal trail or lost in one of many boulder fields that stretch from high up the canyon side to the stream's edge. The terrain was rugged and remote in ways I hadn't remembered, steeper, bigger, more broken up, and wholly wild, as if the last people to have come through here were Pete and Nor and me in '89, and for the first time since I got Will's letter in January it wasn't just my imagination of fear I worried over.

At one point Will dropped his pack in the middle of our path and I saw him down among laurels with his bad foot dunked in the cold stream. I splashed my face, removed my shoes, and dipped my feet in, too. Sting, throb, then numb.

"Mom says it's not Reverend Holland anymore."

"True."

"How'd that happen? I mean, how'd you get into it?"

"Faith, you mean? Or the pulpit?"

"We go, or Mom does anyway."

This surprised me. Years ago I'd not known her to keep anything but a polite remove from what Pete termed "Joe's business."

My ready explanation was all bones, no flesh: church as extended family—my Boys and Girls Club, summer camp, and field of play. Later, when the existential business loomed, I found myself drawn to a familiar architecture, some way of anchoring a life of meaning and purpose. Some way to know and explore more than what I could manufacture on my own.

"How's this?" I said. "I met your dad in church. Before we put the climbing thing together. Freshman year. Not a church, really, just a house whose garage had been converted into a chapel. The Presbyterian students hung out there, and coming from where I did, I wanted to check it out."

"And Dad?" he said, but I went on.

"So later, way later, it seemed the kind of place I could imagine returning to. I'd been running around with your dad a long time. A lifetime. Then we were living in the pinyons here, me in a tent near the trailer, and I felt stuck. I needed a big gesture, something to lever against all the fright and challenge and beauty he liked to remind me we'd been enjoying for almost ten years."

Will looked puzzled.

"I needed to get on to something else, and maybe it had to be something that made no sense to your dad. Otherwise he'd have talked me out of it."

"Jesus. I figured it was all about climbing, you guys."

"Is it ever?"

A dipper fluttered into our shady glen and with darting gestures bobbed in and out of the creek. We watched him, as if through glass, his beak poking in the streambed for bugs.

"But you're no longer . . ."

"No. And not on account of one thing." I lay back on the

grass. "Maybe 'As it was and ever shall be' doesn't leave a lot of room for 'is.'"

"Man, you're a type around here."

"I'm basically a nurse now. Old people. More or less what I was doing before, but better. I'm useful, it pays okay. It's cleaner, the work for hire. Even with soiled underwear and dentures in a jar."

We dried our feet, reassembled gear, and started up the canyon again. We'd get a first look at Moriah's shaded Northeast Face inside of three hours, and in four we'd take off our shoes in the cool grass of the meadow where Pete and Nor and I had camped, my feet raw and legs rubbery for fatigue. In five we'd be slurping steaming bowls of ramen, and shortly after, with the sun still bright on the craggy high ridge to the west, we'd crawl side by side into a small tent. But all we saw and did and said had been altered—stained, decorated, I couldn't tell—by these exchanges we'd been having around the edges of our preparations. Will wasn't just Pete and Nor's son, and I was no longer just Pete's longtime friend and partner, but an older man and another type of seeker, each of us stepping into some unanticipated place vis-à-vis the other. I'd thought our talk would compass little more than strategy and gear and weather, but now I wasn't even thinking of this as a climbing trip, and even bone-tired, I couldn't relax. When we finally got inside the tent, dozens of mosquitoes buzzed around the netting and Will fell into steady, quiet breathing. The sky turned a deeper blue and in time black, the starlight so brilliant the boulders around the edge of the meadow cast shadows.

An hour or two later he awoke and looked at me like he wasn't sure where he was.

"You sleeping tonight?" he said.

"Hope to."

He resettled, his breath going easy and slow again.

"In church? You and my dad met in church?"

"It was a girl. He was trying to get with this girl who was there."

"Oh. Goodnight."

⟞

It was as in a dream that the cliff appeared at sunrise—brilliant and colorful in first light where it had been dark and distant and unchanging the previous afternoon and evening. I'd slept well if not long and was making coffee when sunlight turned the summit yellow and then, over the next hour, steadily pulled the shade aside to unveil Moriah's grand face. The upper third appeared first and full of dazzling variety, blond and sculpted and unquestionably worthy, this morning for me as it had been for Pete upon his very first assessment. Then the middle band glowed, blank as ever, as when a hot iron is run across the midsection of a badly wrinkled shirt. And in another half hour the bottom, less steep and more generous, cut up by those clean corners and shadows that make vertical topography visually pleasing and, to a climber's eye, alluring.

Will stirred well before he emerged from the tent. Whether he was resting or reading I couldn't tell. At one point he was sitting up, massaging his sore ankle with both hands, and some-time later he emerged barefoot and wandered off to the edge of the meadow to pee. The sun was on us now, already starting to shade the left side of the cliff and trace the long arc of the day. Will made a cup of coffee before he said anything more than good morning. His undershirt was stained with salt and his hair matted and sticky for all the work of getting here.

He blew on his mug. "Recognize it?"

"Prettier, maybe."

He sat on a sleeping pad, his legs straight out in front of him, the one foot visibly puffy. "That's a lotta work, humpin' up here. I'm thinking our 'is' today doesn't include climbing."

"Fine here. I can haul some things to the base. You can rest, and dunk your foot."

He started to refuse my suggestion, but then didn't. It was a good idea. With a load or two in place, we'd be on the route earlier and fresher the next day.

"So now we have all the time in the world," he said. "More coffee?"

I saluted the idea with my mug, and Will set some more water to boil.

"You said your mom's a church-goer."

He sat cross-legged on a sleeping pad, leaning on two ropes he arranged as a kind of backrest. "Yep. Years now. When I was eleven or twelve, not super clued in, she was in some kind of ditch. Suddenly Judy's around all the time, from the hospital. I barely knew her before, and the next thing we know Mom's gone. In treatment, alcohol. The babysitter who used to help with Astrid came for a month, and Karine was around a lot, too. They drove us to Palmdale to visit. She seemed totally normal to us. But I guess that's normal, too."

Will talked without embarrassment or shame, like he was describing something that happened to someone he hardly knew.

"So anyway, she gets home and we start going to this church, where Judy goes. Mom's a regular. Astrid and me, sometimes. I think it's a good thing, even though when I got a little older and started asking questions, Mom and I would get into it. Around the details."

"Like?"

"Afterlife business. The saved and not-saved. It's pretty amped up in there sometimes. You know, your 5.13 believers."

"Your mom?"

"No. She's calm. But she credits it for having saved her. I don't know about a next life, but this one."

"Proximate salvation. Sounds good to me."

"It just gets a bit over-the-top. When we go, it's for Mom. Apart from that we don't talk about it. Least not when I'm around."

Will lifted his eyes to Moriah. I turned, too, the sunshine illuminating just the right half of the face now, our part. We'd be up there shortly, tethered together, Will trying to piece together the puzzle that had confounded his father, me merely to assist. Or to bear witness. Or maybe just to appreciate the work, whether or not he managed to complete it. That's all Pete had wanted of me—not even to finish the route with him, but to have me there when he put himself through the paces of trying.

I organized piles of our ropes, the gear and water and extra clothes. I intended to reduce it by half or more in a couple of trips to the base. I wasn't going to do much to advance our progress on the route, but I could lighten our load for day one.

Freighted with three water jugs, two ropes, and most of a rack, I threaded a path through the long talus slope between the green meadow of our camp and the bigger boulders under Moriah's face. Every five steps I stopped to breathe, temples pounding, vision blurred, impressed I had ever been, like Will, at home here at ten, eleven, and twelve thousand feet. As I drew closer, the wrinkles and scars of the Northeast Face fell into relief, familiar if more formidable and alien than last time. The typical cliff backs off as you get closer, becomes a tamer version of the imposing impression you get from afar. The Diamond in Colorado is this way. The Hulk. Even El Cap, at least its bottom third. But Moriah remains as sheer up close as from the first vantage down the canyon. Apart from these initial few hundred feet—the one section we had successfully ascended—it seems beyond vertical, a sort of Leaning Tower of the alpine zone, and I wondered if there was another such cliff in all of the High Sierra.

When I got back to the meadow some two hours later, Will was asleep in the tent. I drank from a water bottle and quietly loaded for a second trip. It was midafternoon, cloudless and cool—the type of weather that "locks the window open" for days of uninterrupted climbing, Pete would say. True in our time, but weird things were happening with weather. Soggy New England winters. Consecutive years of California drought—hence the dry spring at Moriah's base. And yet record precipitation in the North Cascades. In one of our phone conversations I recall Pete saying the eschatology he'd mused over in college was mere meteorology nowadays. He cited not Yosemite's Lyell Glacier, whose shrinking proportions he documented in annual photographs, but those in the Andes and Greenland. A weak Sri Lankan Monsoon and vanishing reefs in the South Pacific. He wasn't surprised this was happening—he'd been reading about the phenomenon his entire adult life—just impressed at how fast. "If he cares to bother," he once said, "Will won't have a bergschrund to step across to get to North Palisade."

Was this depressing? I couldn't tell anymore. As a pastor I had felt some kind of peculiar responsibility—the institution whose pulpit I occupied had had plenty to say about the end-times for two millennia and yet now that it appeared to be coming not with thunderous rapture but in a steady simmer everyone was stymied or, worse, in denial. To be relieved of my little church was to be let off that hook, at least. I was just part of the picture now, both of the warming globe and on it. As was Will. As was this unclimbed cliff I was hauling our gear toward.

I tucked the load under a tarp at the base of the route, then lay down on the very slab from which Pete belayed and Nor watched me start up the first pitch in '89, resting my head on the empty backpack.

Holy God—Moriah soars. With the sun west of the mountain now, a shimmer of golden light skittered off the summit in a halo obscuring the upper reaches.

The section in front of me, even these first two hundred feet, looked more challenging than even the hardest things I'd climbed with Jeremy in '05. But above that—what did Pete have in mind, thinking he'd get back here with me? I squinted to make out the pillar from whose top he drilled the bolt and then pendulumed in futile search of a passage through the part where the wall swells in an emergent granite cornice. Only now did I see we had gotten barely a third of the way up. Will might readily clamber to Pete's high point, but that next section, decorated with yellow lichen, appeared smooth and impenetrable as ever until giving way to the magnificent, steep black-and-white towers above.

In the '80s my hands grew sweaty for such a sight. Now they were cold and dry, worry compounding worry. What confidence we had. What faith. What a gift we enjoyed, Pete and I, a marriage of form and capacity, blessed with ignorance, courting delusion. I'd come to know loss in the years since—Pete, spouse, church, father—my spheres grown limited. Here on this slab of granite I wondered if Pete's had, too. Had the struggle been not just to make ends meet and be happy and available to Nor and their son and soon-to-be daughter but with something else—some darker contender? Had he been soloing Clyde not to express who he was but to recover something of what he'd been? And what of this was tearing at me now?

꘎

Almost a week later we drove back to Mammoth in the dark, me at the wheel, Will resting his sore foot on the dashboard. Twice he hobbled out to deal with the hub locks, but shortly after we hit the pavement of 395 he nodded off.

I didn't know I was all that tired, but then, north of Bishop, forgot myself, slowed and moved to the right lane as if to get off at the Gorge access road and from there up towards the trailer. I swerved back onto the highway and opened the window to cool off and keep alert. Less than an hour to Mammoth.

Not long before midnight we pulled into Nor's. I killed the engine and Will woke up. The porch light flicked on. Nor was at the door in her pajamas, her face in the dark.

When she saw Will try to stand she came swiftly to aid him. The ski poles he'd been using for two days clacked on the driveway.

"It's nothing," I heard him say.

I ferried a couple of loads to the garage, and when I brought Will's pack inside Astrid was wrapping ice packs in a towel. She shrugged, as if to indicate Will had come home like this before.

Nor was down the hall waiting for him to come out of the bathroom. Then they disappeared into his room. Astrid delivered the ice, and in minutes I lay in my sleeping bag on the living room carpet. I could hear Will and Nor's muffled voices for a while, and then someone turned out the lights and the house was quiet and there was only the hum of the truck's engine still ringing in my ears and my heart thumping restlessly.

Early the next day Nor stepped through the living room in her green scrubs. When I turned over and reached for my glasses, she said, "You around for a while?"

"I go Sunday," I said. "What's this, Thursday?"

"Yep. I'll see you later."

When I woke up again, it was Astrid and Will heading out the door, she with his bag, he on some wooden crutches I'd seen in the garage. They were headed to the hospital for X-rays.

⌒

I didn't tell Nor everything, but neither did I dissemble. I even shared some frightening details, if in a sanitized form. She wasn't interested in the mountain or the route or the weather. She wasn't invested in whatever it was Pete and I had spent months preparing for, much less the memory of the week she'd spent there with us back in '89. She was curious only about Will, and she wanted a frank assessment. As I explained how dialed-in he was, how focused and efficient—around camp, with the gear, in strategy—she interrupted: "Does he toe the edge?"

I met her eyes. Whatever I said, she needed to believe me.

"You know what I mean better than I do," she said.

We were on her porch in the Adirondack chairs, a pitcher of lemonade on a little table between us. She gestured with her hand toward the crest in the distance. "Does he cross that point, you know, where you care more about what you're doing than taking care of yourself?"

I said he's a climber, so yes. But he's at ease on the cliff and takes nothing for granted. Double-checks systems, sets anchors like a guide, warned me to be careful when I had to squeeze by him on a stance or run the risk of a big swing if I fell. I told her how readily and capably Will could place a bolt—though he added just three in our several days on Moriah. What I didn't say was that his attention to a climb was like Pete's—entire. That he wastes almost nothing—energy, water, words—in the service of his project, and that if he has his father's savvy and resolve he also has something of her quiet concentration. Will had us start the route at an hour he'd calculated to give us the warmth of morning sun for the first several pitches followed by shade and colder, stickier rock for the section around Pete's high point. I didn't tell Nor how he hiked the first six hundred feet of the route, and when he saw how shaky and worked I was he didn't bother with the formality of offering to swing leads. His foot didn't seem to even annoy him at this point. On the ledge before the unfinished pitch, he changed into tighter climbing slippers and took the bolt kit out of the pack I was hauling. "Gear?" he said, leaning out to admire the odd column that is the fifth pitch's distinctive feature.

"I don't know. I didn't even clean it. I think it's there, maybe small cams in slots. At some point your dad got a sling around the pillar, and at the top there's the single bolt. But unless someone's replaced it, I'd be surprised if it's not rusty."

I didn't tell Nor that nothing I'd read about or seen of Will's climbing prepared me for how he ascended the round-edged column—without hesitation or even indication of effort, much less distress. Pete had spent much of a day inching up this feature, cautiously if impressively, pausing wherever he could to assess the next little bit and fiddle with gear he'd readjusted twice already for fear this might be his last good protection. To watch Will was to witness a finesse and proficiency I'd only heard rumor of. The column tops out like a telephone pole, flat and not quite big enough for two feet, above which the wall begins to swell out. Where Pete had been precarious and purposeful, both in gaining the perch and in steadying himself to drill the bolt from the meager stance, Will seemed almost to hop onto the circular top. With a bit more care, he shuffled his feet and turned around to face out, palms pasted against the rock at his thighs. Then he lifted his arms, as if in praise.

Looking down and cupping his hands around his mouth, he hollered, "Not only no bolt! No hole!"

"Then get to work," I muttered.

I told Nor how he drilled the three-eighths bolt into a harder, smoother layer of stone because twenty-five years of rust, rain, freezing, and thawing had calved off not just the shallow scar of Pete's bolt but an entire saucer of rock.

Then I spent most of three subsequent days at that same belay beneath the fifth pitch—Saturday, Sunday, and Tuesday. On the first, Will had done exactly like his father: lowered off the bolt and pendulumed left at various levels in search of a friendlier set of features. Nothing. On the second, colder day, he swung to the right to explore the improbable, steeper wall on that side and here managed to find and link together moves sufficient for sixty feet of upward progress—only to be shut down just above and well to the right of the bolt at the top of the pillar. He'd worked for six hours on this terrain off to the side where most of the time I could see only a slice of him or nothing at all. Swaddled in several layers of clothing and his jacket too, including two hoods, I felt like I was belaying him from inside a cave. Later he told me he'd protected the section with two small cams placed in pockets, a frightening #3 behind an exfoliating flake, and two hooks "that wouldn't hold a flea." The hour-long delay was on account of his standing in etriers to drill a bolt, at just about the elevation of the middle of the pillar but fifty feet to the right. From there he gained another thirty feet, but in the end was whelmed on delicate holds just two body lengths above and right of his, and his father's, high point. Here he was again firmly back in my line of sight.

"Watch me!" he shouted.

Twenty minutes later I was still watching. He didn't appear stressed, but neither did he make gestures indicating a way forward. He seemed mostly to be studying the steep, blank section to his left, above the pillar. Finally, he looked down, hollered a warning—"On yellow!" Then he jumped. He had brilliantly elected to climb on two ropes, Euro-style, with the yellow one clipped through the gear from two days before. Leaping from the cliff, he flew outward like a skydiver, but after just thirty feet was buoyed by the yellow rope, which he had never unclipped from the new bolt above the pillar. In the hush of the aftermath—relief, humiliation—we listened to the pinging of dislodged hooks and gear sliding down the blue rope to our right.

I lowered Will to my level and pulled him into the anchors. He had been underdressed, and now his teeth chattered and his skin was cold to the touch, like he'd been working in a refrigerator all afternoon. His fingers were too stiff to handle the gear, so I dealt with his knots and assembled his clothing. Then I unzipped his pants so he could turn and take a pee. He stuttered, "I'll have to c-c-clean that gear later. I c-c-can lower once we're above it."

Awhile later, as we were descending, we met again at a stance some two hundred feet above the ground. He was still shivering but leaning away from the cliff and looking up again, still trying to problem-solve the route. "Only thing left to try is straight up," he said. "You just never know, right?"

You don't, of course. But you know neither Pete nor Will nor anyone else who had gotten this far saw anything to suggest a way through the band of blond rock bulging out from the mid-section of Moriah's right side. So I figured this was it—sure, we would be back here again soon but the score was already settled, the journey effectively ended. Will hadn't been able to find a way through the very stretch that stymied Pete. Neither would he aid through it. "All free or forget it," he'd said. "No point just punching a way to the top." I was relieved. I'd gotten the letter and accepted the call. We'd worked hard, gave it an honest attempt, and now it was done. All that was left was to clean up our mess.

We took a day off. A calm, warmer day—the kind that ordinarily burnishes whatever plot you're hatching. I woke up with the sun. Will slept until midmorning and emerged only after the cliff had fallen into shade and looked cold and frightful again. Leaning over a heaping bowl of oatmeal, he said, "Sabbath, even if it's Monday." He had been working so much harder the past two days. Where I had only to trudge to the base and hump up the first several hundred feet on top-rope, stand on a narrow ledge, and adjust my belay seat from time to time to keep my legs from going numb, he was on his fingers and toes for hours. The superficial evidence was abundant—raw fingertips, scraped knuckles, abrasions on his arms and calves—but the muscle fatigue had to be profound. In order to rise he rolled onto his side, paused, then pressed to his knees. He seemed to place his feet delicately as he walked to the edge of the meadow to pee, limping on the swollen left but probably no less sore in the right for all the hours in climbing shoes. To stir cocoa he reached awkwardly so as not to strain a tender shoulder. I napped restlessly in the afternoon, my sleeping bag in the sunshine, and when I awoke Will was back in the tent. I boiled pasta. I figured the flutter of the stove or the smell of pesto would draw him out but ended up waking him at dark just to eat.

"Let's take another day," I suggested.

He was starving. I wondered if he hadn't heard me over his chewing. He spooned himself another bowl of the noodles and drank half a liter of water in one take. "We could," he agreed. He put his food aside for a moment and matched his fingers to one another, testing the tips. "But we have momentum."

I'd never heard anything more ridiculous, but I wasn't bothered. Unless he'd had an entire change of heart about aid climbing, we were done here soon. Shortly after sunset we were in the tent together, and minutes later Will in a deep sleep. I used a headlamp to read, and with the light on Will's stray left hand studied the cuts and stains and scoured patches there. I wondered if he would be able even to reach the start of the fifth pitch again.

But it wasn't tender hands or sore muscles that ended our attempt. Neither, I was startled and disappointed to learn, the blank rock above the pillar. It was his foot. And not from one thing, like catching it on an edge or re-spraining the ankle on approach or descent. Just the accumulated damage—the several days of ferrying supplies followed by several days of clinging to edges the width of a half dollar, smearing, pivoting, and jamming in a climbing shoe that provides no more support or protection than a ballet slipper. On Tuesday Will hiked to the base so slowly it seemed most of the time I was watching him from a half-mile above, and when he got his hands on the rock he remained slow and deliberate—everything hurt. But by the time we were situated in our familiar stance he had become reconstituted, and I wasn't there five minutes before he had rearranged his clothing, reracked, and started tying into the end of the yellow rope that had held his jump on the last attempt. He got to the top of the pillar quickly, and from there he began a daylong battle to see the route through the sheer band: thin edges, sloping pockets, a dynamic launch from tiny holds to a Thank God incut he had discovered on Sunday's foray—and from which he stood in slings for nearly two hours to drill two bolts, about eight feet apart, to protect a section of rock his father and all but a handful of climbers in the world would believe, even upon close inspection, unclimbable. In a day and a half Will gained sixty additional feet, placed just the pair of additional bolts, and left a wide swath of the blond cliff dangling with wires and hooks and long colorful slings as on a sparsely decorated Christmas tree. All the while, and steadily, his left foot swelled. He had spent much of Monday evening plunging it into the icy stream by our camp and felt encouraged when it was smaller again in the morning, but by Tuesday noon his climbing shoe was entirely unlaced and yet still so snug that helping him peel it off at a belay late that afternoon was my most strenuous accomplishment of the day—and I nearly lost the shoe to the big air behind us when it suddenly came free.

He had gotten within thirty or forty feet of what he thought would be the end of this rope-stretcher "mega-pitch"—two hundred feet whose every segment presented something harder than what came before. The start, these first gestures off the ledge where I'd now spent nearly a week of my life, was accessible 5.10. "The pillar is soft 11," Will said, "and then it's an elevator ride through the grades."

Back in Mammoth he said, "The hard bit is right there, where I kept peeling. I think I see a way. It's doable. But I have no idea if I can do it." So that's what he was up to in that last half hour on Tuesday before he lowered: standing with his good foot on the decent-sized edge without any hint or gesture of prospective upward movement, just committing to memory the patterns and possibilities that might bridge him to a promising dish at the upper end of this bulge.

"5.13?" I said.

"If we can do it, it'll have a question mark. That's all. Like what they have for Tour de France cyclists—'beyond category.' Until someone with a better yardstick comes along, it will be that."

⤴

"He jumped?" Nor said. She was stuck there, on the second day, when Will leapt from the cliff.

The skyline ridge was black now, but just two hundred yards from her porch we could make out golfers strolling down a final fairway in the twilight.

"What else could he do?" I said. "He'd climbed out that side. He was stranded."

"He really trusts you."

I thought, but didn't say, my part was trivial.

"Was it scary?" she said.

"Only before. Only for seven months. Once we were up there and done with the first day, it made sense, my role here. It's not like with Pete."

"Which was scary."

"Wasn't his fault, Pete's. It was just more shared. Not entirely, but enough that I was scared, too."

"Was he scared?"

"Pete?"

"Will."

"Just enough. Just what you need to stay alert. I never saw him shivering with fright. He's way ahead of where Pete and I or any of our cohort were."

She went inside. When she came out again she had a bowl of fresh ice and a manila folder. "Lemonade?"

I drank some. It was thin and tart.

Nor opened the folder and handed me a photograph. It was of Pete and her and me outside his trailer on the cold bright morning after the Solstice party in '88. We were posing for a camera Nor had balanced on the motorcycle. Pete's head was wrapped in a scarf like a turban, our arms around one another and our mugs raised. Steam poured off the coffee and out of

Pete's mouth. I remembered our posing, and feeling bugged, less for being in the vise grip of another of Pete's plans than for the forgiveness I knew I'd extend to him.

"It was the night before," I said. "This rumor in the air around the trailer. That was the first I heard of Moriah. It took me a while to get it that Pete hadn't been blabbering that night."

Nor looked puzzled, copper eyes framed with wrinkles.

"He was roping me in. When I first figured it out I was angry. Way later, on the phone, I confronted him about it. He didn't deny it. Or apologize. He said he was worried I was already out of there, and he was too chicken to straight up ask me because he thought I'd say no. He said if it was a congregation I was itching to please, he'd get one excited about our project."

Nor smiled in recognition. I didn't need to tell her how stupid I felt—both for being readily manipulated, and for blaming Pete.

"When he and his mom came through he asked, only half-seriously, what it would take to get me back here.'"

"Well, I guess that's been figured out."

"I know," I said. "We tell ourselves, 'Could have been a car accident, or cancer. Even a broken rope.'"

She appeared to wonder where I was headed with this.

"I wasn't thinking much about Pete, coming out here. But when I got to the top of that third pitch with Will Saturday, well, I was just glad he had climbed through. Because there I was again, right in that little cramped dish where Pete was taking pictures of me, on the last day, the cold one. But there weren't any. He was just watching me through the long lens. He knew I'd find the mail in my tent, and I'd be gone. So when I got there this time I just lost it. Of course Will had no idea what was going on with me, no more than I did with Pete back then."

Nor seemed curious, but not really moved.

"It hadn't hit me," I said, "not until then. What I have here, it's not finished."

"You mean something more than grief?" she asked. "God knows that doesn't happen on any kind of schedule."

"Yeah. But also, and I don't mean to make it about me. But when your partner dies because he's unroped . . ."

"Stop."

"I wish I could even believe it doesn't make sense. You know, watching Will up there all the time, but thinking about Pete an awful lot of it. Say what you or anyone else can about him, he got me. And he got me to feel a lot."

Nor lifted her eyes to the dark crest. "He loved you," she said. Her confidence seemed to poke at something else, some reservoir of doubt.

We sat quietly for a while, the air growing cold, and when Astrid got home we ate a supper the two of them threw together of grains and toasted nuts and salad. Afterwards Astrid made herself a protein shake and Nor explained it would be Astrid taking me to Reno on Sunday—that she had to be at the hospital after church, and Will was coming too, for treatment for his foot.

On Saturday I heard the familiar sputter of Will's truck. I went to the door. A friend was grabbing the crutches from the truck bed and coming around the side to help him out.

"Ricky, that's the reverend there," Will said. "Goes by Joe."

"Hey Rev Joe," Ricky called. He was scarecrow-thin with a patchy, goatlike strand of beard at his chin. We shook hands. Will was wearing a plastic cast twice as bulky as the one he'd had last week.

"Your mom said the X-rays look good."

"Just the soft tissue, they say." He rested his leg on the table. "Must have a lot of it. Foot's like a marmot."

Ricky called from the kitchen, "Not much doing here. Let's go to town."

"Come?" Will asked.

"Thanks. I'm good. Nice to be inside."

He sighed. He seemed, if just out of sympathy, tired as well. "We'll be better next time."

I smiled. I didn't say I'd heard his dad say the same thing and more than once.

"I'll keep the jumars handy," I said.

"That's right," Ricky said. "A rope is for climbing."

"So we'll be in touch?" Will said.

"Yep."

I waved to them from the front porch.

The following morning I was drinking coffee at the kitchen counter, reading the *LA Times* and wondering if I should wake Astrid when she came in the front door in running clothes. Shortly we were driving north toward Reno in Nor's Subaru. I asked her about the East Coast colleges she was interested in and got a little about their church, but in between polite, tidy answers she would turn up the music. Astrid was lean and long, and if in person she still had her father's eyes it wasn't quite the duplicate face I got from that photograph of her racing. She drove faster and more confidently than her brother, and when we stopped in Lee Vining she seemed grateful to see people she knew at the Mobil station. In these gestures—her ease in her body, her affability with friends—Pete again, and as she zipped north I found myself at times spellbound by the transmutation, through gender and generation, at my side. North of Conway Summit, I tried to draw her out. I asked how often they saw Will, considering how busy their mom was with work and church and her meetings.

She turned down the music and sat up a little straighter.

"I didn't mean to pry," I added.

"Will tells anyone."

I didn't mention her mom had been fairly forthcoming as well.

"If he hadn't told you," she added, "you'd be the first."

We were quiet for a while, then Astrid switched from the music to an audio book about Roger Bannister and the four-minute mile. It was the middle of the story—a lot of pseudoscience about how the barrier was physiologically unbreakable interspersed with details of Roger's quiet, methodical training. Just before we got to Reno he ran three laps at a sub-four pace in a workout and told a friend he believed he could have done it that very morning. I wondered if Will didn't think the same about the breakthrough he hadn't been able to achieve, that fitness and good conditions might matter less than just being relaxed. At the airport curb I thanked Astrid for the ride, and for the book. I told her I'd get it at the library, even if the outcome was certain. I suggested she let me know if she came east for college visits in the next year. She thanked me, but her eyes said she wouldn't call me if I were the last person she knew on earth.

It had been a kind of ditch, Nor's. It's the other thing we talked about on the porch before Astrid got home two evenings earlier. There had been two stops by the Mammoth police—"Kind of rolled through that intersection, Nor." Then Judy, a charge nurse and someone she'd known for years: "You're 100 percent on the ball at work" (which Nor said wasn't so). "It's after work I worry about."

Not long after, Judy and Nor's friend Karine "staged the coup." It was a weekend, Will away at a gym climbing competition and Astrid farmed out somewhere for a slumber party. "They practically banged the door down," Nor said. She was lying on the couch, neither asleep nor really awake, an empty bottle of Chardonnay on the counter and an open if mostly full flask of bourbon nearby. There wasn't anything to protest. "The classic, if banal, cry for help. A few weeks later I even got mad at them for taking so long." Friends rallied, kids were taken care of, and Nor went headlong into the regimen. It was in the aftermath that she felt she needed something else, some way of keeping a higher power in view. She started going to Judy's church, and hasn't stopped.

It was the best part of my trip to California, this exchange with Nor. I hadn't seen her in nine years—since the summer I visited when Will was away at camp. She was her same captivating, hard-to-read self, but calmer and more available. In college and after, Nor was in high gear all the time, ever-organized and always hurrying toward something, and in her late thirties still a whirlwind, though only now did I understand it was less to pursue than to avoid. This time she seemed right here, on the porch, hands curled around a wet glass of sour lemonade, her eyes reflecting the falling light of the evening, her rendition of her life frank and more or less unashamed and her smile easy and full when she heard the door slide open behind us and Astrid's voice, "Hi, Mom. Hey, Joe."

Nor asked about me, too, and I gave her something more than the customary, curt summary. At some point she admitted it was she who had suggested Will write to me about Moriah. "And not because of any rights thing you guys have about your routes." Neither, she said, because she wanted a more mature and cautious partner to look after Will. "It's 'cause we've got a lot of history, Joe."

Then the door opened, Astrid poked her head out, and they made the dinner.

∽

When we'd gotten to the bottom of the last rappel on Tuesday, Will's foot was thick and numb, but an hour later, back in the meadow, the feeling started to return. We were late getting him the Advil. He lay in the grass, his head resting on a coiled rope. I gathered cooking equipment, stuffed sleeping bags, folded the tent, and packed our gear. The wind had kicked up and it felt like it might rain; if we weren't heading out now, I needed to re-pitch the tent. But Will was determined, and half an hour later he said his foot hurt less walking than it did when all he had to do was think about how much it hurt. I didn't remind him he had taken four pills.

I carried as much of the heavy stuff as I could fit, and Will used the ski poles to ease his load. We moved slowly but steadily down the canyon, the rain spitting unevenly and at times blowing sideways from somewhere farther off where it was raining hard. Every fifteen minutes or so, I stopped to wait for Will and listen to thunder rumbling around the high peaks.

At one of these rendezvous points, he said, "What's the name you had in mind for this?"

"Your dad called anything we were working on 'A Fine Line.' One of his little rules: can't name 'em till you know 'em. He wondered if people ought to do that, too. He said if my parents had done that, my name would be Solomon, and everybody would call me Solo."

Will appeared bored by the lore of old men. "So you never got a 'Hunter-Holland?'"

"Almost. Early on, something on Williamson. We should have, but we kept waiting for the right one."

We both looked up the canyon. Moriah had already fallen behind an intersecting ridge and would have been obscured by the weather anyway.

"Maybe this is it," Will said.

"May be," I said.

That little exchange was as close as we got to discussing whether it might happen again. You get down from a project like that and for a day or two you're giddy for having two feet on flat earth. You're alive and sentient. You have running water and easy shelter. And then it hits you in a wave: you're so tired it takes an effort to raise your eyelids. Brushing your teeth is an athletic event. Direct sunshine burns the skin. It wasn't until Astrid and I were headed north that I had some wind again, and only at the airport did I notice my legs and back were no longer aching for even the most rudimentary gesture.

I'd never headed east from Reno but from under a cloud of fear and grief and regret, so it was strange to be feeling only wonder, and mostly for any of the little things: Will's acumen for climbing, like nothing his father or I had had the temerity even to imagine. Astrid's cool focus, and these little proprietary maneuvers around her mother. And Nor's open confession and quiet scheming: this whole arrangement, engineered by her. And the not-little things too: the unchanged, grand Eastern Sierra, more rugged and remote and magnificent for all I'd been avoiding in these many years Will and Astrid were growing up there. The scale, above all—the months of planning and training and packing and more than a day of steep hiking just to get within the vicinity of a cliff so imposing and proud that were it anywhere near a maintained trail, much less a road or national park visitors center, it would have the unmistakable visual signature of Half Dome or the Eiger. And finally, the rock face itself, accepting only fingers and toes but demanding every inch of sinew and ounce of muscle and bone, every piece of you engaged in some shamanic choreography—and still, it won't go.

Yes, I thought, as the plane taxied out onto the tarmac, *it's not finished. So long as Will has the appetite for it, I'm in.*

PART THREE

~

Hunter-Holland

Some have high blood pressure. Others a predilection for accidents. My thing: I am slow to learn. Throw a baseball, ride a bike. In seminary I got a sympathy credit for Beginning Hebrew, less for earnest trying than for naked displays of futility. Once, when young, I overheard my mother trying to get me some cover for the long battle with arithmetic: "Please," she pleaded with my father. "He's not fast. But he's not stupid." Neither grateful nor hurt, I knew, even at seven, mine was a pledge to perseverance.

(This proves a useful attribute for a climber, not least on the wide, dirty things that have fallen out of fashion. Even if Will's "Maybe this is it" was sufficient to keep me on a tether for another round with Moriah, the prospect of off-width cracks and chimneys in the big features on the cliff's upper third appealed to whatever part of my imagination could still be quickened by climbing.)

So it's taken me a long time to get what this whole business is about—the ten years of single-minded focus with Pete, followed by nearly twenty-five of avoidance, and now the week with Will. Most of a lifetime. I got back to New England with the energy of the born-again, restlessly alive and shot through with enthusiasm, and even weeks after returning I merely had to bring Moriah to mind to feel a jump in my heart and a flash of moisture in my hands. It was coming together for me at last, that what I got from this—the connive, prepare, ramble, and recover—couldn't compare to what it asked of me. And it's the asking that holds you.

I devoted myself to saying yes. I whittled two pegs out of wooden dowels and began making regular forays to a pegboard in the old Dartmouth gym. It's a conscription-era conceit: parallel lines of holes drilled into wood panels, these mounted on a cinderblock wall of the gym not fifty feet from where students swipe their cards to gain access to the adjacent, newer facilities—the exercise machines, pools, and glass-walled squash courts. Here in the tired foyer lay a stack of discarded wrestling mats where runners stretch before going out in the cold, and this vestigial climbing contraption that rarely sees any action. And here, one evening, I met Emery, an affable sophomore from California.

"Where'd you get those?!" he said, pointing to the old EB's I stuffed my feet into for laps on the pegboard. "They should be in a museum."

"I wear them to keep myself out of a museum," I said. Really I wore them just to keep my feet accustomed to the tight quarters.

Emery had come to Dartmouth partly on account of the college's vaunted mountaineering club, but so far he'd been underwhelmed.

"We weren't impressed in my time either," I said. "We ran into the Dartmouth guys. Their nice cars, their better, or at least newer, gear. They always seemed to be standing around talking about what they were going to do."

He laughed. "We *do* talk! You can't climb a pitch without having a slideshow and a feed about it."

He invited me to tag along with him and another of his pals one weekend, and then it was usually just the two of us—several autumn weekends at Cannon Cliff and Cathedral Ledge. Emery had learned to climb at Joshua Tree. He had logged time at The Needles and made a couple of pilgrimages to Yosemite. Shorter and slighter than me, he was several times stronger. He was quick to smile and, near as I could tell, constitutionally noncompetitive. Emery knew his way around rock and, like me, preferred mileage to pushing hard grades, and in just three months I climbed more and better than I had in twenty-five years. It even started to feel something like natural again. Sometimes midweek we'd throw a rope on Bartlett Tower, a stone and mortar obelisk on a small rise east of campus, and run laps at twilight. From Emery I learned about the "buildering" routines around the college where you could get a good pump for just traversing a granite-block wall for twenty minutes. And when the snow started falling, we began making weekend forays to Boston for marathon gym sessions.

It wasn't long before Emery pieced together my story and guessed at what I was up to—this being the age of instant, abundant information. He was sheepish about inquiring and said he wouldn't have started poking around but for all the questions he got in Boston about why we had to climb for three or four hours at a time. "Getting your money's worth isn't all that convincing after a few visits," he said. We were driving back to New Hampshire. "Just give me something: is it that unfinished route from the late '80s you're gunning for?"

I hesitated.

"I won't tell," he said.

"It's not aspiration I want to advertise."

"But are you? Did I get it right?"

"No: I'm assisting. And trying to assist in something less than fully humiliating style."

"Assisting? Who on earth would you be assisting?"

A couple weeks later I ran to campus through a light snowfall and was resting between pegboard reps, flat on my back on the mats. "Will!" Emery hollered, rolling through the turnstile with friends. "Will Hunter! It's poetic! Positively poetic!" He disappeared with his companions and I didn't see him again until after the Christmas holiday.

Home for three weeks, Emery spent a stretch of it in Joshua Tree with old climbing pals, and when he got back from California he was feeling gloomy in the snowy Upper Valley. On a drive to Boston he told me he used to read about Will when he was just starting to climb—this phenom on the comp circuit. "He was going to be our generation's Sharma," Emery said. "I can't believe you're climbing with him. But then, of course. Pete Hunter's son!" One Saturday he helped me build contraptions like Will's under the back stairs of my apartment building, a set of hangboards and an awkwardly angled "crack machine" I readily fell out of, and he found a mattress outside a frat house so I'd have something to cushion the blows. He started a list of the things we'd climb after the spring thaw and seemed less enthused about his own business than in setting me up for summer. In Emery's eyes, anyway, I'd been transformed from a has-been to an *is*.

But winter has a way of freezing you out. If I had been keeping up the exercises with a kind of liturgical devotion, by February my verve was waning. Straddled between the summers, blowing on my fingers between reps, my mind wandered less and less to the mountain and all it would entail and demand and more to that last evening on the porch with Nor. She'd been awfully honest, and I felt bad for having dropped out of their life all those years after Pete died. I had figured I was part of the problem, and at best an unwelcome reminder of her broken world. I'd had my own grief and guilt to duck and dodge, but the excuses I'd summoned to avoid Nor now felt not just coarse but cruel. In July she seemed to see in me something else, and now when I hung from a fingerboard or ran to the gym I was often as not recalling the twilight on her face and wondering what she was doing now, this moment in Mammoth, where the time was three hours earlier and the snow ten times deeper.

In December she sent a thick envelope, separate from the annual card with a picture of her and Will and Astrid. Inside, a wrapped present. I leaned it against the potted plant in my living room and waited until Christmas to open it. I was surprised at how aware I was of the colorful package there in the sunlight and figured it was probably another artifact she'd unearthed from the old days, a photo of Pete and me or maybe one of his early and heavily annotated Sierra guidebooks. I'd known Nor for more than thirty-three years, but mostly through Pete. She was one year ahead of us at the little college where I was one of too many men who locked onto her when we saw her gliding purposefully across campus and where we went to parties both hopeful she might appear and certain she would not. I learned her name when it appeared underneath her picture in the college news-paper—an article about Eleanor Rhodes' exploits on the New England Nordic skiing circuit. She was disciplined and aloof. She seemed the type who belonged at a larger, more reputable school but on account of some familial connection or maybe generous financial aid, ended up at ours. Then, sophomore fall, she was in my philosophy class. I sat nearby, introduced myself, and toward the end of that soggy semester even got her to hike with me.

Late one night in early spring I returned to Pete's and my third-floor dorm room and there she was, on our couch. They were sitting side by side but not close, and Pete greeted me too enthusiastically, as if relieved I was back. It seemed he'd gotten to know her well enough to get her into our room but now needed some kind of cover or assistance until he could figure out what to do next.

It was like that for a while, a long while really—they were a couple but we were a threesome. Whatever jealousy I felt was eased by gratitude for their not dropping me. And I could see Nor smiled and laughed way more with Pete than she had on our tame little outings. That spring she came along on several of our weekend road trips to the Adirondacks and the Gunks, and in August she joined us in Colorado after the summer session. On these trips Pete seemed as wary as he was enamored of her, worried he was showing symptoms of who he might one day become—cautious, respectful, grounded. He knew this reserve was a contrived disposition, and one he'd need to molt out of if he and Nor were to have a chance, but he didn't want to scare her off. So I was the useful companion. Nor shared a tent with Pete, but she talked to me as much as she did to him.

When we got back to school that fall she was a little harder for Pete to reach. Her goals were explicit—to win a lot of ski races in this, her senior year, and to get into medical school— while ours were couched in the aimless, noncommittal chatter of climbers. We talked less of the near term than of the absurdly ambitious and probably unaffordable post-college climbing itin- erary we were starting to sketch out. Next to Nor we were a couple of hippies. Now she came with us only sometimes and always with schoolwork and some kind of training agenda. One of these was the Columbus Day weekend when we drove all the way to North Conway, way too far for just three days. Pete and

I climbed all day Saturday while Nor sat at the table with her chemistry books in our gorgeous campsite on the Saco River. When we got back to camp late in the day she asked if one of us would pick her up on the Kancamagus Highway the following afternoon—she wanted to do a long trail run. A little row ensued over the logistics, Pete going on about how unnecessarily complicated all this was, how the ride arrangement would pinch our agenda, and why climbing now was better than training for races three months hence, and eventually why climbing was better than skiing, period.

I cut him short. "I'm not good for another huge day. I'll pick her up."

He glowered. We'd set Sunday as the day for the Airation and Lichen Delight double feature we'd driven all this way for, and even if the two routes shouldn't take but a few hours, Pete wanted nothing competing for our attention. Or for mine, anyway. His wasn't at stake.

"You can get on Lichen before the sun hits the wall," I said. And to Nor, "I can pick you up any time after noon."

Pete tramped off to the river to wash up and Nor unfurled a map to show me what she had in mind—an impressive trek, really, more than twelve miles of White Mountain trails and then five more on a tamer stretch beside the Pemigewasset River. We agreed to meet right where the highway crossed the river at 3:00 P.M.

Everyone was on edge in the evening, what with the ordinary climbing-project nerves and this overlay of tension about colliding agendas, but the morning was crisp and routine, and by 10:00 A.M. Pete and I had sent two routes that were as hard as anything we'd climbed to that point. I had trouble on Airation—stalling in the middle, fiddling with nuts and finally hanging on one—while Pete had been clean, fast, and confident on the longer, stiffer Lichen Delight. We were lucky with the weather, a final stretch of Indian summer, and from the belays above the canopy we admired patches of ochre and red and yellow stitched into the green blanket of conifers in the valley. It was a cool morning, but Pete climbed shirtless and in cut-offs and appeared to sail through the thin crux sections as if pulled along on invisible wires from above. We were nearing the end of almost six months of more or less continuous climbing; he was feeling the fitness and coming into his own. It was about then that he developed the grip strength I never managed to achieve, but even more: a balletic way of arranging fingers and toes on unlikely chips and crimps to complement whatever holds lay on the obvious line, in this case a half-inch crack that splits the face. In just fifteen minutes of glory our 5.11 barrier was broken.

We were in camp before noon, arriving just as Nor was getting ready to head out. She wore a little hip belt with a map, some gorp, and a small water bottle tucked inside, and she carried two long ski poles. She wasn't going to lope along easily but rather bound up the steep sections and trot the downhills, taxing herself as she would in a marathon ski race. She appeared a little anxious and distracted—this would involve a lot of effort—so she asked Pete about our morning but didn't penetrate his veneer to see how enthused he really was, and in a few minutes she was gone. In another hour I was, too.

Rather than sit by the bridge waiting for her I decided to run Nor's route in reverse, intercept her, and then keep her company for the last few miles of her long jaunt. The trail there is an old logging road—the forest long ago plundered of old growth, the great trees dragged out of the wilderness along this very route. Still, the forest was huge compared to our upstate New York woods, dappled with light and airy and inviting, the road moist from shade and covered with fall leaves. The afternoon had warmed up, and it felt good to amble along a flat route with an even breath. Climbing is a yo-yo activity. You're on or you're off, working intently for a section and then hanging at a belay while your partner takes over. Running is regulated and meditative. I took off my shirt and tucked it into the back of my shorts. I trotted along restfully, lost in my mind. Then Nor—at first hardly distinguishable against the palette of autumn, and then plainly visible, and then audible as well with the clacking of her poles as she hopped along toward me with a big grin.

"Am I there?" she said.

"Not quite. But it's less than an hour." We took off together.

She was a deer next to me, but with so many mountainous miles behind her I could keep up almost comfortably, and running in the opposite direction the trail felt fresh. The wind picked up, and for the last two miles we ran side by side amid swaying branches and swirling leaves.

In Conway we stopped for hamburger meat and other supplies. Everyone had completed a project today; we'd cook up a good feast in the campground. Nor asked which of the beers Pete liked best, and she tossed into the cart a bag of the chips she'd ordinarily rib him for eating.

He was at the table beside a stack of books when we pulled in, still barefoot and shirtless as when we left him but now with an open down parka draped over his back like a cape. He was so glad to see us I figured he had grown worried about the plan Nor and I had made to meet beside the highway. Maybe he felt bad about not consulting on it, or even about not coming along. Nor limped out of the car, stiff from her long run, and Pete tended to her—got her sandals out of the tent and helped her into warm, dry layers. In an hour we had a fire going and dinner underway and everyone was relaxed and restored and in the twilight the air away from the fire turned crisp with a bite of fall. Pete was tending the grill by headlamp when Nor said, "Hey, nice work this morning." I had told her on the drive what we had done and explained why it mattered.

"We're not bad," Pete said, "for a couple of gumbies from the East."

"So what'd you do all afternoon?" she said.

"I read. Got bored. Had some more juice, so I put a rope on Kill Your Television."

"Alone?" Nor said. Her voice rose up out of her ordinary register.

"Yes. It's called a rope solo. Very safe. Kind of tedious." He enunciated like he was talking to a child. "It's a hard pitch, and too sketchy for me to lead. So I thought I'd get worked on it."

He could see that she was frightened, that she didn't understand the distinction between a rope solo and a free solo. I appreciated his taking the time to explain the systems to her—how you hang a single strand from the anchor and use an ascender attached at your chest in case you fall. And, critically, you stop every ten feet or so to tie into the rope beneath you as a backup, which of course results in dragging a strand that gets in the way of your feet, among other annoyances. Nor listened carefully. She'd had a beer and was feeling pretty relaxed ten minutes before, but now her attention was fixed on Pete. She needed to understand how climbing 5.11 alone could ever be rendered safe. From time to time she looked at me to verify Pete's version. After a while she seemed reassured, if not satisfied, and then I asked Pete a couple of perfunctory questions about the route, whether it would go ground-up, about the gear and stuff—but what I didn't ask in front of Nor was how he had got the rope up there, whether he rapped down from above or soloed to the ledge where Kill Your Television ends. Not until later, when Nor disappeared to the restroom before bed, did I seek confirmation of what I suspected. I didn't even give him a chance to lie.

"Practice Makes Perfect or Pine Tree Eliminate?" I said. These were the easier routes to the left and right of Kill Your Television.

Pete was stirring the coals with a long stick. I was sitting at the picnic table, facing the fire. He met my eyes briefly, then returned to the hot charcoal at his feet.

"Don't," he said.

"Pete."

"It's my business. It's our business."

I was quiet.

Then he said, "Pine Tree. I floated it. Though I had to wait two hours for three guys to get off it. Didn't want them dropping anything on me."

Pine Tree was a straight-in hand crack, if stout at 5.8, perfectly manageable at this point but still not the kind of thing either of us had ever soloed unprotected. I couldn't tell if I was scared for Pete or just mad that he'd crossed a threshold without me, and when Nor returned I said goodnight and withdrew to my tent. It took me a while to get to sleep, and when I finally did I had a little nightmare—Pete and me in a car and suddenly going too fast, and yet laughing, too engaged by one another's conviviality to bother with the prospect of a crash. When I snapped awake I could hear them talking and quietly laughing from their tent on the other side of the campsite.

⌒

Only in retrospect do I see what a crossing it was: Pete elevating his approach, climbing unroped and insecure even if in service of setting up a top-rope on a nearby test-piece; Nor assuming a whole new level of wariness about Pete; and me aiding and abetting the secret. She never learned that he actually free soloed something on that Sunday, though even his climbing alone was to her a rent in something she'd thought inviolable, akin to driving drunk or diving in the shallow end, and she began to rely on me for trip reports and reassurance as to his prudence. So when they fell out of one another's orbit some two or three years later, I was relieved. I never had any illusions about controlling Pete, and now I didn't have to massage facts, much less pretend I was influential. And some part of me felt I'd won. I had Pete to myself again, and we went all in: weeks on the road, full months in Colorado, Utah, and California, living in campgrounds and out of the backs of cars from Chamonix to Chile, our bodies as rough and brown and hard to the touch as the rock we clung to. During that stretch—'84, '85, '86—we were frequently unroped, hyperaware, absurdly confident, and horribly vulnerable, light and fast and often at altitude, tethered to one another not actually but in quiet conspiracy, a confidence game shot through with exhilaration in the moment, though later, and often at night, the sort of thing you have to push to the side of your mind in order to rest.

For years after, I wondered whether I might have saved Nor a lot of heartache if I'd been forthcoming about Pete—not even about the incautious risks, just those we embraced as a matter of course. The third morning in North Conway was cool and blustery, and with a six-hour drive ahead of us we decided just to put a top-rope on adjacent hard 11's, Play Misty and Pete's Kill Your Television from the day before. This time I led the 5.8 to the ledge at mid-cliff where these routes end. I blew on my hands and tried a little too hard to keep calm, but even in the first twenty feet I couldn't get it out of my head that Pete had soloed this line, and when I stopped in awkward positions to place protection and felt even a bit stressed I told myself at least he hadn't had to fiddle with gear. Then I took stock of the exposure, the ways my toes were awkwardly wedged in the crack or tenuously straddling an edge, and I felt sick inside. The eighty-foot pitch may have taken twenty minutes but it felt like three hours, and when it was my turn to have a try at the hard routes I was useless, unable even to get into the crux sequences. Pete lapped both, then we packed our gear and headed down the trail.

I took the back seat on the drive home, purportedly to do homework. They were enjoying one another, taking turns driving and singing along to Woody Guthrie and the Grateful Dead—Pete had used some of his dad's money to outfit the Datsun with a good stereo. I held an open book on my lap but didn't read three pages. Pete was passing me by. He'd soloed a pitch I found gripping. He'd punched through to another grade and pulled up the ladder behind him. There had always been a gap between us, but now it seemed a chasm, and it would be only a matter of time before he'd find another partner. This was okay. I had other interests, and even if I appeared as devoted to our bigger objectives as he was, part of me was provisional and detached, with secret plans of my own I imagined I would execute in the event one of us got hurt or disillusioned, or worse—I'd even thought my way to that. The drive back to school was endless, the two of them chatting easily, laughing, the weather turning colder and windier the farther west we got. At a gas stop near Albany the air filled with flurries, which Nor greeted excitedly, her arms thrust into the air, while Pete turned to me with a pouting lower lip. I found myself clutching—thinking about training harder, even furtively. I would double down for five months and see where we were in spring. I didn't see yet that I had become indispensable in this other way, as cover for Pete.

So two years later, when they split up, I felt better. And when they started writing letters again in '87, and got back together in '88, well, I wondered if I'd failed her.

~

I work the holidays. With no one to see and celebrate with, and the nursing home paying time and a half, I spend a long shift there and do my tending with a measure of cheer—at Christmas in a simple Santa's hat and cotton beard. It's a hard time of year to be old. Residents with visitors have been anticipating them for days, while others, those sharp enough to know they don't have anyone, feel the sting of isolation all the more. What do Thanksgiving and Christmas and Easter do but galvanize the memory and stitch the years together? For most at New Horizons, holidays bring to mind the chilling proximity of lost things if not last things. Even the modest decorations we drag out for such occasions are faded and sagging.

So it wasn't until late on Christmas that I opened the present from Nor. I'd walked the two miles home under cold, clear starlight, scooting well off to the side of the road when a car passed. My apartment was warm but my fingers numb as I tore the wrapping paper. Inside, a guidebook, but a new one: *Fifty Day Hikes Worth Doing in the Eastern Sierra*. And a card:

Dec. 12, 2014
Merry Christmas Joe—
Come early this time or, better, stay later. We can hike a couple of these. It's a collection my friend put together.
I can't quite believe you're doing this with Will.
Hope you're having a warm time of it there, warm as possible.
                                                    Nor

P.S. Astrid's looking at Middlebury. There's a terrific women's team there. If she comes east in the spring for a visit, I'll holler. May need some help with #2 now too!

I kept the book on my bedside table and turned to it every evening for fifty nights in a sort of compline. I was familiar with many of the hikes and enjoyed rediscovering these, but all the new territory was intriguing—though it wasn't the promise of an aspen-lined canyon or sublime alpine bowl but the idea of being out there with Nor that left me equal parts eager and scared. Like climbing. I continued workouts on the equipment at home and at the college gym, but when I drove to Boston with Emery or, on a couple of sunny and not-too-cold weekend days in February when we met on campus to traverse the exterior of the math building, I found my thoughts of summer were less about Moriah and Will but of Nor and tart lemonade on the porch and what it might be like to watch a sunset together again and not get on a plane the next morning. Lundy Canyon, George Creek—any of these would do. I had been sure the gift was a memento, something she couldn't bear to throw out but was eager to part with, but the simple guidebook she'd sent was a forward-looking gesture that altered the way I looked forward.

⤴

As with dancers and musicians, the climbing partnership is an intimate affair. Preparation, challenge, performance—you embrace, enjoy, and suffer these together, you depend on one another entirely and cover for one another endlessly. But where musicians have the advantage of complementary instruments, and dancers their distinct choreography, climbers share everything, not least the unique challenges of every move on every route. Before long, the nature of the enterprise yields a stark fact: one partner, nearly always, is the stronger. This was Pete, and it was a circumstance about which he was expressly ambivalent. He coined the acronym SPS, for "Stronger Partner Syndrome," to describe what he believed were the limiting effects of imbalance on both climbers, but especially on the weaker partner. "A guide," he declaimed, "is one thing. That's prostitution. An above-board arrangement. No feelings attached, and ratified by an exchange of bills once you're all dirty and tired. But SPS is like, what? Maybe marriage, but a marriage all awry. The energies working for half the duo." In sum: a good partnership doesn't just support, but pushes and inspires, while an SPS arrangement tends to exaggerate respective strengths and weaknesses until the lesser climber might as well be a mere afterthought for all the influence he has over what they do and the style they do it in. In the best of arrangements one climber might be generally stronger but the other better with a particular technique, as in off-widths or slab climbing or technical face. In the worst—a not uncommon circumstance—the weaker partner devolves to a BB, Pete's lingo for "belay bitch."

With Pete I was only occasionally at risk of becoming the latter (if with Will there was never any pretense I could be anything but). Still, he was anxious—not just about my growing too comfortable in a lieutenancy, but also about his being held back. So more than a few times we split up, and always on account of some arrangement he cooked up with another pair in another dirty campground—with Lester and Bill at Indian Creek, with Rafael and Jean-Paul at Smith, with George and Aaron at Eldo. And he was right: partnered with someone weaker, I was more in charge, more challenged, and on balance a better climber in my own right. But neither as productive or satisfied as usual.

Pete's appetite was expansive—eight, ten, fifteen pitches a day, where most climbers are happy to tick four or a half dozen and head back to camp. I had the stamina and fervor to keep up with Pete, even once in a while to push him, but I didn't have the drive to impel anyone else.

And then Argentina, and Pete's hand. The plan had been to get back home and, on the basis of our Southern Hemisphere doings, be poised for a best-season-ever, but Pete's treatment was crippling. He was incapable of climbing until the sutures came out and found mere sunshine unbearable for all the antibiotics he was taking. Still, once he was switched over from IV treatments to pills we left LA and drove straight to the Valley. Pete sat under the trees in Camp 4, showing off his fat hand and telling war stories from Patagonia. I hooked up with others we knew and even a few strangers. By early summer, with the Valley dust-filled and overheated and Pete just starting to climb again, we headed to the high country with two objectives in mind: some long, fitness-building moderates for him, and a pair of first-ascent prospects we had discovered two years before, these on Peak 13,242, just north of Royce Lakes.

Off the meds but still sunlight-sensitive, Pete dressed like a Bedouin: hood and visor, dark glasses, and white fingerless gloves. Even the exposed knobs of his ankles ached in the sun, so he wore socks inside his climbing shoes. What an odd-looking creature at the other end of the rope—fingers and toes adhering to white granite and yards of fabric luffing about in the wind. But in just days we were swapping leads on easy routes and eager to test ourselves on the line we would name Mistral. It should have been a forgettable route, despite the gorgeous aspect that first drew us to it—a scimitar of an arête on the peak's northeast side. The rock was weirdly granular and brittle. Where most Sierra granite cleaves thoroughly and cleanly, this face had weathered in rounded patterns like folds of old skin, making for tricky foot placements and long, hard-to-protect sections. But we were committed, and in a single day we established the first seven hundred feet. Just beneath where the ridge joins the mountain proper and the route rears up, we stopped, left our gear on a ledge for the next day's push, and admired the much blanker and more compelling three-hundred-foot headwall above. It was on the rappel from there that the wind kicked up several notches, Pete was blown about like a spinnaker torn from its moorings, and "Mistral" came to mind.

This next would be my pitch—Pete had been out of commission for more than two months—but still, early the next morning, he did me the courtesy of asking: "You want it?" Of course, I said, but not until we were walking out of camp did I realize that I actually did, and not on account of anything I saw or expected, but just because I believed I was the better suited. This didn't occur to me until later. At the time I thought I was taking care of Pete, nursing him back. But really I was becoming Pete: the confident, insistent, stronger partner. I'd shown myself capable; I was exercising my capacities. He'd revealed a need; he was along for my ride. And in the morning, as he had done in like circumstances, I let him lead most of the way to our high point, establish a secure and comfortable belay beneath the steep section, and, upon my arrival, hand over a neatly arranged rack as a surgeon's assistant delivers a tray of instruments.

This was hardly the first time my climbing was abetted by Pete's watchful eyes, but this was different: not just the uncharted territory, nor the weird outfit enveloping him in a billowing canopy. Different because it made sense for me to be advancing our progress and completing the route.

Which I did, and it wasn't without fright or challenge. But neither was it very good. Even on this vertical section the cliff was disconcertingly friable, the holds rounded and knobby and the protection adequate but hardly abundant or easy to come by. I got my courage from two tied-off horns and staked my confidence on the rare combination of terrific fitness from months of constant climbing and Pete's odd status as supporting actor. And it would have been forgettable but for what happened on top.

I set up an anchor in an alcove to stay out of the wind, so I was over the lip and couldn't see Pete. I got him on belay by means of the tug-on-rope signals we used in hearing-impaired circumstances, and then I sat and settled down, taking in the rope a few inches at a time and hoping he'd find the pitch satisfying if not worthy. I admired the broad sweep of the granite basin more than a thousand feet below and the rippled sheets of wind on the Royce Lakes.

And then a heavy weight on the suddenly taut rope. Pete had fallen. But of course—he was out of practice, climbing on muscle memory a pitch that requires muscle. Or maybe a hold broke under his toes. In just seconds the rope was light again, and the few feet I pulled in indicated he was through the part that had given him trouble. Then again, and twice more: the rope strapped over the edges at my feet, the gear at the anchors strained for the sudden tension. There was no cussing or yelling from below, no indication of pain or frustration. Some stalling, longer periods of hanging on the rope, and then incremental progress. Pete spent twice as long following the pitch as I did on lead, but when he emerged onto the ridge he didn't appear anything but relaxed. He was neither winded nor wet with sweat. He sat in the shade of my little cave and calmly handed the gear to me piece by piece.

"Kind of grainy," I said.

"Kind of hairy," he said.

We changed into approach shoes and took some water.

"I counted five distinct cruxes," he said. "And how many flares?" Later, he allowed he might have died on that pitch if he'd tried to lead it, so crappy was the gear.

I had nothing. It seemed he was talking less about the particular climb than about what a finely tuned instrument a climber is and how out of sorts he was from his recent convalescence. We poked around on top for a summit register and, finding none, headed down a scree-filled gully on the north side of the peak, and in two hours we were back in camp. After a nap I felt fresh, already eyeing the other line we had in mind and gathering a rack for what appeared to be larger fissures and blockier, probably easier climbing.

From inside the tent, Pete said, "I'll need a day."

"I'll handle things," I said.

"No, I really do. I'm fried. And raw."

I knew exactly what he was talking about, but it was no less unthinkable—that I was pushing him, that he was having to go as hard as he could just to stay with me even as I was poised and rested and eager for the best and harder pitches.

We were almost five years in at that point, and this inversion of SPS didn't last long. Nor did it ever happen again. By September he was back in shape, and I don't recall a balance-point period of perfect compatibility we should have enjoyed before Pete once again commandeered our climbing. But he never again sought to moderate the discrepancy by climbing with others and only rarely made noise about the SPS phenomenon. The second route we did, following the rest day, was technically easier but physically more demanding than the first, and in the aftermath whenever I needed a break I'd find the photograph I took of Pete from above, his arm, shoulder, and one leg wedged in a fissure of bewildering, exhausting size so that all you see is a rope stretched down to a plume of fabric that seems flowing out of the rock itself. He was so useless afterward I had to undress him for bed, and a few months later and ever after, safely established again as the weaker partner, I needed only to produce the picture to get a groan, an expression of sympathy, and some kind of adjustment to the agenda.

⤳

I heard from Will just twice—first around Thanksgiving, an Ansel Adams postcard of Mount Williamson: *"Namesake covered in snow. Moriah too. See you on the other side of the melt. News alert: sometime this winter everyone will be watching Tommy and Kevin free the Dawn!"* Then again in early June, and this time just a scrap of paper he slipped into an envelope: *"Joe—Got your flight info. See you in Reno. N.A. 2: Dawn done! How great is that?"*

I was aware of the latter, had read about it online: Tommy Caldwell's project to free climb a line on El Cap made famous for the siege style of its first ascent. That one, in 1970, was a twenty-eight-day push, a rescue-defying, bolt-profligate pounding of the Dawn Wall by Warren Harding and Dean Caldwell. No maneuver in modern American mountaineering so cleaved climbers into two distinct camps, the purists and the summit-seeking rebels, and no gesture did so much to establish the context for the modern soloist—Bachar, Croft, Hersey, and Potter, only one of whom survives into middle age, and now Honnold. Tommy and Kevin weren't of this latter tribe—they'd been roped up—but they'd pushed Sharma-like grades on the biggest stone and stage of all, projecting dicey sequences on nearly featureless rock, and because they were sponsored professional climbers, there had been cameras in the meadow and more than a little attention by the regular press during their much-publicized ground-to-summit push. There's never an Olympic year in rock climbing; whatever the latest and greatest are doing, you pursue your objective on your own terms and in your own arena, and if you learn about the great achievements at all it's well after the fact and through the grapevine or from one of a couple of glossies that are always at the edge of going out of business. That we'd known about the Dawn Wall so far in advance suggested this was something else—a bold and worthy endeavor, yes, but also a production and some kind of marketing machine.

I wondered how Will really felt about this, devoting his own energies to completing a remote and obscure High Sierra route of his father's with his dad's elderly friend instead of a fellow hotshot who could, like Kevin for Tommy, join him in the free climbing both to appreciate and verify the bona fides. But I was above these scruples, and overly invested myself. Will had several years ago positioned himself outside the minuscule if crowded corner of the climbing scene that involves cameras and reports and documentation of derring-do, and now, for this project, he had elected me to accompany him. Whether he was envious of the Dawn Wall business or merely impressed—none of this mattered. For this turn, anyway, he was stuck with me.

⤳

Reno in mid-July was ablaze. Wildfires closed 395 in two places, news I picked up on a phone message from Will. He suggested I get a room at one of the cheap casinos downtown and sit tight to await further instructions. I took my duffels to the curb and got into the first free shuttle, this one to The Virginian.

Vegas has tourists. Reno, refugees. I walked the pavement by the Truckee River, meandered through a homeless encampment, and spent two afternoons in the Washoe County Library, mostly vacant but for a few families coming in and out to exchange books and, in an alcove of comfortable chairs, napping drifters.

Like others of the downtown hotels, The Virginian encases a vast, windowless gaming floor, colorfully lit and noisily chirping whether there are twenty or two hundred gamblers at play. And not a clock anywhere, the card tables and craps rings as likely to be clustered with activity at 3:00 A.M. as at 3:00 P.M. At one of the slot machines, a lady didn't mind my watching. She sat half-perched on the stool, her hair arranged into a willowy cotton ball, nails long and lacquered. She kept a cigarette burning in the ashtray but rarely paused to take it up. The dollar slot seemed perfectly designed to tease her along with a periodic pair of lemons or tangerines and subsequent, burping payout, but it was clear this game goes only in one direction. Her little bucket of tokens grew visibly shallower in the ten minutes I stood nearby. When I took a step to move along, she said: "You just doling out bad luck?"

I must have blushed. I kept still.

She fed the machine and hit the button. "Won't be much longer, now."

A dozen pulls later she got three bunches of grapes and the machine lit up, grinding and expelling tokens, coins piling upon coins until I was helping her pick them up off the floor. An attendant brought a second bucket, and other casino-wanderers gathered to admire the gleaming bonanza.

Everything tidied up again, she turned to me. "Belinda," she said, extending her hand. "Thanks."

I took her cold fingers in mine. "Joe. I'd say 'Good luck' but I don't want to jinx you."

"Don't believe in it, Joe," she said. "Anyone who believes in luck here is a sucker."

"Then why thanks?" I said.

"It's entertainment, is all. Sometimes the entertainment goes a little better with an audience."

She winked at me, took a long, satisfied pull from her cigarette, and slipped back onto her stool. She was set for another couple hours before whatever modest initial investment was exhausted and she too could move on.

When I got into the lobby, I saw I had a message from Will. He was headed to South Lake Tahoe and suggested I get there on a casino shuttle. We could spend two or three days cragging—"*Get our bearings,*" he said, "*before we get to work.*" I packed, hauled my things around the corner to Harrah's, and inside of an hour was headed up Highway 50 east of the Tahoe Basin. Others on board the minibus, none with luggage, wondered at my heavy duffels and less tidy dress.

I hadn't come all this way to stay in casinos, but when I found they were practically giving away rooms I took one for the night. Will was delayed—horrible backups just getting to Highway 89 on account of the fires—so I told him my room number and spent another evening wandering about. At least up here there is the magnificent lakefront, families of ducks chugging along the shore.

After midnight I heard a knock at the door and stumbled there in my underwear.

"Room service," Will said. Framed by the bright light of the hallway, I couldn't see but the outlines of his shaggy hair. "Holy Jesus," he said. "What did you do to Joe?"

It took me a second to get it.

"Did you hurt him?" he asked. He carried his pack on one shoulder, entered the dark room, and tossed his things onto the bed by the window.

I crawled back under the blanket.

"Seven hours," he said, pulling his pants off.

"Wow. That's love."

"No, that's bad luck, or stupid planning."

"Don't believe in luck," I said, recalling my friend in Reno.

"Well, I know you believe in stupid plans. Or at least used to. Anyway, I'm glad you're here."

"Glad you're here, too. Even if here is here."

In the morning we skipped the mounds of sausage at the casino in favor of Starbucks on the California side of town. On two good feet Will wasn't the measured, wounded warrior I remembered but a happy dancer, supple and light on his toes. He also seemed quicker to smile and easier to laugh. Outside it was cool and clear, but Will thought it would get too warm at Sugarloaf, the massive granite formation twenty miles west.

"Grand Illusion," I said, referencing the area's very famous, very hard pitch.

"Our illusion's plenty grand," he said. "Let's try this little sport cliff. It's closer. I heard it's pretty good."

After assembling quickdraws, a rope, and water on the shoulder of Highway 89, Will reached into the back of the truck bed to move my duffels into the cab. "Whoa. You get a big payday?"

A steep hike up a scree gulley on the east side of the valley got us to the base of a pair of hundred-foot cliffs, the Distillery and Detox Walls. And here a further indication, Will's climbing, of just how hampered he had been last summer. He was quick, smooth, and fearless. He used his toes like the front points on crampons. In climber-speak this type of precision is called "quiet feet." Will's were silent. By noon we had ticked eight of the cliff's ten routes, me leading the easiest—Methadone, Jonesin', the Betty Ford Route—Will taking the others, and each of us climbing everything. The 5.11s gave me trouble, but I managed, and it was all very encouraging to be so efficiently disposed and roped up together again.

In the early afternoon we drove south to a swimming hole on the Carson River within view of the towering, lichen-splotched spires Will had in mind for the following day. We plunged into a deep pool in the cold stream, then lay naked on the warm rock. Will was brown as a wild animal.

"Seriously," Will said, looking at me. "Steroids?"

With the roar of the water beside us we had to talk loudly. I mentioned he seemed healthy, too. Maybe more cheerful than last summer.

"Her name's Al," Will said. "Or Allison."

A while later he leaned forward and smiled. "She's not from central casting, but we did do the Harding Route on Conness last week, to celebrate ten months."

"Tell me," I said.

"She's a bit older. An EMT. Solid on rock."

"Sounds serious."

"Oh man. Like nothing I've ever known."

"How'd she end up on the Eastside?"

"Like everyone. SoCal refugee." He chortled. "Mom introduced us. Al's at the hospital a lot, hauling the incoming. She's got a place at June Lake. Or pays rent there, anyway. But since winter she's pretty much been at the cabin. So you're in a tent this time, or at Mom's."

I wanted to get the climbing business done first.

"You're doing better at the house," he said.

"Nice. I could use some help with your sister."

"Thank the boyfriend. She's gone gooey. Still training, studying and all that. But you can just tell, she's not all there."

"A virus in the Hunter children," I said.

"I thought Mom was catching it, too. Someone she met in winter. Seems to have cooled off, though."

The river went quiet, and I became aware of the warm wind blowing down the canyon and cottonwood leaves shaking overhead.

Will lay back down. I closed my eyes too, trying to adjust to the sudden stir in my gut. A splash followed, Will taking another dip. Then he stood before me, drying himself with his T-shirt and stepping into shorts and sandals.

We found a place for the night nearby in a Forest Service campground. He had brought a stove, a few pieces of wood for a fire, and a couple of camp chairs. He also had fishing line, hooks, and salmon eggs. While I got dinner going he set out a couple of lines, and before the pasta was ready he had two little trout to go with the noodles and cheese.

"Woodfords here," he said, gesturing to outcroppings on the ridge behind us. "It's one of those areas, you know: best climbing you've never heard of."

"Sounds good."

"What was that, in your day? For you and Dad."

"Needles. The Sequoia Needles."

"This isn't The Needles," he said.

"Thankfully."

"The long approach?"

"No. I liked that. It's just there's nothing, well, easy there."

He was gutting the fish. "Was it ever, with him, easy? Or always go, go, go?"

Will arranged the splayed bellies of the fish in a pan to sizzle.

"There wasn't a lot of standing around feeling full and satisfied."

"I'm like that. Except once you've been on the comp scene, with all those eyes on you, and people in your business, other stuff feels casual. Even bouldering was a circus."

"Well, yeah, it's not like skiing. Or running. No one cares about climbing, 'cept climbers."

"Someone cares about Nordic skiing?"

"There's someone at the finish line," I said. "Someone with a clipboard and a watch. He cares."

"Plenty of those in El Cap Meadow last winter. And some cameras."

He had a point.

"It's different," I suggested. "Tommy was at it for years, and no one cared till the end. It was a Moby Dick, and that was the chase."

Will didn't disagree, but neither did he appear to be all that interested. He assembled a plate of noodles for me and with two fingers put a fish alongside. We sat in the camp chairs, resting our feet on the grill.

He nodded at the little pile of wood. "I cart these boards around and never have a fire."

"You come by that honestly, too. 'Only for warmth,' he used to say."

Will set his plate on the ground. "You know, that's not why I asked you to do this with me. Mom thinks she engineered the whole thing."

"Easy. I'm here. I don't need everyone squeaky clean and clear about motives."

"No, I mean it. People who know what we're up to, there aren't many, they think it's all sweet. Me getting a chance to hang with my dad's best friend."

He paused, chewed, and seemed to expect I'd have something to say to rebut this angle.

He continued. "All I'm saying is I meant what I said: it looks like a quality route, I want to finish it, and you had first rights of refusal. And now you've gone all, what's his name? John Long?"

"Largo."

"Him."

He stripped his fish of its spine and ribs with a single pull. "Okay. So what's the deal with campfires?"

"He wasn't religious about it. We had blazers at the solstice parties. But most of the time he felt, why bother adding to the smoke?"

I told him about the early reports Pete had read about the "greenhouse effect." "Ever heard of eschatology?" I said.

Will shook his head.

"One of your dad's things. It's at an intersection—religion, philosophy, science. In college he got quite into it. For someone who didn't think himself so hot a student, he was fairly decorated. He had a professor counseling him to go to grad school."

"But climbing got in the way?"

"Of grad school, but it wasn't just academic. It was reality, even then. Now it's just better documented—the melting glaciers, rising seas. Extinctions. Give him that much. He loved things. Things he didn't want to lose."

I could see Will wondering about this, how someone who loves things he doesn't want to lose takes a seven-hundred-foot fall.

"So Dad could have been a professor," he said. "Instead of the guy the professor pays to haul him up the East Face of Mount Whitney."

This seemed far-fetched, but I didn't complicate the picture.

"But you two weren't in touch so much later on."

"Not enough. But we made a point of it, and we were honest with each other, which is more than I can say for a lot of us. Men, anyway."

Will adjusted his feet as though settling in and wanting more. But then he sprang up, took my plate, and walked off to the spigot to clean our dishes. When he came back he shared options for the morning on pages he'd printed from an online guide. We agreed to "climb the stars," the most favorably rated routes, and before dusk we retreated to our tents.

The evening air was warm and fresh, a breeze nipping at the fabric of the tent. I lay on top rather than inside my sleeping bag, listening to the stream, tired from the day's doings but not too sleepy to wonder whether I'd made a crippling mistake in imagining myself into Nor's life these many months since winter.

⌐∽

In the morning Will showed me how Moriah would go.

He had spent more than two months with his foot in the cumbersome cast and wasn't able even to walk without discomfort until winter, but the limited mobility and long sabbatical from climbing only intensified his training. He got to the point where even legless workouts were aerobic—lap after lap on crack machines with just one foot, reps of pull-ups with weights strapped to his chest. Hangboard routines he'd found torturous in the past became "practically casual." But all of this was incidental, in his view, to what he did at night: the nettlesome ritual of rehearsing in his mind the choreography that got him to his high point, the fifteen or twenty gestures above the top of the pillar to where he was finally stymied. He slept restlessly, for weeks, and if he blamed the aching foot he suspected his dreams were the real trouble—which frequently had him stranded beneath that thirty-foot band of lightly overhanging rock he'd studied so carefully before lowering off for good last summer.

"Then, right around Thanksgiving," he said, "I got it. So clean and natural I didn't even wake up."

"You got it." I didn't mean to sound skeptical.

"We'll see, of course. But it's the foot. Not the injury, the placement." Waiting by the stove for coffee water to boil, he showed me a sequence that started with his left heel on the edge of the picnic table: "Lever here, a back-step with the right, reach through to that sideways crimp, but with the left hand, not like I kept doing it last time. A long reach, possibly desperate, but nothing I haven't done elsewhere."

"Some dream."

"Maybe all it is. Helped me sleep, anyway. And then I was with Al and didn't have any more trouble sleeping."

But I wasn't doubtful. I'd been haunted in a like manner, if never for anything so improbable and impressive, and climbing lore was full of these tales: Kauk unlocking the solution to Midnight Lightning. Lynn Hill deciphering the Changing Corners way up on El Cap. Everyone relishes the onsight send, but legends require failure, and blood. The climbs that stay with you have kept you company for such a good long while before you complete them you can't remember in the aftermath which was the essence—the climbing, or all the angst and preparation and problem-solving. Will was eager to get back there and get going, so I was surprised and even a little disappointed when he said he first needed some time to help Ricky move his equipment into a new shop. "I want to be careful, too," Will said. "Which means no hurrying. Thinking two days."

We found Woodfords as advertised—uncontrived, fun lines on steep rock. Will was as generous as a guide, giving me the pick of leads and not objecting when one after another I elected the better pitches. And part of me was reveling—I was nothing special, but compared to last summer's apoplexy this was something to enjoy, and I felt a measure of the old pride for being able to shoulder a load, however modest. By midafternoon we'd had our fill, and after another dip in the Carson we headed south through the smoky evening, finally intersecting with 395 just after nightfall. With fires raging to the north the highway was almost empty. The moon rose over the eastern hills, and as we snaked over Conway Summit and down into the Mono Basin a long veil of white satin shimmered across still water. Will pulled the truck onto dirt east of the highway and we stood outside to stretch. Down by the shore tufa towers cast shadows in the moonlight and gulls cackled in the night, the warm air rank with dead brine shrimp.

"What's that thing you said? What Dad studied?"

"Eschatology. End-of-times stuff."

"Paiutes have been here forever. He figure them into the equation, about everything falling apart?"

"Canaries and mines. That's how he saw it."

"Ricky's girlfriend gets a check every few months, something to do with the casino in Bishop." He touched his toes and raised his arms to the sky. "She looks about as Paiute as I do."

"You might pass."

"Her mom says it used to be something you tried to hide. Now you have to prove it, least if you want the check."

In another hour we were grinding up the steep dirt to Will's cabin. Al's car was there. Will kissed her bumper with his own. As we unpacked the truck she emerged in pajamas and a headlamp. He refused her offer for help, and she went out back. I assumed she was using the toilet, but when I unfurled my things for the night I saw they'd set up a tent for me, now glowing with a battery-powered lamp. The pines, the quiet, sore fingers and fatigue—a happy, familiar formula.

In the morning we sat outside the cabin in camp chairs. Al had round, expressive eyes and the copper-tinted skin of someone at home on a sun-bathed cliff. Most of her hair was tucked underneath Will's trucker hat, but the ends spilled out the back and sides and these too were sun-stained. Will told her what we'd been up to the past two days.

"So you've been on the scene a while, I hear," she said.

"On it, sure. Not of it."

"He's a hair-splitter," Will said.

I sipped the coffee. "How about you? How'd you make it up here?"

"Same as Will. My dad."

Will protested. "Got some genes from my dad. Al got the real deal. Hers took her up the East Face of Whitney when she was twelve. A couple of years ago she returned the favor: East Butt of El Cap. Those are family values."

"Dad was a Tahquitz, J-Tree guy," she said. "An engineer. Loves the gear. Now they're all into surfing, my brothers and him."

She got up and went inside. I pulled the smaller and heavier of my duffels from the back of Will's truck and dropped it between our chairs. Soon Al was popping out with one pancake after another, a grainy version of her own devising that clearly pleased Will. He gestured to the bag with his fork. "So much for light and fast.'"

I unzipped it and pulled out a smaller, interior sack whose side bore a faded logo: "Great Pacific Iron Works."

"Proto-Patagonia," Will said. "Intriguing."

"The gear, too," I said. "Most of it, anyway. He never threw anything out."

"Dad's?"

I nodded.

"Mom said she gave it away."

"To me, a few months after. She probably doesn't even remember."

Will dragged the bag closer. He pulled out a frayed, home-made gear sling that, but for old-style stoppers and a few oval carabiners, was lined with what you'd expect on a mid-'90s rack. He held it up and ran his fingers through the gear as though assessing a jeweled necklace. "I played with this stuff when I was little. He'd walk in from wherever and drop it on the floor."

Al stood behind him, her hand light on his neck.

"Smells the same." He engaged the action on a couple of the old cams, which were sticky. "And these blocky stoppers."

"He said they never improved them."

Will pulled out a second sling with a set of first-generation Friends, their rigid stems drilled with holes to lighten them.

"They got better," I said. "But we still used the old ones."

Also in the bag were pitons and etriers, a hammer and other aid gear. Slings whose knots Pete had tied, and odds and ends of webbing whose ends he'd burned with a match. Finally a harness, the gear loops frayed and droopy. A belay device was clipped to the side and a chalk bag tied at the back.

Will stood. He stepped into the harness, wriggled it up, and cinched the waist-belt tight.

"Think it's safe?" he said.

Al looked doubtful.

"It's probably fine," he said, unclasping it and letting it fall to the ground. "But it's stupid."

He looked at me. "What's your point, Joe?"

"No point. Just returning it."

Will piled most of the gear back onto the bag.

I reached for the set of stoppers. "Put the number five on our rack, anyway. Your dad placed it all the time. Said it never held a fall."

"I know one time he didn't place it."

"Or don't," I said. "Your call."

Will dropped the rest onto the open bag and left it in the dirt between our chairs. "I'm headed to Ricky's. You want to stick around here, or should I take you to Mom's now?"

"I'll take him," Al said. "I don't start till noon."

She followed Will to the truck and stood a few minutes beside him. Then he drove off.

When she came back I nodded to the open duffel. "That didn't go well."

"No." She started gathering the plates and mugs. "But how could it?"

I wondered what he'd said to her.

"He wants to get back up there with you. You know how that goes, pushing aside the other layers. This," she said, nodding at the bag. "It's always here."

After ferrying dishes to the side of the cabin, she said, "I know Nor encouraged him to contact you. But that's not the whole story. He probably didn't even know when he wrote you, but now he does. You know, about being up to something more than the route."

She stood behind the chair Will had been sitting in, her hands folded at her waist.

"He talks about you. You and his dad. It's all, I guess, more available."

"Same here."

"Tell him. I think he'd find it, well, reassuring. Anyway, he said to tell you he's aiming for Tuesday. Walk in on Tuesday."

Al went inside, then she disappeared. I moved into the shade beside Will's training equipment. Will had left me the topo Pete had started, now embellished with his own drawings and comments. "Improve it," he said, handing me a sheet of paper decorated with detail far greater than anything I could have recalled, and not just because only he and his father knew the hard section that had shut us down. I couldn't tell who wrote what on the creased and dirty paper—their handwriting angular and neat. Next to the start of the third pitch one of them had written "small TCU," indicating the sketchy protection on that short lower crux, and other places were scribbled with laudatory remarks, "clean corner" and "fun, steep!" Like his father, Will had this uncanny grasp of a route's dimples and cavities. Where most see mountains and cliffs, they saw intricate features and, closer still, the cracks and buttresses and lines of weakness that portend a passage, and then, on the rock, the distinguishing, often cryptic arrangements of holds—a jagged sidepull, a solution pocket. They could also enumerate from memory the gear they used, not just which pieces but which order and why and what to save for where. I might register a route's character, but Pete and Will recorded the useful data.

Across the top of the topo Will had written, "A Fine Line (unfinished)—First attempt: P. Hunter and J. Holland, 1989. Second: J. Holland and W. Hunter, July 2014."

Sometime later Al trotted up the drive in running shorts and a sports bra, skin glistening. Earlier she'd seemed compact, another of the proverbial gymnast-climbers. Now she appeared looser and longer if no less composed. I moved to the front of the cabin so she could shower, and soon we were putting my things into the back of her car. She wore a blue jumpsuit, scissors and bandages stuffed into bulging pockets. Easing her car down Will's steep drive, she told me she'd seen Nor at the hospital the day before, and she was excited I was back.

"How much does she worry?" I asked.

"She's a mom. It's the same thing I hear in my mom's voice,

even if I don't always want to. How grateful she is my brothers are into surfing."

Where the road bends close to the lake I could see picnickers by the shore, already settled at tables not far from where we had held the service for Pete.

"It's nothing about Will," Al said. "You know that. It's just climbing, something about it. Even when a sport climber makes a mistake, usually dropping a partner or something else pretty dumb, it gets tabulated in the wrong column. Like it's Alex Lowe on Shisha Pangma."

Neither of us referenced the unique shadow Pete cast on Nor's worries.

Pulling into Nor's driveway, she said, "I look forward to more."

"Same." I grabbed my bag and backpack from her backseat.

She leaned across to the passenger side window and took my hand. "I might see you again before you guys head off, but if I don't, I hope it goes well. That it's whatever it needs to be to make you happy. Meaningful or whatever."

"Beautiful's good. Maybe doable, too."

～

My life at home, predictable and prosaic as a monk's, suits me poorly for a period of such concentrated activity as the days that followed. I had to remind myself several times just to go with where I was and hope to remember a few things I might arrange and understand later. When I heard Will's truck Tuesday before dawn, I was in a restless half sleep. Will and Nor and I converged at the front door, and after a brief exchange of goodbyes he and I headed out just as the black night to the east was recast in cold layers of dark blue. We were quiet. In the previous forty-eight hours we had talked only on the phone. While he was busy with Ricky I had used the truck to go to the market and spent long stretches in the garage sorting and packing our food and gear. Nor was enduring a not-uncommon busy stretch at the hospital—summer visitors falling to earth from their mountain bikes and skateboards—so I saw her mostly in passing, though one late evening she brought me a sandwich and sat on a bear bin while I ate. If it didn't feel easy or natural in the way I had fantasized about in the winter, there was still something more than gracious about Nor's attention, maybe just tenderness.

Around Crowley Lake I noticed Will tracking his mirror. "I don't mind when Clyde disappears from view," he said.

I glanced at the mirror on my side. The Minarets were gone.

"Not that I'm thinking about him every time I see it," he said. "But still . . ."

"Some monument."

"Exactly. An eleven-thousand-foot headstone."

Will slowed a bit. He sat lower in his seat and lifted his foot to the dash. "You know, I've never done it."

"You don't have to."

"I know I don't." Then, more quietly, he said, "I couldn't tell Mom."

"No." I felt my hands flash with moisture. "But if you need somebody to tell . . ."

Will interrupted. "You said you saw him just once more, right? After you left here?"

We were bending toward Bishop now, still tucked in the shade of the Whites but with Humphreys' proud summit blazing in the first light off our shoulder. In moments we'd slow to a crawl through town, catch a whiff of bread from Schat's, then roll past Miguel's and Wilson's and other venues Pete and I frequented. The Sportsman's Lodge where I'd made beds had fresh paint and a La Quinta sign out front, and a block farther a few backpackers were already lined up outside the ranger station for permits. I didn't launch right in, but over the course of the morning I told Will about Pete's visit in '95, when I was in my first year at the church and he drove his mom through Vermont. His mother's health wasn't good. Something spooky, autoimmune-related, and she wanted to see the fall colors once more while she could still get around.

Pete let me know they were on their way, but I didn't expect them that Sunday. They slipped into the back during the organ prelude and I didn't notice them until I was at the pulpit for the prayer of invocation. It took me a moment—it had been seven years—but the interval contained a void sufficient for me to play through possibilities: a youngish man, perhaps a local farmer or maybe even a professor, someone new to the area. With his aunt or mother. No, those eyes, that's *his* mother. Pete's mom. Pete. And then the part I didn't tell Will: that after he died the gap was there all the time, a confused space of looking and trying to locate but never landing, never settling on features I knew as well as my own and then, the recognition, and his reciprocated smile. In the feverish space after he died I wrote down most of what I could remember. But then I learned to train my mind elsewhere, to shut out the vacancy. It took half a dozen years, coming back here that summer Carol was in Berkeley, to reclaim enough of his territory even to begin to look again. So I felt something of what Will contended with all the time—growing up amid the loss and the looking but without a topography of firm memory on which to know and exorcise grief. For me, Pete was right here, amid sage and stars and the unmistakable signature of the Sierra crest. For Will, he was everywhere and nowhere.

After the Sunday service, Pete and his mom were last in the line of two dozen or so parishioners I greeted at the door. We hugged. He felt for my arms underneath my vestments, not sizing me up but just confirming I was in there. Then he placed his palm against my chest and said, "Divorcees allowed. I respect that."

I gave a start, but when I saw the confusion on his mother's face I understood he was joking—referencing not him and Nor, but us, him and me.

We stood awhile in front of the church, getting caught up, and when they circled back to the Upper Valley a couple days later we met for dinner in Lyme. "You were barely one year old," I told Will. "He laid pictures of you on the table in the restaurant, which your grandmother and I studied. She fingered them closely. At some point she said, 'I hope I get to know him.'"

"And she's the one at my high school graduation," Will said.

"Yeah, amazing." She outlived Pete by sixteen years.

"It's cool you guys could just pick up again."

"We were a long way from the pinyons. Further than either of us expected, I think. Your dad had you. I had this tiny church. All the sudden everything feels like a long time ago."

What I didn't tell Will was that Pete seemed a little subdued, even solemn, which I attributed to his mother—to her declining health, and her being so matter-of-fact about a nearness to the end. Nor figured into our exchanges very little. I remember her coming up only in regard to one medical angle or another on Pete's mom. Still, he seemed eager to get back home. His face was tanned from Sierra sun, his hair bleached and a little ratty at the ends, and his hands were still leathery and cracked while mine had relaxed into soft, ministerial harmlessness. If we'd each assumed domestic duties, his did little or nothing to cleanse him of these touches of the wild.

"So that's all?" Will said. "The next time you're out here it's for the funeral?"

"We talked on the phone."

Will looked at me in a way that seemed envious.

"He'd tell me about mountains, routes, snippets of what he was up to. He'd always talk about you, little proud-dad stuff. I remember he described having you at some crag."

Will nodded. "That's about all I remember. Horseshoe, Clark Canyon. Even Gong Show. Can you believe he'd haul me up there? Toys too."

"He took you backpacking."

"That's the one everyone likes, the normal-dad story. Mom says we were 150 yards from the car. I don't remember. Campfire, marshmallows. Teddy bear in a tent." He looked off at the eastern hills. "No projecting climber whose kid's covered in dirt at the base of the crag. And you get to forget for a minute he'll be dead in a year."

The upper third of the crest turned amber, and Will slowed down. We'd be leaving the pavement in a few miles, heading west on a rutted road that ends where the mountains rear up out of the desert, then hiking up the canyon under heavy loads for the rest of the day. Will grew quiet. He seemed to savor these last moments of comfort before his attention shifted entirely to what we intended rather than to what he called "all that slop" of what he doesn't remember or never knew. On the dirt he drove in first gear, not much faster than a walking pace, and when he got out to secure the hubs he stood a moment beside the truck to admire the canyon whose mouth was pink with the morning sun.

I don't know if we exchanged ten more words that day. The hike last year was plenty strenuous but unfreighted with expectation. This time we had an agenda, or Will did anyway, and even with the first steps from the truck he surrendered to the tacit anxiety and concentration that is the climber's familiar province in advance of something you know will tax you—not just in all the ways you've dreamed about and planned for but in so many others you can only worry over. It's a visceral stir of anticipation and a constant conversation you have with yourself: I'm ready. Ready as I can be. But what if it's beyond me? I can aid it if I have to. But if there's bad gear, or no gear? Or the weather turns? Pete called this the gallows walk—less because you feel you may be walking to your execution than on account of the light-making remarks and stabs at humor climbers indulge in these circumstances that are clumsily rendered and grossly inadequate. So this seemed another of the gestures Will inherited from his dad: rather than feign calm, he consented to the focus and fret, and as we worked our way up along the stream on the narrow mountaineers' path he drew farther and farther away from me until I could only occasionally see his light frame under the giant gray backpack, ducking through a boulder field or skirting a stand of willows, and finally, for the last several hours, not at all.

৹

Three days earlier, on Sunday morning, I had been deep into the *LA Times* at Nor's dining room table when Astrid emerged, dressed in a tracksuit and pulling her hair back into a tight ponytail.

"Hey," she said.

"You're at it early."

"Long run. Have to eat first."

She pulled several jars out of the fridge and cupboard and started scooping things into the blender.

"How about you today?" she said.

"Your mom and I, taking a hike. Other than that, just getting stuff together for this week. Will's helping Ricky."

"Ricky," she said. "Will really collects them."

I figured "them" included me too.

Astrid poured a purple smoothie into a plastic cup. "You know, they really like you. Will and Mom."

"Thank you," I said, sitting back in my chair. "Thanks for telling me."

"I guess what I mean is, I wasn't super-friendly. Last summer."

"Stranger shows up. Gets more attention than anyone deserves."

"Okay, but maybe more about Mom feeling Will is safer with you, and I'm just thinking whatever climbing he does, you know, it just stresses her out. Especially when he disappears for days."

"You haven't changed your mind."

"You know what's helped?"

I didn't.

"Al." She tapped the side of the cup with a spoon. "She's got all the same stuff with her mom, and it was like I finally got it. It's just normal. And not just 'cause, like Al says, there are so many other scary things he could be into."

I hesitated, but then said it: "That your dad didn't do."

"Yeah." She paused. "Imagine, for Mom."

"I do."

Astrid stepped into the laundry room, then headed out in a white hat and brightly colored shoes. "See you, Joe."

When Nor emerged I was in the garage scooping cereal and powdered milk into smaller bags per Will's instructions. He'd covered the floor with two large tarps, one littered with piles of climbing gear, the other with camping equipment and food, and on each a list of what we needed.

We hugged.

"Sorry it's so late," she said. "Even Astrid's out and about before me."

She turned back into the house. "Let me grab some toast," she said. "How about the crest? I haven't been up there this summer. Flowers should be out."

"Great."

Nor threw energy bars and water into a daypack and tossed me a bottle of sunscreen.

We parked in Nor's friend's driveway above Lake George. The trail starts nearby in a dry meadow with lupine and mule ears and gently rises through a yellowing forest of dying lodgepoles. "Beetles here," Nor said. "Same as Yosemite."

The air was acrid and sappy, the forest floor padded with fallen needles.

"Julie says it's like living in a box of kindling. She gets a wisp of smoke, just someone's weenie roast by the lake, and her heart's racing."

Pete again, in the alacrity of Nor's gate, in the cobalt sky, and down here among the dead trees. Even in the '80s he believed it was climate change. Swaths of brown pines and piles of beetle casings. A few years after I left he ran into the Tuolumne ranger we'd see in summer, a shy, ruminative woman who looked the other way when she saw us carrying our sleeping bags into the woods by Pothole Dome. The science was in, she told Pete: a die-off so vast a park biologist predicted the range would one day be botanically akin to Nebraska—dry grasses where conifers once thrived. Only the rocky alpine realm would bear any likeness to the Sierra John Muir and Clarence King explored a hundred years before us. "Minus the glaciers, of course," Pete added.

Walking, Nor was quiet. Only later did it occur to me she was working herself up to say something—something she wanted told. Still, it took a couple of hours for her to get going. Not until we'd ascended the switchbacks above the trees and were stopped on broken, metamorphic plates. We stood still for a moment, looking west, where Clyde's black face cut the horizon.

"He figured I was next, you know," she said, continuing up the trail.

She was in front of me, and in the wind I strained to hear everything she said.

"Pete," she repeated. "He wanted us to be partners. After you left."

Nor stopped again. "He had this idea that we'd be one of those climbing couples. Not right away. First it took a while for him to get it that he wasn't going to find anybody else, anyone to replace you. So then me, next in line. I was deep into the hospital, but you have to come home some of the time." Looking off at the higher peaks, she seemed pained for what she remembered. "And we needed something, something together. So I tried."

"Just This," I said, referencing a route attributed to Hunter-Rhodes.

"That was a good one," she smiled. "Down there on Lone Pine Peak. As good as it got—just this day. But Pete was very insistent about, you know, the rules: swapping leads, sharing everything. He had me drilling bolts for anchors, which took five times longer. He was guiding then, so there was this rigid distinction between 'partner' and 'client.' It was nonsense, of course. He was driving everything. Finding the routes, dealing with the gear. Sometimes he'd pre-clean the lower pitches."

"Making the rules," I added.

"He knew better than to exhaust me on that score. I did as well as I could, but whenever I felt measured, I let him have it. And we both knew I could never be depended on to care as much as he did."

"A real party."

"But you know who really made me mad?"

I stopped to tie my shoe. I thought to myself, *When I was with Pete, who'd I get mad at—besides Pete?*

Nor didn't notice I'd paused, and now she was a ways ahead, ambling along the rocky trail, swift and relaxed, possibly still talking. I stayed for a while and watched the rippled back of her windshirt. She had that darting energy again, the eager, breathless aspect I recognized from when we were young and she always knew where she was headed and most of the time seemed glad for it.

By the time she stopped and looked for me I was two hundred yards back. Nor threw her hands up and started in my direction. She turned the bill of her hat around to keep it from blowing off and leaned into the wind, hair whipping around her head.

I started as well, and we met in the middle.

"You okay?" she said.

"Shoelace."

"Where was I?"

"Mad at someone. You were telling me about being mad at someone other than Pete."

"You!" she shouted. She was smiling, but she was adamant. "At you, Joe!"

"Me?"

"Yes! He was trying to, you know, reconstitute something. What he had with you. So whenever I felt myself verging on what he'd call 'client behavior,' I'd get mad at you."

In the order of things I felt responsible for, this felt small, even good, though it seemed my debts here had just been compounded in ways I didn't fully understand.

"I had to live with him," she added. "Forgive me."

"Done."

We stopped for a minute on top, the wind hammering at us and deafening. On the gentler, east shoulder, stretches of alpine grass broke up the rocks, and soon we were pausing to admire the flowers Nor had promised—sky pilots, clumps of dwarf penstemon, and the infrequent splash of Sierra columbine tucked in the lee of a boulder. I think she recognized it as Pete's favorite, though neither of us said anything.

Then Nor told me about a climb they did together in the fall of '93. She started by saying they hadn't had a great summer—a spat about her being less invested in their adventures, which she readily admitted, and long stretches of feeling like they were leading parallel lives. She was working fifty- and sixty-hour weeks, doing her best to keep up with what she called the "Second Somethings"—established doctors, all men, with their second homes, second wives, second ski boats, or some combination. "No wonder health care is expensive," she said.

"So I'd get home at nine or ten, on my feet most of the day, and Pete would have us packed for an alpine start." Still, she tried. In late summer they attempted but didn't complete a line on the back side of Red and White Mountain, and in September they managed the third ascent of a harrowing route on the Dana Crest that nearly undid her even though Pete did pretty much all of the work and took all the falls. "He was like a badger, just throwing himself at the cruxes. Every time he fell he'd shed a layer. When he got the last one he was down to pants. I don't think it was fifty degrees."

Then the one he'd been ogling for several years, an almost invisible line on the upper half of the Wheeler Crest that takes hours just to get to the base of. It was mid-October and cold, but the window wasn't shut, not entirely, even if they'd missed a perfect stretch of Indian summer a couple weeks earlier on account of Nor's schedule. "And to top it off," Nor said, "I'd been feeling sick." They went anyway, starting in the dark from an alfalfa field deep in the valley in spitting hail and trudging up a steep, scree-lined drainage amid flurries. "The forecast wasn't any better for the following day, so we agreed just to get a good look at the buttress. Then at least Pete would have something to stew about all winter." But the clouds broke before they reached the cliff, and when Nor started up the first pitch she felt relieved, even inspired. "I thought maybe it will go more or less easy and fast and Pete could get what he wanted and we'd be done with it."

"But of course, that's always a recipe for disaster," she added.

I must have looked confused.

"The need for it to be something."

They swapped leads on the first four pitches, and while these went fine, she noticed something strange: friable patches of rock and lichen were everywhere, as you expect on an unclimbed route, but not in several of the harder sections of the first few hundred feet. Pete had been here already with his wire brush, cleaning these sections and previewing things.

"I didn't say anything," she added. "Not then, anyway."

At about the midpoint of the formation, the cliff rears up like the upper half of a cresting wave and, from there anyway, the rougher rock and plant life was intact. A fist crack splits the cliff for forty feet and then opens into a squeeze chimney, above which the last several hundred feet of steep face is decorated with so much gold and iron-stained patina it's like climbing a ladder. "This was where he got the idea for the name," Nor said. "The last third, the part that looks so unlikely from below, it's so easy Pete said you had to invent the difficulties to make it fun. But first you have to get there."

The wind picked up, and shortly clouds and flurries again, and by the time Pete was racked and ready for the steep fifth pitch they were in full storm mode and eager to get it over with. He scampered up the crack with ease, the snowflakes melting off his hands and face. But a squeeze chimney is a funny thing, very size-dependent, and this one was just the width of Pete's chest. He slid up and inside without strain, and by breathing in he could be perfectly secure. But when he exhaled he didn't have enough room to get any purchase. Ordinarily he'd have moved to the outer edges and used off-width techniques to climb outside the squeeze, but flurries melted by the scrum of his activity had left the rock slick. To Nor's eye he looked tentative and unsteady. He paused and strategized. She wondered if he was scared. He wriggled deep inside to place a large cam in the shadows, emerged and paused again. Finally he hollered, "Here I go," and by means of exhausting chicken-wing and knee-bar maneuvers appeared to be making steady progress. Then, about eight feet up from his gear, he slipped out and fell almost upside down. With just two or three pieces of protection between the belay and the big cam, it was like catching a shark, Nor said. She was jerked off the ledge and for a moment hung to the side until Pete righted himself and unweighted the rope.

"Fuck me," he moaned.

"We could come back," Nor hollered. "In the sun."

But Pete was having none of that. It had been a disappointing season, light on accomplishment, tainted by strain. He wriggled back into the chimney and reached in to slide the cam up a few feet, but he found it was already dangerously close to tipping out, so he ended up lowering it even further to a more secure position. This time he lined up at the outer edges of the chimney, intending to lieback the thing. Watching him closely, Nor was terrified. If Pete succeeded with this technique, he'd have to run it out almost thirty feet before he'd have another chance for gear. If he failed, he'd pop off with tremendous force and end up in her lap, or worse. So when his feet peeled off the slick rock after the first couple of moves, she was adamant: "Let me try!" she hollered. "The size seems more like me!"

She lowered Pete to the belay. She'd never seen him look more defeated, the backs of his hands raw, his face pink for the cold and exertion. "He was like a little boy," she said. "I would have insisted we just bail, but I thought he might cry. I figured if I gave it a try at least he'd have a chance to get cold and uncomfortable."

For Nor, it was the lower crack that was formidable, wider than her fist but too tight for an arm-bar. She managed it by wedging a knee and pulling on both of her hands, one clenched and the other flat, worried only about the blood seeping through her pant leg and whether this would eventually make her knee a greasy liability. With Pete's gear still in the chimney, at least she had the security of a top-rope until she got to his high point.

"The chimney itself was a snap," she said. "Almost relaxing. For one thing, it was warmer in there, out of the wind and snow. I could sneak inside and be perfectly still." About halfway up she got gear in a smaller crack and even left a chain of clove-hitched slings in the event Pete had to aid through it. Her belay at the top was secured only by tie-offs—webbing laced around natural protrusions—and she agreed with Pete's characterization of the face above: so dazzling it seemed almost unnatural, a mosaic of colorful, highly featured monzonite. But Pete would have to get through the tight chimney, and then they still had four hundred feet to the top of the formation. Standing in the wind again on a four-inch edge above the maw, secured by slings tied to untested features, Nor's mood darkened.

"I think that was the moment for me, one of those times you just say, 'What the hell am I doing?' And I never really resolved it. Pete got through the chimney, didn't spend three minutes with me on the ledge, and the next I remember talking was on one of several rappels down the gully. Must have been four or five hours later. It's almost like he knew."

The gorgeous part of the route was made trying by the worsening weather. The snowflakes got big and soft and then turned to spit in the warming afternoon and finally a steady drizzle. "But we were right at the freezing line, so snow would have felt warmer. When we topped out, neither of us had any feeling in our hands and toes. Pete was coiling the rope and kept dropping a loop. Finally he just stuffed it into the pack. It took twenty minutes at the first rappel to untangle it, but at least we were out of the wind."

It was early evening when they slogged back through the valley, watching for the dark edge of the alfalfa field in order to find the car. The skies had grown calm, and in holes between clouds there were stars. They were warm again, or at least not miserably cold. From time to time Pete would turn toward the mountains to take stock of their accomplishment, though the crest remained mostly shrouded. Nor was quietly seething, almost sick with fatigue but even more just furious at Pete. Still, she was careful not to say anything. She could see he was more tickled than chagrined about that trouble in the wide part and in any case basking in a measure of satisfaction—they had ticked another wild route on a hard-to-get-to Sierra cliff. They'd added to the résumé. They were a climbing couple.

Pete said something complimentary to Nor. She chafed, not with anything definitive or even testy, but he sensed her rage.

"He stopped there in the desert, and made me stop, too," she said. "He put his hands on my shoulders and looked me in the eye. He had these little salt stains along the edges of the wrinkles in his forehead." She ran her fingers along her brow. "After a breath or two, he said, 'Just give me a few more hours of joy and pride. Then you can have the rest of our lives for regret and anger.'"

"We didn't talk again until the following afternoon. It was a Sunday, I was off, and we were kind of wary around one another. We were exhausted, but also, you know, that post-climb adrenaline buzz."

I knew what she was talking about—the mind's still excited but your body's paralyzed.

"At some point in the afternoon I found him lying on the couch in the living room. He said, 'You okay?'

"That's when I told him: 'I'm pregnant.'"

Nor looked at me, as if expecting I'd be aghast, but what I felt was a pang of jealousy.

"He was quiet for a minute," she said. "Then Pete said 'pregnant,' like he wasn't sure what the word meant. 'I didn't think it would be like that.'"

"What?"

"I don't know. Regret. Anger. I thought it would be, well, flintier."

She drew near, took his hand, and put it on her belly. "No," she said. "It's soft, and it's right here. And it makes my boobs hurt."

Pete smiled, but Nor said he looked kind of scared. "Talk about inventing the difficulties," he said.

"Everybody has a specialty," Nor said.

"And that's mine?"

"It's ours," she said. "Now, it's ours."

At this point we were hiking down into the forest again and Nor seemed eager to get back, bounding along. Then, in a dry clearing decorated with powder-blue lupine, she stopped and faced me. "I think that really was a turning point, Joe." She pulled her hair away from her face. "Maybe not that ledge, the sketchy one where I belayed him, but that day, or at least that summer."

She looked over her shoulder to where the trail disappeared into the trees.

"I've been at this alone so long I sometimes wonder if he'd have made it if we just split up then. I never really had any hope he'd get on board, you know. I don't mean quit climbing, or even get a normal job. I mean liking it. Having a home, being a father. Being with me."

"But Astrid," I said.

"Astrid," she sighed. "I don't know if we had sex ten times in the next four years. But that was once, anyway."

"I always felt bad about missing the wedding," I said, stupidly. She chuckled. "Wedding? We got married. Just the two of us, down there next to Vons, in the city offices. I remember afterwards we went into the supermarket and Pete ran into three guys. Climbers, all gritty, just back from a day in the Gorge. One of them said he'd never seen Pete in a shirt with a collar.

"I wasn't right there, but close enough to hear. Pete told them he was grocery shopping. Said he liked to dress up for a little shopping. They laughed, and then they started telling him about what they'd climbed. I had the sick feeling like how I felt early on being pregnant. Except now it was spring, and I was due in a couple months."

Nor stepped down the trail, then stopped and turned around. "I don't know why I'm telling you all this, Joe." She looked at me as if I might know.

I shrugged.

"It's not like I haven't talked about it," she said. "I guess I'm just thinking you've been there."

"Trying to make sense of things," I said. "With Pete."

"Yeah."

"He made a crack about us being divorced. More than once."

"Whatever," she said. "So you divorced the man I married. It's not that you left him. It's that you loved him." Her eyes welled up. "Then, now. I remember. How you had to tear yourself away. The most I managed was try to hold it together."

She pulled her hair back to retie the ponytail. The wrinkles in her brow ironed out.

"You know," she continued, "when he died, it was plenty awful, but there was relief, too. I know it wasn't deliberate. Maybe not even reckless, at least by you guys' standards. But there's something about Pete's taking a long fatal fall that just kind of makes sense. Like someone who's been out at the edge of a diving board for a long time."

I felt protective. I fought the inclination to protest.

"Not deliberate," she said, "except if you've got something you're really connected to, at home, or wherever it is, you're gonna get there intact."

"Will," I said.

"And then, having Will grow up here. If I'd been even a little bit sober I'd have had the guts to move."

"There're rocks everywhere."

"It's not that. It's the air. It's everything around here. It's not even that it stings. More like it's stained. And the kids, they don't know anything else."

"What about you?" I said.

She looked puzzled, like she'd been talking about herself all this time. "Inch by inch," she said, staring off at the trees. "It's all I know about letting go."

"Yes. Miles don't work."

Our eyes met.

"Someone with all that life," she said, "and a wake of such, well, sadness. But maybe that's how this goes. Sometimes I feel really lucky to have had the years with him, even ones that weren't so good."

"Me too."

She reached for my hand. "He's this thing we have, Joe. Just us, really. We'll always have Pete. And we'll always be losing him."

Nor gave my hand a squeeze, turned around, and started down the trail toward the lakes.

I don't believe in an afterlife, not of the conscious, individuated-being variety anyway. Still, I couldn't help thinking about what this must look like to Pete, Nor leading me down a dusty trail in the light of a late-summer afternoon twenty years later. And each of us a little stuck. And these awful things I'd foisted on him, not loss and sadness but the other stuff, the regret, and shame, the nagging feelings of responsibility. On him who showed me all I needed to know about how good it can feel to be alive.

In the next couple of days I saw Nor sporadically and briefly amid comings and goings, and as I packed food and sorted gear in the garage or sat at their counter over eggs and toast or in the living room with a book, I came to realize the ideas I'd nourished about her over the winter were wide of the mark, that what I imagined didn't account for the intimacy we already shared— and this is it, and it's all there is, a deep and true and unshakable communion of grief.

⌒

The shadows were long but the air still comfortably warm when I lumbered into the meadow where we would again make our camp. Will had set up the tent and arranged much of the gear on a tarp. He'd changed into dry clothes, set out the stove, and cut a brick of tofu into an aluminum bowl over which he'd pour steaming ramen when I was ready. Earlier in the summer he'd hiked up this far with the plastic jugs we'd left in the miner's cabin over winter, and now these were lined up on the edge of the tarp, each filled and treated with iodine.

"How you feeling?" he said.

"Same. Same as last time."

He gestured to the mounds of gear. "It's all this."

"It'd be rough with a fanny pack," I said.

I splashed my face and arms at the little stream and stripped off my sweaty clothes. Moriah had been black in shadow since we could first make out the mountain, but with the sun bending west the face grew brown and orange and finally amber in light reflected from a farther ridge. I stood in the grass next to the stream, naked but for my hat. Will reached into a pack for his new, more compact binoculars, a Christmas gift from his mom. The route was in full relief—crack system at bottom, bulging wave of the midsection, and the steep buttresses and dark corners of the upper third we had yet to explore. As Will lingered on the intricate band he had been plotting for all winter, I wondered if he was daunted, or even scared. From inside his snow-banked cabin he had been a boy on a boulder with only a dozen moves to accomplish with fingers and toes and the levering maneuver he'd devised for his left heel. From here, he was an insect on the side of a cathedral.

Without lowering the binoculars, he said, "What do you want?"

"Which pitches?" I said.

"No. I mean, what do you want? Like, why are you here again?"

I gathered my clothes.

"I want the route," he said, his eyes locked on the mountain. "I want to punch through that part." He kept raising the binoculars to his eyes and then looking on without them, satisfied with neither perspective.

"It could go smooth," he said. "And then what? We don't have those two Brits along to spice up the story."

It took me a second. "Oh, Lester, Lester and Bill." I smiled. "I can do without the spice."

"A regular boring climbing story," he chuckled. "Really?"

"So long as it's one I can believe."

"Meaning, not like the others? The ones you made a living from?"

I didn't answer.

"Have a look."

I took the binoculars. "No," I said. "Not like those. Any bloody hands in this one will be yours. Or mine. Probably both."

The shadows had reclaimed the left side of the cliff and in minutes would fold the remainder in darkness.

"Let's eat and get to bed," he said. "If there's going to be blood, we might as well fortify."

We crawled inside the tent with the first of the stars. Will lay down, his hands behind his head. "You ever miss Carol?"

I told him no.

"I miss Al. Even now."

"That's lucky."

The wind tugged at the tent flap.

"Did you?" he said. "You ever miss anybody?"

"Pete."

He was quiet for a while. "Is that lucky?"

Before I answered he said, "I'm tired of everyone's fairytales about my dad."

"I'm guessing they're sincere."

"They think I'm missing something. Something I should have or need. But they don't stick, the stories."

I turned off my headlamp. "I've got one that's no fairytale."

"Yeah?"

"That photo of us, in Argentina. The one in the hall."

I could see Will's profile in the dying light.

"There's more," I said. "Shortly after your dad hurts his hand, on some garbage pitch, we're out of food, and we have to hike all our gear to that little outpost at the edge of the mountains where we took the picture. We were there two days. Every gesture a constant, mostly unspoken negotiation about what's next. He wanted more, but his hand was messed up. I wanted to want more, but I was done. We'd spent months making plans. Years really. Not to mention a load of money. And your dad, a big amortizer."

I could feel him listening.

"We get to that little inn next to the bodega. And, well, your dad's trying too hard. These little demonstrations of how harm-lessly his hand is hurt. Chatting up the others there like it's some kind of Camp 4. I see where this is going, and I'm just about to burst. I don't think I slept two hours in the most comfortable place we'd been in a month. In the morning I find him pumping someone with a radio for a weather report, and a little later he's inspecting shelves in the bodega for stuff we could cart back into the mountains. At some point we're out front, watching the sky. A few others are out on the porch, old guys. It's dramatic, these massive cumulous formations rolling over the pampas like on a time-lapse, and, in the breaks between clouds, luminous beams of light. Calendar material, otherworldly. Your dad points to a couple of puddles in the muddy road, steam pouring off them. He says, 'Look, Joe. It's drying out!'

"For a second I was blind. Then I just went for him."

Will turned his head to hear better.

"One minute we're watching the sky, the next we're hammering at each other in the mud, limbs flailing. At first he fought back. Just enough to compound my fury. None of this lasted long. He was hurt, after all. But before we were through I had him on his back, my knee on one arm and his bad hand wedged underneath him. I remember pulling away just enough to see his teeth were clenched and thinking, that's all he's got now, he's gonna bite me."

I felt my voice cracking.

"Too much?" I couldn't see Will's eyes.

"No."

"I put my forearm across his throat. Anyone looking at us, the guys on the porch, they probably thought we'd given up, we were so still. We could just as easily have been lying there recovering. But it was like being inside an off-width, everything pressed hard just to keep from slipping, and you know you can't hold on much longer. So I leaned harder. I could hear him struggle for air. Then something cracked, under my arm. Like shellfish, something fragile along his windpipe. Then these other hands are pawing at me, mercifully. *Chicos* from the porch taking big folds of my jacket. '*Tómalo con calma, amigos. Calma.*'"

I fought the impulse to apologize or explain. Will's breath was steady and quiet.

"When we got back to the States I was rattled. Not just in LA, where he got treated, but for months. It wasn't that I could have really hurt him. It's that some part of me wanted to. Because he had me pinned too, and it wasn't until South America I saw the only way out was for one of us to die. The story your dad always told about the trip was that I'd saved his life, or at least his hand. That if we had left Argentina any later he'd have lost one or both. But the part he'd always leave out was that our rolling around in the mud reopened the wound and filled it with grit. And he never even seemed to register the habit he had, even months after, of massaging the side of his throat, right where I nearly crushed it."

We lay still, just the ripple of the tent and our breath between us. I braced for something, an "I don't want to be here with you," or something to position himself with his father. I wondered if maybe that was the one favor I could do for him.

Will sighed. "That's more like it," he said.

Then he adjusted the jacket he used for a pillow and turned away.

My heart had been ratcheted into a disquieting thump. I could feel my pulse in the raw patches of my feet. Altitude, exhaustion, simmering apprehension—these were incidental. I cast about for palliative thoughts but kept getting pulled back to Will's question: *What do you want?* I worried I'd given him part of an answer, bludgeoning him with confession. I knew the pretense I assumed, of being here to help Will, was hollow. He didn't need me. And yet my eagerness to get this over with rivaled a desire for it to last forever. But I couldn't name the "it." It wasn't the climbing. It wasn't to bury Pete, or to resuscitate him, if perhaps some of each, but rather a confusing admixture of needs and motives—and no less vexing and potent than twenty-five years before. Back then I thought myself stunted for feeling so raw. Now I felt alive, and there was nothing to do but surrender to newly enhanced jitters. I studied my watch from time to time. I marked Will's breathing. His focus was like Pete's—as was his leaving the angsting and breast-beating to me. I wondered what would happen if Will got this, Moriah—how he'd react, how he'd recover, what he'd do next. I knew this wasn't a beginning, but I couldn't tell if it was the middle or end of something, and I felt pretty sure he didn't know, either.

At some point I got up to have a look at the night sky. The tent's zipper startled Will. "Time? Is it time?"

"It's not even two."

"Oh good." He rolled away. "I'm not ready."

As I stepped onto the cool grass, I heard him mutter, "I'll be ready. Just not ready now."

"Nothing's going anywhere."

But to be barefoot in the meadow under a dense wrapping of stars, you'd think it was—gentle breeze in willows and stream gurgling past our camp and sky crisscrossed with randomly etched lines of shooting stars and only the craggy gray ridges and dark mass of Moriah static and lifeless. Now it seemed not frightening but merely foolish that we should be here again, not for what we risked but simply for all we had given to get here. I felt envy of Pete—for the first time in more than twenty-five years—though not of the wit and joy and abandon I admired, couldn't match, and didn't try to. Nor his talent. Nor the regal authority other climbers foisted on him without his wanting it or even seeming to care. Just the appetite he fed, even to the end. I was wrapped in a down parka and just one thin layer from waist to feet. I lay down on the tarp where Will had arranged our gear, resting my head on a rope to watch the night sky. Only now did I see that this was to be Pete's venture, Moriah with Will, and how insufficient I was to either role—the climbing partner who could hold his own, or the proxy father. I felt a stab of self-pity about the small and forgettable part I played on a big stage, but sorrier still for Will, and for the summit-less solitude in and out of which he climbed as on a treadmill to the sky.

"Hey," he said from inside the tent. "You coming back?"

"Yeah. Just enjoying the stars."

I sat up to move back inside, but Will emerged, lurched a pace or two, regained his balance, and lifted his eyes to the sky. After a minute he said, "All right. Let's get this started."

I figured he was just remarking on the favorably clear night. I made a move to the tent.

"You can sleep?" he said.

I stood still but didn't answer.

"I'm done," he said. "We could send today."

I hadn't slept an hour and wondered if it wouldn't be worse than painful, but dangerous, to proceed.

"No pressure here," he said. "Whatever you like."

I lay back down on the tarp. Will sat at the edge of the tent.

In a few minutes I said, "Okay."

In an hour we'd had coffee and oatmeal and packed the gear. In two we were threading our way by headlamp through the upper boulder field. The air was strangely warm and soft with a whispering breeze that kept our faces dry. Of the weather Will said it was summer's Indian Summer. "More water, fewer clothes," he advised.

At the base the darkness grew close. We spread our gear on a slab of granite and flaked two ropes. Then Will stripped to change into dry clothes. With his headlamp on the gear I noticed he had brought the #5 stopper and a few other pieces from Pete's rack. I slipped into my climbing shoes and took the rack. I wasn't going to be much good later, so I'd try to be useful now.

Climbing by headlamp, and carrying a pack with food and extra clothes and a rack too plentiful for these lower pitches, I was startled by how readily I ascended. It was as if the surface of the rock had been weathered to a stickier texture and the angle of the cliff backed off a few degrees. I hiked through sections that had asked so much of me the summer before, surging with gratitude for Emery and wishing he were along to share this small slice of glory that would be mine. When he arrived at the first belay Will said only, "Way to hum," and later, at the third, suggested we simul-climb the fourth pitch, which, as the stars blinked out and the sky turned purple and finally blue, we did.

We built elaborate anchors and removed most of what we'd carried in our packs, arranging everything on a sort of clothesline stretched between gear at either end of this ledge Will dubbed the "launching pad." Back in Mammoth we had discussed moving the next belay to the top of the pillar so he could pull a lighter rope and carry less gear through the bulge, but he elected to proceed as we had last year—less to maintain the character of the long, varied, and perhaps impossible pitch than simply to preserve the style of the first ascent. I didn't bother to point out we hadn't actually ascended it. While Will changed his shoes and arranged his rack, I added a couple of layers, thinking I could easily be here the rest of the day.

Sunrise bathed us in yellow just as he set off for the peculiar column whose top marks the middle of unfinished pitch five. He was even more sparing with gear this time, placing two pieces on long runners in the first fifty feet and just two more as he clambered up the rounded edges. Unworried about a mistake, he was thinking more about the dicey section above, where even modest rope-drag could pull him off. I leaned out, straining the anchors to take pictures in the golden light of dawn. In twenty minutes Will stood on the pillar and clipped the bolt he'd drilled there with a double-sized runner. He spent a few minutes rearranging gear, then reached to the back of his harness and opened his chalk bag for the first time. He removed the rack for a moment to strip down to a single T-shirt, tying the windbreaker around his waist and leaving his heavier shirt wedged in a crack by his feet. Reassembled, he dipped his hands in the chalk bag and slapped them together. Puffs of powder surrounded him—a prizefighter at the edge of the ring.

However improbable the first moves off the column appeared from my vantage, Will had shown little indication of trouble there last year, and again he launched into the sequence that would position him for the crux. Thin edging and a couple of long reaches up and right, and from what looked like a strenuous stance he placed a micro-cam in a seam. He clipped this and repositioned his feet. Then he was airborne, his entire left side off the cliff, but somehow the fingers of his right hand remained attached and with a barn-door pivot he swung around until he was nearly facing out. "Whoa," I heard him groan, swaying back into the cliff. He re-placed his feet on the bad edges, swapped hands a few times on the better hold to recover. Then he moved into the heart of the bulge. Two moves put him within reach of the first of the two bolts he'd placed around the crux, and when he clipped this I felt a warm surge of relief—at least he'd be safe for this next little stretch. Finally, and almost without pause, he accomplished the very sequence he had dreamed up back in November and pantomimed for me in our camp a few days before: where last year he had faced right to grind up spare edges and side-pulls, now he turned the other way, levering off the left heel and back-stepping with his right toes on smears to reach past former nemesis holds to where the great incut marked the end of this sequence. In seconds it was over. Will let out a little whoop, clipped the second bolt, and manteled onto the good hold until his feet gained a stance he could maintain nearly hands-free. I should have been inspired—we could top out today—but instantly felt the full weight of my exhaustion. The lids of my eyes grew heavy and my hands went limp around the rope. While he fumbled with gear, I wondered if I might fall asleep here in slings.

Will was jazzed at the prospect of completing the pitch, craning his neck to get reacquainted with the next section and quickly rearranging the rack to have key pieces at the ready. The crux may be behind him, but there were still forty feet of shallow pockets on vertical rock to get to the dish he hoped would mark the end of the pitch. "All right," he shouted. "Watch me! Looks harder than I remember!"

He scooched his feet to the right until just the left remained on the good ledge, and with his left hand crimping an undercling he managed to place a small stopper in a shallow crack. I shook my head to stay alert and palpated the rope; if I gave him too little slack I could pull him off—too much and I would just add to the fright and danger should he fall. We were in the shadows again, and even in still air I couldn't imagine he wasn't freezing in just a T-shirt. He stepped out and up, committing to the face, each move wary and deliberate. A vertical rib was within two body lengths, and with his fingers pressed onto tenuous holds he worked to keep his feet as high as possible both to avoid slipping off and to readily gain the advantage of anything better within reach. He looked like a frog traversing a garden wall. And then, with signature dexterity, he faced the opposite direction to better utilize the crummy pockets and then lengthened to place one more piece before gaining the rib.

And then he started to shake. At first it was barely noticeable, just a shiver and possibly a consequence of strain alone. But as Will adjusted positions to gain a more relaxed posture, his toes scissored more violently. Pete's long plummet off Mood Management came to mind, and I took in a few inches of slack and prepared to haul in more should he come off. With the left foot he heeled a nubbin that seemed to do the trick, and now he could fiddle with the placement. Efficient as a surgeon, he blindly reached for the right-sized cam and in seconds had the gear and confidence requisite to completing the pitch. A dab of chalk with the left hand. He hiked his feet up under his butt and reached for a thin edge. If he could stick this move, he'd gain the conspicuous feature. He appeared to caress a sidepull, as if afraid he'd peel it off the face, and then with an upward burst Will's legs extended and his right arm shot up to the rib, which he grabbed like a loaf of bread. A spray of something like chalk now, to the left of him, and he hollered. He hung on with his right hand for a couple seconds, then flew out and backward. I cinched and waited. The cam held, the nut snapped out, the rope went taut, and Will swung across the cliff right to left about a hundred feet above me. It took me a second to see the dispersed speckle was blood.

He dangled for a minute, groaning, then lowered. At the level of the top of the column he hollered for me to pause so he could pendulum over and rig up the trail line to rappel to me. But first he reached for the shirt he'd left there, which he wrapped tightly around the bloody hand—the middle and ring fingers of Will's left, sliced as if from a careless slip while cutting an onion.

Will untied from the rope that had held his fall, pulled it through the gear above him, and reattached himself to stay on belay while descending these last eighty feet on the other cord, wisely mistrustful of a one-handed rappel. He backed down slowly and appeared even to be admiring this lower part of the pitch he knew best. Dangling a little ways above me, he paused. "I guess that would have been too easy."

"Didn't look it. You all right?"

"I don't mean it wasn't hard. I just mean we're cooked."

"Our why and wherefore," I said.

But feigned levity wouldn't stick, each of us alone now with our private thoughts—his that this could very well be a whole other cycle, possibly a year, before he had another shot at it. Mine: I'm done. Finished. Throw myself into nursing. Maybe that's what I've been doing all along—first and most inadequately with Pete, then with the college kids. More or less ineptly in a parish, somewhat better at New Horizons.

For safety's sake, I lowered him through the bottom pitches two at a time, minimizing instances he'd have to use the injured hand. He seemed unrattled, walking slowly backward down the face, less defeated than amazed. You plan, you train, you anticipate and worry—but it's always something else, something you can never imagine. He kept his left hand wrapped and lifted above his heart, from time to time looking at it, and with pity, as though tending a wounded pet.

We were on the ground and barefoot before noon. Will moved onto a slab in the sun and waited for me to coil ropes and pack our things. We had stripped the cliff of most of the gear, all but what remained above Will after he fell, and cleaned the ledge of our supplies but for one of the water jugs, which we left secured by a single stopper on the large ledge because, he said, "One way or another, someday I'll get back here." He was scratching dried blood off his arm. "If only to have some water." I prepared a huge, heavy pack for myself and outfitted Will's with just the clothes and some food, but there were still three plastic jugs at the base.

"What about those?" I asked.

He studied the question. Emptied, the jugs would be painless to carry, just clipped to the outside of my pack.

"Leave 'em," Will said.

I didn't press the point. It was his business.

He continued to hold the bloody hand in the air as we ambled down across boulders and scree and tufts of alpine grass back to camp. It was a sunny, almost windless afternoon, the pleasant weather a kind of salt in the wound whenever we glanced back at Moriah's shaded face—a two-or-three-times-a-year day for a route like this. But I was wrecked, too, more or less sleepwalking at this point, and when we got to camp and dumped our stuff beside the tent, I tended to the deep, clean cuts on Will's hand with antibiotics and bandages, then went to sleep. When I awoke I looked for Will through the mosquito netting. He was leaning on a pack in the warm meadow, facing the mountain, his elbow propped to keep his hand raised. The fingers had bled through the gauze. Once I saw him peering at the cliff through the binoculars. I asked if it hurt. He dropped the glasses for a second and looked at me with a sort of bewildered glance, as if unsure what I was talking about.

When I emerged in the late afternoon, the meadow had fallen into shadow and Will was asleep where he'd been sitting. I covered him with an unzipped sleeping bag. In moments Moriah would shine once more in the last of the light. I got water going on the stove and retrieved food from the bear canisters. I was starving and figured Will would be, too, but he might not wake up until morning, so I made a meal I could store and reheat, ended up eating most of it, and then made some more. The evening turned softer and still brighter than yesterday's and I was thinking it was probably better Will didn't have to admire the glorious cliff when, without moving, he said, "We'd be topping out right about now."

"Food here. Hungry?"

"The upper section, it's steep. I could see it all this time."

I put a bowl together and sat beside him. "Someday," I said.

"Some. Day."

"Can I rewrap that hand?"

"Tomorrow. What's the hurry?" He balanced the bowl on his legs and took a forkful of noodles. "Thanks for the grub."

We were in the tent before dark, each drifting in and out of sleep through the night. At some point Will allowed that his fingers throbbed and I got up for some Advil. It was a night of blazing stars, and when I reported this to Will he muttered a phrase I'd only ever heard from his father: "Made-to-order weather."

"Well, like you said, maybe it was going too well."

Sometime later, as if to himself, he said, "It's all small."

"How larger be?"

"Huh?"

"Something Carol used to say. I think it's from Dickinson."

"Never heard of him."

"What is it, that's small?"

"You get born," he said. "You see the big rocks, maybe you remember your dad on them. Or maybe you just remember what everybody tells you. Anyway, they're outsized and scary and all over the place, and then you figure out how to do it, how to make your way, and you get a lot of encouragement. But it's all small, really. All of it."

"You've been thinking about this," I said.

"Hmm."

"You sound like me, when I was here. Not last summer, but with your dad."

"Whatever."

"I know what he'd say, if you care."

"Go."

"It's the trying, trying your hardest. That's what makes it matter."

"As in Fail Better, that crack you couldn't do at the Creek?"

"Exactly."

"Too bad you guys used that one. The name, I mean. Might have been handy here."

He fell asleep, then I did, and next we talked it was over coffee well after dawn. We discussed packing up and starting down, but just to think of it made us lazy. We were comfortable enough, and Will said the last thing he wanted to do was spend the balance of the day in a waiting room at Urgent Care. We lay about in the sun, and at around noon I had another turn at Will's fingers. I'm not a medical person, but you see a fair number of skin wounds working with old people. Will's cuts were parallel and oblique, clean as sliced salmon. I couldn't tell if he'd need stitches but agreed he'd at least have to get his mother's opinion. He said he'd been aware of the sharp edge—he intended to release it just a tad earlier in order to avoid getting cut. A little lower the hold was blunter and more secure, but he was launching onto that rib he'd never touched and had no idea whether it would be rounded and smooth or have the positive edge he was thrilled to find on the other side, so he elected to ride the left hand as high as possible for more extension. Even after he got the great loaf he thought he had stuck it, but then there was this sting and so much blood, and then his right foot peeled and he let go.

"Anyway," he said, "I was thinking more about that stopper, the one that popped, and the cam at my knee."

"Naturally."

"Lamely."

"That hurt?" I was coating the fingers with Neosporin and wrapping them again.

He pounded his chest lightly with his good hand.

A couple of times Will ambled shoeless about the meadow. For more than an hour he sat by the water, dipping his feet in and out of the cold stream. He seemed always facing the mountain, tracking the long day's play of light across the great face.

Toward evening I tidied up and had most everything but the tent and our sleeping gear packed for the hike down. We had brought a red-beans-and-rice mix Will liked, with the thought we'd have something to celebrate with. I went ahead and made it for dinner, a gesture Will didn't register one way or the other. He picked at the food. We'd been up here for forty-eight hours. We were finally rested and well fed, and yet the only thing left for us was to gather our things and walk down the canyon. Will was quiet. With his right hand he grasped the forefinger and thumb of his left, the uninjured digits, as if pressing them into service.

The golden light lingered on Moriah, finally flickering to brown and black. I washed our dishes and repacked the bear canisters, coffee and cereal on top for the morning.

Sometime after the first stars appeared Will said, "Give me another day."

"For what?"

"I mean, I think I can do it. But I need another day first."

"Your fingers, Will. They're pretty messed up."

"These aren't," he said, raising his bad hand with just the thumb and forefinger extended. "I can do that move with these. I can try, anyway. And then we're done with it."

"Done? We're seven hundred feet under the summit on God knows what. What if there's some cranky thing up there? A 5.11 finger crack, say."

"All right. How about we take another day, and you talk me out of it."

I said okay, but I saw where this was going, and in the moment, anyway, I resented the jolt that would make for a restless night. We were in the tent with the dark. I could tell he was sleeping lightly as well—that the mood had shifted, no longer rangy and ruminative but lassoed again to purpose, even our smallest gestures now assigned to the go or no-go sides of a scale each of us was tabulating. Deep in the night I heard him mutter, "I'm crazy." I didn't respond and never determined whether he'd been talking in his sleep.

Clouds moved in overnight and dropped to our level, so at dawn the meadow was an island from which we couldn't see two hundred yards in any direction. When I noted the weather Will said, "It's what got wicked out of the ground yesterday. You get mornings like this on the best summer days."

Later it was still gray, but a light breeze indicated a change, and before noon the cloud layer was entirely dissipated and the sky brilliant blue. I wasn't going to take a position on whether to give the route another go. Will's attempting it with half a hand was no more ridiculous than his climbing with one foot the summer before. But I should have thought longer about what another attempt might presage for the upper pitches instead of, like Will, focusing merely on whether he could do the move-in-question without further wounding himself. Like the day before, Will alternately rested in the meadow and took little strolls nearby. Once when he was off a ways I looked at the notes and additional scribbles he had added to the topo of the route. He had drawn in some of the features on the upper third, and that's all I needed to know he was serious. I started rearranging and packing the gear we'd need. Midafternoon I made a move to haul a load up to the base.

"You don't have to do that," Will said.

"I know. That's probably one reason I am."

"What if I change my mind?"

"Then I'll get it again in the morning," I said, and headed off.

Better to be moving, whatever for. This was the sixth or eighth time I'd hiked to the base of Moriah, and as with other approaches to other remote cliffs I found myself tracing a familiar path between boulders and pockets of meadow and across small streams, touching the same rocks to hump up through steep sections and even finding the faded imprint of a foot now and again in soft, moist earth. A mountain of this stature that sees so little activity—and yet if the Grand Teton itself were ten miles farther from a road it too would be reserved for the adventurous and hardy. I thought about Pete here, alone on his first foray. I wondered if Pete had charged through these boulders with a mind to climb the whole thing—just get it done and not even involve me, and only when he got up under the fifth pitch did he see he'd need a partner.

That Pete's route should remain unfinished a quarter century later was amazing enough. That I should be here with his son— well, like Emery said, "positively poetic." Breathing hard, making good progress toward the cliff, I began to get lathered up, not just with enthusiasm and courage but a dash of pride, too. Maybe Will was right—we could tick this thing. Maybe I was finishing something here, too, not the route but whatever it once trellised for Pete and me even in the time we were coming apart. For so many years I hadn't felt much other than loss in association with him. But here, once more at the base, something else—a splash of Pete's spirit.

I dropped my pack. I had hauled two ropes, all the gear, and our harnesses, shoes, and climbing clothes—everything but the food we'd carry. I sat to rest. From down valley Moriah is shadowed and formidable. From directly underneath the cliff is attractive, even friendly—clean features on blond rock, at least for the first few hundred feet. I could see why Pete hadn't waited. He'd arrived here to discover a made-for-climbing rock face that would shortly be ensconced in winter. Walk out without a taste? Not weighing the considerations any self-respecting soloist keeps in mind, I found myself changing into climbing shoes and strapping on a chalk bag. I could never be here like Pete—first and alone—but I wanted my own taste, and in moments I was ten, twenty, then thirty feet up the first pitch, telling myself to turn around now. You're high enough.

A ropeless ascent either tears at your guts or feels secure as a walk across the living room. I relished the razor focus, and shortly passed the first belay stance without pause. The one distraction I allowed was the caution that I had to reverse each move, and downclimbing is half-again harder. Most of the time my feet were locked in a crack, but from time to time I took an edge nearby and by blurring my vision replaced my yellow

La Sportiva shoe with Pete's gray Fires. Stacking fingers in a secure jam, I felt them warm, as if the hold had been preheated. Between the second and third belays a little bulge and narrower cracks comprise the crux of the first six hundred feet. I had been sure I would turn around far below this point and in any case hadn't any notion of climbing through this steep, thinner section, but in minutes I was passing the third belay and clambering up the fist crack Pete called "the grody part."

At the "launching pad" ledge I took a swig from the jug Will had left tied there and sat down, facing out, legs dangling. I loosened the laces on my shoes and zipped up my nylon jacket against the wind. The meadow was more than a mile off, a bright green gem set amid white rock, Will a twig now strolling to the upper edge. I remembered his mumbling "It's all small" in the night when he was sure we were through here, everything he'd trained for and dreamed about for a year foiled by thin slashes on two fingers. From here it felt anything but, with the sun bending far to the west and Moriah's shadow marching steadily across the valley.

I relaced my shoes, tighter still, and reminded myself to lock into each move. The downclimbing felt no harder or less secure, if unnerving—my downward focus included inescapable glimpses of the boulders several hundred feet below. Twice my foot slipped, but neither time did I feel fear, much less the visceral clutch and panic of losing my grip one can suffer even on a protected ascent. I trusted my fingers and hands, and when my foot popped I simply fastened the other, even if to a smear or chip, until I could reestablish the errant limb. This should have been horrifying, particularly the moves through the bulge, and in retrospect I found it nauseating just to think of it. But in the moment I was calm as I'd ever been on rock, not perilously confident but quiet, easing myself down as if through memory, section by section, pitch by pitch, passing belay stances without rest and reversing the choreography move by move until, not an hour later, my feet were again joined to the flat slab of granite at the base.

I took a few breaths, changed my shoes, and started down toward camp.

When I crossed into the sun it felt twenty degrees warmer. I tied my jacket and both shirts around my waist and rolled my pant legs into knickers. At the first little stream I splashed my bare skin and cupped hands to throw water into my hair. I was unfatigued, encouraged about our prospects, my steps light and balanced between boulders. I hadn't cheated death—I'd just been entirely alive, and now basked in a feathery afterglow.

Two hundred yards from camp I could see Will hunched over the stove in the meadow, a little cloud of steam pouring off water he was tending. He didn't look up as I approached, didn't remark upon my odd outfit. I went past him to wash up, dropped my feet into the cold stream near our camp and changed into the clean set of underwear, tights, and shirt I'd wear to bed.

Will was making noodles and tofu, his go-to meal before a climb. I got my bowl and sat nearby.

"Thanks," he said.

I was confused.

He snorted, as if blowing his nose. "I mean thanks. . ." He did it again, like he was about to sneeze. "For scaring the crap out of me."

His eyes had welled up.

"Oh God, Will."

"You're all right," he said. "I can see that."

He didn't look at me, but continued stirring the pasta.

"Maybe you did that kind of shit with Dad all the time."

"Well, no."

"Maybe. . . Oh, fuck it."

"Sorry, Will. I wasn't thinking about you."

"So what's that, some sort of agreement you had—forget the kid in the meadow? Fuck you, Joe. You and your old gear that never held a fall bullshit. One of you's dead and the other. . . I don't know, what are you?"

"I'm glad you didn't fall," he said, slobbering over his words. "But fuck you, Joe."

He reached past me for a container, dropped a gob of pesto onto the noodles, and handed the pot to me. "Eat up. 'Nother early start coming." His face was red and streaked.

Soon after he went inside the tent. It wasn't 7:00 P.M. The binoculars lay next to the matted grass where he had spent much of the afternoon. He'd been watching—sitting here in the grass getting reacquainted with his imagination of what happened when his dad had set off ropeless on a familiar route on a calm summer afternoon. I was glad he was asleep when I got inside, and relieved to discover I was at least as tired from the day's outing as agitated for what I had put Will through.

It was later than the first day but no less dark, Will outside the tent when he called me awake. Even in the cold I could smell coffee. He set my bowl next to a steaming mug and half-filled it with already cooled oatmeal. I took sips while changing into climbing clothes. Will sat on a bear canister, bandaging his fingers by headlamp. This time he taped them together tightly in a single stiff splint. Whatever he managed to do, it would be with just the thumb and forefinger on his left hand.

He walked out of camp before I was ready, and by the time I left the meadow his headlamp was ducking in and out of boulders half a mile away. I hadn't been able to gauge his mood, but mine had shifted—yesterday's lift dampened not by fatigue or some deferred trepidation but remorse for what I'd put Will through. He'd been watching through the glasses when my foot popped, and if the prospect of my soloing wasn't alone sufficient for consternation he surely felt, in those two instances, calamity is at hand.

And yet some other part of me had had an out-of-body experience, and I didn't want to let go of it. I had run up and down six hundred feet of rock I could only claw and shake my way through the year before, and not with the dangerous abandon or delusion of the reckless but with measured movement, even grace. I wondered if this is where Pete had been—not brooding about big life questions as he did on the phone with me but throwing them off for a while to exult in a summer's morning on the grand Southeast Face of a nearby favorite. A fatal fall generates pretexts and stories, and I'd always had my own for Pete's. Not a suicide, but not a not-suicide either. A dead soloist's survivors tend a colder brew of grief. Did he think his life dispensable? Were we so insufficient?

Now I wondered if Pete wasn't just fine when he lost his grip.

Will's light flickered around the dark base of the cliff. When I got there he was in harness and shoes. I changed into dry shirts and slipped into my harness. Will said, "I'd suggest let's not bother roping up, 'cept I'm not sure what this will be like for me."

"Sorry," I said. "Honest. Also, I forgot about the binoculars. Didn't occur to me I wasn't alone."

He was tied in now and turning toward the cliff.

"Anyway," I said, "That's done. Not again."

"So you *were* gripped?" He studied my face in the dark for a moment but didn't wait for me to answer. Then, in what I took for a forgiving gesture, he added, "You didn't look it."

Will started up the first pitch before I was ready. He hiked it in ordinary fashion. By the time I got him on belay he was thirty feet up, and when I saw him at the first stance and asked how it went, with the bandaged fingers, he said he couldn't really tell. He wouldn't know until we got on something hard.

Not long after first light we got to the big ledge. Will changed his shoes per usual and stripped off the thickest of his three layers. I added the discarded things to the pack I would carry if indeed I got the chance to aid through the hard pitch.

"I'll give this a good go," he said. "But I'm not gonna work it. If I can do it, I can do it. If I can't, we head down. And home."

"Roger."

"But if it goes," he added, "wrap everything up here. We're walkin' off the top."

In Pete's and my day you approached a hard pitch with a bit of bravado and some hope for luck. The difference between punching through a crux and flailing felt less contingent on preparation and talent, much less beta, than chance—the appearance of a critical intermediate hold or a clever if improbable liebacking maneuver you contrived in order to bypass a tips crack. The next generation—the sport climbers and high-ball boulderers—they're more clinical and calculated. Theirs is artistry, too, but the foundation is engineering. Will was of this school, climbing very much within the range of conscious command, executing a plan, blithe to context and largely unruffled by surprise. So long as the route was one he believed within his capacities, he was like a great musician: a single rehearsal got him all he needed to link the components in seamless orchestration.

Minus the two fingers, which jutted stiffly from the left hand like a small ivory horn, Will played the pitch perfectly. From a hundred feet below I couldn't hear clinking gear and labored breathing, nor the grunts and periodic reminders-to-self—"Steady," "C'mon!" Watching through the camera's long lens, I could see only efficiency: almost hopping through the part off the pillar where he barn-doored two days ago, levering up the crux as if it were an apparatus in his backyard gym, and then dancing through the small dishes until he had the great loaf solidly in his right hand. If he even touched the sharp edge of the setup hold, I didn't see it. Nor was there any prolonged and anxious windup for the move. He coolly fastened to the blunter bottom of the curved feature with the forefinger and thumb of his wounded hand, hiked his feet up, and launched. Once he established his right heel over the long rib as well, he paused to place a small nut, then hauled up the dike until he was standing on the long-sighted but never before touched cavity that marked the end of the pitch.

Moments later he hollered off belay and the deed was done. I dug into the pack for my watch. It wasn't even 9:00 A.M.

There was no point in my trying to repeat Will's hijinks. It was so absurd a prospect we didn't even discuss it. But I wanted to try my hand at the bottom half, if only to see if I was as futile here as before, with Pete. I changed my shoes and stripped down to two layers. I clipped the jumars to my harness and attached the pack to the haul line Will had fixed to intermediate anchors at the top of the column, then summoned whatever I could by way of a game face.

Even the moves off the belay are devious, but as much from watching Will as from the year of training I stitched them together and shortly got my hands behind the generous flake where Pete was when I snapped the photograph I have of him at home. It's a ridiculously secure feature, and I finally understood why Pete felt emboldened to continue, even if to look ahead is discouraging: barely visible flakes and incuts that lead to the strangely inverted funnel, which from directly beneath seems even steeper and nearly detached from the face that produces it.

With a top-rope I was nearly fearless, and in just minutes I had fingers in a narrow slot behind the bottom of the pillar. So far as we knew, only Pete and his son had ascended this section—Pete three times in three days, August 1989; Will, multiple passages over several days last summer, and now this time, twice in four days. I felt a surge of determination to join them, and again, largely by means of mimicking Will as well as several times encountering a fortuitous gap and decent hold, I managed to thrutch and scrum nonstop to the upper third. Here a small cam required me to reach and fidget with one hand while secured by just two fingers of the other, these slipping in an awkward flare, and I fell. The rope stretch was such that I was instantly ten feet under my high point. Will couldn't see me but figured where I was. He hollered, "Get above it and reach down!"

After a rest, I did as directed. The final twenty feet proved a frantic fight up the increasingly polished and bewildering feature, as hard and weird a thing as I've ever attempted, and here a fresh reminder of Pete's pluck—no wonder it took him several hours—and Will's savvy: he monkeyed through here without pause. In time I too stood on the small, flat top, panting, a self-satisfied grin on my face.

The shiny bolt Will had placed here last summer was at navel height. I secured myself and hauled the pack from below. When I shouted to Will to fix the lead line to his anchors, he hollered a caution: I could take a wild swing to the right when I left the stance. I attached my ascenders to the rope, ratcheting in as much slack as I could, then leaned off a perch I intended never to visit again.

The bulge up here is less pronounced than it appears from below and only now could I see this is an optical trick due less to a change in angle than to the arresting blankness. The holds are limited and obscure—not a pattern so much as a contrived smatter of small, oddly angled edges and chips I could detect only on account of splashes of fresh chalk beside each. I surrendered my full weight to the rope and gently bounced across the cliff until I was well beneath the section Will had been working. To my eye it didn't seem possible anyone could climb through here. As I pushed the jumars up I studied the wall for things I must be missing—the pockets or flakes that would pull this back within the range of feasible. Even the crucial incut hold from which Will drilled the bolts last summer wasn't two knuckles deep, and the moves above, those that culminated in the tricky lever he had devised for his left foot, seemed pure sorcery. Then I encountered the curved edge where he cut himself and a black stain of blood that appeared to have seeped out of the crack itself. Above there, near the loaf-shaped dike, I paused to study the pitch one last time. As from beneath, beyond belief.

I stopped once more, ten feet under Will, to get the camera out of the pack. He was leaning from the anchors and facing right, his arms crossed casually, and smiling. He appeared, in a word, satisfied—feet bare, climbing shoes clipped to his side. I dangled beneath him on the single strand, performing the very offices I was to have executed for Pete—witness, documentarian, admirer. Only the looming distance and uncertainty of the cliff's upper half prevented me from feeling like I had accomplished my purpose.

"Holy smokes," I said.

"Yeah. Surprised here too. Relieved, but even more surprised."

It's a cramped little stance where Will was anchored but the gear mercifully big and secure, two large cams in the bottom of the corner and crack system we would ride to the summit. Will had a sling for me to clip into, and after a peanut butter sandwich and some rearranging I was hot to set off on the next section, a manageable ramp and corner not unlike the very bottom of the route. It was still early, and though the top remained beyond view, it was just a matter of time now, and the prospect of several hundred feet of steep, featured rock not daunting but delightful.

"Hey," Will said.

"Yeah?"

"How's it feel?" he asked.

"Ask me in a couple of hours. Anyway, nice work."

In the moment I thought it curious he should be asking me, but later I understood: he figured I had the longer investment. But that's just how young Will was—not seeing that what he'd done in just these two attempts wasn't merely more objectively demanding, but that what he'd put into it, both on the route and off, was vastly greater than anything I had to offer.

The rock here changes character—grainier, pock-marked, and decorated with splotches of dark lichen. More friable, too, weathered plates and chickenheads on either side of a generous crack. Not wanting to send anything down on Will, I was careful, avoiding easier features on the face in favor of the cool, dark crack and glad to be off belay again inside half an hour. More of the same lay ahead in a steepening double dihedral of the sort that appeared to offer many options for a painless and relatively quick path to the top. When Will got to me he said, "Why don't you?" We switched ends of the rope rather than restack, and some part of me felt emboldened merely for tying into the end he'd worn through the crux section below. With the climbing right in my wheelhouse—parallel crack and corner systems that make for a playground of stemming and jamming, and protection most anywhere you want it—I felt I could go on forever.

But of course you can't, and neither did the amenable fissures and features. I ran this pitch the full length of the rope, belayed from a comfortable eight-inch ledge, and leaned a little left to see the trouble ahead: the overlapping corners continued to the sky, but only fifty feet above me the deep cracks and mottled features appeared to close down to seams for a hundred feet. Higher still there were fractures again, and even farther up an array of larger cracks, possibly even a chimney. But between here and there lay another smooth baby's butt not unlike the one that had stymied us below. I belayed Will on auto-lock, indulged worried glances upward, and finally told myself just to bring him to me and what will be will be. With the sun at apogee, the boulders in the valley were nested in tight, dark shadows. A whisper of wind seemed laced with briny grasses and alfalfa from the deep valley many miles to the east.

By the time Will got to me he too had taken measure of the trouble. He was neither sweating nor breathing audibly when he clambered onto my little ledge but, businesslike, clipped the pack to the anchors, took the rack, and started rearranging. Without lifting his eyes, he said, "Celebration premature?"

"I've been looking at that, too."

"But you never know."

"Right."

He tightened his shoes and set off. I dug into the pack for my watch—just after 2:00 P.M. The part right above our ledge was more of the same, and in minutes Will was fifty feet up with just three pieces of gear between us. But the steady progress ended there, and once again a hundred-foot band of Moriah's Northeast Face eclipsed proximate segments by orders of magnitude in difficulty. Here at least there were corner features that brought to mind the Zig-Zags on Half Dome: famous overlaps of vertical slabs whose friendly, hand-sized cracks lure you in for some spectacular climbing before things get messier. You're right under the visor there, with hikers lying prone on the summit's edge to mark your progress up the last four hundred feet. Under so many attentive eyes you can work yourself into a heroic lather on the first of the Zig-Zags, but then the cracks go to fingers and tips on the second pitch and only the very strongest don't whip out their etriers and aid the remainder. Will wouldn't have any audience here but me. Neither would he have the option to aid: these features, it turns out, are not like the Zig-Zags but more akin to El Cap's Changing Corners—devious, symmetrical, steep, and smooth. Scantily protectable and only with tiny stoppers, and climbable only with talent and temerity if climbable at all.

I watched Will until my neck hurt from craning backward, then figured a way to rig a sort of headrest with spare slings attached to the top-most gear in our anchor. Will's progress was slower than gradual. Twice he hung on gear to scrape at the rock with the small brush he kept in his chalk-bag. At one point he worked for ten minutes placing a brass nut in a micro-seam off to the right, which he clipped to the rope via two long runners—psychological protection at best. The climbing itself involved none of the dynamic gestures he'd employed through the lower cruxes but these inscrutably cerebral maneuvers, pressing and stemming and balancing amid blunt features—lieback to face chip to mantel—and it took him nearly two hours to get two-thirds through these hundred feet. Through the camera's long lens I caught glimpses of the strain and concentration on his face, and surely his toes were screaming for all the continuous, pressing footwork. Another long pause yielded another piece of protection, this a tiny cam he tested by repeatedly yanking hard.

Then he bellowed "Take!" and weighted the rope. For a while he just dangled. He was studying the section above, arms folded across his chest, and he looked defeated.

"Lower!" Will hollered.

When he got to the bottom of the blank part he fixed the haul line, untied his lead rope, and rappelled to me. He was quiet. He seemed exhausted. He removed his shoes, toes red and raw. The cuts on his left hand had reopened, the splinted fingers oozing through seams in the tape. I'd have thought we were in retreat but that he had made no effort to clean the gear. Still, if I aided up to where the fixed line was anchored I'd be able to gather most of what lay above us and we could descend with little lost and only minimal litter.

"Should I clean it up?" I said. "Best I can?"

Will was leaning down, straining the anchors to massage his feet. He had drained the last of a liter of water, leaving us just a third of a bottle. He didn't reply, but slowly lifted his head and brought one foot up to rest sideways against the other knee.

"Hungry?" he said.

"What are we doing?"

He seemed still to be figuring it out. "The cam I lowered on is bomber." He sighed. "But I don't know if there's any more gear above it. Least not till where you see things open up again."

"So?"

"So I'm going to try. If I take a sixty-footer, you'll catch me. If I don't, maybe we watch the sunset from the top."

He thinned his rack to less than a third of what remained— the smallest nuts, a few tiny cams, and some bigger pieces for the next belay, should he get there. "I don't think I'm being stupid," he said. "I saw some things that make it look doable, and the rock's pretty solid, considering no one's harrumphed through there."

I pointed to the oozing bandages. "Help you there?"

"It would just make more trouble, I think." Gesturing to the sky, he added, "And it's getting on."

He stuffed his feet back into his shoes, grunting with the pain.

"Keep those headlamps handy," he said.

When he left the ledge again I felt less anxious than exhausted. I knew if Will spent anywhere near as much time on the pitch as he just had we would be dangling in slings through the night. While he was still on the easy part I dressed myself in more layers and rummaged deep into the pack for the headlamps and spare batteries. The first I moved to the top compartment of the pack. The second I only now remembered I'd forgotten in camp.

But Will, a true clinician, was far faster this time in regaining his high point, and so now the entire route lay in the balance of these forty feet above him before the cracks again open up a promising path to the summit. As he had below, he backcleaned certain pieces of gear to arrange a clean, largely friction-free path for the rope, even adding protection in two places and all the while reenacting move by move the bold and mysterious sequence between holdless corners and invisible features that had worked earlier. He backed up the top cam with another just beneath it, equalized these with another sling, and added a second carabiner as insurance against mishap. Then he paused. I expected he'd shout me a warning, a "Watch me!" or "Here it goes!" but instead he seemed just to be gathering himself, his gaze not lifted but level, maybe even eyes closed. There wasn't anything to figure out from here—it would just be a matter of finesse, psyche, and luck.

I could see from what followed why he'd stopped and lowered from there: to get above the two little cams required a kind of circus technique, bridging himself sideways across the cliff, his hands on the larger corner to the right, his feet out left on a dike I wouldn't have been able to discern but that his toes were massaging some kind of protuberance. Getting into this arrangement required of Will a cryptic negotiation between sinuous elasticity and boardlike stiffness, but once he was established the climbing itself appeared repetitive and straightforward, if strenuous—padding and toeing out left, pushing and pressing on the right. I was cautious in using the camera to watch—I had to provide a more nimble belay now—and when I did glance I looked ahead for holds that might provide an exit from the Houdini-like posture he had assumed. Unable to hear him, I couldn't tell how hard he was working, but one thing was clear: with each gesture he was farther out from the two cams, and if he didn't find a way to reposition he had little hope of placing additional protection even if a crack or seam were at hand. I found myself breathing deeply, as if for both of us.

Because Will was sideways, I couldn't gauge the extent of his progress—the ordinary body-length measurement was void. I snuck a quick peek through the camera, looking above him for something to hang hope on. If anything, it looked still smoother, and Will appeared stuck, as if he'd reached a dead end and the only thing left to do was resign himself to flight. He inched still further, his toes working the invisible edge at the left, and then, with his good hand firmly pressed on the corner to the right, he reached up with the bandaged hand and appeared to curl his fingers on something I couldn't see. In what seemed an effortless gesture, he brought one foot from the feature at the left to an edge directly beneath him. Instantly he was right side up and seemingly relaxed, studying the wall above him.

"Holy God," I muttered.

Will fingered the gear on his sling for the right-sized piece, but he didn't take anything off. He continued to study the next section, and with measured, self-assured moves climbed the vertical face on tiny crimps, these interspersed with just two or three decent edges. He had to be thirty feet out from those two micro-cams, but to watch him from my vantage you'd have thought he was on a sport cliff near home. Finally, with his right fist, he was joined to the unequivocal security of the crack. In two minutes he hollered off belay, and only after I detached him from my belay device and leaned out to confirm did I feel the extent of my relief—my "Belay is off" caught in my throat and lost in the breeze.

The light was low now—but no matter. We'd summit, even if by headlamp. I stripped down to climbing layers. I'd jumar the lead line to Will, pausing only to clean the insufficient gear and, here and there, to admire his genius. Then I'd lead the next pitch, or even the remainder of the route.

Eager to set off, I neglected to weight the rope gradually this time, so when I detached from the anchors I slid and sagged well to the right and fifteen feet beneath my belay. I could hear the snapping and sliding of gear above, the shoddier placements dislodged by the suddenly taut rope. In the light of the early evening the cliff's ruddy, pock-marked complexion grew smoother and more severe. As I worked the ascenders up, my toes barely glazed the cliff and I felt I was dangling in space, as on the famously exposed headwall pitches of El Cap. The eastern sky had turned rosy, a sort of refracted sunset, but the rock we clung to lay in a shroud, and when I got to the two little cams that marked the bottom of the last section I had to strain even to make out the feature Will had pawed at with his toes. The corner itself, the one he'd been pressing on with his hands, was polished as glass, every nubbin and crevice coated with chalk and the last twenty feet so steep and featureless I didn't even try to make sense of it but shuddered a couple of times for fright of what he had managed to do just half an hour earlier.

Nearing his small stance, I said, "You okay?" The laces on his shoes were loose and dangling. I could smell the stink of his feet.

"You kidding?" he said, his voice calm. "Never better."

"Never? Wow. Even if for you that's not so long."

"It's enough. It's what I got. It's all I need."

I smiled and slid up the rope to join him. "I won't even ask."

"I wouldn't know, if you mean how hard it is." He couldn't mask his joy. "All I know is we didn't do the next guys any favors here."

"No, you didn't. But you can come back."

"Let's just top off, before we get into any coming back. Headlamps handy?"

"Right here." I tapped the top of the pack. "I blew it on the batteries."

"We can conserve."

Only then did I smell it, acrid iron. It was dark enough I hadn't noticed the bandages on Will's left hand were fully red and dripping.

"Ouch," I said.

"Yeah, no two-fingering that last part."

I slipped the headlamp over my helmet, flipped it on, and looked down. The crimps and edges beneath us were slightly better than I feared if still dreadfully thin. On the one side they were white with a dusting of chalk, on the other slathered with pink goo.

I shined the light up. "Let me have at it."

"All you," Will said. He placed the rack over my head. "Run it to the end if you can. Looks like two pitches, maybe less."

The transition from aid to free climbing is always awkward— from gear-dependent to self-sufficient, muscles reengaged, balance reestablished. For the first few moves I was scared. To compensate I dug further into the crack with my feet and fists and consequently moved slowly. I needed the headlamp less to identify holds than to calm my nerves. When I placed a cam I inspected it too long; when I got above a piece of gear I looked down to see that the rope wasn't running over the gate or getting tangled in a sling. I told myself it didn't matter how fast I moved so long as I kept moving.

The buttresses and dihedrals that mark the upper reaches of the cliff are steeper than they appear from below, and were they not cleaved with deep cracks and cavities they would present a whole new round of the insurmountable. With soaring corners and roofs to either side and above me, I was grateful for the merciful cocoon in which I climbed, darkness interrupted only by my flickering headlamp. The fist crack off the belay is continuous for the first hundred feet or so, but then opens into something between an off-width and a chimney. This was more secure but slower still, and several times I paused to rest, always scouting for the next placement and too many times fiddling with nuts in order to keep the bigger cams at hand for what might lie ahead. Finally the wide stuff closes down again in a cleaner corner and hand crack, and right when I heard Will holler "Thirty feet!" I happened upon a triangular block wedged among other broken features that would make for a safe belay. Pitch ten of the route had taken me more than an hour and a half, and we were still well under the summit.

The wind kicked up, and as I belayed Will I grew cold, eager for him to arrive with the pack and extra layers. With the headlamp I attempted to take in the surroundings, but my little alcove was like a closet in a skyscraper. I turned off the light, leaned against the wall, and took in the rope. Will moved along steadily and without difficulty.

Then a sparkle, followed by another, like fireflies off a ways in the dark. Lights in the valley, in the vicinity of our meadow, it seemed—two, no three of them. Backpackers, most likely, this being an infrequent destination for climbers. I couldn't tell, but it seemed the activity was near to our camp. I had to squelch a fear of marauders. Having marked our sluggish progress all afternoon and evening, they were now rummaging through our food and gear for what they could scurry off with in the night. A couple of high-end sleeping bags. A beat-up tent. Dried pasta and tofu cakes. Spare batteries.

But this was unlikely, and then I began to question whether I had even seen lights down there. Only the stars broke the black of night now, with Will not bothering to deploy his headlamp but rather climbing by feel. Then I could hear him breathing. He was right under me.

"You see that?" I said.

"Can't see my hands in front of my face."

"Down by our camp. A little while ago. Lights."

"Well, mine's dead. How's yours?"

I flipped it on and off.

"Oh good," he said. "That'll be helpful."

When he got onto the stance and clipped himself to the anchors I started re-racking by feel rather than draw down the batteries. Had the cuts on his fingers not reopened, there wouldn't have been any question as to how to handle the next pitch—it would be his. But now we had to choose between my halting, phlegmatic pace and his doing further damage to himself. He grew quiet. I assumed he was debating our options as well. Then he said, "Turn that light on again."

I did. His good hand was deep into an interior pocket of his wind jacket. He pulled out two small Nalgene containers, like miniature water bottles, each with a screw top.

"Let's do this here," he said.

"What?"

"It's Dad. The last of him. Ashes. Mom gave me one of these when I turned sixteen, the other to Astrid when she did. Told us to scatter him in a place we love."

My eyes grew moist, my breath short.

"Astrid gave me hers, last summer, before we came up here," Will said. "And now we're here, right where you two were headed."

I nodded, the light of the headlamp bobbing up and down. Yes, I thought, and someone's missing.

"I never thought about it being anywhere else. So let's do it, before we top out."

The wind blew up the cliff from below, promising to send the ashes skyward.

"Take it," he said, handing me one of the containers. "You want to say anything?"

I didn't reply, my breath coming in uneven gulps.

Will waited. "Take a minute."

I leaned away from the anchor and looked up at the night sky. "Your dad, he was the easy one. Or at least he could talk up anyone about anything. He used to say he'd take care of the proximates, while I was busy with the ultimates."

"Where's this going, Joe?"

"I just mean I think he was right. He was onto something."

"Okay. So does this count? This an 'ultimate'?"

"No. It's a proximate. That's where I got it wrong." I fell into a full cry for a moment, then caught myself. "It's good, really. Feels good to have him again, even like this." I wiped my eyes with my fingers, then again with my shirt to massage away the sting of chalk. "What he was so good at, you know, it was the living. And really loving it. No fairytale. All in."

I shined the light at Will. His eyes had softened. I felt if I kept talking he would stand by all night.

By the light of my headlamp he unscrewed the cap from his little bottle and looked inside at the gray flecks of Pete's remains. He upended the vial, the contents falling out in a spray like coarse salt in air. With a finger, he reached into the bottle to break up a stubborn clump, and then this too fell out in several pebbles bouncing lightly off the face of the cliff beneath us.

I did the same with the other bottle, and Will tucked the empty vials back inside his jacket.

"I'll take it," Will said. "Let's get this done."

I handed over the rack and the headlamp, and then I was alone and cold again in the dark.

∽

Why I should have felt gloomy in the aftermath of this little rite I didn't know—until I realized I felt I was seeing it through Pete's eyes, or at least persuaded myself I was. The grief I'd known until then had been mostly a private, even selfish affair. However deep, even disabling, it resolves itself in time—as the distressed child is palliated not by anything so much as the exhaustion of crying. But here, in these sensible, tender, wordless gestures of Will's—the resurgent sting of Pete's death. I was seeing the loss not to Will and Astrid and Nor and me, but to him, to Pete. And from here the loss felt not predictable or tragic or any of the other coddling explanations I'd used in the past but simply sad.

I marked Will's progress through the dark above me, the clinking of gear, the flashing of the headlamp. I shivered. I wept. At some point the light dimmed and then went out altogether—I figured he had transitioned onto lower-angle features beyond my view. But the rope continued to play out slowly, and it was quite a while longer before I heard a distant "Off belay" shouted into the night. I blindly cleared the anchors.

On this pitch—a rope-length shaft of cracks and corners, steep but manageable—I had to work to contain my eagerness to get it over with and slipped a couple of times for trying to move too quickly. When I weighted the rope it snapped loudly on the cliff. I liebacked a twenty-foot section I would never have climbed so boldly in the light, and when I made out decent horizontal holds amid the blockier sections I fairly lunged for them, heedless of consequence. It turned out the angle doesn't back off at all, but the line bends to the right in the upper half of the pitch where I'd lost Will's light earlier. A right-facing corner up there proved tricky, at least in the dark, and then I was surprised to find myself standing on a large ledge on whose other side I could vaguely make out Will sitting cross-legged. It was no ledge at all—but a flat slab at the edge of Moriah's broad summit.

"Ahoy," he said.

"Hey."

"Nice work."

"You too," I said. "Give me a little light here, will you?"

"This one's dead, too. We're fairly skunked for light."

My flat soles on a secure slab, I didn't care. I untied.

Of the descent we knew only it was said to be an easy, scree-lined walk-off if you picked the right chute on the southeast side, and Class 3 or quite a lot worse if you didn't. So this part we didn't need to discuss—there would be no going down in the dark. It was nearing midnight, cold but not freezing, and all we could do now was gather our things and find as protected a place as we could to curl up and wait out the night.

We changed into approach shoes and coiled the ropes. I consolidated gear and stuffed the pack. Will padded around for a bivy site. The sky was starlit, with wispy, translucent clouds blowing quickly by, but with no moon the broken granite beneath our feet was faint at best. We each reminded the other to mind the lip of the cliff—you can get turned around in conditions like these. Will disappeared for a while, and just when I started to worry and thought to call to him I noticed he was ten feet to my left, shoulders framed by the black night.

"There's some sand over there," he said.

We hauled our things in that direction. It took a while to find the place again. I happened upon it first. It wasn't quite flat but sandy in places and protected by a two-foot wedge of granite on one side. We set the coiled ropes down for our heads and pawed at the surface to move smaller stones aside. Will lay down first.

"Cold?" he said.

"Gettin' there."

"A hold-me night."

"Yeah."

"Last time I did this was on Sentinel," he said. "Some German guy I hardly knew. Met him at the The Cookie a couple days before."

I was quiet.

"You?"

I had to think about it. It was with Pete, but I couldn't quite remember when or where. "In the trailer, I think. One of those crazy cold snaps you get over here. We'd burned through the wood inside and neither of us could persuade the other to stumble out to get more, so we just hunkered down in our bags on his bed. I remember waking up with your dad wrapped around me."

We lay the empty pack across our lower legs and feet. Will drew closer. I folded him inside my arms. We fell asleep like this and then alternated for several hours—me holding him, him holding me—some of the time at least one of us asleep but often both awake. At one point he told me about something he remembered from when he was small, something that happened on one of those outings with his dad when Pete and his partner were climbing and Will was at the bottom with his toys. It was in the Owens Gorge, he thought. "I guess I waddled off from where they were climbing. I had a stick. Something to mess in the dirt with. Then this loud buzz. Didn't even scare me. A fat rattler just a few feet away, curled up on a rock ledge at about the level of my face. Big wedge of a head, tongue darting. I watched it a minute. Then it slipped behind a block and I got busy with something else. I don't know if I ever told Dad. Or if I did whether he believed me."

I was lying face away from Will, his knees tucked behind mine. In a little while he was asleep, and the night grew colder around us. The wind died. Time slowed down. When we flipped again I slipped a hand inside his jacket. I hadn't realized how cold I was until the feeling started to return, first in the tingle of my skin and then, a heartbeat, faint for a while but with another adjustment palpable and steady as a drum. I pressed my fingers around Will's side until I could feel the curl of his ribcage. His heart, yes, but Pete's, too. Ashes tossed from a cliff, body in a refrigerator—they were no more, but this life, right here beneath my palm, inextricable. My breath grew short.

"Y'all right?" Will said.

I said yes, but it was cut with feeling. He covered my hand with his and seemed to mind me until he drifted off again.

Later still we flipped back and forth more frequently to ward off the awful contrast between body-to-body warmth on one side and frost on the other. Sometimes I could hear Will's deep and steady breathing—he had to have been spent—and then he'd say something as if he'd been alert for hours and knew I was, too. At one point, he said, "We're on top."

"Yes."

"I was dreaming."

"Here," I said, flipping over. "That better?"

His knees pushed mine onto rock, but I didn't bother to readjust.

"What are we calling it?" he said.

I lifted my eyes to the sky, the stars burning brighter here at the bridge between the deep of night and dawn. I didn't care what we called it. I was sad it was over. I wondered if anything is sadder than finishing.

We missed the narrow band of purple sunrise over the Whites. Our sky went from black to primrose in just minutes, and soon there was enough light to make out the cramped features of our summit bivouac. Then it was gray and cool, like twilight, and sufficient to see in all directions. I sat up, waking Will, and in minutes we started down.

We were even colder now, but at least we were moving. I had the pack and a rope. Will carried most of the rack and the other rope, clinking and jingling with each step. Where the broad summit falls away to the west a series of steep chutes drop down the side. Will led the way in picking one of these. Our hope was to slide through scree rather than have to use our hands on anything crumbly and exposed. After a couple of false starts we seemed to alight upon a good option.

"Hey," Will said, pointing to the high peaks to the west, their rocky summits yellow with first light. On one we could see a band of blue ice in the upper lip of a snowfield and two deep crevasses where the whole thing appeared to be coming apart. The sky framing the ridge was the bright baby blue of new morning, but the watercolor fantasy only reminded me how heavy I was with fatigue. We were finally in view of easier walking beneath us, Will more buoyant than I, relieved, proud, eager to move along. Several times he waited for me to catch up.

We crossed a sandy plateau on the mountain's western flanks, angling around toward the upper reaches of our canyon until our own Northeast Face began to emerge again, first the far, more formidable side, then the back sides of our buttresses and corners, and finally the route itself, all aglow in the early morning sun. Will got the camera and worked to balance it on a boulder. He wanted a photo of both of us with yesterday's handiwork soaring in the background.

"Got it yet?" he said.

I didn't know what he was talking about.

"The name."

"You did the business," I said. "You name it."

He was fiddling with the camera.

"I'd say 'The Withholder,'" he said, "except it's too good for that."

"On account of the blank parts."

"Hah!" he crowed, trotting toward me as the camera blinked. "On account of you! Has there ever been someone who had so little to say about himself?"

I knew it wasn't a compliment, but it was touching to me. "Well, either way you're right. That isn't it."

The shutter snapped. "We'll figure something out," he said.

Now we were nearing familiar territory, the line we had trod many times from camp to the base of the cliff, and shortly we got separated amid boulders the size of trucks. I emerged in an alpine field beside one of several patches of snow that feed the stream by our camp. Soon we'd be able to see the meadow in the distance. I turned to look for Will. Nothing. Then I spotted him quite a ways back. He was standing on one of the boulders and looking off into the distance. He waved. I waved too, but it seemed he wasn't waving at me.

I heard them before I saw them, not far off, a cackle of voices.

Then bright jackets, knit hats—alpine wear and enthusiasm. Even before I could see their faces I could tell it was Nor, Astrid, and Al, hiking up toward us. The lights I'd seen the night before, theirs.

Will caught up to me when they were just a hundred yards off. Al was in the lead. Their appearing fresh and happy, summer hikers greeting the day, reminded me how beat up I was, and when we met in the talus I felt I might collapse amid the combination of exhaustion and relief. Al embraced Will, Nor tended to me, and Astrid stood to the side waiting for the hullaballoo to subside. If Astrid had had worries she didn't let on, but the other two were effusive in relating theirs, less on account of our failing to show up in Mammoth earlier in the week as planned than the vacancy they'd encountered when they arrived at our empty camp late the previous afternoon. It was Astrid who first spotted headlamps on the upper reaches of the cliff. They marked our progress into the night, and when the lights flickered out they figured we were on top and felt reassured for the first time in days.

After some debate about when and how to treat Will's hand, and then another round of photographs, most of just Will and me and Moriah, we started down to the meadow together. Al again took the lead and Will went last of the five of us, a steady train across alpine fellfields and sandy stretches dotted with glacial erratics. Each of them had taken something to lighten our loads, and they talked readily among themselves. I felt encased in a bubble, my face growing hot the lower we got, and when we finally made it to camp I dropped the pack and collapsed inside our tent without removing even my shoes.

Late in the morning Will shook me awake. I said I needed another hour—I could imagine getting up but not hiking out. Several hours later it was Nor waking the two of us. Someone had to get going, she said. She'd told a neighbor to alert Search and Rescue if she didn't call by this evening. We roused, they made us coffee and oatmeal, and in the midafternoon we packed our camp and started down. Now I wasn't just tired but sore, each step a bit of labor, but with the five of us our packs were lighter and the prospect of food and a bed almost enough to keep me going.

At some point I heard Will rebuffing Al's suggestion that he'd just ticked his own Dawn Wall.

"Minus the circus, too," she added. "No meadow clogged with TV trucks."

"Tommy's the man," Will said.

He looked at me. I shrugged. I wanted to say you're pretty special, too.

Later, just before a bend in the canyon would put us out of Moriah's range for good, Will had us stop once more for a picture. With the afternoon sun behind the peak, the cliff looked black and blank and cold. We posed, arm in arm, haggard and happy. Without breaking his smile or taking his eyes off Al's camera, Will said, "How about 'Heaven'?"

I must have looked doubtful.

"You know, with some of Dad up there now?"

"Come on, you two," Al shouted. "Lighten it up a little."

"Then help me," he said.

"Hunter-Hunter," I suggested, nodding back toward the peak. "You can add Holland in a parenthesis if you need to rope me in, but this is your dad's and yours."

Will grabbed my pack and turned me around. "There," he said.

We looked together, the setting sun touching just the top.

"Hunter-Holland," he added. "Straight up."

Will faced me again for a moment, his eyes wet. Then he smiled, nudged me with his shoulder, and we started off again down the canyon.

We had a route, we had the name, and in four or five hours we'd have a bath and a beer. Astrid scooted by us on the left and set the pace. Layered with two ropes diagonally across her shoulders, she looked like an advertisement for a Swiss holiday. Al and Nor got well ahead of us, too, and in the early evening a hot wind blew up from the valley, whipping at the laurels along the creek. Will and I moved slowly. We had grown quiet—each of us in a kind of dream state, clinging to the minutiae of the climb lest we lose it forever but no less grateful it was safely behind us and beyond view. I found I had to think to step forward, lurching along on bone. Then, with the last of the light, we emerged out of the mountains on a broad, sandy alluvial fan, Will's truck and Nor's car glinting in the sagebrush half a mile off, and here at the end of the day the great eastern escarpment stretched north and south farther than the eye can see.

AFTERWORD

༄

Autumn 2017

Headlamps hang from a nail above the bed. A hand crawls up the log wall in the dark and a light snaps on. Al groans and whispers. She's been in a deep sleep. For a second she can't remember what they're doing and why the alpine start.

Will steps barefoot onto the wooden floor, then into his pants and sandals. He's been awake for hours. Outside, between the pines, he can see stars. It's a cold, calm morning in early autumn. It's just right.

They ease down the steep drive in the dark. In minutes the truck's cab is warm and Will's are the only headlights on the paved road to the ski area. With the summer season over they're allowed to drive all the way to Agnew Meadows—one reason he wanted to wait until fall, not to deal with the shuttle. Another, the weather. Few thunderstorms this time of year. But mainly he wanted the chance to have it all to himself, undistracted and alone.

On the west side of the pass the road drops steeply. Will slows. He slips a tape into the old-style stereo Ricky installed two years ago so he could listen to his father's music—the three dozen or so tapes and CDs that were in Pete's truck when the Forest Service towed it from the trailhead. He's cued this one to something called "Fake Plastic Trees." They've only a few miles more, and Will knows whatever he plays last will be looping in his mind all day. This is the loop he wants. He doesn't know what it's about—much of his dad's music is like that—though he can tell it bleeds disappointment, and it's a lyric for Will that both memorializes his parents' marriage and hardens him against it. *It wears her out, it wears her out.*

Will and Al look ahead. He slows more, wary of deer. She's been working for days not to freight Will with her worry, and as they start the hairpin turn from which a dirt road leads to the trailhead he reaches for her hand. It's cold. He steals a glance. Her eyes are wet. Down in the valley here the grass at the sides of the road is splashed with frost.

She never tried to talk him out of it. Even when they made their "no hard soloing" agreement last year, there was an unspoken understanding this could be the single exception. Easy things were still fair game. In just the last season they'd done three laps of Cathedral unroped and both the ridge routes on Conness. A highlight from the year before was the long north buttress on Bear Creek Spire. Nothing bold or dangerous—just long, easy, free, and fast. They both felt this was about as good as climbing got these days, and a rare perk of their partnership. But a corollary is that they tend to rope up only for something serious and challenging—no Third Pillar of Dana or Sun Ribbon Arête. No Southeast Face of Clyde.

If I could be who you wanted, if I could be who you wanted. All the time.

A couple of times she even proposed they do it together, though not unroped. How appropriate, she felt. A statement of intimacy. But Will never went for it. He only said, "If I get around to it, my mother can't know."

Al agreed.

The dirt parking area is empty. Will kills the engine. He wonders if he's pulled into the spot where his dad left his truck. In the quiet he feels his heart thumping unnaturally again, as it had during the night. The only way to relax is to move, he thinks.

Al has agreed to wait, all day. Whether he changes his mind and turns around in the first half mile or summits and walks off, she'll be here—seven in the morning or seven in the evening. At some point she might walk around, but she'll never be gone from the area around the truck for long. If he's not back by midafternoon she might hike in. No farther than Shadow Lake.

Will is grateful. He's told her he doesn't really know how far he'll get with this. He only knows he wants to do it alone.

In the bed of the truck is a small pack with a windshirt for climbing and one other warm layer, energy bars and water, rock shoes and chalk bag. He grabs the pack and leans over to tie his shoes. He knows Al's anxious. He wants to get going.

Will pulls her into him, his back against the warm engine. Her lips near his ear, she reminds him, "Don't do it unless you're sure. It'll always be here."

He holds her tighter for a pace, then kisses her under her eye.

"See you later," he says, backing away but taking her hands in his. "And thank you."

Will wears a headlamp, but he resists disturbing the dark merely to find the trail. It's a sandy stretch through a meadow, cold with frost and canopied with stars.

Al can hear him longer than she can see him. She pushes aside the awful thoughts that play through her head. Was that the last time? How unthinkably unfair for Nor. She gets back inside the cab of the truck and unfurls the sleeping bag and pillow she'd cradled on the drive. With her feet by the steering wheel and her head at the other door, she curls into the remaining warmth and hopes for sleep.

There aren't five miles of trail within a hundred miles of Mammoth Will doesn't know by heart—but for this stretch. He may have hiked the first bit as a kid, if not with his father when he was small then possibly with any number of the family friends, mostly men, who came around those first few years to take Will away for a few hours, give Nor a break. But he's avoided it since he was nine and learned the details of Pete's death, the when and where and what he'd been up to, and in the years since whenever he drives past here to get to Reds Meadow or the Postpile he notes this little trailhead but never stops. Clyde is another matter, of course, the proud dark spire on the horizon. Unavoidable as the Eiffel Tower to a boy from Paris.

Will is fine with the cold—he'd be soaked with dew from so much overgrown deer brush but that it's frosted. He avoids putting his hands in his pockets should he stumble in the dark and wishes he'd brought gloves. Like Al, he trains his mind from the histrionic—doesn't allow himself to think about his father walking the same path on a July morning nineteen years ago, doesn't wonder what time of day—much less if—he'll be walking back in the opposite direction, nor how he'll feel. He's moving easily, following the plume of his own breath, his quickened heart finally in sync with his intention. He knows the topography, so he's unsurprised when the trail rises sharply out of the valley, and with just a few hundred feet of elevation gain the air feels ten degrees warmer. Sunrise isn't until 6:45 but already there's a lighter band of sky in the east, and though the trail is rockier here Will can see almost fine.

He knows Al is more nervous than he. The curious thing, he thinks, is he wouldn't be doing it but for her—not for her support and encouragement, but for what he feels about the future. Clyde's been on his mind for a long time, but he's only recently trusted himself to consider it. These days he's a bit haunted by some of the things he did when he was fourteen, fifteen, and sixteen—the highball boulders, sometimes with four or five pads and several spotters twenty, thirty, even forty feet underneath him. Stuff he'd never do now, and not for lack of appetite or ability. It's just that back then he felt he could afford to fall, could get hurt, or worse. Now he's got something to keep it together for, something more than climbing to do today, which is getting back to Al tonight. And, in Will's mind, it's the getting back undamaged that makes the solo reasonable.

Plus, his dad used to solo the route more or less regularly, as much as once a year. What could be the problem? What *was* the problem?

Only when he intersects the stream does he realize how noisy his head has been for the last many hours. The music here is a relief—splash, tumble, cascade. He cleans his hands at one of the crossings—the water warmer than the air. There's sunlight on trees farther up, and Will starts to feel this is it, I'm on my way. I'll be warm soon.

Just a few yards beyond the outlet of Shadow Lake, Will steps onto a granite boulder. The water at his feet is green in the early morning but the rest of the lake black and still. He stops here, as planned. He's told himself to have a couple of these moments to pause, and if it doesn't feel right, reconsider. It's momentum that's dangerous, he believes, the tease of false urgency, the heedlessness of *go, go, go*. No matter how this day unfolds, he wants to be in it. He sits cross-legged on the rock. A ripple of breeze on the lake and some bird activity in nearby trees. When he was young Will felt disdain for the day hikers for whom an alpine lake was sufficient. Now he envies them. The adequacy of a captivating slice of wilderness, the safety of a trail. The severe beauty of the vertical backdrop, minus any inclination to join oneself to it.

He carries on, the trail here cut by roots and rutted through meadows. A single yellow tent is tucked amid trees on the north shore but there's no evidence of movement nearby. Probably backpackers on their first or last night—climbers would be camped farther in. Will looks closely just to be sure there isn't a rope or rack or some other indicator lying around. He's told himself if anyone else is on Clyde, it's not his day. The Minarets are known for having loose rock. But that's not it. He just doesn't want any distractions. If this is as close as he can get to summoning the spirit of his father, he doesn't want to have it mucked up by, well, other spirits.

He wonders about that, a something that lives on. It didn't bug him when he was younger, and when his mom went all-in at church he even grew skeptical—all that confidence seemed to poke at a deeper anxiety. He was doing risky things then, and it felt easier not to ponder the cosmic unknowns. You don't stick a V9 on tenuous crimps twenty feet off the deck but for surrendering to the business of now. Later, though, he started to wonder. He'd thought he might get something more on this on Moriah, a big project like that not just with Dad's longtime partner but a minister, or ex-minister, besides. All those logistics and long approaches, nights in a tent, rest days. But no. Not even Joe. Everyone is tentative, coy, or vague on the matter—apart from the "He's alive in you" gestures he and Astrid get from all sides, which to Will feel no less vacant and obligatory than "Merry Christmas."

He's read about this stretch of trail between the first two lakes, Shadow and Ediza. Someone wrote in a magazine it was the most pristine three miles of the entire Sierra Nevada—and overnight it was anything but, and not long after the shuttle became a mandatory part of the equation in summer. But Will finds it no more trampled than any other reasonably accessible part of the wilderness, and it is gorgeous: a steady rise up the Minarets' principal drainage, a dancing creek just off to the side. In early summer there would be wildflowers. Now there are dried stalks of shooting stars and in open stretches clumps of the dun, desiccated leaves of frostbitten mule ears. He thinks he'd like to get back here earlier in the season, when it's wet. Then he remembers what he's doing.

It's an hour to Ediza. In the warmer air he starts to tire. He knows he didn't get much rest last night, and now wonders just how many nights it's been since he slept well. The restlessness predated his telling Al it was time. Later this month. Time for Clyde. It had been stirring in him all season, a kind of foreknowledge.

When Will phoned me in July, two years to the day since our summit bivy, we talked mostly about other things. The call wasn't out of the blue; we'd been in touch from time to time. He'd grown more interested in his father since our time together. He said he'd become less afraid of what he would feel for looking. And in finding himself more connected, he also felt freer. Now when someone referenced him as Pete Hunter's son it felt like a happy connection rather than a dark twist of fate.

But this time he talked mostly about what was going on now. He gave me the latest on Al and Astrid. He wanted to know if I'd gotten started. I said, once again, I've got notes. He wanted to know what was keeping me from writing it out. I said I wasn't sure.

"Not enough of a story?" he said.

I thought about that. "No, it's too much."

He chuckled. "I'll say. Lotta time in slings, at least in your version."

"It's not that," I said.

"Well, when you get to it I hope you'll just tell it straight. You have a way of being, you know, roundabout."

I laughed.

"You don't have to make sense of it, Joe. Just project it. Get it written down."

Then, in a near whisper, he told me he was going to do Clyde. In the fall.

I grew quiet, my throat tight.

"Joe?"

"You don't have to. You know that."

"I know."

"Your mom?"

"She'll never know."

In the quiet I could hear him breathe.

"Unless . . ." I said.

He sighed. He didn't like me pushing back.

"In which case," he said, "she's got more practice than anyone else. More important, I think she'd even understand."

"And Al?"

"Supportive."

"So that leaves me."

"It's not for permission, Joe. I'm just telling you."

I didn't try to talk him out of it. I just said I hope you're careful. "And please," I said, "Let me know when it's done."

"I wanted you to know," he said. "I guess I figure it's part of the story."

Without thinking, I said, "So long as you get back all right. I'll need the details."

"And say I don't. Nothing to say then?"

I was quiet, suddenly choked up.

"Then just make it up."

❧

In the last little while before Lake Ediza, Will's eyes are so dry he sometimes walks with one closed. Full sun, nearly warm. He's amazed at how tired he is. The lake is blue and still and deep, the trail skirting the southern edge through pine-dappled light and then veering away from the shore to climb out of the basin. Will leaves the trail in search of a patch of grass in the sun. He's two-thirds of the way to Clyde—time for another session to sit and consider. There's a dry meadowy area just feet from the water where a broad granite slab forms a tiny amphitheater of still air and sunlight and heat. Will drops the pack on the stiff, golden grass. He doesn't sit but lies down, head on the pack. He closes his eyes. He feels as though his muscles aren't resting on the ground so much as sloughing off his bones. It's not the day, he tells himself. I don't have the juice, or not the right juice anyway. Now that he's decided to turn around, he can finally sleep.

When Will wakes he is initially disoriented, not with *Where am I?* but rather *What happened that I could sleep so deeply?* He's not sure what time it is and didn't bring a watch, but the sun is not where it was before. He doesn't remember anything he dreamed. He sits, then stands, puts the little pack on and starts up toward the trail. He's a little stiff. He thinks he may have been out for a couple hours, even. He thinks if it's an encounter with his father he's after maybe this is as good as any—to wander into the wilderness and sleep so soundly and go some other place so fully you can't even remember, or know, what was there.

He sees the trail thirty or forty yards before he joins it and thinks at least Al will be happy to see me. And like she said, it will always be here.

But when his foot falls on the worn path he turns right, toward Clyde, not back in the direction he came from. He wonders for a moment if this is "Go, go, go" and quickly pushes the thought from his mind. The trail is steeper and less well maintained from here, but he's got wind now, and a lightness to his step. He'd thought about this day years ago and started planning for it earlier this summer, and always imagined he'd feel this way on the approach.

Iceberg Lake comes quickly, then Cecile. The first is at treeline, the second above. These are larger, more austere alpine basins than Ediza's, the lakes frozen as much as half the year. Even in autumn Cecile has a snowbank above the shore on the far side. Will stops nearby, cups his hands together, and splashes his face. He knows the next snowfield is the massive one he must ascend to get under Clyde's Southeast Face. So this, Will feels, more than any first moves on steep rock, is the start of the climb and a sort of point of no return. If he turns around above here he will be downclimbing, retreating. If he turns around now he'll merely be changing his mind.

What to do?

The morning's song comes looping back—*A green plastic watering can. A town full of rubber plans.* He wonders if his is another rubber plan, no more or less meaningful than kicking around the town skate park all day on his BMX bike when he was seven, eight, and nine years old. No more or less a rite and ritual, this climb, than any other. Just an idea. An idea slathered with other ideas. It's too neat, he knows. Possibly too dangerous. In any case unforgivably rude to his mother, and not very kind to Al.

But he's curious, too. Whatever his avocations, attitude, voice—all the little ways, he's told, you're your father's son—he's never been all that identified with Pete. His dad is someone he vaguely recalls, a supposedly important someone who one summer afternoon neglected to come home, and was no more. Was, and is not. Is not, and somehow never was.

Only in the past two or three years, since Moriah, or maybe to make Moriah happen, maybe to make Joe happen, and now with Al, especially with Al—he's grown curious. Or rather he's felt curious, something welling up in him not to learn who and how his father was but to express something of what he already knows. Yes, it's in me too. A recognition he feels—and at odd and surprising times. Opening the door for Al. Calling Joe on the phone. Holding the rope more attentively when someone he loves is on the other end.

Except here. The part he doesn't know is the last part. So the idea Will has, the dangerous idea, is to become acquainted not with his father but with himself. With this one other piece, the one he'd told himself was off limits. Not the most important piece, he knows, but it's the one he has obediently avoided. So he needs to do it now, he thinks—before there's a somebody else whose childhood could be punctuated and mercilessly length-ened under the long shadow of a vacancy.

Now his breath is full and deep and eager. He's above ten thousand feet, shoes sinking into the sandy moraine between the lake and the snowfield, and in another ten minutes he's on it—placing his feet carefully at first where the scalloped edges are more ice than snow, and then moving easily up the lower camber of a gentle ramp that will take him up to the edge of dark rock. He's avoided even glancing at the cliff until now, not just out of habit but worried he won't be able to look at it with-out bringing to mind his father plummeting off. But soon he needs to gain the advantage of this full frontal view to line up the cliff's larger features with the topo map he carries in his pocket. A single page, xeroxed several weeks ago in town from a notebook where his dad catalogued years of routes in hand-drawn maps, annotated and idiosyncratic, with rack informa-tion tidily delineated in the corner and brief descriptions of the approach and descent. This one: *"App: 3 hrs. from Agn. Mdws. Descend SW from summit to notch. 3ʳᵈ to snow. 4+ hrs. from the top."* And below that: *"Car to car: 9 hrs. solo. ~15+ w/ client."* Pete's topos themselves tended to less detail than those in published guidebooks, but they're better in rendering particular parts of a route—the hard or best parts, usually—and Will is frequently impressed at how readily his own tastes are matched to his dad's, as well as how well his father gauged the time to get any-where. But this, of course, just another indicator. Lungs, legs. Your father's son.

Halfway up the snowfield Will pauses. He reaches to his back pocket, pulls the paper out and unfolds it. When he lifts his eyes to the mountain, his heart is beating fast, but not from feel-ing, and he's surprised he doesn't feel something—so proximate now to what he's averted his eyes from all these years. The steep dark face. The scene of the accident. If anything, the looking is ordinary, and inspiring. He locks onto the signature corner two-thirds of the way up, a blocky hanging buttress, big as a freight train standing on end, and traces the route down from there—all of it so obvious he doesn't even glance at the map. All but that midsection three hundred feet above the traverse, which, he knows from the report, is where they believe Pete fell from. Believe, don't know. And not from anything forensic, not from blood or a piece of torn fabric left behind. Not even because of where on the snowfield his body was found or in what condition. Just on account of that part of the cliff's reputation for friable rock. They may merely have been burnishing his reputation, Will thinks. Keep the mythology intact. No way Pete could have fallen off anything solid.

At the upper lip of the snowfield, just a step-across to the dry ledge that is the bottom of the Southeast Face Direct, Will turns to have a look back. He'll be locked in for the next two or three hours, and if he pauses again to take in the view it will likely be from the summit. The snow is a mirror for the sun—Will's face grows hot—but the glare doesn't blot out Mammoth's broad shoulders in the distance and the cobalt-blue surface of Cecile Lake in the foreground, small and still and neatly contained as a birdbath. Hard to believe he was there an hour ago. He leans over to stretch, his knuckles scraping granules of corn snow beside his shoes. He unties these, and moments later, when he hops across the bergschrund, nearly loses one in the frozen maw between ice and rock.

Barefoot now, Will sits on the rock ledge. He closes his eyes to quiet his mind, slow his heart, and try as best he can to join the moment. Before he'd made the pact with Al he'd done other long solos of this type, only a few times of routes more difficult and only once on something he hadn't climbed before with a partner and proper protection. Dark Star, on Temple Crag, and it was scary. As here, the crux comes early and the route is long. As here, Will carried a copy of his father's topo, which he consulted several times. But he never felt secure, not on the easy first moves, nor on the 5.10 pitches, nor higher up, where he intercepted a party of two who had camped at Third Lake and were making good time but still going nowhere near as fast as he was alone and unroped. They had a tidy alpine rack and a bulging pack. Each wore a white helmet, the older guy's heavily scratched and scarred. Will caught them right when the leader was moving onto the sixth pitch, and he knew he should have scooted along and been glad to get above lest they dislodge a rock or drop some gear. Instead he felt grateful for the company, even half-wished he could tie in and do his part for the team. Climbing near to them for a while, he realized it wasn't the rope. Just this proximity to others conferred a measure of security. He waited for them at the seventh belay, not just for the leader but for both. The older guy sensed something, and before Will set off again, he asked, "You all right?"

"Yeah, thanks. Have to say, it's not as much fun as I expected."

"Kind of a dirt pile, this buttress."

Will was sitting on a little pillar, fifteen feet above their stance and well over a thousand above the base. He didn't make any gesture to move along.

"Need anything?" the older guy said. "We've got food and water."

Will was carrying just a windbreaker, approach shoes, and a chalk bag.

"No. Thanks."

"You know, if you like you can join us. We can even tie you in. There's webbing in the pack here."

Will appreciated the gesture. He'd once done the same for a guy gripped on Cathedral—who, an hour later, was effusive in thanking Will but couldn't bring himself to look him in the eye even as they shared the tiny summit block. Will had the feeling the man on Dark Star had taken care of someone like him in the past as well.

"No, I'm good. Thanks."

"All right. Have fun. Change your mind, you know where we are."

Will is remembering this exchange as he slips his feet into his climbing shoes. Then he rises, opens the chalk bag and slides it around to his sacrum. He clips his approach shoes to a piece of webbing on his waist and cinches this tight. The little daypack with food, water, and another layer of clothing he leaves on the ledge for later.

Will faces the cliff, then bows his head. He caresses the rock lightly, like a pianist at the keys, then blindly inserts his fingers into the shallow slots that are the first decent holds. These feel secure, but the feet are the telltales. Are they precise and tacky, or are they like hooves? You know only once you're on them—the micro-edges, jams, and smears. Solution pockets and friction. Today Will can't tell—not just yet. The first hundred feet ascend a splotched granite corner of a type he'd be nearly comfortable downclimbing, '5.10 minus' or no. The crux passes mysteriously—no part harder than any other, maybe a bit steeper for thirty feet and no doubt trickier to protect but of course this is as irrelevant to Will as it was to Pete, and in twenty minutes he's three hundred feet up. Here a generous traverse swings left, transitioning onto the famous mahogany rock that looks black from any vantage but this, your eyes inches from the broken plates and manifold holds that make a passage up these vertical fifteen hundred feet not only plausible but fun. "If Half Dome were made of this stuff you'd have to take a number to get on it," Will remembers one guidebook reading.

He agrees. After pausing to adjust a shoe, Will is slotted into the conspicuous wide crack directly beneath the great face from which his father is believed to have fallen. The crack is perfectly sized for Will and easy to manage on account of various holds on either side of the dark interior. Twice he stops. Expanding his chest with a full breath, he's fully wedged and weightless, his arms entirely at rest. He could even remove his feet from their tiny crimps, but doesn't. He leans his face against the rock to admire the southern half of the magnificent wall he's halfway up. He's not thinking of his dad, just resting and enjoying the view. He's knows where he is. He knows the upper end of this crack pinches off, and then he's launched into the three or four acres of vertical terrain where his father last clung to life. Will reassumes the rhythmic mantra of "three limbs on" that is the soloist's only safety, and continues.

This part, well, it's fun. So perfectly steep, so amply featured. Several times he reaches for holds with positive edges of the sort he would ordinarily seize powerfully and even lean out on to stretch, rest, and revel—but here he treads lightly and always with at least one good foothold. Then, in the upper half, the song again, and a line he's not sure he has right but can't believe he'd be so clever as to make up: *But gravity always wins. And it wears him out. It wears him out.* A jet is streaking overhead, barely audible and probably ten thousand feet above, probably on approach to San Francisco. Will sees himself as someone from the plane would see him, which is to say, not at all. A terrific black tower soaring above a snowfield, a series of shimmering lakes in the distance—a gorgeous, formidable landscape. Too high for any kind of life form, even the birds.

The plane speeds along into silence. Will continues to rise. It's almost too easy.

Off to the left and only a little below a single swallow darts and dives and snickers agreeably in the mountain air. Will stops. He's got good holds, the right and more secure hand on a flat edge, the left curled onto a smaller but even better fissure, this one tingling as it does ever since he sliced the two fingers. His weight is comfortably distributed on four holds, none of which is larger than half an inch. And here he thinks of his father. Did he pause to enjoy the birds? Did he get this far? Is this lone swallow a descendent of others that played here in summer nearly twenty years ago? The thoughts play across his mind, and as Will starts to see himself from the inside, he grows wary, even a little frightened. He's more than a thousand feet off the deck. A single misstep, a sudden distraction, a fractured hold—he's joined to oblivion. He raises his right foot higher onto a thinner edge, stretched beyond comfortable, and cautiously levers onto this hip. The bird's gone quiet, replaced by another sound. Something strange, like air through a pipe. It's the wind. It's the wind penetrating the wall, blowing through the very cracks and crevices that make the cliff climbable. It feels as though the whole thing could peel off and him with it—but then, too, he's light as the wind in the rock, and now easing through the upper part of the great face without further thought or hesitation.

The massive dihedral marks the last part of the climb, two walls joined at ninety degrees. Will stems through this corner eagerly, pausing from time to time to look between his legs at the dark cliff and splash of snow far below. Twice he liebacks through sections he could more securely jam, and always he sets his toes on the better edges for safety. He has the sense he's nearly finished here. He reminds himself, *Stay till the end*, but this is futile. Summit fever. He can't see it but he can practically smell it, and the last hundred feet of the great corner are as perfunctory and unmemorable as walking from his cabin to the truck before dawn.

He's been scrambling for a while before he realizes his hands are beneath him, pressing on blocks for balance rather than reaching above for holds, and here a little surge of feeling. He's safe. He's alone. He's nearly on top. He thinks of Al down there, waiting. He thinks he must hurry so she too can know it's done. But first, tag the summit, and have a look.

～

When Al wakes again the windows of the cab are wet with her breath. It's cold inside. She wishes she'd moved the truck into the sun. Even as she glances at her wrist she reminds herself to avoid marking the time. He'll be back when he's back. Not a minute before or after.

She wanders down the road with a yoga mat to a dry, sandy patch beside the long meadow that's now bathed in sunshine. She's instantly warm. She lays out the mat and sits a while, facing the light, her feet crossed in unmatching socks. The point is to spend time. Wherever he is now, he's still on approach—the earliest he could be on the cliff would be midmorning. Still, not to know is annoying. To worry is hard, as to be happy is its own burden. She remembers. She was unburdened before she met Will. Restless maybe, but free. *I know too much*, she thinks. Rock fall. Getting off route. She sees it all, and all the time. Gear failure. A patch of black ice on 395.

They'd come to the agreement about soloing almost simultaneously and without conflict, each seeking another level of insurance for nothing so much as the other. "Just this," she said, curling around him in bed.

He cupped the back of her head with his hand. "And this."

He'd been moving in this direction for some time, she knew—dangerous boulder problems already years behind him, but now cured even of reflexive disdain for carrying an extra rope so they wouldn't have to downclimb the so-called easy fifth-class. Will was no less confident than at any point in his life. Nor was he anxious about mishaps and anomalies. He was just more alert to his own dimensions—fragile as anyone else's. The clients he guided. Al's. His father's.

Another part of the story is one she hasn't told him: how when they were in Tuolumne a year ago and Will was off guiding a father and son on Third Pillar and she set out to do Lembert Direct alone and unroped and nearly died for fright. Her hope had been to be on the dome's west side in the late afternoon and to walk down the slabs in the yellow light of evening, arriving back in camp not long before Will or perhaps even after. There wouldn't be anyone above her at that hour, nor the clot of beginners on the adjacent easy route who might raise a cackle over someone soloing something hard nearby. The Direct may be the hardest route on the wall, but the cruxes involve steep cracks, whereas Crying Time's are on spooky, delicate knobs. Al knew both routes well and never felt anything but secure on them.

This was different. Even walking to the cliff she found her heart leaping along. Then, lacing her shoes at the base of the slab, she noticed her fingers kind of dancing involuntarily. She didn't so much as pause on the first, fourth-class section but thought it felt somehow slipperier than in the past and made a mental note to keep her feet under her should she start sliding down the initial groove. Then the first pitch. It's nothing, really, just a trough that steepens and becomes a seam adequate for fingers and smearing feet. It felt slick too, and as she approached the first crux, where you step left on good feet to do an insecure move and pass a bulge, she found herself panting. Twice she stepped onto a nickel-sized knob and then eased back down. She questioned not just her competence but her sense of her own judgement—how can this feel so sketchy? Then she allowed herself to imagine the consequences of falling. If her head weren't severely injured she might live. Whatever happened, it would be beyond ugly.

She scooched back into the seam and started down, at first quietly relieved for reversing course. But where the crack closes up and becomes more of a friction climb, she felt shaky again. Like a first-time climber, she leaned into the rock and thereby became still more slippery, and now she clutched with her fingertips, trying to wedge them in the tiny gap where two bulbous masses are joined and where on roped ascents she'd placed stoppers more for practice than any need for security. A foot skidded. She gave a little shriek, ripping her pants on a crystal. The other foot was safely fastened, and in just two or three moves she was back on the lower angle section below.

At the base Al changed out of her climbing shoes. She grew angry she had so underestimated the route, if still a ways from *What was I thinking?* She imagined walking back to their empty camp. Instead, she moved fifty yards to the right to the standard beginners' route, changed back into her climbing shoes, and went through the same mental checklist as before. Here, on Northwest Books, she encountered no trouble, nor any anxiety about the big air beneath her. In thirty minutes she was on top and in an hour halfway down the slabs when she saw Will's truck sweep past toward the bridge and turn into the campground.

He was at the wooden table in their campsite and glad to see her. When she drew closer, he noticed the bloodstained flap of fabric near her right knee.

"You okay?" he said.

"It's nothing. Just nicked it. Northwest Books."

This felt a little dishonest, but she wanted to figure it out for herself—what had happened up there today?—before parsing it with Will. And then, in November, the rule about soloing—his idea, and the perfect chance to tell him. But this seemed its own thing, their agreement, not something to sully with her stuff. And then winter, spring, and summer—days and weeks and months coating over her fright and even the little scar by her knee undetectable except after a long soak in a hot tub. And now, here, in her imagination of Will today.

When she gets back to the trailhead the truck is in the sun. She sits nearby in a foldable camp chair with a book and her journal. The book is *When Things Fall Apart*. It's by a Buddhist nun, and it seems to Al mistitled—the little homilies more about how to live than how to survive hardship. When she finds herself reading the same paragraph over and over she turns to her journal. She writes "Ten things I want to do with you." The first seven come fast, and soon she has fourteen. From these she picks and reorders another list on the adjacent page. She can't get it to ten. Number three is "Hold you." Thirteen is "Try that thing your dad said to Joe about it being awesome enough just to enjoy your life." Fourteen is "Get a puppy."

At midday she sets off to walk the perimeter of Agnew Meadows, intending to move as slowly as possible. The meadows themselves are green but everything around the edges where the trail goes is dried out and brown, and she finds it hard to meditate on dead things. Her heart leaps unnaturally—she knows where Will is now. She considers walking normally, maybe doing a couple of laps—it's more than a mile around—but decides instead to go no more than twenty steps without a pause. Some of these stops last just a few seconds, but most of the time she finds something to engage her attention for a minute or two. The stream is nearly dry now. Not far from where it trickles into the meadows two butterflies dance around the bushes. Their wings, bright with color and large as she's ever seen up this high, seem almost too heavy for them. She wonders if they know enough to migrate across the pass to lower elevations and warmer climes, or whether they'll simply freeze up here in the next few weeks. She sees only a few other bugs, and not many birds, winter hanging in the air even if it feels warm in the sun.

Al left her watch behind on purpose. She carries only Will's key in her pocket and a long-sleeved shirt tied around her waist. From the position of the sun she knows she's approaching the truck but has no idea how far off it is. She entertains a picture of Will, back already, legs dangling from the open tailgate—unhurried, unharmed, happy to be through with it. She quickly pushes the thought away. She knows Will has to stay in the moment, not just to avoid catastrophe but to get what he calls "full value." She is pledged to join him in at least that much—staying present, whatever the discomfort or danger.

Then she sees the truck. It's been at least a couple hours since she left, and she had expected to be grateful so much of the afternoon was behind her. Instead, she wells up with worry. Where is he? She feels a surge behind her eyes.

And she's tired. Al hasn't slept well either lately, in anticipation of today. She sets her yoga mat in the half-sun between clumps of laurels, spreads her sleeping bag on top, and lies down with her book. A dragonfly zips into view, then rests in shade nearby. She recalls another time she was waiting at the base of a cliff, a long time ago. It was after a rappel. Her father had gotten some gear stuck at the anchors. He was far out of view, and she had no idea what the holdup was about. It was the end of the day, and she thought she was just hungry and tired but really she was scared.

It doesn't take long for her to drift off. Not a deep sleep, but still, what relief.

Al is awakened by something moving. She lifts her head and holds her breath to hear better—it's the wind blowing laurel branches against the truck, or maybe a squirrel scurrying about. Not what she hoped. Now there's a fright in her gut. It's after five—sunset's in an hour. She puts her pad and the other things into the cab, stuffs her extra clothing into a daypack, and locks the truck. She wears a headlamp loosely around her neck and sets off on the trail Will had taken in the morning. It feels a little better to be walking, but there's still this fight in her. He could be fine, could appear any minute. He could be hurt and need me. He could not be. This is how grief feels, she thinks, for one who is not yet grieving.

The light is lower, the air cooling, as she rises out of the valley. She told Will she wouldn't go any farther than the outlet to Shadow Lake but now thinks she might have to continue on toward Ediza just to keep moving and warm. She tries to look past this feeling, to where everything is resolved or it's much, much worse, but she cannot get to either. She stops twice to look back at the valley, and on the second pause she feels tears on her cheeks and the halting, shallow breath of crying. She must slow down. There's nothing to do but go slowly and wait.

The trail parallels Shadow Creek for the last mile and the stream is fuller than expected. The noise is a kind of salve, though now Al keeps lifting her eyes to look ahead because she wouldn't hear him over the falling water. To distract herself she decides to think about how they got to this point, and soon she is smiling. She recalls their first time in the backcountry together. How shy they were swimming naked. Their first time making love, in a sun-splashed tent that grew hot as a sauna. Learning their way around one another in the morning. He seemed to her a strange mix of young and wise, quick to delight but also a bit weary. She learned about his father within their first few hours together—on the hike they took for a first date. She'd had a rapport with his mother for months, a directness and confidence she rarely achieved with the testier male docs who seem always to second-guess details she relates when bringing in the sick and injured. When Nor said, "I have a son," Al said, "I know. I climb." She'd even seen him, once in the Gorge, a couple of times at Stellar Brew in town. But her first feeling was reluctance—she didn't want to mess up what she had with Nor. Plus, he was younger, and at least in her mind only a little older than the kid she'd read about in climbing magazines when she was in high school.

That was a year and a half ago, and now they were having family dinners and such. And Nor, like a mom, but even more a dear friend. So much to live for.

And how could I ever tell her?

The long shadows cast by the lodgepoles are gone, the sun completely obscured by the knife-edged peaks Will should have descended by now. But maybe he missed the notch. Al's heard people do. They leave the summit and walk too far to the south, some even returning by way of Minaret Creek. That would put Will several miles lower than Agnew Meadows when he got down to the valley, in which case he'd hike up behind her once he got to the truck and found she wasn't there. *He'll know how worried I'll be*, she thinks. Unless he's flat worn out. It's not like he's had a lollygagging day like mine, with a decent nap besides.

The outlet comes sooner than she wants, and with this new thought—that he descended by way of the other drainage—Al decides to go no farther than this first set of rocks that jut into the dark lake not far from the trail. *This is it. I'll be here until it's too cold to wait any longer. And then what? I'll go back. And then what?*

I don't know what then.

She sits on the cold rock.

Was he telling her something, she wonders? Was there an indication of fear, or even intention, that she missed? She wonders about this, what they know and when. She's usually among the first on the scene of the accident, and if it's climbing-related she's often first because the firemen and even Search and Rescue folks rely on her to steer them to the mountain or crag or boulder—all these place-names only another climber could bother to know. But these are young people, and usually just broken bones. It's the car crashes, the heart attacks and strokes—the silent, sudden disasters. Did they suspect anything awry? Was there a premonition, or even a vague feeling?

It's after sunset. The lake is black and the surrounding forest colorless if still visible. The rock tilts slightly toward the water. Al sits cross-legged, grateful for the relative comfort of her perch. She thinks she can wait here for quite a while, even hours. There's no wind, and only the stir of water at the top of the outlet disturbs the silence. It won't be long before there are stars. She consoles herself with the thought that she'll see him again. *One way or another, I'll touch his face. I'll move his hair away from his eyes, and wish for him he's not cold. I'll place my hands on his cheeks. I'll wait. And waiting, I'll try not to be afraid.*

In the forest, not seventy-five yards off, something moves, a flash like a deer or bird between the trees. Again.

Will, walking.

He's seen Al before she sees him but his pace is unbroken. He's smiling to himself, and then not. His eyes are full and wet. Al stands. She waits on the rock in the water. She's choking over her breath and tears, and then they're folded into one another.

"It's done," he says. "Sorry I took so long. It's done, it's okay."

GLOSSARY

AID, AID CLIMB—to use equipment to hoist oneself up a cliff, as opposed to free climbing, wherein the equipment is used only for protection in the event of a fall or as an anchor for belay or rappel.

ANCHOR—two or more bolts, pieces of protection, or slings around a rock or tree for secure attachment at a belay stance or rappel station.

ARÊTE—a steep or vertical edge on a cliff or mountain.

BELAY—letting out, taking in, and/or locking the rope to secure a climber and minimize the distance of a fall.

BELAY DEVICE (e.g., ATC, or GriGri)—the rope is threaded through the belay device, which is secured to the belayer's harness; the belay device facilitates locking off the rope, akin to a cleat, in the event of a fall. Most belay devices can be used for rappel as well.

BERGSCHRUND—an open, often deep cavern between the upper edge of a snowfield or glacier and the rock cliff above it.

BETA—information about a climb or a particular sequence of moves on a climb. (From *Betamax*, an early version of the video recorder, because good "beta" is akin to a film rendering of a route or the moves on a route.)

Bivouac, or **Bivy**—mountain camp, usually exposed and uncomfortable, sometimes on a cliff's ledges or hanging in a hammock.

Bolt—a permanent, drilled anchor, usually placed where no natural features (e.g., cracks, fissures) exist for "clean" protection (cams, nuts).

Boulder (v.), **Highball Boulder** (v.)—to climb technically challenging routes without rope or protection on a feature no higher than fifteen feet (bouldering) or thirty feet (highball bouldering).

Buttress—a square-edged aspect of a cliff that stands out from the rest.

Cam—ingenious device invented in the late 1970s for protecting cracks; brand names include Friends, Aliens, and Camalots.

Carabiner—oval ring, made of aluminum alloy, with a gate on one side through which a rope or sling or other piece of climbing hardware can be readily attached or detached.

Chalk, Chalk Bag—chalk is used to keep hands dry; the chalk bag hangs from a climber's waist.

Choss—Poor rock, friable and dangerous.

Class 3—a rating indicating two things: the terrain is such that hands are used as well as feet, and no protection is necessary because the climbing is easy and a fall possibly quite dangerous but less than catastrophic; as distinguished from Class 5, which involves various levels of more difficult climbing and requires protection in the event of a fall. Also a verb: "We class 3-ed the route," meaning climbed unprotected, i.e., free soloed, whatever the route's rating. (A fuller primer on climbing ratings follows the glossary.)

Climbing Shoe—tight-fitting shoe with a smooth rubber sole and stiff insole for edging, smearing, and jamming (in cracks).

Copperhead—an obscure piece of aid gear; a tiny wedge of copper, attached to a thin cable, which is hammered into a small crack or seam.

CORNER—feature of a cliff formed by vertical rock at right or oblique angles; ascended via techniques like stemming, jamming, and/or liebacking.

CRACK (also: tips crack, finger crack, hand crack, off-width, chimney)—a fracture or fissure in a rock face, fingernail-width to body size, that climbers utilize to make upward progress and/or for gear/protection. Different sized cracks call for different climbing techniques.

CRAMPONS—metal spikes attached to boots for traction on ice and hard snow.

CRUX—the hard moves, or the hardest move, in any section of a climb.

DIRECTIONAL—a piece of gear placed to reduce rope drag and/or to keep the rope moving in a straight line.

DIRTBAG—low-budget lifestyle of climbing devotees; includes illegal camping, eating leftover food on cafeteria trays, dumpster-diving, etc.

EB's—a popular and widely available technical climbing shoe, 1970s.

ETRIER—a ladder made of webbing; used in aid climbing.

FIX—to place gear that's difficult or impossible to remove, as in old-style pitons or modern-day inadvertent placements, like a nut that's too securely slotted into position or a cam placed too tightly.

FLARE—a crack of any size whose sides are angled and oblique, making the climbing more difficult and the protection (cams, nuts) hard or impossible to secure.

FREE CLIMB—to use one's hands, feet, muscles, and acumen to ascend a cliff; the rope and gear are utilized not to facilitate upward movement but to prevent injury or death in the event of a fall. The converse of Aid Climb.

FREE SOLO, or often just SOLO—to climb without protection (gear, rope) on a route from which a fall would be catastrophic.

GRIPPED—climber jargon for scared; comes from hanging on for dear life.

JAMMING—a technique for climbing cracks; involves wedging fingers and/or hands and toes or feet into cracks of various sizes as a means of ascending a cliff.

JUG—a very generous/favorable handhold.

JUMAR—a micro-toothed device used to ascend a rope; used in aid climbing. "To jumar" is to ascend a rope using jumars and etriers.

LEAD, LEAD CLIMBING—to climb first, which requires placing the gear/protection and risking a leader fall (roughly twice the distance the climber is above the last gear placement or bolt).

LIEBACK—A climbing technique, often insecure, in which the hands side-pull on a crack in a corner while the feet push on the wall; often used to bypass sections where jamming, a more secure technique, is not possible because the crack is too small or too large.

NUT, STOPPER—aluminum alloy or brass wedge placed in a crack for protection; a nut is the original type of passive or "clean" protection (1970s), designated such because, unlike a piton or bolt, a nut or stopper does not disfigure or scar the rock and can be readily removed by the second climber who "cleans" the route of the gear.

PENDULUM—to swing back and forth from an anchor or gear placement in search of a climbable line on either side of one's current position.

PITON, PIN—an iron blade hammered into a crack or fissure; old-style protection.

PITCH—the distance between belay stances, typically 100–200 feet.

PROJECT (v.)—a verb born from a noun: to work a route (i.e., "my project") over time, with many hangs (weighting the rope) and falls, in order to solve it—and then to climb it in a single push.

PROTECTION, also called **PRO** or **GEAR**—cams, nuts, bolts, pitons, slings around natural features: any number of ways to secure a rope to the rock face and thereby protect the climber in the event of a fall.

QUICKDRAW, or DRAW—two carabiners at either end of a short sling; used to clip the rope to a bolt or other type of protection.

RACK—the gear carried by the leader on a climb, usually including nuts and cams and customized according to the what the lead climber judges necessary for the next pitch.

RAPPEL; RAPPEL DEVICE or ATC—to rappel is to descend by sliding down a rope; the rappel device or ATC is a small metal apparatus attached to a climber's harness which generates friction to facilitate a mostly effortless, controlled descent.

ROOF, OVERHANG—a feature on a cliff that juts out.

ROPE, also CORD or LINE—in free-climbing, means of preventing catastrophe; made of colorful Perlon; typically 200 feet long.

ROPE SOLO—to climb alone with protection (as opposed to Free Solo).

RUN OUT (v.)—to get far above the last point of protection while lead climbing and thereby risk a long, dangerous, and possibly catastrophic fall. Sometimes unavoidable because of insufficient features or fissures in which to place gear. Also used as a noun ("that pitch has a bad run-out") and adjective ("the run-out section is scary").

SEND (v.)—to successfully climb a route (often used in conjunction with the nominative form of project, as in "She sent her project.")

SIMUL CLIMB—a technique to move quickly over (generally) easier territory with minimal protection; two climbers are roped together, the first placing gear and the second removing it, but no static, attentive belays are offered nor any anchors utilized.

SLING, or RUNNER—an extension used to reduce rope-drag, especially on routes that zig-zag; made of a sewn loop of strong nylon.

SOLO—to climb alone; variations include 3rd Class, Free Solo, Rope Solo, Aid Solo.

Sᴘᴏʀᴛ Cʟɪᴍʙɪɴɢ—bolt-protected, usually single-pitch climbs, as opposed to "trad climbing," where the leader carries and places protection and the follower removes or "cleans" it.

Sᴘʀᴀʏ—self-aggrandizing remarks or humblebrags referencing one's climbing accomplishments.

Sᴛᴇᴍ, or Sᴛᴇᴍᴍɪɴɢ—climbing technique in which the feet apply pressure on opposing features, often used on corners.

Tᴏᴘᴏ—a detailed drawing of a route's features and difficulties; a form of "beta."

Climbing Ratings—YDS Primer

Several ratings systems are used around the world. In North America, the Yosemite Decimal System (YDS) is predominate.

Class 1—hiking on a trail.

Class 2—hiking or scrambling off-trail; hands used occasionally for balance.

Class 3—climbing on secure handholds and footholds; exposure can be severe.

Class 4—steeper rock, smaller holds; a fall can be fatal or worse. A rope may be used for safety.

Class 5—technical rock climbing; a rope and gear are generally required for safety because an unprotected fall would be catastrophic.

Class 6—aid climbing; gear is placed and weighted for upward movement.

Class 5 is subdivided into roughly twenty subgrades from 5.5 to 5.14d:

5.5–5.8—moderate rock climbing; requires experience and general fitness.

The Grand Teton's easier routes are in the 5.5 range. The East Buttress of Mount Whitney goes at 5.7.

5.9–5.10b—challenging rock climbing; requires strength, flexibility, finesse.

Royal Robbins established the country's first 5.9 on "Open Book" at Tahquitz in 1952. The East Buttress of El Capitan, an eleven-pitch route on the shoulder of the great cliff, is 5.10. The Regular Northwest Face of Half Dome is 5.10 if you aid several pitches (or 5.12 if all free).

5.10c–5.11b—increasingly thin, sketchy, strenuous, and/or dynamic technical climbing.

Can be hard to protect, as one must let go with one hand to place gear.

5.11c–5.12b—A tiny fraction of climbers climb at this level.

512c–5.15—A still tinier fraction, including most any contemporary climber you've heard of.

ACKNOWLEDGMENTS

∽

With gratitude to these –

Fellow roamers and friends, the ones at the other end of the rope, more or less in order of appearance:

Tim Loughlin, Harry "Huck" Yim, and Mark "Coz" Neuweld. Joe Hunter, Steve Longenecker.

David Goldstein: for the early outings and far more for roping me back in and showing me what's what when I could stand it again.

Matt Hern, Jason Wells, Jonny Kwong, Kevin Friedrich, Bill Beckwith, Linda Jarit, Erin Neff, Michael Rieser, Pat Meezan, Tyler Mugg, Kevin Starr, Dennis Van Denbos, Chris McElheny.

And Bill Zildjian, Bob Hoffman, Jamie Bourret, Chris Stone, Al Ramadan, Julian Pollock, Danny Tesfai, Mike McCarthy, Geoff Ruth, Dan Rampe, Leon Sharyon.

And, in loving memory, Bill Beckwith, Jason Wells, and Mark Neuweld.

For friendship and kinship in art and life: Bej Tewell, Brian Cohen, and Bill Stanisich.

With love and gratitude for my children, Emily Howland Rhodes and Noah Howland, for Brian and Luka and Renata Rhodes, for my siblings, Steve, Ben, and Barbara, and for our father, Robert Howland, who is all over this book in Joe's sensibility, though Dad would have advised he be funnier.

My mother, Mary Howland, read each section of the novel as it was completed and offered suggestions and pointed to problems. Amy Cunningham Atkinson read the first final draft; her affirmation was exquisite. Lauren Gersick, Nicholas Thomson, and Bill Broder read first runs, too, and each was generous and helpful.

Austen Rachlis offered excellent editorial help and sound suggestions.

Dan Duane hit me hard about some inattentive writing. His writerly counsel and steadfast support have been huge.

Jimmy McClements was avid in editing and wrestling with me over details, spending days on the manuscript and long sessions with me on the porch of his home in Boulder, Colorado.

Amanda Moore—great poet, dear friend—inspires and encourages me. Jennifer Starkweather, too—a great friend and luminous artist. Jennifer and her partner-in-art Amanda Hughen composed the book's cover, and Jennifer did the savvy pen-and-ink drawings for the pre-glossary. Greg Monfils as well—steadfast support and encouragement through the years.

I'm immensely grateful for Bill Finnegan's generous reading and advocacy.

Big thanks to Danielle Svetcov, my literary agent, an early advocate of the novel and an insistent, wise guide all along.

Dede Cummings, publisher at Green Writers Press, expressed immediate and fortifying enthusiasm for this novel and shepherded the book into publication. Rose Alexandre-Leach, editor at GWP, worked closely with me on the manuscript.

Her insight, sensitivity, exquisite suggestions, and insistent revisions were nonpareil. Michael Fleming's keen and spirited copy-editing down the home stretch improved the manuscript palpably, and Chrissy Yates gave the book still further attention— and the green light.

Deep appreciation for Chrisandra Fox, Peter Wright, and Robin Duryea—three in a constellation of great teachers.

Courtney provides more than I can say much less know by way of insight and wisdom and judicious suggestion. Our shared endeavoring made it possible for me to care and invest enough to get started and stick with it and move along toward a finish and even enjoy much of the doing.

ABOUT THE AUTHOR

JONATHAN HOWLAND lives in San Francisco, where he alternates between climbing trips in western states and writing, gardening, and playing with two grandchildren at home. Also: cooking, yoga-ing, and coyote-sighting in the Presidio of San Francisco, which he frequents with Courtney and their dog Ike. His favorite writers include Melville and Morrison and Marlon James, Faulkner and Woolf and Chekhov, though if limited to just one, Emily Dickinson.